THE PROPOSAL

MAYA HUGHES

THANK YOU FOR READING

Maya Hughes

Cover Designer: Nail Qamber, Qamber Designs

Editors: Lea Schaffer, Tamara Mayata, Sarah Kremen-Hicks, Sarah Polcher

For my biggest cheerleader, Mr. Maya

1

ZARA

Steam rose through a subway grate and the wet pavement made my heels extra slippery. Taxis were sparse on the roads this early. Garbage men loaded up the dumpsters in the alley between not-yet-open sandwich shops and my glowing beacon of a destination.

My scavenged coffee cards were tucked in my pocket, each with a single coffee cup-shaped hole punched out. Other coffee drinkers' garbage was my cherished treat. Why did people throw away their punch cards for a free coffee? Because they hadn't survived on ramen and discount green beans for months at a time. The baristas didn't bat an eye anymore when I showed up with my nine separate cards to claim my free coffee.

Coffee *and* a chocolate croissant. Small pleasures in life to keep the slough from drowning me.

The two reports due on Bill's desk by eight am only needed a few final touches and a spell check I could run while I sipped my warm, chocolatey drink. Nothing went wrong on Coffee Day. The universe looked down on me with my size-too-small shoes, threadbare blazer, and pilfered coffee, and waved its hands to give me a small window of perfection.

Only, today my happy day wasn't starting out all that promising. The usually non-existent line was nearly to the door when I stepped inside. Why where there so many people here this early? I yawned, covering my mouth with my arm and whacking the suited man in front of me with my bag.

He glared at me with bleary eyes.

I cringed. "Sorry." My mumbled word was lost to his grumbling.

We inched forward. That comfortable cushion I'd thought I had ticked away. I shifted from foot to foot, craning my neck to see what was going on—couldn't they call in whole office orders ahead of time to keep from over-taxing the baristas at the beginning of the morning rush? Checking my emails on my phone, I answered a few to keep from eating up time once I was at my desk.

I'd left last night's company event less than five hours ago, but the deluge from work had begun. How was my inbox already a horror show? Ugh, and was everyone in front of me ordering coffee for a construction crew? I checked the time. It was cutting it close. Bill would freak if the report wasn't on his desk before he got in.

Emails from florists, caterers, and linen providers clogged my inbox with questions I was copied on. Questions I was supposed to sit back and watch as they were handled by a pro, but after two years, I knew the drill. Nothing would get done and I'd get blamed if I didn't respond.

Someone cleared their throat and I hopped forward into the three-person-sized space in front of me.

"Sorry," I said over my shoulder to the disgruntled man with his arms crossed over his chest.

My phone rang in my purse. The only ringer I hadn't set to silent in my contacts blared in the coffee shop filled with sleepy-eyed business drones like myself. More throat clearing and narrowed gazes. One look at the screen and I didn't care what anyone here thought, I wasn't missing this call.

"You're up early." It was barely six am there. Fourteen-year-olds aren't known for waking up at the crack of dawn.

"Hey, Z! Awesome, did you see the pics I sent from my trip last week?"

"I did. It looks like you're having loads of fun."

"It's the best. I'm sneaking this call in before homeroom. I got an email from the financial aid office. They're sending a new tuition package for next semester this morning. They mentioned it would be a little more than last semester. That'll be okay, right?"

While those words would normally fill me with dread, I'd been tucking away every bit I could to make the payment. I'd thought in a few months I could upgrade to a non-pilfered cup of coffee and not filling my refrigerator with leftovers from our events, but I could hang on a bit longer. The lease on my apartment ended in a couple months, and I could downgrade to something smaller. Maybe a studio. Or I could look for roommates again.

"I got my first test back for AP Chemistry."

He'd gotten emotional when he'd started boarding school two years ago in seventh grade, worried he couldn't get through the intensive work like the other kids, but by now I knew the hedging tone he took when he'd knocked it out of the park.

I sucked my breath through my teeth. "That bad, huh? Did you barely pass? Scrape by with a 65, maybe a 66?" I put on my understanding big sister voice.

"A 66?!" His voice pitched up an octave and cracked. Ahh puberty, keeping little brothers adorable into their early teens. "I got a 96, Z! The highest grade in the class."

"And you doubted yourself."

I covered the phone and handed over my cards. The barista chuckled and shook his head without me needing to say anything. It was a dance we'd done before.

My drink and croissant order in, I was dancing on the inside in anticipation of warm layers of flaky dough wrapped around yummy chocolate.

"And you told me to take a few deep breaths and ask my teacher for some extra help. They're all so nice here. We went over everything every day after school for like two hours. They didn't try to kick me out or anything. And I talked to our dorm dad and he said I can stay over winter break this year."

His last visit back to our parents' house a couple hours outside of Chicago had been a disaster. My car had died a few months before, so I couldn't make the drive there to be the buffer for him. Even the bus and train tickets would've meant making the choice between my meager groceries and straight ramen, plus missing out on extra event work, which paid enough overtime to pay for Tyler's spring break class trip. Had I known, I'd have chosen six months of ramen. It had taken Tyler nearly a month to shake off the cloak of sadness weighing him down.

"My teacher also said by the time I graduate high school, I'll have enough Advanced Placement credits to be a college junior. I could get my bachelor's degree and a masters in the time it takes most people to graduate from college."

"Sarah." A droning, mildly interested voice broke through my conversation.

I lifted my finger and grabbed my drink and warm

chocolate croissant off the counter. Even when I spelled my name, they never got it right, so I'd given up trying. I added three sugars and took a long whiff, closing my eyes and savoring every second with this glorious cup of coffee—still too hot to sip, dammit—before popping the lid back on.

"If there's anyone who could do it, it's you." When I'd told him to apply for the boarding school located two hours from home, I hadn't thought he would. But being away at college, I'd needed to throw him that lifeline for when things went to shit at home. Mom and Dad, when they weren't buried at the bottom of a bottle, were pros at losing whatever money we had for things like food and keeping the lights on. They couldn't stop gambling—whether it was scratch cards or bingo nights. Before I left for college, I'd tried to protect my little brother as much as I could, but I needed to keep *my* head above water. And I'd done it by coming to Philly for college.

Growing up, I'd thought about running away from home more times than I could count, but I hadn't wanted to leave Tyler behind. My going away to college had hit him *hard*.

It hit me harder.

There had been so many sleepless nights staying up with him on the phone to help him through homework. Dates or evenings with friends skipped to talk Tyler through making dinner. Watching cartoons together as his states-away babysitter while everyone else was in the library studying or working on class projects.

The guilt had nearly ended with me dropping out, but he'd told me how proud he was of me and how great I was for going to college. He squeezed me so tight at the curbside outside our house on my last day. I held back my tears, saving the sobs for once I turned the corner and his small waving figure disappeared. I couldn't disappoint him. My going to college intensified his determination to leave.

Within two months he'd completed all the forms himself with a little guidance from me. He'd gotten in and made it through the rigorous entrance exam. Then came the tuition bomb. Even with a generous financial aid package, a private boarding school wasn't cheap, but this had all come in right as I was graduating. My job offered me a salary, which barely made it work, but I didn't have the luxury of shopping around for something better. Every penny, except for my rent, was squirreled away for Tyler's education and maintenance.

My phone pinged with the notification from Tyler's school. Someone in the financial aid office was up early. The email came in from them. The screen went white as the scan of the financial aid letter downloaded like it was running on dial-up.

Taking my croissant and coffee, I balanced my blazer over my arm and my bag on my shoulder.

I bumped the door open with my hip and looked up at the early morning sun. It was still warm out, but orange and yellow peeked from between some of the branches. The crunchy fall leaves always made even a walk to my parents' house much more fun. A perfect crunch under my shoe reminded me of hiding out in the piles of leaves as a kid, not wanting to go home, staring up at the sky, watching planes pass overhead and wishing I'd get to fly in one someday—still wishing.

Tyler's excited chattering broke through my memory rabbit hole.

"My cello teacher said he'd tutor me before classes. I've got to go. I love you, Z."

"Bye, Ty. Be safe!"

A woman who looked more like she was going clubbing than mixing in with business professionals stood on the corner, handing out fliers and talking up how the charges in their club came up as a steakhouse if the men's wives had any questions.

Real nice.

I slipped on a wet patch on the sidewalk, my heels wobbling. I should've worn my flats to work, but I'd forgotten them in the office last night.

The tasty smell of the coffee and croissant made my mouth water. Maybe I should've sat inside to eat my croissant at least. But I didn't have time. Besides, the perfect blends of sweet and savory would no longer be burn-the-roof-of-my-mouth hot once I got to the office.

My stupid data finally loaded. The scans finally came up with full resolution.

Lightheadedness blurred my vision. That wasn't a small bump in our expected family contribution. Holy shit! Did they think we'd won the lottery since the summer?

A deep voice called out his love of steak to the woman standing by the street.

Turning the corner with my phone in hand, I slammed into a man. But a wall probably would've had more give. The full contents of the furnace-hot cookie crumble cappuccino escaped my cup, blasting the lid straight into my face. My eyes opened through the spray of cookie flecks in time to watch the rest of the now crumpled cup splash all over the front of my white shirt as my feet shot out from under me.

As if a burning hot coffee shower weren't enough, I watched in slow motion as my chocolate croissant fell out of the brown butter-soaked paper bag like a lover slipping out in the dead of night and bounced on the sidewalk before being promptly trampled on by a pair of shiny black shoes.

"Oh shit," he yelled. "I didn't see you—"

"Yes, I know you didn't," I shouted right back from the ground. "You were too busy trying to pick up the blonde wearing a bandana for a dress."

He glared down at me like he wasn't the reason I had wet sidewalk water seeping through my clothes and touching my ass.

"Me? I'm walking around the corner having a friendly conversation with someone on the street. You're the one not looking where you're going."

Leaning down he offered me his hand.

I smacked it away and pushed myself up off the ground and glared right back. If I weren't so pissed maybe I'd have noticed his light brown eyes or his perfectly imperfect five o'clock shadow or the close curls on his head, but all I zeroed in on was the way he'd somehow managed to keep every droplet of coffee off his buttoned-down shirt (with the rolled-up sleeves revealing his muscled forearms) while burning hot coffee continued to soak into my shirt.

The one luxury I allowed myself drenched a shirt I couldn't afford to have dry cleaned. My rare-treat croissant was now squished on the bottom of his shoe.

"I didn't expect someone to be charging down the street like a linebacker."

His scowl deepened. "I love how this is my fault when you ran into *me*. If I were in a generous mood I probably would've offered to buy you another coffee—"

"I don't need your charity." Tugging my shirt from my chest, I searched my bag for napkins to sop up some of the mess.

"Good, because I didn't plan on offering. Did you want

what was left of your croissant?" Pointedly following my gaze with his, he lifted his shoe, showing off my formerly buttery, flaky, pastry.

I'd never wanted face-melting laser vision more. Or a magical hammer to harness the power of lightning and turn him into a smoldering crater in the sidewalk. Instead, I gritted my teeth with my arm out to the side to keep my blazer from getting covered in coffee too. "Have a nice day, asshole."

He brushed past me. "Have a nice life, lady," he called over his shoulder.

I glared before turning back to my trashed treat, splattered and smooshed all over the ground. It would be my last one of those for a while. I stared longingly at the one perfectly intact chocolate chip sitting straight up on the sidewalk. Poor guy, made it this far only to end up as pavement paint.

Checking the time, I could add 'almost late' to the list of the ways my life had been thrown into a tailspin. And I'd been doused with an entire cup of mocha cookie crumble cappuccino. I needed to change—fast.

2

LEO

'Sorry, careful!' had been on my tongue before she'd opened her mouth and unleashed on me like the crash had been all my fault.

Yes, I'd been on my phone and distracted before our collision, but so was she.

Yes, I'd failed to catch her or the cup of coffee that had splattered all over her.

Yes, I'd been kind of distracted by her wide green eyes with lashes so thick there had to be glue and one of those caterpillar fake eyelash things involved.

Yes, I hadn't helped her up the second she'd fallen.

It had happened so quickly I'd been in shock for a solid two seconds before offering her my hand like I would any player on an opposing team I'd knocked off their feet.

She'd smacked my hand away and scrambled back up, laying into me.

It was already a day and I didn't need to add someone's crappy bullshit to the smoldering pile of rubble that was my life.

So, her "Have a nice day, asshole" put her at the top of

my shitty day shit list. At least I had someone to be the focus of my frustration. Had it felt nice to snap at her? Hell yeah, it had.

In the coffee shop, the vacant, half-lidded stares of business professionals milling around staring at their phones, the whirring crunch of the coffee grinder, the overpowering smell of ten different types of beans, and the cringe at mispronounced names scribbled on cups only meant one thing—Monday.

September should've meant training camp for me. Instead I was in line with everyone else trying to figure out how the fuck my life had turned out this way.

"Aren't you that guy?" An insistent tap on my shoulder.

My head dipped for a second before I turned to the woman peering up at me over the top of her glasses. She didn't strike me as a football fan.

"What guy?" her friend unhelpfully offered, staring at me like a zoo exhibit.

My jaw clenched and I stared straight ahead over the heads of the four people in front of me.

"The guy who got wrecked last season by, like, three guys during the Super Bowl? Remember, we watched the replay ten or fifteen times?"

My fists clenched at my sides. "No, that's not me."

"Are you sure? There were so many close-ups on your face when they pulled you out of there on the stretcher."

"I'm sure." I glared at them before facing front, not needing to relive the unceremonious end to my career thanks to a nosy woman in line at the coffee shop. I'd learned over the past few months that my face had become much more recognizable in the time since I'd been booted from my team than it had been the whole three seasons I'd played for them.

It wasn't like I blended in, though. Once, sticking out like this had been all I wanted; now fading into the background was what I needed.

The exit path for former players was a crash course in how not to live the rest of your life. People flamed out like an overworked engine reaching its breaking point or parlayed their experience into something more. Every waking moment had been layered over a football backdrop. Practices. Playbook reviews. Traveling for games. Recovering from games. For eighteen years, since pee-wee football began when I was eight, I'd devoted myself to the gridiron— what the hell was I supposed to do now?

Sports commentary was the only way to stay close to the game for me. My attempts at coaching had flamed out spectacularly. College hadn't been my forte. My college transcript wasn't winning me any coveted positions anywhere. My face wasn't even recognizable enough to start up a car dealership like a lot of guys did when they left the pros. Besides, you need capital to jumpstart a business fast, and all mine had been sucked away with one signature on a dotted line.

My agent had worked out a deal with an accountant to protect me from myself. The money I hadn't blown through while playing was locked up tight, only accessible in monthly payments of just enough to keep me afloat. The contract was ironclad. Waiting around for a check wasn't my style and my skills were limited. Sports commentary was the only way to keep myself from going off the deep end, but no amount of resume sending had gotten me even a 'fuck off' in response.

Sam had said I could stop by at eight, and I wanted to grab him a coffee first. It was the least I could do.

He'd been pale and skinnier the last time I'd seen him

and guilt bore down on me like a whole squad of offensive linemen prepared to take my head off. They should. It would hurt less than knowing how I'd let Felix down before he died.

Brushing past the sidewalk surliness, I went inside to get a couple cups of coffee, if only to have something to do with my hands when I showed up at Simply Stark.

A text rolled in.

Hunter: You're still coming to the game this afternoon

Me: Of course.

August: He's trying to get out of it.

Me: Isn't that Everest's job?

Everest: Fuck. Off.

Me: Shocking language from such a posh guy.

Everest: I have a few other choice words I can pull out of my hat, if you'd like

Jameson: Children! Focus! We have the court reserved for 6. Brady's saving our booth until 7:30. The Wing Night Special ends at 8:30.

August: Thanks for keeping us on track, Jameson

Jameson: It's what I do

Hunter: It's settled then, everyone will be there.

A chorus of yeses happened right as I got to the counter.

Walking past the barista set-up after placing my order, my shoulders tensed. Eyes were on me. I could feel them with every step I took. This was what I got for not wearing my baseball cap.

"Leo Wilder. I knew it was you." The woman from earlier in the line had her phone up to the side of my face, not taking my denial lying down.

My shoulders sagged. So much for a quick trip into a coffee shop.

"Can I have your autograph?" She clambered half-up

onto the counter to grab one of the barista pens and held it out to me.

You'd think in Philly, they'd hate me forever for being a hometown boy who was playing for the opposing team that beat them at the Super Bowl, but five signatures in, no one seemed to mind. At least some things never changed. City pride over all else.

How many more months until these reactions were wiped away? The next season started in a couple weeks; there'd be a new clip played on repeat and I'd be another has-been peddling signatures no one wanted, instead of basking in the dying light of my former glory. I hadn't even stood on the field when the confetti cannons had gone off and they'd hoisted the glistening trophy into the air. I'd been in a CT machine and a neck brace, not knowing my football career was over.

But everyone loved a recognizable face. I'd need it to kick start the next stage of my career. Being up in a booth talking about the games was nothing compared to being on the field using my body to gain one more inch for my team, but it was all I knew. Football was where I no longer felt like a mere mortal, so I'd get back to it the only way I knew how.

With my coffees, a hand cramp, and phantom flashes dancing in my eyes, I made it back outside. There was no sign of the woman other than a dried coffee splatter and remnants of her croissant on the sidewalk. Her seething anger hadn't distracted me completely from how pretty she'd been—or would have been, if not for the sneer and need to jump down my throat. Too bad. With over a million people in the city, it wasn't like I'd be seeing her again. I headed to Simply Stark.

"Look what the cat dragged in." Phyllis tugged her horn-rimmed cat eye glasses down to the tip of her nose.

"Hey, Phyl."

Her gaze narrowed. "Stranger, I'm surprised you remember my name."

I pecked her on the cheek before holding onto both her hands and perching on the edge of her desk. "How could I not? If I was forty years older…"

She lifted an eyebrow and threw her head back, glasses sliding back into place. "Who said I'm not into younger men?" Pushing at my shoulder, she shook her head. "Laying it on pretty thick aren't you, kid?"

"You know I love you. When will you finally accept my offer and run away with me?"

"Don't let my husband hear or he'll run you out of the state, but if *I* were forty years *younger…*"

"Then we'll be sure to keep that our little secret." I winked and she swatted at my leg. "How's he doing?"

"As good as he could be, considering." A hint of tenderness she almost never let show broke through. "Things have been rough lately."

The desks in the small office behind her were all empty. The last time I'd visited, there had been flower display samples, mini tasting cakes, and brightly colored fabric all over the office. Their twenty employees had been either staring intently at their computers or gathering things up and rushing in and out of the office.

Now there was a dark void between Phyllis's desk and the single office in the back with a faint light shining through the cracked door.

"It's pretty quiet around here."

"Did you bring him a coffee?"

"Yeah, although it's stupid, he's already in the office. He

probably already has one. I didn't want to show up emptyhanded."

"Go back there. He'll be happy to see a friendly face."

The overhead lights flicked on as I passed through the vacant office. I tapped my knuckles against the partially opened door.

"Hey, Sam."

Sam, my uncle by marriage, looked up from the stack of papers on his desk. There were bags under his eyes and his salt-and-pepper hair leaned more toward just salt these days.

"Leo." He scooted back from his desk and hugged me tight. "You look good."

"So do you."

He motioned to the seat in front of his desk and took the one beside me. "You're lying to an old man. I look terrible." Raking his fingers through his hair, he sank back in his seat.

"I brought you a coffee." A curl of steam wafted up from the mug on his desk.

"How thoughtful of you. Thank you. To what do I owe the pleasure of you stopping by?"

"It's been a while. I haven't seen you since... How are you holding up?"

"As good as can be expected." His sigh was bone-deep weary.

"Where is everyone? What's going on?"

"Your uncle...well you know how he was. But one thing I never thought he was great at was keeping secrets. He always had so many big ideas. It was so clear to him. And he painted big, beautiful pictures for everyone around him and you couldn't help but follow along. Who wouldn't want to?"

"He did have a way with all this." I motioned to the swatches and sketches up on the wall.

"Reaching for the stars was his hallmark. He couldn't stop himself, and when he was doing well and was here in the office everything worked smoothly. But all you need are a few clients to go back on their word and you're stuck holding the bag—or the table linens and custom centerpieces.

"To execute his vision required a few loans. We had a few employees who needed advances on their salary, and even when I said not to, he put things on credit cards. Business credit cards. Personal credit cards." He pulled off his glasses and squeezed the bridge of his nose. "The statements didn't even arrive until after he was gone. I told him he was working too hard. I told him he needed to take care of himself. And he'd turn and pat me on the cheek and say that was what I was here for." Sam's voice tightened and he rubbed his eyes.

"He didn't listen."

"I told him we were overextended with the salaries going on and the events getting bigger. We had to front even more of the deposits ourselves. So I'm about to lose the house and I'll lose this place." He looked around at the walls covered in Felix's inspirations and ideas. "And the five people I've managed to keep on part time will lose even that. What do I do, start over from scratch? Doing what?" He lifted and dropped his hands to the desk. "I have no idea."

"Let me help."

"There's nothing you can do, unless you know an event planner willing to work for free for a while and salvage our biggest account."

"Is that a real opportunity to save the business?"

"Winthorpe Hotels is forcing us to team up with Easton Events. They don't trust us to pull off a few small, employee-focused events and—" He let out a weary sigh. "I don't know if we can. I can sell the desks and other things around the office to see what debt I can cover." His shoulders sank lower.

Felix and Sam's birthday cards had always been well-stuffed and the presents exactly what I'd wanted. Throw in the catering trays of mini brownies and they'd been the best uncles in the world.

When I'd needed help putting together my college applications to make my football scholarships official and my dad had been an ass about it, Felix had come down and helped me. And once I was in college, he'd let me drop into events to serve as a waiter for some quick cash. My football scholarship covered almost everything, but two-a-day practices and traveling for games, on top of being a normal college student, meant without his help I'd have gone to bed hungry more than a few nights.

Felix had come to me. He'd asked me for a loan a few weeks after I'd gotten out of the hospital. And I'd had to tell him no. Not because I didn't want to, but I couldn't—not then, and not now. Locking my money away from myself had kept it away from him too.

A decision I had no idea how much I'd regret making.

Had the financial stress led to his heart attack? The weight of responsibility on his shoulders and on his heart? That stress hadn't gone away.

I hadn't helped him like he'd always helped me. And now Sam was about to lose possibly the last two connections he had to Felix.

"I can do it." How hard could catering be? Order food, tables, chairs, beer.

"Help me sell things? That would be—"

"No, not help you sell. Help you salvage the account."

"You have experience with event planning?"

Football parties, barbecues, I'd been to enough booster club events at college. It was food, some nice tablecloths, maybe an open bar if whoever it was felt generous.

"Absolutely. You think after all this time Felix didn't rub off on me? I can do it and I can work for free." At least for a couple months while I worked the Sports Center angle. Working here would keep me busy, push me into a business setting and I could help when I hadn't been able to before.

Sam sat up in his chair. "Are you serious? You'd do that?"

"Give me the details and I can get to work."

"Bill from Easton said he's sending someone over at nine. If it's his pain-in-the-ass daughter, you've got your work cut out for you."

"Don't worry, Sam. I've got it covered. There isn't a woman I haven't been able to charm."

"Too right. Phyllis threatens to run most people over with her car on a first meeting, but she's always had a soft spot for you."

"I'm sure working with whoever they send over will be a piece of cake."

3

ZARA

In my office, I slammed my bag down and changed into my emergency work shirt. My supplies were dwindling low—this was my last spare.

Kicking off my heels, I sat at my desk and fumbled around with my feet. Target acquired. My secret flats were a soft, cool, and comfy release from my high-heel prison.

My desk lamp filled my dim office with enough light for this early in the morning. It had to—the overhead fluorescent light flickered and buzzed. No matter how many times I'd asked for it to be fixed, old blinky up there continued to let out a low, droning wail, driving me to the brink of slamming my head into the keyboard by seven pm.

I blinked hard, trying to clear the haze in my vision. The coffee I'd hoped to cherish during this early morning quiet had been stolen from me by an asshole with gorgeous eyes and a rock-hard body that were spoiled by his shitty attitude.

Somehow the walk from my coffee-and-croissant funeral to the office had refilled my inbox. The work never stopped.

I'd rushed the report to Bill's office and sat back in my chair less than sixty seconds before Bill breezed past my open door without a sideways glance. *Good morning to you too, Bill. Yes, I had a great night. Slept like a log after cleaning up all Valerie's work she left behind at the gala last night.*

Resting my head on my hand, I clicked through the nine hundred RSVPs one by one, since no one had thought to have them all imported into a spreadsheet to begin with.

Why do something efficiently when you can force me to do it at a painstakingly slow pace?

The names blurred together and my eyelids drooped like there were tiny eye-sized sandbags attached to them. Over four hours last night, I'd broken down the last of the flower arrangements and ensured the chair covers were returned. After hour two, I'd given up on the heels, but my feet still throbbed.

Who said event planning wasn't glamorous?

My head dropped off my hand and my bangs brushed against my spacebar. Slamming the heels of my hand down, I saved myself from a keyboard facial.

"Sleeping on the job, Zara?" The nasally, grinding voice was accompanied by a flood of light.

Lifting my head, I squeezed my fists together.

Valerie stood in my doorway with her oversized purse and latte. She dropped her hand from my light switch.

"No! I haven't had my morning coffee, Valerie." I clenched my fists and cursed the giant asshole from this morning. Someone his size should be used to watching out for fleeing villagers lest he smoosh them. I wasn't tiny by any stretch, I stood up to most men eye-to-eye, which hadn't won me any flirty-girl-of-the-year awards. Sometimes I thought those genes had been deleted from me entirely at birth.

She examined the purple streak she'd added to her hair a few weeks ago. Was that allowed by the company dress code policy? No, but she did whatever the hell she wanted. Rules like those were only for peons who didn't coast on daddy's bank account. She glanced up like she'd remembered I was there, even though she was standing in my office doorway. "My dad needs to see you in his office in five minutes. Something about reports you prepared."

My stomach plummeted as my indignation soared. I'd triple checked everything. I shot up from my desk, slipped my feet into my heels, wincing as the Band-Aids barely gave me enough padding for the blisters, and grabbed my blazer.

She looked me up and down, lips pursed, but I kept my shoulders straight, not letting myself shrink under her caustic gaze.

"Good morning, Valerie." Andi walked behind her with a huge smile. She was one of the only friendly faces in the office and made coming into work less hellish every day.

Valerie's gaze narrowed and she turned, hair flipping in the air, and walked off.

"Really nice use of the company copy machine last Friday," Andi cupped her hands around her mouth with her coffee cup in her hand, amplifying her voice throughout the office.

I held my blazer in my teeth and grabbed a notepad and pencil off my desk.

"What did Cruella want?" Andi leaned against my doorway in her t-shirt, jeans, and sneakers.

"Telling me Bill wanted to see me and making small talk." My longing for those comfy shoes knew no bounds as I struggled to get my arms into my sleeves and winced, nearly rolling my ankle in my office-approved heels.

"Oh, I didn't know you spoke bitch. Have you been taking lessons?"

"You're hilarious. I can have a mean streak when I need to."

"You mean when you gently lay your pen on top of your notebook? Or maybe when you push back your chair angrily before neatly tucking it back under the conference room table?"

I'd learned to keep my snapping replies to myself. I needed this job. There wasn't any room for me to fly off the handle when Tyler's future and my ability to eat hung in the balance.

"I'm not always like this."

"I'd pay for front row seats to see you snap. It would be a spectacular thing of beauty and the mushroom cloud would blanket the whole city. Where are you off to? Weren't you working until the ass crack of dawn?"

I peeked out my office door and popped my head back in for a second to cover my yawn. I leaned back out and grimaced. "Yes, and now I'm meeting with Bill."

Peering into my office, she searched my desk. "Isn't today your Mocha Cookie Crumble Cappuccino Day? The last day of the month?"

"You remembered that?" Did I talk about Coffee Day that much? Did Andi think I was crazy for making such a big deal about it?

"Hard to miss the way you cradle that thing like you gave birth to it."

"I'm trying to keep my budget balanced."

She lifted her cup to her mouth before hesitating and holding it out to me. "Do you want this? You look like you could use it more."

"No, I'll get one from the coffeepot after my meeting."

"Lucky, lucky you. You know where to find me." She backed away, not glancing behind her once. "My IT cave is quiet and I have candy and gold stars in my drawers."

I walked down the hallway toward the glass-walled office with the panoramic view of the city. The assistant waved me through to his office door. Bill stood inside, pacing, with an earpiece in, tossing a baseball from hand to hand. He was an inch or so taller than me. His sculpted salt-and-pepper hair went along with his game-show-host suit. If I'd seen him on the street, I'd have pictured him at a car dealership, shoving people into overpriced cars while he fanned himself with his commission checks.

He stared at me like he was struggling to place my face. Understandable. I'd only been working here for two years.

My wave was met with a slight head tilt before he turned his back to me and kept on pacing and tossing.

A full seven minutes later, laughing and smiling, he opened his door and rushed me inside, still on his call.

"Pebble Beach is so much better this time of year. I'll hold you to that bet. Bring your son along, I'm sure he and Valerie have tons to catch up on."

Poor guy, whoever he was. I sat in the overly slick office chair in front of Bill's oversized glass-top desk. The leather squeaked and my butt slid forward. I wedged my elbows into the sides, bracing myself in the chair. The interior design of his office screamed, "I'm insecure and I'm going to shove my position of power down your throat every chance I get!'

"Zara." He'd finally hung up, and now he sat behind his desk and steepled his fingers in front of his face. A glance down at the papers on his desk and back at me.

"Bill." I pinched my lips together. My stomach knotted and I forced a neutral but pleasant curve to my lips. My grip on my pen tightened. "If there was a problem with the reports…"

His gaze swung from me to his wall of accolades. He kicked up his feet on the desk and leaned back in his chair.

"I have an assignment for you." And he didn't sound the least bit happy about it.

"An assignment?"

"I reviewed your application. You applied here as a planner two years ago."

"Yes, I did."

"But you're working as an assistant."

"Yes, I am." I schooled my features and kept my tone even. The temporary position I'd taken to learn the ropes had turned into full time purgatory. I hadn't taken a day off in two years, taking every overtime opportunity I could, which left little time to apply and interview for other jobs.

"It's working with a client."

"Can I see their file?"

He pursed his lips exactly like his daughter. No question where she got it from.

"There have been some missteps with them in the past and they're giving us a chance to restore the relationship. Unfortunately, all the full-time planners are working on other events or they've been unable to meet the exacting requirements of this client.

"So that means you're the best option we have."

I wasn't going to let his dig at my competency or his backhanded compliment deter me.

"You'll be working alongside Simply Stark on two events over the next month. You'll have to work together, since they want to use Simply Stark's vendor contacts and our logistic skills for the event."

He cut his eyes to the side. "And as per our company

policy, you'd be entitled to a bonus of five percent of the net of the events." He quoted me the minimum value of the events like it was pried out of his mouth with a crowbar. "As we'll be sharing the account, it will be half the sum."

My heart beat hummingbird-fast in my chest. Tyler's financial aid letter. Those dollar signs weren't mind-explodingly huge anymore. Even half a bonus would be enough to more than scrape by. There might be enough for the slimmest amount of savings. Maybe I could bump myself up to a purchased croissant and coffee once a month without the punch card theft. Who was I kidding? Free was better than not free.

"The event is for the Winthorpe."

My perch on the edge of the seat became a full slide. I barely kept my ass off the floor and scooted back into my seat before Bill turned his head.

"They're planning some events for their staff and management to boost morale ahead of their winter season, so they're looking for outside staff to handle everything."

The historic hotel chain was a staple of the city. Their interiors were beautiful and had an old-school charm many had tried and failed to replicate in newer builds.

"Do you think you can handle this?" His tone said he didn't think I was up for it, but I didn't care if he believed in me or not, I'd throw my blood, sweat, and tears into making this happen.

"I can." My voice was firm and absolute.

"Fine, you have a meeting with Simply Stark at 9am. You'll need to go over the division of work, and Zara..." He held out a thin manila folder. I took it from his hand, but he held onto the edge. "We want to keep this account. The whole account. Bring your A game so Winthorpe sees we can handle their account outright. Do you understand?" He let go of the edge and I nodded, trying not to let his supreme asshole tendencies kill the high I was riding.

"I can handle it." I rushed out of his office and down the hall on the verge of tears. And, for once, they were tears of determination and joy. Maybe things were finally looking up for me.

I had less than twenty minutes to get to the Simply Stark offices. I ducked inside my office and grabbed my flats and my bag. These heels could suck it.

As I rounded the corner to the elevator, a shape loomed, and then my entire chest was on fire—again. From my neck to my belly button, straight-from-the-pot-hot coffee splashed all over the front of my new emergency shirt and blazer. I stood, arms out at my sides in the frozen horror as scalding liquid dripping down between my breasts for the second time today.

"Oops." Valerie stood holding a still-full cup of coffee. Why'd she need two if she didn't plan on making it to her office with both?

Biting the inside of my cheek so hard the warm metallic tang of blood lingered on my tongue, I jabbed the elevator button.

"My dad gave you the Winthorpe account." She leaned against the cubicle behind her.

"Yes," I bit out, seething. There wasn't time to change here, I'd have to rush there and get changed as quickly as I could at the Simply Stark offices.

"Good luck." The smug smirk dripped from her voice.

Turning, I let out a deep breath and brushed past her, taking the stairs. I grabbed a handful of napkins from my bag and jammed them down the front of my shirt. Fighting with my bag like we were going toe to toe in the middle of a ring, I wrestled a water bottle I'd had stashed in there and dumped it on the front of my shirt, trying not to get any on my blazer.

In the lobby, men and woman in suits stared back at me —the woman throwing a solo wet t-shirt contest in the lobby on a Monday morning. I shoved my portfolio under my arm and ducked past everyone and straight out to the street.

This would've been the perfect time to throw my arm up and hop in a taxi, but I didn't have the time or money for that, and I hadn't been bestowed a company expense account. Instead, I hoofed it the ten blocks. Sweat mixed with stale coffee and water wafted off me with every step.

The doors opened on the Simply Stark Events floor. The blue and white silhouetted sign to the left was the only good news I'd seen all day: I bolted into the women's bathroom.

Inside, I yanked off my blazer and hung it on the hook on the back of the door.

My shirt was a splotchy mess of stains and now dissolved granules of instant coffee. Had Valerie purposely filled her mug with sludge to dump on me? Anger threatened to bubble over. I wouldn't put it past her, especially if her dad was giving me her old account.

I braced my trembling hands on the edges of the sink and took a few deep breaths like I used to do back when I lived at home. My fight-or-flight mode kicked in hard when someone pulled nasty shit, but I didn't have the luxury of reacting. I needed to paste a happy smile on my face, walk in there, figure out how to work with whoever had been assigned to this at Simply Stark Events, and blow everyone away with my work so I could keep a roof over my head— and my brother safely at school in Chicago.

Turning on the faucet, I ran my wrists under the water to cool and calm myself down.

The caramel on top of my latte had been a nice, extra touch to my white button-down, and added a lattice pattern to the spot already over my left boob.

Sugar and dried coffee coated my skin as I peeled the shirt off. I ran the sticky damp spots of my shirt under the faucet. There was no way this would dry in time for my meeting. Dabbing at my chest, I cleaned off the coffee as best I could. Who didn't want to smell like a traveling coffee cart?

I evaluated my black camisole. It had hidden the coffee stains fairly well. A glance at my blazer showed the same thing. Did I really want to show up to one of the most important meetings I'd ever had in a tank top that was practically underwear? Did I have a choice?

The heavy thud of feet broke me out of my will I-won't-I tug of war with the mirror. I wrung out my shirt and shoved it into my bag, grabbed the blazer off the back of the door, and threw it on.

4

ZARA

Simply Stark had been a staple on the events scene for a while when I first started. Everyone at Easton fumed about losing out on jobs to them, but they'd fallen off the radar recently. Of course, I'd also been buried under a mountain of tasks that left me dead on my feet and sometimes nodding off in meetings, so I hadn't paid as much attention to which jobs we'd won, just the eighty things standing between me and the end of my to-do list each day.

But my job here was simple. Find a way to make sure Easton Events came out on top in this pitch, steal away the Winthorpe account and get my bonus. Ty's spot at his school would be safe and I wouldn't have to deal with the eventual scurvy after being reduced to getting my vitamin C solely from drink garnishes stolen off picked-over catering trays.

If I'd missed Mr. Hosken, it wouldn't kick things off on the right foot. I hadn't even remembered hearing his name before in relation to Simply Stark, but my competitor research wasn't as sharp as it could've been.

My phone flashed the time. Two minutes after I was

supposed to be meeting him, although from the glare the receptionist had given me when I walked in, I didn't think she'd do me any favors by letting him know I was in the bathroom.

"You're in the wrong place for sex appeal to work, sweetheart." She leaned back in her chair with her arms crossed over her chest.

After buttoning my blazer, the frilly edges of my camisole weren't exactly providing full coverage.

"It's been a long day and someone spilled coffee on me *twice*. Trust me, I don't normally head into meetings like this."

Her eyebrows were like a scrolling electronic billboard across her face and they spelled out, *I don't like you and even if you'd walked in here on fire, I'd possibly spare you a wet nap to blot out the flames.*

"Is Mr. Hosken in?" I craned my neck to look through the double glass doors behind her.

She set down her nail file. "You're the one from Easton Events, aren't you?"

"Yes, we have a meeting at nine." Could she see the bead of sweat rolling down the side of my face? Good thing I never wore foundation anymore. It was too expensive when I was already using out-of-date mascara and eyeliner.

Keeping her gaze locked onto me like I'd sprint through the doors and start toppling desks and flower arrangements if she averted her gaze for a second, she lifted the phone. "I have someone here from Easton Events to see you."

"It's Zara." I leaned in.

She covered the mouthpiece of the phone. "I didn't ask. You can go in. It's the office at the back. Don't touch anything." Her voice was crocodile friendly.

The lights flicked on as I moved past the empty desks.

Was everyone already out on site for the day? There was a
stillness to the space like no one had moved around in it for
a while. Taking a deep breath, I stood outside the open door
and tugged my blazer lapels closer to cover the black lace
trim of my top. I rapped my knuckles against the wood.

A gray-haired man looked up from his desk, took off his
glasses and smiled. It was a jolly one, instantly melting
some of the tension wired through my muscles. Maybe I
wasn't about to walk into the lion's den.

"Zara." He wrapped his hands around my extended one.
"Bill said he was sending over one of his best, so I'm happy
to have you here. I'm Sam."

His kind eyes immediately made me feel like shit for
what I'd been thinking about in the hallway. He actually
seemed happy to see me.

"Yes, I'm Zara."

"Take a seat." He motioned to the one beside me. Instead
of settling behind his desk, he sat in the second well-worn
chair across from mine. "I'm so happy you're here. The
moving parts are hard to juggle, and I'll admit I'm a little
lost."

Guilt rode in right behind my flash of excitement at him
not knowing what to do next. Swooping in and stealing this
account would be easy, but an uneasiness sat heavy in my
chest after only a few seconds of meeting him. He'd made
me feel more welcome than I had in two years at Easton and
here I was trying to take away some of his business. I smiled
and nodded, focusing on what he was saying.

"Together, we can pull this off and enjoy a wonderful
long-term relationship."

Was he hitting on me? I leaned back in my seat, the
leather squeaking under my shifting. I wasn't getting creepy
lecherous vibes like I got from some guys at the events we

held. His gaze hadn't once dropped to my almost-underwear camisole.

"Felix was the design and execution brains, so I've brought in someone new you'll be working with." Sam lifted his coffee cup high and took a sip. "He stepped out to go grab some breakfast and get a coffee for Phyllis out there, but he'll be back shortly."

The ding of the elevator echoed through the nearly empty offices. I craned my neck to get a look at who I'd be working with over the next few weeks. The person I was supposed to outshine to win the account outright. Sam had said they were new—maybe I'd have a shot. Unless he meant an established rock star planner, but new to Sam? My designs and event execution were still green, but I could hold my own. I hoped they weren't a seasoned pro.

Tyler's financial aid letter with the giant bolded dollar sign at the bottom opened the bottomless pit in my stomach. All I needed to do was win the job of one of the most historic hotels in the city, win them over to Easton Events while screwing over Simply Stark, and collect my check. Piece of cake, right?

I swallowed past the lump in my throat and tried to focus on what Sam was talking about.

"And we're ready to put in as much work as needed. You'll have the full resources of Simply Stark at your fingertips."

The heavy footfalls signaled the arrival of my competition.

"Leo's wonderful. You two should get along well. He's an absolute sweetheart."

The footsteps ended outside the doorway.

"We're in here, Leo. The associate from Easton Events is already here," Sam called.

"Phyllis is already devouring her short stack of pancakes. For some reason, I had a hankering for a chocolate croissant. I got one for you too." A syrupy thick voice poured through the doorway and the hairs on the back of my neck stood up.

The entire doorframe was filled with a guy who would have been more at home on a football field than in a room filled with fabric swatches. He filled out the suit well. Broad shoulders without a hint of shoulder padding. They were all him. The cut fit him perfectly, leaving just enough room while staying taut, almost like it concealed a brick wall.

Sam stood to stand beside the guy who was a head taller than him. "Leo, this is Zara. Zara, this is Leo."

My eyes landed on the same chocolatey brown ones that had twinkled with laughter after ruining my first shirt of the day.

I shot up from my seat.

We both shouted, pointing accusatory fingers at each other, "You!"

5

LEO

"It seems you two have met." Sam turned to me with a tentative smile and a question in his eyes.

"Briefly," the woman gritted out. "This morning."

I slipped a chocolate croissant out of bag with a napkin.

Her gaze darted down to the buttery soft, flaky dough wrapped around a center of chocolate.

"I got this for you, Sam." Without taking my eyes off the interloper, I handed the croissant to Sam.

"Thanks, Leo. I told you he was a sweetheart." Sam walked between us and sat behind his desk, oblivious to the palpable tension filling the room.

Keeping my eyes on my new events buddy, I lifted my croissant and took a hearty bite. "God, this is fan-fucking-tastic. Don't you think, Sam?" It was actually pretty damn good for a coffee shop pastry.

The woman's gaze narrowed and her nostrils flared.

"It's delicious. Oh, I feel terrible. Zara, did you want some?"

"Don't worry, Sam. Z's not big on accepting offers from others. I'm sure she's fine."

Her jaw clenched. "He's right, Sam. I'm fine. I've already had my breakfast. We should get started on our presentation. I have other work to do today."

"You two can take the corner office."

"Thanks, Sam. We'll get to work. Don't worry, I've got this handled." Food. Booze. Music. It was all people needed. "After you." I held out my arm, stepping out of the doorway.

Zara yanked her portfolio up from its spot leaning against the chair and stormed out of the office.

I let her go and couldn't stop myself from watching her walk away with unbridled fury.

She had nice legs. Long and shapely, powerful even, with the way she was trying to stomp her way through the concrete floor.

I cleared my throat. "Z, it's this way."

She stopped short, her shoulders so tense I expected a tendon to pop. Whirling around with fire in her eyes, she stared at me expectantly.

"In here." I took another massive bite of my croissant.

"Don't call me Z." She swung her portfolio in my direction.

"Why not? We're all friends here." At this rate, I'd have her quitting the job in a few hours. Then I could figure out what the hell I was doing, get everything smoothed out, and put Sam and Simply Stark in a better position.

"Not even co-workers. You could've mentioned earlier that I was headed in the wrong direction."

"I could have." I shrugged and pushed open the office door, wearing my smuggest grin. The one that had my sorry ass running five laps around the football field during freshman year of college when I decided to show up to practice hung over. My college coach had wiped it off my face until I was drafted, but that didn't mean I couldn't whip it out for special occasions.

"Let's get this over with." Her biting smile leached hostility into the air.

I gave her an hour tops. With her put-together looks, towering heels, and perfectly primped hair, she wasn't someone used to getting her hands dirty.

~

"Those napkins are the exact same color." We'd flipped through three stacks of vendor samples to find the perfect shade of pink for the table cloths. Was this what my life had come to? This was the guy I was now. Instead of committing eighty different plays to memory until I could run them in my sleep, I was fighting over fabric samples with a woman who hadn't sat down in the five hours we'd been cooped up in this room.

She pored over the sample books. Her lips did this thing where she sucked in one half of her bottom lip and then the other half. They were full and constantly shiny. Soft and pink.

Her head snapped up. "They're completely different." She held up two identical squares of fabric. "Light rose and light raspberry. They're completely different."

I needed out of this room. Staring at her lips, getting sucked in when she was the most infuriating woman ever, was a sign we'd been at this too long. "They're pink."

She gritted her teeth and sunk her head, running her fingers across her forehead. "They're not. You know what?" Her deep, heavy exhale ratcheted up my anger. At every step she treated me like I was a moron. "Let's move onto something else. The tables."

"Fine. There will be 150 people, so we need 15 tables. Done."

She scowled. "This isn't a simple, seventh-grade math problem. We need to decide how many cocktail tables we need, if ten person rounds are appropriate for what we have in mind..."

I picked up the glass paperweight and tossed it from hand to hand. "Have a few of each and people will figure out where they want to sit. We're not solving world peace here."

She slammed her hand down on the table. "Is this a joke to you?"

I palmed the weight and leaned over the table. "Of course not, but I'm not going to obsess over every miniscule piece of these events. Do you think anyone cares about the napkin colors? Will they be able to tell the difference between rose and raspberry? Are they going to storm out and kick us off the job if there are twelve round tables and no cocktail tables? No. People want to have fun, eat good food and drink, even better if it's an open bar."

"People also like being surrounded by nice things. They relax people, help them have fun. Do you think we should set up some milk crates and turn over garbage cans and everyone would be happy?"

"I didn't say—"

"You may not care about this, but my boss does—and the client does. If you want, you can sit the hell down and I'll handle it." She leaned in closer, nudging the table straight into my balls.

She thought she could scare me off with boring ass linen decisions? *Game on.* I jammed my legs against the table. The feet squawked against the floor.

Zara stumbled back a half step.

"And take all the credit? I don't think so."

"Then choose a color." The sounds escaped through her gritted teeth. She flung the sample book to my side of the table.

My jaw popped. "Raspberry."

"Wonderful." A calculating, furious narrowing of her gaze, and the list of decisions got longer and longer. She'd never met a decision she could get through the easy way.

"In what world do you think ax throwing would be the best event for a hotel group like Winthorpe?"

"Who wouldn't want to throw axes? This was a huge hit last time I included it." After we won our conference championship a couple years ago, the QB rented out the entire facility for the team party, for a chill night. BYOB plus axes had been a guaranteed night of fun in the off season. There had been people from all walks of life every time I visited one. Corporate suits. Husbands and wives. Bachelor parties. Bachelorette parties. It crossed all demographics.

"I could throw an axe right now, for sure." Zara dropped her pencil and leaned back in her chair, squeezing the bridge of her nose.

"You two are still at it? I'm turning in." Sam had his jacket draped over his arm and a briefcase in his other hand.

"It's only—oh wow." Zara gestured to the windows and froze.

The night sky was pitch black, the autumn sun long gone below the horizon, creating the perfect black mirror to reflect our shocked faces.

I snatched my phone up off the desk. "Shit!" Stacking the papers, we worked on with one hand, I typed out my reply to the twenty unanswered texts lighting up my screen. I wasn't missing tonight. I'd missed out for the past year, I wasn't going to be the one who skipped out on stuff until everyone stopped inviting me. Nope, I wasn't going to be the one left behind. Snatching my jacket off the back of the chair, I threw it on.

"You're leaving?" Zara stared at me, palms flat on the large conference room table covered in sketches, abandoned scraps of paper, and empty coffee cups.

"We can pick this up tomorrow."

"Thirty-six hours. That's all we have left. We don't even have a draft proposal completed." She stood in front of the doorway with her arms crossed over her chest. Her favorite pose.

"Finger food. Booze. Axe throwing. Presentation. Throw some bows on it and call it a day. It's not complicated. Excuse me."

She squared off in front of me. "We still have vendors to choose, menus to sort through, and we need to figure out what we'll be doing to entertain everyone."

"Tomorrow is a new day. Why don't you sleep on it? That way you'll have more energy to jam your color palettes down my throat. You're in my way." I nudged her out of the way and jogged toward the elevator.

"Tomorrow at eight am," she shouted after me.

I stepped into the elevator. "Wouldn't miss it for the world."

Sneakers scuffed and squeaked off the lacquered wooden floor. Four nets had been lowered from the ceiling for two parallel games on the courts. The entire place smelled like sweat, lacquer, and a dirty gym bag.

I kept my right foot planted, spinning from side to side with Everest guarding me. Even his gym clothes were starched to within an inch of their life.

"Are you washing clothes with all this spinning? Or are you going to shoot sometime today?" Everest kept up his coverage of me.

"Like you've ever seen a washing machine, let alone used one. You'd better protect that watch face when I knock your ass over."

He froze for a second and looked at his wrist.

It was the opening I needed. Throwing a wide elbow, I pulled the hit a bit, but that didn't mean I didn't smile at his *oof*. Lifting my arm, I pushed through the groan of my muscle and let the ball go. It sailed through the air and past Hunter's attempt at a block, hit the backboard and fell into the net.

"And the crowd goes wild." I cupped my hand around my mouth and imitated the roar of a stadium full of fans. August and I high fived. He spun the ball on his finger in our victory dance. We grabbed our water bottles. It had been a while since I'd worked up a sweat like this. It felt good to be out of breath after an hour of game play, even if it wasn't my game of choice.

Hunter jogged across the gym to grab the game ball.

"The reigning Thursday night basketball champions," I put on my best echoing announcer voice and added in more fan cheering before taking a gulp of water.

Everest slipped his watch off and shoved it into the zipper pocket of his bag. "That's the closest you'll get to a crowd saying your name anytime soon."

I tossed my water bottle down and it bounced in the gap in the bleachers. "What's your problem?"

August and Hunter got between us.

"My problem is you show up throwing elbows and throwing off the team dynamics and can't even be humble about a win. This isn't a stadium. This is for fun. We're blowing off some steam, that's all."

Throwing off the team dynamics. They'd found their groove without me, all hanging out at college together. But fuck him, I was part of this group too. Our weekly game was a way to keep us all from drifting into the solitude of adulthood. A friendly—okay, sometimes not so friendly—game of basketball, followed by wings and beers at The Griffin.

"Sorry we can't all be as refined as you, Everest. My etiquette lessons were cancelled because they clashed with my riding lessons."

He cut a gulp from his water bottle short. "You're such an asshole."

"I'm the asshole? We can never go back to a city—hell an entire state—because of you."

Everest wheeled around, eyes blazing, and shoved his finger in my face. "It wasn't my fault."

Jameson nearly tripped himself climbing over our gym bags on the bleachers. "Is this about Milwaukee?"

The name sent a bolt of fear through me. I looked over my shoulder like even mentioning it would summon the consequences of our last night there. Everest, Hunter, and August had the same stricken look I was sure I was wearing. "It's about nothing."

I flexed my hands at my sides.

Jameson looked from me to Everest. "It's been almost four years. It can't be that bad. What happened?"

We all turned to him at the same time. "Nothing."

Some of the anger in the room deflated. If there was one thing we all unequivocally agreed on, it was that we never talked about Milwaukee.

Everest picked up his water bottle again, but his eyelid twitched.

I probably got too much satisfaction out of pissing him off.

"Since everyone's sufficiently wound up now, let's get to Barry's before he gives up our booth." Hunter dribbled the ball and slung his bag over his shoulder. He lifted his arm and took a shot in the basket closest to the locker room door. It sailed through the air, completely missing the hoop and bouncing against the wall. He shook his head and jogged for the ball. "Plus, our court time is almost up."

As if summoned by his words the double doors on the side of the court banged open.

The doors to the hallway opened and a voice called out, cutting through the squeak of our sneakers on the court. "Nice air ball. You guys are still here? Stick around next time and we'll show you how to play." The tallest one stood with his little bird arms—seconds away from snapping—crossed over his chest, surrounded by his friends. He only came up to Hunter's chest.

"Don't start things you can't finish." Hunter bent down, glaring at the seventh grader.

"I can finish anything you can dish out, old man." The kid scoffed and looked to his teammates over his shoulder.

"Old man?!"

"Are you seriously about to scrap with a thirteen-year-old?" Jameson grabbed Hunter's bag, pulling him away.

"He started it."

"If I hadn't seen you walk across the stage at our graduation, I'd swear you were thirteen." Jameson dragged Hunter toward the locker room exit.

The kid cupped his hands around his mouth. "Next time. Me versus you. *Mano a mano.*"

"Let me know when the other *mano* arrives," Hunter shouted over his shoulder as the locker room door closed.

I nudged Hunter. "You're the worst person I've ever seen with kids."

"They weird me out. They're like adults, but small." He said it with a completely straight expression and slightly disgusted face.

I grabbed my clothes out of my gym bag. "It was your idea to play at the Y."

Hunter shrugged. "I got a good deal on our family membership."

"What the hell kind of screwed up family would we be?" August tugged his shirt over his head.

"The best kind—one that can go to different houses at the end of the night." Everest slipped on his shoes. They were probably Italian leather flown over from Milan on a private jet encrusted in jewels. The rest of the guys I played basketball with got big pro contracts rotating out every month or so. But I wasn't one of them. I'd gone to school with them and worked just as hard—if not harder—to get where I was at today, and it would never make me one of them.

And no, I wasn't bitter.

Not one damn bit.

6

ZARA

Most of the lights were out when I got back to the office. Had I known I was going to be gone all day, I'd have brought everything with me. The stack of invoices to process from vendors, Valerie's expense reports, and the vendor samples to organize would only be waiting for me in the morning, if I didn't take care of them tonight. Somehow my position had become the catch all, but maybe not for much longer.

A sneaky yawn escaped. I cracked my back, blinking hard to keep my eyes open.

"Nice of you to show up."

My neck and shoulders tightened. Since a massage wasn't in the cards, finding relief would mean grinding a tennis ball and my back against the wall like a grizzly bear in those toilet paper commercials.

Every word was a grating, passive-aggressive, back-handed comment, but I bit my tongue like I'd done since my very first day. What choice did I have? She was a known entity. I could handle her and let every insult roll off my back—at least, I could try to. This job was what I needed to keep Ty and me off the streets, and I'd do everything in my power to keep it and not let him down.

"I had some things for you to do." Valerie's nasal, entitled voice was like needles to my brain.

"The Winthorpe project took longer than I thought to set up. I came back to finish a few things, but now I'm going home." I shut down my computer.

She was in full make up, a shimmery, sequined dress, and heels.

"I stopped by to pick up Daddy's company card. Mine is maxed out."

From the stack of receipts I'd gone through, I didn't doubt that.

"Have a great night." My cheeks ached at my forced smile.

She held up her freshly manicured fingers in front of her. "Entertaining clients requires a certain level of expertise. Maybe someday you'll understand."

Was she entertaining them with her mouth? "You're right. Maybe one day I'll be as good as you."

Her dismissive snort was her way of saying goodbye. Thankfully, my doorway was empty by the time I stood up; she'd only stopped by for snide remarks. At this point, I didn't care. Nothing mattered but getting this account. Winthorpe would be mine. The bonus would be mine. And for ten whole minutes, I'd feel like the world wasn't on the verge of crashing down around my ears. The way things had been going, I'd take it.

Walking home, I went over everything we still needed to hammer out tomorrow before our meeting on Wednesday. Every idea I'd thrown out had been shot down by Leo. What the hell did he know? What was his experience? Could he sense my inexperience? Did I not actually know what I was doing?

Don't let him get into your head. You've been around the busi-ness for two years now. You know this stuff. He's an asshole and you don't need him. By the time I made it to my apartment I'd funneled all my day's shittiness back to Leo.

In my apartment lobby, a guy held the elevator open for me. Wow, an actual gentleman.

"Thanks," I mumbled and jabbed the button for my floor, leaning against the wall to stay on my feet. Had I even slept last night? Could I have one day where my feet didn't feel like they were angry after everything I'd put them through?

Feed his tie into the shredder. Or maybe use the stapler to—

"Are you talking to me?" The guy with the loosened tie and briefcase asked with his shoulder pressed hard against the wall opposite me.

"What? No, sorry, I was talking to myself." More like grumbling out all the ways I'd murder Leo if he screwed up this pitch. Once we won the job, all bets were off, but I needed him until then. Winthorpe wanted Stark and Easton on this month-long event extravaganza, but it didn't mean I was above letting everyone know, once we'd won, how much of the work I'd done on my own. Rose and raspberry are the same? Was he out of his mind? Okay, they were close, but come on. These were important details in our industry.

The doors opened and the guy sprinted into the hallway with his briefcase clutched against his chest with a single look back, like he wanted to be sure I hadn't followed him to carry out my plans of homicide.

He jumped at my apologetic smile as the doors closed.

Ha! Welcome to feeling like a woman, buddy.

Trusting Leo to help me pull this off would end up like

every group project I'd ever been involved in. Never trust
someone else when your ass was on the line, or you'd get
burned. A lesson I'd learned early and often.

The *ding* for my floor zapped the energy out of me. My
apartment had never been a refuge and now it sucked my
will to live like living on the edge of a hell mouth or with a
succubus.

"Zara!"

I jumped at my name shouted in the previously vacant
hallway. Her Spidey sense tingled the second I stepped off
the elevator and, no matter what, she always grabbed me. It
probably wasn't the worst thing to know someone who
always seemed happy to see me, but did she always have to
be so excited?

"Hey, Stella." I stood in front of my door with my key in
the lock, not opening it. I'd stand out here until I grew
cobwebs, rather than let her catch even a glimpse inside.

"Can I talk to you for a second?" In her plush ducky slippers and matching robe, she waved me into her apartment.
With a quick glance down the hallway, she widened the
door for me to come in, while keeping her gaze locked onto
the elevator like we were about to do a drug deal.

"What's up, Stella?"

"Your shirt's different from this morning."

I squeezed my forehead, warding off the pounding
headache threatening to send me into lights-out territory. A
dark, quiet space was what I needed. And sleep. "It's been a
day." The words leapt from my mouth, sharper than I had
meant them to.

Her shoulders dropped.

Fuck. Stella was the nicest, sweetest person ever and I
was an asshole. "I'm sor—"

"I think Adam's cheating on me."

I couldn't have been more surprised if she'd walloped me with a thirty-pound tuna. At least my snapping hadn't been the sunny mood killer.

But then my brain cycled back through her words.

"Adam? As in your boyfriend, Adam? The one who learned to braid your hair when you sprained your wrist?"

She toyed with the end of the French braids hanging down over her shoulders and nodded.

"The Adam who nearly got frostbite when he went out in last winter's blizzard to get you a box of Butterscotch Krimpets and hot chocolate because you ran out?"

She bit her bottom lip. "He's being so weird lately. And he flies out this weekend."

"For his first residency interviews. The same ones you forced him to take since he only wanted to apply to schools in the tristate area to be near you."

Ducking her head, she crossed one foot over the other, smoothing the poor plush duck head under foot. "I know, but he's been so off lately."

"Maybe he's nervous about the interviews. They determine whether he'll get a residency placement and become a doctor. He's the sweetest guy ever. Don't work yourself up over something that's most likely nothing."

She released the knot she'd been twisting in her sweatshirt, worry swirling in her eyes. "You think I'm being silly?"

"I get being nervous. You have a good thing with Adam —you're afraid of losing it because you value the relationship. Don't let your worries ruin it." The words rang hollow to my ears, but she didn't seem to notice. Everyone always let you down. The only person I could count on not letting me down was me and, hell, even I sucked. "He'd never cheat. Talk to him, if you're worried, and let him know how you feel."

Her smile brightened. "You're right, I'm being stupid. Did you want to come in and watch some TV?" She pulled the remote out of her robe pocket and waved it at me like she'd hand over control and we could watch whatever I wanted. Another reason Adam was a saint. Her bloodthirsty love for WrestleMania knew no bounds, and he never complained once, even though he was more of a nature documentary kind of guy.

"It's been a long day. I'm headed to bed."

"Okay, goodnight." She waved the remote at me again.

I turned the door knob and stepped into the hall. Seconds from freedom.

"Any leads on a new roommate?"

So close. I turned as she opened the door wider. "Nothing yet. You know how hard it can be to find a good one." More like impossible, and letting someone back into my place wasn't high on my list of things I wanted to do right now.

"I don't blame you. Jeannie was a fucking mess."

My jaw dropped and a laugh escaped me. "Language, Stella."

"She was. Get some rest, Zara. You look like you're about to pass out."

"Will do."

She closed the door.

I took my chance and rushed across the hall to my apartment before she changed her mind. Kicking the door behind me, I dropped my stuff. The absolute stillness and silence should've filled me with joy, but instead a creeping dread about what hid in the dark tightened my throat. I didn't turn on the lights. Why blind myself with the horror show after the day I'd had?

This is what I got when I let other people help—a kick in the teeth.

No. Shower, bed, sleep. Tomorrow, I'd do it again. Two more days until we presented to Winthorpe.

This was my life now. I had one chance to pull this off and I wasn't letting Leo steal even an ounce more of my sanity. I'd be calm, professional, and double and triple check everything he did until the account was *mine*.

Tomorrow the war was on. And I knew one thing for sure.

Leo Wilder wasn't screwing me.

7

LEO

The mountain of extra spicy buffalo wings sat in the middle of the table. The flats versus mini drumstick battle had begun, with everyone staking their claim to a section of the pile. "She screamed at me like I was trying to mug her, spilled coffee all over herself and blamed me."

Hunter waved over the waitress. "We're going to need more blue cheese. A lot more. Put what you think is an excessive number of cups on your tray, and then double it. Not telling you how to do your job, just trying to save you a few trips." He winked and she laughed, winking right back.

She walked away like she knew he was looking—and he absolutely was.

The bar with live music had become our go-to after games. Not only was there killer food, but the owner didn't care when we showed up sweaty and barely presentable.

Using the muscles I hadn't worked out in a while kept me focused and as close to sane as possible. I was an event planner now. It hadn't been what I'd seen for myself when

I'd been carted off the field on a stretcher, but neither had walking and talking, so I counted myself lucky.

Jameson slid his almost finished cup of blue cheese closer. "Leo is telling us his story and there are wings on the table. Can you concentrate and not flirt for a whole twenty seconds?"

Hunter leaned back with his patented smart-ass smile. "No, it's genetically impossible. I've been tested. Do you want to see my doctor's note?"

August leaned closer to cut through the squabble. "And now you're working with her?"

I threw down my wing. "For the next month. If I don't get this account and more work, Felix's company is gone. It's all Sam has left of him. I can't let that happen."

Everest butted in with his ever-helpful commentary. "Weren't you going on and on about looking for a sports-caster job? Trying to get Hunter to set you up with connections to get in there. Something about the financial well drying up?"

"I'm working on it. Hunter's working on it."

Hunter gave me a wing salute. "Pulling strings as we speak." He moved his fingers through the air like a puppet master. "Is she at least cute?"

Cute. I rolled the word over in my mind. The way her skirt skimmed across her thighs, the shoes with the high thin heels. Those were legs a guy couldn't not notice. "She's got great legs, but she's also got a serious shrew vibe." No longer bathed in a cloud of annoyance at her presence, I could see how someone might think she was cute. Faintly red hair, mossy green eyes. If it weren't for her inability to drop the scowl, someone might even confuse her for pretty. Maybe even more, but I couldn't afford distractions right now.

August stole some fries. "Does that mean you get to tame her?"

Hunter leaned back in the booth opposite me, trying to get the server's attention by "subtly" flexing his biceps. "I'm sure those legs will look wonderful when she's standing over your charred body after she figures out you have no experience whatsoever."

"I planned killer parties in high school. What about the day before spring break senior year?" If you gave people good food—and even better, alcohol—no one would complain about anything.

Jameson clutched his stomach. "Killer was right. I had my head out the window the whole drive down the shore the next morning."

August blew the paper off his straw in Jameson's direction. No one walking by would mistake us for guys only halfway to thirty, but something about hanging with old friends made reverting to those childhood roles so easy. "What are you moaning about? I was the one who had to clean the puke up before it peeled the paint off the walls."

The server came back with a tray practically swimming in blue cheese.

"Thanks, darling," Hunter's slight drawl amped up whenever he got his way.

I'd seen women punch guys for less than a darling, but the server was practically glowing. Her cheeks turned red and none of us missed the neatly folded napkin shoved into Hunter's hand.

August shook his head. "Do you emit a pheromone? Or have hypnosis skills we don't know about?"

"It's called game. And I've got a football field's worth of it."

Everest's head popped up. "Is that where Leo's went?"

My fingers tightened around my beer bottle. His perfect white teeth wouldn't be so straight when he picked them up off the floor.

"Everest..." Jameson went full-on Dad Mode with his chiding, which made me feel a hair better. "Everyone will eat their wings, drink their beer, and have a great night, dammit. I only get one of these a week. Don't make me find new friends." He dragged his fingers through his hair and served up a searing sigh.

We all buried our faces in those wings or beer bottles, trying to hold back the laughs. *Don't make eye contact. Don't make eye contact.*

My eyes connected with August. Tears swam in his eyes and he choked back his laugh. That broke the dam, and we were rewarded with a spray of beer from Hunter, who'd tried and failed to drink his way past laughter.

The forks and knives jangled as Hunter pounded his hand on the table.

Jameson slammed Hunter on the back. "It's what you all get for stressing me out on my night out."

Hunter coughed into his napkin. "If this is the best evening entertainment you're getting, we need to find you a date. I've never been able to pin down your type."

Jameson dragged his fingers through his hair. "It wasn't an invitation to matchmake."

"Who said anything about matchmaking? I'm talking straight up." He grabbed an onion ring and slipped his finger inside, knowing all Jameson's buttons.

Jameson slapped the onion ring out of his hand, sending it flying into Everest's lap. "Stop it."

"These are cashmere." Everest jumped up, knocking the greasy onion ring from his lap—and sending a full bottle of beer onto its side. It spun, facing his legs. He froze, staring straight ahead. The pitter-patter of ice cold beer splattering all over the floor, his pants, and shoes, warmed my cold heart.

Keeping his laughter-filled mouth hidden behind his fist, August righted the bottle and handed Everest a stack of napkins, which he snatched and dabbed at his pants.

Jameson and Hunter were fascinated by something happening behind the booth. I sat grinning from ear to ear, taking another bite of my food. I leveled a chicken wing at Everest. "They make cashmere sweatpants?"

Everyone lost it. The whole place was looking at us now, trying to figure out who'd died as we all doubled over gasping for precious breath. Even Everest cracked a smile.

More wings and drinks arrived before the happy hour special ended. A kid, (I'd need to check with Harold, the bar owner, to see if he was indeed an actual child), got onto the stage with a similarly-aged girl in a bright orange shirt who was moving around the cables and cords.

"Have you heard this guy before?" Hunter asked over his shoulder, already turned towards the stage, wings forgotten.

"No, is he any good?"

"He's phenomenal. I might have put in a word for him with some people I know."

Hunter, always the string puller and connection maker.

The girl in orange hopped down and stood at the side of the stage with another guitar at the ready.

The guitarist would've fit in with the D&D mob we'd played with for a few years in middle school. He wore an Avengers t-shirt, cargo shorts, Converse sneakers and an uncertain look that disappeared the second he opened his mouth.

A shiver ran down my spine at the first note. Everyone at the table looked at one another. Was this insanely talented kid for real? Now that he'd opened his mouth, he sounded at least eighteen.

All conversation stopped. Some people were watching mid-bite. Nacho cheese slid off tortilla chips all over the place until he sang the last bar.

"He won't be playing here much longer." Jameson shoved two fingers into his mouth to whistle in the way that had made me jealous since middle school.

Someone on the way up. The world was his oyster and anyone could see his talent would take him far.

After four more songs, the young singer spoke to the crowd. "I want to dedicate this set to my best friend, Riley. She convinced me to ask Harold if I could perform and she always has my back." He peered at her, still standing on the side of the stage.

She gave him two thumbs up, grinning from ear to ear.

"Aww, puppy love." Hunter laughed, clapping before cupping his hands around his mouth and joining the calls for an encore.

We paid our tab and left the bar before Harold could kick us out.

"Same time next week?" Hunter looked up from his phone.

My empty apartment called my name. That had been a shit ton more excitement than I'd had in months. "Penciling us in?"

He shrugged. "Everyone knows I'm a busy man."

"Same time every week."

I got back to my apartment and dragged out my laptop. Cracking my knuckles, I fired up my web browser, typing in 'event planning'. How much could there be to this?

Tomorrow, I'd lay out all the ideas and drag Zara along if

I had to, because I wasn't losing this job, especially not to a ball busting, barely ginger with killer legs.

Scratch that last part.

I wasn't going down without a fight.

Zara Logan had met her match.

8

ZARA

We met outside on the steps to the Winthorpe's flagship hotel. The gravel driveway led to the grand entrance with stone and marble steps and doormen in tails.

Unable to endure the stone digging itself into my arch a moment longer, I set down the portfolio and kicked off my shoe, emptying it. He'd wanted to bring the presentation, but I'd told him to leave it to me. I'd switched out the boards and put them into the still-pristine portfolio I'd never used for a client presentation before.

"Where are the boards?" Leo hissed and stared into the half-unzipped portfolio.

How hard was it to see inside a bag? Did I have to do everything, including *see* for him? "They're right—" Blood drained from my face. The new car smell from the never-used portfolio was even stronger, since it was totally empty. I lifted it and turned it over, shaking it.

My lips were numb and the entryway to the hotel blurred. "I grabbed the wrong portfolio."

It was the showing-up-to-class-and-there's-a-pop-quiz-I-didn't-study-for nightmare, only it was real and happening to me right now. In my stupid rush this morning, I must have left them sitting on the floor where I'd pored over them last night in my bathroom, which was the only room with a functioning light bulb where I had floor space to work.

"Go get them. I'll stall." He glared at me and rushed to the top of the steps of the hotel.

I'd never screwed up like this on a project before. I wanted to crawl into the empty portfolio and die.

"Zara." Leo shook me, staring into my eyes. "Can you handle this? Get the boards and get your ass back here."

I nodded dumbly.

His arm shot up and a taxi pulled forward. He shoved a couple twenties into the driver's hand through the open window, and pushed me into the back of the taxi and we hauled ass to my place.

Sweat poured down my back as I jabbed the elevator button five times in a row. Of all the days to forget the boards, this had to be the day. I could see Leo's condescendingly smug face looking down at me when I got to the meeting with minutes to spare.

Squeezing through the barely opened doors, I yanked my bag free and sprinted to my door. The telltale squeak of the door opposite mine almost had me flinging myself into my apartment, but it was too late.

"Zara," Stella squealed.

"Hi. I'm insanely late. I've got a big meeting." I blew a strand of hair out of my face, doing the dance of impatience, but trying not to snap at her. It wasn't her fault she had bat ears and the excitement level of a six-week-old Yorkshire Terrier.

"You know how I said I thought Adam was cheating?" She was doing a little dance on her tiptoes, squishing the unicorn faces into the carpeted hallway. Her hands were cupped in front of her.

Hell, I couldn't leave her *now*. "Yes. What happened?" I shoved my key into the door. A clear sign to cut to the chase for any normal person.

She glanced around at the completely empty hallway and leaned in close. "I went snooping." From the way she was *beaming* she hadn't stumbled into a treasure trove of kinky clown porn, a burner phone, and weeks' worth of text messages from another woman. "And I found this." She thrust her hands toward me and opened them, revealing a black velvet box. Her eyes dropped to the box and snapped back to mine.

"Can you believe it?"

"Awesome. Earrings? I told you he was a keeper." I turned the key in the doorknob.

"Oh my god, no. It's not *earrings*." Opening the box, Stella's eyes got wider as the angle of the box's opening did. And standing in the empty hallway, I was suddenly afraid guys in ski masks would show up, taze us both, and run off with the ring.

I was happy the landlord kept the hallway lighting to night-club dim. The sparkle on that thing in the light of day would've surely blinded me.

Taking a breath, I set down my portfolio and gave her a hug. Yes, I was in a rush. Yes, my future hung in the balance, and yes, Stella always cornered me, but this was great news. For once, I completely got why she couldn't keep it to herself a moment longer. They were great together and they'd get their happily ever after. At least someone should. "I'm so happy for you two. See, I told you, you didn't have anything to worry about."

She ducked her head, cradling the ring box in her

hands. "I know, but he's so sweet and so good to me, I was waiting for the eventual let down." She squashed one unicorn head with the other slipper.

"You two were made for one another. It's a gorgeous ring." It really was. If I weren't on the verge of a heart attack, I'd probably feel self-pity I'd never find someone who got me like Adam got Stella. Relationships were a no-go zone for me. I wasn't going to fall into the same trap my parents had. Being alone was so much easier than depending on someone else for your own happiness.

She lifted her head with a wide smile. "Isn't it? I've been staring at it, imagining what it'll look like on my hand." Cupping it to her chest, she gazed down at it like she was holding a day-old kitten.

"You haven't tried it on yet?" I turned my doorknob still needing to get the hell out of here.

"What? No, I couldn't. I want the first time I wear it to be when he puts it on me when I accept!" Her eyes lit up and she took a step closer, thrusting the box in my direction. "But you could try it on."

I had to open my big mouth, didn't I? "No. Absolutely not. You're playing the part of the wacky neighbor across the hall perfectly right now, but I'm so late, Stella."

"Please. Pretty please." She bounced up and down, pressing her hands together around the open box. "Just let me see what it looks like on, maybe take a picture, and then when I'm tempted to take the ring out and look, I can look at the picture instead."

"That's the worst idea ever. And makes no sense. Wait until he asks you!"

She slipped the ring out of the box, walking it toward me like she wanted me to join her on her quest to Mordor. "It could be months before he proposes, and what if he moves the box between now and then?"

I backed up until my back hit my door. "Then it'll be an even bigger surprise."

"I'll lose my mind, Zara. This ring is the proof he loves me. Proof there's no other shoe waiting to drop."

The poor thing. I squeezed her forearm reassuringly. "I know, but you shouldn't need the proof of a photo now. You—"

She grabbed my hand and shoved the ring on, using some Hulk strength I'd never seen her display before.

"Ow. You don't know your own strength, woman." I snatched my hand back and shook it, wincing.

"A few pictures and then you can take it off."

The foreign weight of it made me acutely aware of every part of my hand. I set my hand into Stella's outstretched one and let her finish the world's weirdest hand modeling session. I'd never known there were so many angles you could snap a picture of your fingers.

My phone buzzed in my open purse. Leo's name flashed up on the screen.

"Stella, as much as I want to stand here for another hour having every crease and fold of my fingers documented for posterity, I have to go." I wrapped my fingers around the ring and twisted, trying to pull it off. All I managed to do was smoosh all the skin against my knuckle and send shooting pain through my finger.

Oblivious to my growing unease, Stella swirled in a circle staring at her phone, flipping through the pictures.

"Ugh, Stella?" The space behind my knuckle where the ring rested throbbed to my increasing heartbeat.

"Yeah?" She held her phone up in front of her hand, staring at it adoringly.

I licked my entire-sleeve-of-saltines dry lips. "It's stuck." I bent over, twisting and twirling the symbol of her commitment around my ring finger, only managing to redden the area more. The thump was like a telltale heart under the metal band.

"Oh my god." She dragged me into her apartment finger first, and squirted soap on my hand like I was being deloused at a prison. My finger was now spotless, wrinkly, and still sporting a sparkler worth more than the GDP of a small island nation.

The clock over her stove flashed its bright and angry numbers at me. I had—

"Shit, eighteen minutes. We can figure this out later." I tried to pull away, but her grip on my hand was iron strong.

"You can't go!" Her shrill shriek rang in my ear.

"I have to. I have what might be the most important meeting of my life going on in—"

"Adam is coming back in two days."

"Exactly." I grabbed both her arms, trying to break the hysterical trance. "We have plenty of time to get this off. But if I don't go *now*, I could lose my job. I promise, I won't let my hand out of my sight. I promise." Backing out of her apartment, I didn't give her a chance to respond. The door slammed shut behind me and I threw the door open to my apartment.

Inside, I scanned the room for my old portfolio. Diving for it, I whacked my knee on the stupidest chair to ever exist and rushed back out into the hallway, grabbing everything I'd dumped there and took the stairs. My phone buzzed in my open bag, adding another tally to the five missed calls from Leo.

My day had started so well and here I was stealing someone's engagement ring on my way to a presentation with man-sized pit stains on my shirt. A bead of sweat rolled down my nose at the curb as I flung my hand in the air for a taxi.

Miracle of miracles one actually stopped for me. Maneuvering the unwieldy portfolios in the backseat of the taxi, I swapped the oversized boards to the new one.

Falling out of my taxi, I scrambled up the stairs to the hotel and asked at the front desk for the meeting rooms. The pointed me in the right direction and I took off, my heels squeaking and clacking on the marble floors. Rounding the corner, I took deep breaths to compose myself. My shirt clung to my body with sweat running down my back.

The area outside the meeting room was filled with ten or twelve people. I set down my things and threw on my blazer.

Two people came out of the conference room, pushing a mobile flat screen display and wheeling out a catering cart stacked with hors d'oeuvres. *Holy fuckballs.*

Leo's laser gaze zeroed in on me like an enemy combatant. His jaw ticked in time to each stalking step in my direction.

A suited man and woman entered the room at the direction of an older woman with a tartan scarf, bun, and a clipboard. They both carried large portfolios and sample flower arrangements.

"We're up next." He hissed. "Where the hell have you been?"

9

ZARA

The long, wide hallway leading to the conference room was lined with colorful fall bouquets. Did the flowers give off that fresh floral scent or was it piped in to make everything feel free and bright? It was the furthest thing from my mood, which was a grimier, panicky, sweaty shoe situation.

"You know where I've been," I seethed through clenched teeth. I buttoned and rebuttoned my blazer jacket. Gah! Two empty holes at the top. Dropping my hands, I closed my eyes and breathed through the panic. My heart was racing, sweat pouring down the back of my neck and my left hand throbbed. This ring was going to make my finger fall off.

Opening my eyes, I undid the buttons one more time and I swear, if there was an extra button or hole at the top I was going to burn this thing in a dumpster out back to go along with the raging dumpster fire of my life. Crisis averted; all buttons and holes safely matched.

Leo's simmering stare of disbelief while I searched through my bag for the tablet wasn't on my radar as the biggest problem I was dealing with. I knew I was late. I didn't need his dramatic *what the hell* looks to make me feel any worse.

"You left forty minutes ago." He dragged me by the elbow to an alcove in the hallway a yard away from everyone else.

Kathleen Thomas, who was heading up this project, stuck her head out of the conference room, spotting the two of us.

We smiled and waved. She tilted her head and smiled back before calling in one of the other companies, keeping her gaze on us until the door closed.

Leo snapped out of his smiling mannequin trance first. "I stalled as long as I could, nearly going out of my mind waiting on you. Are you trying to botch this pitch on purpose?"

"We're allies, remember? I'm not going to stab you in the back."

"Yet. After all your freaking out about being on time and prepared, you slink in here with minutes to spare."

"Slink? I didn't slink. I..." *came rushing in here flooding my heels with sweat.* "I got hung up."

Panic mode hadn't only set in for me. Leo was finally out of his cool guy mode. Winthorpe handled high profile events for even bigger clients. We'd been brought in to handle a staff event. It wasn't as glamorous, but I'd treat it like it was a royal wedding. All the other companies brought in a circus, including everything except for the big top and lions.

Vying for their corporate events, everyone pulled out all the stops like this was a multimillion dollar project, because that's how you won lifetime clients. They had their full floral arrangements and catering samples. But the well on our project coffers was filled with dust and cobwebs, although

Bill had been adamant I win this. Win it with shit back-up. *Thanks, Bill.*

"Kathleen came out and said we could present last."

"We'll be fine. I made the tweaks to the presentation in the taxi." My gaze lasered in on him, but I kept my face relaxed, almost pleasant to a passerby. They'd all be laughing at us anyway. Why add watching us throwing down to the list of ways we amused them. My stomach knotted and threatened a total upheaval. Hands shaky and heart thundering in my chest, I couldn't even take deep breaths to calm myself.

"What tweaks?" he ground out the words before he plastered on a fake smile.

"Ones that needed to be made." Three typos. Typos I'd made. I'd used my label maker to fix them. He didn't need to know.

"Without me getting a chance to look them over?"

"Your input wasn't necessary."

"What's that supposed to mean?" He reared back like me fixing my own damn typos needed his authorization.

"We're fine. The presentation is fine. It's been a day and it's not even noon." I jabbed my finger into his chest. Damn! Was he wearing armor under there?

I smiled wide and gripped the lapel to his blazer, smoothing out a fold. "And I don't need you adding to the crap pile. Got it?"

He glanced down at my hand—the one with the huge, honking diamond ring that hadn't been there this morning —and jerked back, pulling me with him, my death grip still tight on his jacket.

I fell against his chest. "What the hell?"

"Did you run home to get engaged? Is that why you were late? Making out with your boyfriend—sorry, fiancé?" His gaze darted around like a groom was going to rappel down from the ceiling and steal me away.

"Not that it's any of your business, but no I didn't get engaged. I'm not even dating anyone. It's my friend's, it's stuck, and it's a long story. Actually, it's a short story, and that's it." As insane as it sounded, that was my life. My gaze darted down to his neck. The fabric was trying to throttle every breath he took.

"Did you get changed in your car?"

He looked down at himself. "What the hell is wrong with how I look?"

"Have you ever tied a tie?" I yanked the knot loose, jerking his head down closer to mine. I whipped his tie out from under his collar.

He braced his hands on the wall behind my head, so he didn't pitch forward. "What's wrong with my tie?"

I smacked his hands away and pulled his collar up. "A standard knot here? At the Winthorpe?" It wasn't as bad as assless chaps and a tiara, but I could at least make it look like something wasn't trying to decapitate him.

My pleasant smile remained in place, but my gaze drifted to the people standing only a few feet away. "Are you crazy? With your neck, you need a half Windsor at a minimum. Maybe even a full Windsor, but this will have to do."

Moving quickly, I looped it around his neck, our lips inches from one another in this tight space.

His were soft. The rest of his face was dramatic lines and squared angles, so they stood out this close. The jaw, the long straight nose, the cheekbones usually hidden behind a smirk. I took one quick peek because I wasn't getting this close again, dammit—his eyes were pretty like caramel drizzled over chocolate fudge framed by thick eyelashes. Why did guys always win out on the eyelash department when women had to buy them? But those lips. They parted, clearing his throat. I jumped, my fingers getting back to work on the tie.

Someone cleared their throat. "Simply Stark and Easton Events?"

Kathleen.

We jumped apart, our heads whipping around.

My cheeks burned and I cleared my throat, stepping out of the alcove we'd been folded into.

This wasn't the time to be thinking about anyone's lips. I was only doing this so he wouldn't be strangled by his own tie.

The tail end of the navy fabric flipped into his face.

My hands tightened around the knot, shoving it right up under his Adam's apple. "That's better. Well, as good as we're going to get."

Kathleen wore a tartan neckerchief with glasses tugged down her nose. Her gaze narrowed when she spotted us. Dammit, so much for keeping ourselves inconspicuous.

I grabbed my bag and the papers. Leo gathered up our presentation materials. He dropped his hand to my waist, guiding me toward the room. I jumped, glared at him over my shoulder and gritted my teeth.

He wasn't even looking at me. He was staring into the room we were walking into like there would be an iron maiden and other torture devices. His hand brushing against my waist seemed completely automatic, not done to screw with me. At least I wasn't freaking out alone. But every team needed one person to keep a cool head—shit, that meant it was me.

We followed Kathleen into the room under the careful gaze of our opponents.

Dread and doom clouded my vision and blood rushed in my ears, drowning out everything else anyone said.

The stapled packets Leo set down in front of everyone around the conference room table paled in comparison to the slick trifold printed brochures everyone had in front of them from the previous presentations. We were the freaking Bad News Bears of event planning.

I unzipped the portfolio and the foam proposal boards we'd put together fell out of the bands holding them inside, hitting the floor with a *thunk*. Leo's fingers gripped the edge of his chair, probably trying not to facepalm. My ribs would be bruised by the time we left with how hard my heart pounded. How could it be in my throat and trying to burst through my chest at the same time?

He crouched at the same time I bent to pick them up. We almost clunked heads gathering everything up and setting it up on the easels sitting in front of the room.

"Shit." My voice was laced with misery and embarrassment.

Could I black out now? Wake up on the other side of this without the heart attack? So much of this prep had been meant to beat down the nerves, but now an about-to-puke feeling hit me. It happened whenever I needed to stand up in front of groups to speak.

Leo picked up the last foam board, keeping his back to the group.

I tried not to cringe. They looked like crappy fifth grade science presentations. We should've done digital—at least appeared modern. Why had I kept this to physical boards? This was my fault. I'd wanted them to feel the fabrics and not have all the colors screwed by the temperamental printer in my office. If we'd gone digital, I couldn't have forgotten the boards and I wouldn't be so hot and sweaty right now.

Leo leaned in close, resting his hand on my shoulder. He smelled clean and fresh. "Take a breath. We've got this."

Get it together, Zara. Mine and Tyler's futures hung in the balance.

"I've got this." I grabbed the last board and set it beside the other easels.

Standing in this bright, sunlit conference room, next to eight people at a table staring at me, I wanted to explode through the door to safety.

"Has anyone here been to summer camp?"

Our presentation was a balance of the old and the new. Leo'd had to fight for every idea and I'd been tempted to rip them off the board on the taxi ride over, but we had a deal and if I was going to get any help from him in pulling this off, I needed his buy-in. But standing here walking them through the day we'd planned felt like a massive mistake. It was getting harder to breathe and my hands wouldn't stop shaking.

"Sorry, what was that, Kathleen?" *Focus, Zara.* I snapped to attention and leaned in, trying to keep my panic spiral from dragging this whole thing down.

Kathleen's glasses slide even lower on her nose. "A paint balloon fight? I do hate being disappointed and dealing with people who aren't even trying." She set down her pen and crossed her arms over her chest.

Everyone else in the room shifted back, similarly. Panic rose in my throat. *We're losing them.*

My gaze cut to Leo's and my fists tightened at my side for a flash.

Leo jumped in. "All the paint is non-toxic and non-staining. There'll be coveralls for anyone who doesn't want to get it on their clothes. It's a new take on capture the flag, and nowhere near as painful as paintball, but with the healthy living ethos and reputation of Winthorpe, I—*we* felt it would be an adventurous addition outside the norm."

Kathleen leaned back with the corners of her lips turned down.

I stepped forward. "And there will also be stations for people who want to opt out of the activity itself. Beauty treatments and express massages. Head, neck, and back massages for participants after the paint battle as well." Every second under their exacting gazes threatened to melt me into the floor.

"We had a massage set-up at our retreat a year ago. There were a lot of long lines." Kathleen tapped her pen on her notepad.

Leo held up his phone and directed everyone to the spot on the handouts we'd given them. "They're express massages, and the company has an app to let people book a spot only a few minutes before, so no wait times. And they can change their appointments depending on what else they wanted to do that day."

Kathleen's mouth tightened and she jotted down a note.

She hated it. She hated everything we'd presented today. Gasoline was pouring out of the wreck of this presentation headed straight toward a lit match on the ground. It was too different. Too out there for a more traditional company. If I could've fit my hands around Leo's neck I'd have strangled him.

No worries, I could always use his tie.

"We'll have a campfire for roasting hotdogs and marsh-mallows?"

"For eighty people? How do you propose to make that

work?" Kathleen rolled her chair closer to the table, tenting her fingers together.

The sun came out from behind the clouds, lighting up the room even more. Like a stage hand shining a spotlight on us to watch me bake in my failure. I swallowed against the anxiety-induced lump in my throat. Why the hell had I been thinking I could do *this*? Bill was definitely going to fire me for not only tanking this, but making us look like idiots. Where would I go? I'd get evicted. My credit would be ruined. Tyler would have to leave his boarding school he loved to live in a cardboard box on the side of the road, or worse—with our parents.

Their scrutinizing gazes zeroed in on every gap of our plan.

I cleared my throat, stepped forward. "We would also have full catering, of course. But for people who wanted to fully lean into the camp experience, we have another option." I pointed to the campfire pictures.

The room was bathed in a cascade of rainbow colors from Stella's rock on my finger. Before I could drop my hand and cover the ring, I nearly blinded Kathleen. She shielded her eyes and locked onto my hand. Her face softened and the corners of her mouth shot up. Looking from me to Leo, her lips parted and the smile widened.

The ring. She loved the ring. And after our tie tying fight out in the hallway, she now thought Leo and I were together. No, not just together. Engaged. And that made her happy. Giddily happy. Her pen was down and she'd rolled her seat forward even farther, taking her steepled hands to the side of her face like she was looking at two lovebirds.

An idea ricocheted through my brain.

I angled myself toward Leo, trying to catch his eye. "Right, hun."

Leo's head jerked back, almost cracking the drywall.

Narrowing my gaze, I walked to him and stood beside his chair.

Kathleen's eyes lit up like she'd stumbled into her own live action soap opera. Three minutes ago I was sitting on a block of ice in Antarctica, but now we were on a rocket fired into the center of the sun.

"We have a strong relationship we know can provide you with the best experience possible."

Leo looked over at me with so many questions in his eyes. Was I having a stroke? Or hallucinating? Was this some head injury-induced lucid dream?

Taking his hand, I squeezed it to snap him out of his stupor. *Read the fucking room, man.*

His gaze shot from me to our hands.

Did I need to hire a skywriter? He hadn't picked up on the whiplash change in mood in the room?

Through clenched teeth with my head tilted, I gripped his fingers tighter.

He hissed. *Whoops.* Too tight.

"I was telling Kathleen about our wonderful relationship." Keep it ambiguous. Couldn't he read the intense arch of my eyebrows?

I kept the pleasant smile on my face, meeting Kathleen's gaze.

She sat up straighter in her chair. It was no longer bored and uninterested, but engaged and total ga-ga smiling.

"What relationship? Working together?" His face was a mask of confusion.

Work with me, Leo, I willed him, but the eyebrow signals weren't getting through.

Kathleen's smile was fading. So much for ambiguous.

Laughing, I threw back my head and turned to our audience. "He's such an amazing actor. I always told him he should take up acting, but he followed me into the planning business. But we're currently working for different companies until we can finally work together. Our bosses don't know."

Kathleen pressed her hands against her chest. "So wonderfully romantic. We'll keep it quiet, for sure, and not let it out of this room." She zipped her fingers across her closed mouth, locked it, and threw away the key.

There was a murmur of approval from the three other people around the table.

"How long have you two been together?"

A small sound escaped my mouth.

Stepping forward, Leo wrapped an arm around my waist and tugged me against his chest.

Then his hand travelled south, cupping my ass. My teeth clacked shut and I clasped my hand over his, squeezing it and dragging it around to my hip.

"It's all new. A whirlwind engagement. Sometimes it feels like we've only known one another a week. Isn't that right, Gingersnap?"

He stared into my eyes and I let loose a glare burning with the fires of retribution. Sliding back into the agreeable fiancée mode, I swung my head around and smiled wide.

"It is new, but when you know, you know." And I knew I was going to murder him in the parking lot. I grabbed his wrist and slid it back up to my waist.

"We know you've had many wonderful presentations today, but we also know how important it is to do things differently and make a lasting impression, especially for your employees. That's why our ideas were so unorthodox. When Zara and I are working together, we can't help but create something long lasting that'll leave everyone screaming for more."

He's certainly taken the ball and run, sprinting, streaking across the field with it.

"Should we go through the rest of the presentation?" I tried to steal away from Leo's Mr. Handsy routine.

"No, it's fine. We've seen enough. There were a few unorthodox things in your presentation, so let us talk it over. If you'll wait outside?"

We gathered up our presentation materials and walked out. Leo dropped his hand to the small of my back to guide me out of the door.

The second the door closed, I whirled on him, keeping my face as neutral as possible. Everyone else was still standing outside the conference room.

"What the hell was that?" I whisper-shouted, backing him into the corner with a smile on my face.

"It's called playing along, Gingersnap. You're the one who sprung the whole 'hey, guess what, I'm engaged to this guy' card like it was no big deal."

"I insinuated it. I was trying to be subtle." I raked my fingers across my scalp. The ring snagged in my hair, ripped out a few strands. "I freaked, okay? We were losing her, so I looked for another angle. Once she saw the ring, her eyes lit up and she was into it. Checking us both out."

He squints. "Hunter said she used to work in weddings before moving to the hotel side of things."

My head whipped up. "You had information on her and what she did before this and you didn't tell me?"

He shrugged. "How was that going to help us?"

"We could've tailored the presentation to play up romance and love versus a paint balloon, capture the flag, testosterone-fueled rave." My fingers flexed at my sides. If his neck weren't so thick...

"They seemed into it."

"We could've framed it as a historical battle or something else. If you have information like this in the future, you need to share it with me." What else was he holding back?

"And if you decide we're moments away from the honeymoon suite, a heads-up would be nice."

My cheeks flushed. "Even if we were engaged, manhandling me in a professional meeting was out of line."

He scoffed. "Hardly manhandling."

I glared, roasting him under my gaze. "Sorry, was someone else's hand on my ass in there?"

"If you want me to—"

The door opened and we both straightened, pulling ourselves out of our *ready to rip each other's throats out* pose.

Kathleen stood in the doorway and she scanned the room.

"Thank you everyone for the wonderful presentations this morning. We've made our decision."

Hope flared in my chest. We were new. We didn't know what the hell we were doing, which was certainly a new direction for them to go in. Maybe I hadn't completely fucked this up.

She glanced down at her clipboard. "We've chosen Oren & Co. to handle our staff event. I'm so happy to be working with you two again."

Zara sagged, her shoulders rounding.

I nudged her with my shoulder. "At least we don't have to pretend—"

"The gala, that is. The Simply Stark and Easton Events collaboration from Leo and Zara? You'll take over our two staff appreciation events. I can't wait to see what the future holds for this union." She winked with the subtlety of a fifty-yard punt return to the head.

We both froze, slack jawed and gaping at one another. From the look on her face I knew I hadn't imagined it. The words Simply Stark and Easton had come out of Kathleen's mouth.

Zara flung her arms around my neck and without thinking, I wrapped mine around her, pulling her close. So much for calm, cool, and collected professionals.

She smelled like raspberries. In a split second, she seemed to realize she'd practically jumped into my arms and she dropped hers from around my neck and slid down my body.

I held on for a split second too long and she gave me a gentle shove in the stomach.

"Just playing along, Gingersnap." I slipped my fingers through hers and we walked over to Kathleen.

Zara squeezed right on my knuckle and I swallowed my wince.

"Thank you so much for giving us this opportunity. We look forward to creating many memorable experiences for everyone."

"I'm very interested to see how you two pull this off, and I hope it'll be the beginning of more than one happy relationship throughout the process. I've divided up the events and you'll have the first one, which will be next Friday. I know it's tight and it doesn't have to be the full event, but it would be wonderful if you two could be our first."

"Of course, we'd be honored." I lifted my hand, draped it over Zara's shoulder, and cupped it. "Wouldn't we?"

Her teeth were clenched hard enough to bite through nails. I was going to enjoy this. Oh so much.

Zara tried to dislodge my hand, but I held fast. "It would be our pleasure. If you give us the details, we can get to work right away."

"I'll touch base with Oren & Co. and then lay everything out for you."

We followed her back into the conference room after the other companies had left. Two events two weeks apart while Oren & Co. would handle the gala in between. Kathleen had hinted not-so-subtly we could end up as the go-to planners for the five Winthorpe hotels in the tristate area, if we proved ourselves through the smaller events.

These events alone would put Stark back on the map and pull Sam out of any financial worries. It was a retainer account, so he'd have a steady cash flow no matter what, which would allow him to bring in the right people to keep the business going.

My phone vibrated on the table as we got the final details from Kathleen.

Jameson: 911. When are you getting here? Teresa's getting restless.

Me: I'll be there ASAP. Wrapping things up now.

Jameson: Hurry!

On my way. Zara threw out another volley of questions to Kathleen. Everyone else had already left. She was the kid who asked the teacher about homework as everyone was already halfway out the door.

"Gingersnap, I have that meeting I told you about, but I'll see you later." I laid it on thick like molasses and enjoyed every eye-dagger she sent my way.

"Really? Right now?"

"We've got all the details. Thank you for this opportunity, Kathleen." I shook her hand and left without waiting for Zara.

But the click of her heels across the parking lot told me I wouldn't be lucky enough to get out of here without a fight. Bring it on, Gingersnap.

11

ZARA

I t had taken me a full ten seconds to stop gaping at Leo and go after him. I said bye to Kathleen and rushed after him. Every time I called out his name, he waved to me over his shoulder with his car keys clutched in his hand.

I opened the passenger side door of his car, leaning in. "Where are you going?"

Leo jammed the key into the ignition and the engine roared to life. "I told you."

"A meeting? That's bullshit and you know it."

"I have somewhere to be."

"We need to talk about this. She thinks we're engaged." I'd never hyperventilated in my life, but there I was, gasping while standing in the middle of a wide-open parking lot.

"So when *you* pull something out of your ass it's fine, but when I do it, I'm trying to destroy things. You said it yourself. We were losing them. You saw an opening and went for it... and so did I."

"That's not fine. If she finds out she's going to lose it."

He shrugged. "You should've thought about that before

you started dropping 'huns.' When's the wedding date, Gingersnap?"

"We don't have much time. We're not through discussing this."

"You can have me all day tomorrow, but I have somewhere to be now." He shifted the car into reverse and backed up a foot, bumping me with the open door. "I'm leaving."

"You're not rolling out of here without talking about this." I flung myself into the car and buckled my seatbelt.

"Get out of my car."

"No. Let's go." I patted the dashboard. "I'd like to see where you need to go that's more important than coming up with our plan of attack for the event in eight days."

"I'm already late. I'd hoped to present first, so we wouldn't be late, but someone decided to take her time and go jewelry shopping on the way here."

"I'm not getting out of this car. We can go over everything in your car, meet at my office or yours. I don't care, but we have eight days. In planner time, it might as well be tomorrow."

His jaw ticked and he glanced down at his watch. "Fine."

"Great." I reached for the seatbelt to unbuckle it, when he slammed on the gas, reversing out of the parking lot. Bracing my hands on the roof of his car, I banged against the passenger side door. "What the hell are you doing?"

"You said we could have our meeting in my car. You didn't say anything about the car being stationary. I said I had somewhere to be."

We whipped past city blocks following signs for the bridge into Jersey. Oh god, he was going to murder me and bury me in the Pine Barrens.

He looked over at me with his smackable smirk. "Didn't

you have some things to discuss that couldn't wait until tomorrow?"

Pressed up against the door at my side, I glanced out the window. Did I need to jump for it?

"For once you're speechless. It's a Christmas miracle." He kept his gaze trained on the road, other than glances at the clock on the dashboard.

Reaching into the wheel well at my feet, I grabbed my tablet out of my purse and made a few notes. "We'll have to confirm everything we put into the presentation. Catering will be hard for three hundred people on such short notice."

"It's only one-fifty at a time. They can't exactly shut down the hotel for our afternoon of team building. It's two shifts, so we'll have to do everything four or five hours apart. It gives us a lunch and a dinner option."

I paused with my stylus above my screen and ran over what he'd said. We could call in a last-minute order for lunch and dinner much easier for one hundred and fifty people. "You're right."

"Turns out I'm not a total fuck up."

"I never said that."

"You didn't have to." His grip tightened on the steering wheel.

Resting my hand against the window, the afternoon sun caught the solitaire cascading the inside of the car in a rainbow kaleidoscope of color. My finger was a charming three shades too dark due to lack of blood flow.

He nodded at it. "When we get there, I can help you get that off your finger."

"With a bone saw?"

He laughed, turning to me before laughing even harder.

I reached out to steady the steering wheel as his deep laugh cut through some of the simmering tension.

"Good one," he muttered, but I still wasn't one hundred percent sure the thought hadn't crossed his mind—it would get me out of his hair, and he could have the account to himself.

We went over many of the other items we'd need for the event. I had confirmations from five vendors by the time Leo pulled the car in front of a white two-story house in a quiet suburban neighborhood. There were colorful flowers lining the walkway up to the house.

I set my tablet down on my lap and angled myself in my seat. "We don't have to be enemies."

"You're the one who started things off this way. You're trying to steal the account for yourself."

My jaw hung open. "I'm...It's..."

"You think I didn't hear all your 'I' talk? Or how you keep trying to shove everything down my throat to get your way."

"I need this to go well. I need my job. This is my one shot to prove myself. I have bills and responsibilities.

"Plus, I wasn't the one who slammed into me, spilling coffee all over my clothes, stepped on my one chocolate croissant, and offered it to me from the bottom of a shoe." I jammed my tablet into my bag, dreading how much a taxi would cost back to the city. Maybe I could take one to the closest train station instead. That would be cheaper.

A small knock broke through the seething tension in the car.

Leo looked over his shoulder and his entire demeanor changed. He opened the door and a small voice filled the interior.

"Leo, you're here! You're here!" A little girl with big black curls under a conductor's hat jumped onto his lap, wedging herself between the steering wheel and his chest.

I stared at her and back at him. Did he have a daughter?

There wasn't a resemblance. We hadn't delved into anything personal, but wow, I'd have thought he'd have mentioned it. Not like I'd given him much of an opportunity.

"Teresa Amelia Asher." A man with thick-rimmed Clark Kent glasses stood at the top of the steps with a kitchen towel slung over his shoulder. "What did I tell you about leaving this house?"

The little girl who looked no more than four jutted her bottom lip out. "Sorry, Jamie."

He came down the steps with a big smile.

Confusion whirled in my head. Who the hell was he? Who was she? Was Leo gay? Was this Leo's boyfriend or husband? Mind bombs were exploding left and right.

Leo climbed out of the car with Teresa. "Happy birthday, Birthday Girl."

She laughed and giggled as he blew raspberries into her neck.

I sat in the car. I had so many questions, smoke was probably rising from my ears.

Leo ducked down through the open doorway with Teresa's arms wrapped around his neck. "You coming or what? I can drop you off back home once we're finished here."

"Sure." I needed answers; I couldn't have stayed away.

"You must be Zara." He covered his laugh with a cough into his fist. "Leo's told us all so much about you."

"Us? Yes, I'm Zara. And you are?"

"Jameson."

He ushered us all into the house and I took everything in in wide-eyed fascination, not wanting to pry, but dying to know what was going on. This was the meeting Leo had to get to? Somehow, it made his adamancy that we not debrief right after our presentation less annoying. I knew all about not wanting to let down people who were important to you.

Inside, there were two other guys, each armed with baking staples. Chocolate, flour, sugar, baking pans, vanilla. Everything was out all over the countertops. A heady punch of testosterone filled the room. It was like an Avengers poster, but they were all wearing regular clothes and somehow hotter when sprinkled with flour.

Leo swung around like he was looking for something. "Zara, I want to introduce you to someone. Where's Teresa?"

The little girl in his arms giggled and tapped him on the shoulder. He jerked like she'd appeared out of nowhere. "This is our conductor extraordinaire and birthday girl Teresa."

I held onto the strap of my bag and shot them a small wave. "Hi, Teresa. Happy birthday, I'm sorry I didn't get you a present."

He'd been in a hurry not to miss her birthday. The last of my simmering anger was zapped away. From how wide her smile was, Leo was important to her and he'd shoved aside his other responsibilities to be there for her. Finally, something we could relate to.

"You can help with my cake. It's the only present I asked for." She beamed. Leo set her down and she ran off to a trunk beside the couch and pulled out a wooden train.

"Guys, this is Zara."

"Zara, this is August and Everest." He said the second name like a swallowed curse. "And you've already met Jameson." Each one waved when Leo said their names.

Everest had on a blue button-down shirt with the sleeves rolled up to his elbows. His black hair made his striking blue eyes stand out even more. And from the way he and Leo kept glaring at one another, he was The Nemesis.

"Your ring is so pretty." Teresa grabbed my hand and rubbed her finger over the stone. "You're engaged." With everything going on, I'd been distracted from the engage-ment ring strangling my finger. Strange how quickly that had happened.

"Yeah, today." I laughed, but no one else did. The air had been sucked out of the room.

August with the tousled brown hair and deep green eyes, skittered over the ring. So, Mr. Commitment, he wasn't. The ring seemed like his kryptonite—he couldn't even look directly at it.

Their gazes bounced from me to Leo.

He stepped in front of me waving his hands. "Not now. Not ever. It's stuck on her finger. We had a few things to go over, so Zara had to ride over with me."

There was an exchange of skeptical looks, but everyone went back to their spots in the kitchen.

"Teresa, are you sure you don't want a smiley face cake or a sun cake?" Jameson with the glasses leaned out of the kitchen doorway.

"I want Thomas the Tank Engine," she singsonged, and sat down at the center of an elaborate wooden train track set.

"Of course you do." Jameson and the rest of the guys ducked back into the kitchen.

Teresa seemed totally content with her trains and the door was locked with the top chain on.

I slipped into the kitchen where all the action was taking place. "Can I help?"

Jameson looked up from the tablet on the counter, playing through a cake decorating tutorial. "Do you have any experience making a 3D Thomas the Tank Engine cake? It says we need dowels. Anyone have dowels?"

Leo patted himself down before snapping, "Damn, I left them in my other pants."

The sink was already overflowing with dishes, abandoned batter in bowls, and utensils, even though from as far as I could tell, nothing had made it into the oven.

Everest followed my gaze and his cheeks pinked up. "We had some slight confusion with the salt and the sugar on the last batch of batter."

So The Nemesis wasn't a good baker.

"Twice." Jameson held up his fingers. "Two times."

"What? No culinary expertise from the help growing up, Master van Konig?" Leo bowed with a flourish.

"F—" Everest peered out the open kitchen doorway, substituting the words for a double barrel single finger salute.

"I'm happy to clean dishes." Lifting my non-ring ladened hand, I broke into the volley of barbs and banter. They were all so comfortable and at home with each other, enough to insult and tease. I'd never had a group of friends like this before. Growing up had all been about keeping my head down and not drawing attention to myself.

There had been no sleepovers or nights out on the town. In college, everyone seemed to have had a much different childhood, so once again, I was focused on doing my work, graduating, and starting my real life. And I'd never thought about what I'd missed out on until now. I guess hanging out with a total of three people ever meant I'd missed a lot.

"Sold to the lady who doesn't want to be responsible for crushing a five-year-old's dreams of a Thomas cake on her big day."

The four of them crowded around the tablet, stopping and starting the video, and moving and reorganizing the cake pans into various shapes before Leo shoved them out of the nest.

"We jump in. It's the only way we know. Let's get started

on the batter—again." He pointed to Mr. Clark Kent Glasses and Mr. Commitment, whose gaze still drifted to my hand every so often.

"Everest can make the chocolate icing."

"I'll butcher the abomination that will be these fondant flowers." Leo stared at the multicolored lumps of fondant on the counter like he was trying to morph them into petals and stems with telekinesis.

I turned on the faucet and sorted out a good soapy needs-a-long-soaking side, and a to-be-cleaned-now side—which was more of a pile that overflowed onto the counter.

Working quickly, I washed and dried the dishes to the sound of tutorial videos overlapping one another from three different phones. Recipe books were multiplying on the counter.

Leo was hunched over looking ridiculous with tiny pieces of colorful fondant, shaping and molding them with his giant man hands.

I took a deep breath. Maybe we'd gotten off on the wrong foot. Maybe he wasn't a condescending and clueless asshole who kept trying to steer my boat straight over the waterfall to my untimely demise. Maybe there was a way we could work together on this project and not rip each other's throats out. And maybe he looked kind of cute rolling out fondant leaves for a five-year-old's birthday. Maybe...

12

LEO

"Yes! That's it. You did it." Jameson ran his finger across the top of the bowl of frosting and Everest beamed like he'd run his first 100m in under 14 seconds.

"Leo, how are the flowers coming?"

My flowers weren't half bad. After the first five video tutorials, I'd gotten the hang of something that could have been mistaken for a flower. But the buttercream roses? Those were dicey.

Zara had finished washing every dish in what seemed like the entire neighborhood, and hadn't complained one bit. Out in the living room, she sat on the floor with Teresa, helping her rework the tracks.

When she wasn't overbearingly controlling, she wasn't half bad.

"So, what's up with her?" August whispered over the cake pan with a steaming, golden brown cake inside.

"I've told you all there is to tell you about her. We're stuck working together on the Winthorpe events for Felix's company."

"What's the deal with the ring?"

"Your guess is as good as mine. She said it's not hers, it got stuck on her finger and she couldn't get it off. During the presentation, the decision-maker's face lit up when she spotted it, so we're stuck playing fake fiancées for a while."

"Fake." Some of the tension in August's body relaxed. He set down the cake pans and picked up another empty set.

"Do you think I'd get engaged and not tell you guys? That I'd show up like, 'Hey guess what? I'm getting married?'"

August's hand jerked and he spilled some of the vanilla batter onto the counter.

"Only an asshole would do that." He didn't look up, but kept pouring into the next pan.

Everest and Jameson shot me looks and my mistake became crystal clear.

"Shit, that's not what I meant," I sputtered, trying to recover.

"Don't worry about it. I was, indeed, an asshole."

"Was?" Jameson threw out, nudging his glasses up higher.

August laughed and set down the bowl. "You're right. It's still in here."

"But we love you, man." I handed him a tiny, half wilted, half misshapen fondant flower.

"Like you guys could get rid of me."

The front door banged open, stopped by the chain. "What's going on? Did I miss it?" There was an almost hopeful hint to his voice.

Zara looked up from her seat on the floor to me.

Hunter had his face smooshed in the open door, lips first.

Teresa jumped up and down, spotting the bit of gift wrapping paper through the gap in the door.

"Move your freaking face and I can let you in." I shoved Hunter's head back and opened the door.

"Hey, Teresa." Hunter crouched down and Teresa flung herself at the present in his hands, wrestling it away and bounding back to her train set.

Hunter's lips creased into a frown and he shook his head. "Always about the gifts?"

"When it comes to a wrapped present on her birthday, it seems so." Jameson walked into the living room with batter splatters all over him and the lenses of his glasses.

Hunter half whispered out of the side of his mouth. "Who's the gorgeous lady playing with Teresa and wearing an engagement ring? Did August pull an August again?"

"No, that's Zara. The one I told you about."

Hunter's eyes widened. "I was expecting some sort of troll-like creature with a hunchback and oozing pustules, not a surprise engagement."

Zara looked up at me.

I expected daggers in her eyes, instead she laughed. I'd never seen her laugh before. It suited her. Her eyes sparkled.

She picked herself up off the floor. "No surprise engagement. My neighbor wanted me to try this on. It's a long story." She waved her hand as though questions about that part of her story could be as easily waved away. "But we got to our meeting and Leo blurted out we're engaged. So now I'm stuck with this ring on my finger that I have to give back, and a fake fiancé with no ring."

"Then it's good I showed up when I did. I can solve both your problems. First, I need my tools." Hunter shot his finger into the air. "To the bathroom."

Everyone hesitantly followed him with slightly

concerned looks. He took Zara's hand and led her to Jameson's upstairs bathroom. He rummaged through the medicine cabinet until he found what he'd been looking for.

"Dental floss? You're going to clean your teeth?" Jameson held Teresa in his arms, so she could see between our heads.

"You have no imagination." Hunter held Zara's hand in his. Putting the stopper down in the sink, he ran her fingers under the cold water. "You only make that mistake once. Always. Always pull the stopper."

Zara looked to me and I shrugged. If I'd had an idea on what he planned, I'd have done it myself.

Pressing on the metal and turning the ring around, he slipped the floss under and wound it around her finger. Slowly, he wrapped the floss down her finger past her knuckle like a mummy. The tip turned a little purple.

I reached for the floss. "What the hell are you doing? Look at her finger."

Hunter shot over his shoulder. "Shhh, I'm working." He turned back to Zara. "How do you work with him? Isn't he a total pain in the ass all the time? Thinks everyone is part of his defensive line."

Zara's forehead crinkled and she chuckled, wincing as the floss was tightened around her finger. "He's mainly a pain in the ass, but he has his moments."

Wow, I'd expected her to go all-in on the Leo bashing. Had that been a compliment? A real live one? Was I a real boy now?

"And voila." Hunter unwound the floss from behind the ring and dragged it along the dental floss mummification of Zara's finger. The smooth floss squeezed down the swelling of her finger and made for a track for the ring. It clattered into the plugged sink.

"You're a genius." She threw her arms around Hunter's

neck. A small bolt of jealousy shot through me, like the one I'd felt when she'd shown up with that ring on her finger, which was stupid.

I didn't even like Zara—what was with not wanting someone else to slip a ring on her, or have their arms around her?

She massaged her hand. The combination of the ring being stuck and the dental floss, had done a number on her skin. At least the color was returning to normal.

I wedged myself between her and Hunter. "Did you want some ice?"

She looked up at me. "I'd love some." Picking up the ring from the sink, she stuck it in her pocket. "What do we do about the ring? Kathleen will have questions if I'm ringless the next time we see her."

"You're on board the engagement train now?" I looked at her over my shoulder as we walked down the stairs. "You're not pissed anymore?"

"You teed up the ball and I hit it out of the park, Kathleen thinks we're engaged and we need to use it to our advantage. We can't exactly show up at our next meeting and tell her it was a joke. You heard her today. We'd be dead in the water." Her lips pinched together like all those memories of why she couldn't stand me were flooding back.

"I can get you a ring." Hunter walked beside Zara and looped her arm through his.

"You can? How much will it cost?" The skepticism dripped from each word.

He patted her hand resting on his arm. "Don't worry about it. I—"

"He knows a guy," everyone chorused as we walked into the kitchen.

Everest set down his bowl of frosting. "You'll learn, Zara,

that Hunter has a particular set of skills. And we don't ask how he gets things done, but they get done. He has connections even money can't buy."

Hunter pulled up a stool. "Can I see the ring?"

Zara fished it out of her pocket and handed it over.

Hunter took a few pictures from different angles with his phone.

He tapped out a few messages with the intense look he got whenever he 'fixed' things. With a sigh, he slipped his phone into his pocket. "It'll be here by the time we sing 'Happy Birthday.'"

"A ring? You ordered a ring through your phone to be delivered here." Zara pointed her finger at the floor between us.

He shrugged and swiped his finger through the vanilla frosting. "No big deal."

"He's also the one who told me about Kathleen's previous job as a wedding planner."

"Even without that piece of *vital* information"—her lips pinched together—" we stumbled onto this." She held up the ring by the band between her two fingers. "Can he really get us a ring?"

"It would be one of the least shocking things I've ever seen him procure. He has a way with things and people."

Hunter leaned forward. "Not kids, though." He shuddered and spooned out his mini bowl of vanilla frosting. "Where's your mom, Jameson?"

"Stay away from my mom, Hunter." Jameson's menacing words were softened by the fact he was holding two massive pans of perfectly-baked cake in oven-mittened hands.

Hunter held up both his hands. "Damn, it was an innocent question."

Jameson slammed down the cake pans. "At work. She

switched from nights to days, so I'm on duty until she gets home."

Hunter's eyes twinkled with mischief and glee at pushing all Jameson's buttons. "Your mom is a beautiful woman."

Jameson grumbled to himself in the corner, flipping the cakes out onto a wire rack to cool.

All the icing was made, and my flowers, fondant, and butter cream weren't half bad. Hunter and Zara helped with the rest of them. We rolled and cut fondant to be the railroad tracks for the train.

Standing in front of mountains of cake, we stared at it like an opponent on the field.

Jameson called out orders like a quarterback. Everyone passed off ingredients, cake, icing, and fondant as he worked. Mounds of cake fell to the counter as he carved it away, layering and stacking. The scraps disappeared as quickly as they fell.

"A little more off the top." Everest closed one eye, standing in front of the cake.

Jameson got to work, sawing and spackling on more icing.

Teresa wedged herself between him and the table, watching her cake come to life. Her eyes were wide and she bounced up and down.

The look on her face when we added the last of the railroad tracks and flowers—that was why we were all here to help.

She walked up to each one of us and squeezed us as tight at her five-year-old arms could. Her thank you melted my heart.

Jameson's mom came in right when we stuck the candles in the top of the cake.

"You all did this?" She clutched her hands to her chest and wiped away a tear. "Let me go change and then you're all getting hugs."

Hunter rubbed his hands together and Jameson punched him so hard in the arm it echoed in the living room. "Jesus, chill the hell out. I'm not going to feel up your mom. Again."

Jameson stepped in front of him.

Hunter held up his hands. "It was seven years ago. An honest mistake. How many times do I have to say it?" He mumbled under his breath, "I thought it was her elbow, not her boob."

August clamped his hands down on Hunter's shoulders and took a seat beside him. "He knows we'd vote him off the island if he crossed that line. You know he didn't mean it. He hid in his room in our apartment for hours until she left."

Jameson sat so forcefully the chair slid back from the table a foot. "Probably jerking off."

Teresa stood on her chair, swiping her finger at the cake. "What's jerking off?"

Coughing laughter and horribly patchwork non-answers only ended when Zara put Jameson out of his misery by asking Teresa about how train signals worked.

The rest of the guys launched into a recounting of the infamous day. They'd all gone to a college without me. I'd gone to the big football school, which led to the pros, but now I was washed up and had missed some of those friendship highlights they'd recount until we were old and gray.

I'd become an outsider with nothing to show for it. It didn't feel like a very good trade-off.

A knock broke the awkward-as-hell tension in the room. Hunter shot up from his chair and stepped outside, closing the door behind him. Five minutes later, he came in with a huge grin, holding a tiny plastic bag. Inside, there was a sparkling ring that looked like a cousin to the one Zara had slipped into her pocket.

Zara's arms dropped to her sides and she stood rooted to her spot on the floor with her eyes so wide she might've strained a muscle. "Is that what I think it is?"

Hunter dangled the baggie from his fingertips. "I never lie. Does it fit?" He passed by, but I snagged the bag from his hand.

"Wait just a minute. Before you slip this on your finger, I'm going to need a proposal to make it official." The warm fuzzy feelings had to go. Once we pulled everything off, I'd be stealing this account from her and leaving it gift wrapped for Sam. The last thing I needed was for feelings to get involved, and what better way to stop that than keep her pissed off at me?

"What?" Volleyed back and forth throughout the living room.

"Zara has asked me to shoulder the burden of playing her fiancé."

Her scowl deepened and her foot beat out a rhythmic pattern of annoyance.

"It's only fair she asks me." I put on my best innocent face. "Unless you want to tell Kathleen it was all a big misunderstanding."

With muscles tense and tight, she stared at me before crossing the room to me in two strides. "You want me to *propose* to you?"

"It'll make a wonderful story to tell if anyone asks. Or we can call the whole thing off and confess, but you're the one who led us down this path with the relationship talk. Kathleen would probably kick us off the project. Or maybe just you."

Her gaze narrowed. "Just when I think you're not a complete asshole. Fine." The word shot out like a nail gun. Covering her mouth, she mumbled into her hand. "Will you pretend to be my fake fiancé for the next thirty days?"

I cupped my hand around my ear. "That wasn't exactly romantic and you're not even on bended knee. Boyz II Men would be disappointed." I dangled the ring in front of her.

She squeezed her forehead and snatched the baggie out of my hand.

I braced myself for her to fling it straight into my face, but she didn't. Hiking up the skirt of her suit an inch, she lowered herself to the floor with her gaze trained on mine. The intensity of her emerald gaze sent my blood thrumming through my veins. Her thick eyelashes framed her eyes and the ill wishes she was trying to sear into my brain.

But damn if her sinking to her knees in front of me didn't flash me into a whole different set of circumstances with her where she wasn't wishing me dead and I wasn't trying to steal this project out from under her.

"Leo—"

"Elizabeth Wilder," Everest supplied from the cheap seats.

Zara's head whipped to his and back to mine. "Your middle name is Elizabeth?"

"No, Everest thinks he's a comedian, but he's actually an idiot. It's Charles. Continue." I waved her forward.

"Leo Charles Wilder, will you please agree to be my fake fiancé for the next thirty days and make me the most miserable woman on earth?" She held out the ring in her palm.

I tapped my finger against my lips and stared up at the ceiling. "When you put it like that..." I took the ring and held it between my thumb and pointer finger. "Yes, I will, and I can't wait to fulfill those vows." I slipped the ring on her finger. There was a smattering of applause and Teresa jumped up and down in her seat.

Jameson's mom came back toweling off her dripping hair. "What did I miss?"

Teresa clapped her hands together. "Leo and Zara are getting married."

After a quick recap of our non- engagement, we sang Happy Birthday to Teresa. She beamed and wiggled in her seat, soaking up all the attention.

We picked at our cake, already having had our fill during the construction and decoration portion of the day, but Jameson's mom wouldn't let us leave without a slab of cake wrapped up to take home.

"This was the best party ever. I want you to make my cake every year."

Jameson, Everest, and August twitched like an old war memory came rushing back. Hunter laughed at everyone's expression. Jameson, ever the dutiful older brother, crouched down beside Teresa.

"You got it, Tree."

We said our goodbyes, thanked Hunter again for his magic-making with getting us the ring, and headed out.

The car ride back to the city was quiet, but not with the tension that had blanketed it earlier. It was more of an exhausted sugar coma than blistering anger.

"Your friends are nice. Did you all grow up together?" Zara rested her head on her hand propped up against the window.

"August and I were friends from the third grade. Jameson transferred into our school in seventh grade. Then Jameson and August went off to college and ended up with Everest as a roommate. Hunter roomed with them their junior year, I think."

"So, Mr. Commitment is your oldest friend?"

"Mr. Commitment?"

"The one who looked at the ring like I was wearing a cockroach."

"August has a history when it comes to commitment."

"So I was right."

"You weren't wrong."

That sent her deep into thought for a while. She stared out the window, watching the city grow bigger as we crossed the bridge.

I pulled up outside Zara's apartment building, not sure how to move forward with our partial truce.

She opened her door. "Thanks for the ride."

"After a mild kidnapping, I figured I owed you. My day is open tomorrow. We can start as early as you want."

"Once I stop by my office, I'll meet you at Stark by eleven."

"See you, Zara."

"Bye, Leo."

"No kiss for your fiancé?"

She froze halfway out the door. "Not on your life. Not a kiss. Not an ass grab. None of that. Thanks for the reminder. Tomorrow, we can go over a few ground rules."

The door slammed.

I pulled away from the curb unable to hold back my grin. The game play had been kicked up a notch. And my skills extended far beyond the field. You've made your play, Zara, now it's time to make mine.

A nd now I was ready to kill him again. Not that I hadn't ever fully not wanted to kill him. All those not-half-bad feelings had disintegrated after five cups of instant coffee. A wilted lettuce leaf from our lunch sandwiches sat abandoned at one end of the table, and my hair should have littered the floor from me ripping it out over the last six hours. The basics had been confirmed, now we needed to get the logistics of how we were running the day down.

My stomach rumbled. Tyler sent me a message about winter ski trip sign-ups. He'd tried to do it in his feeling-things-out, not-directly-asking way. I'd told him yes. He wasn't going to be left behind. The string of emoji had made it worth it, and I couldn't let him down.

"Can you sit down, so we can talk about this?" I slapped my hand on the table.

He tossed the football from hand to hand, pacing in his favorite 'I'm about to come up with something absolutely insane' thinking exercise. "S'mores. Didn't you love doing that at camp?"

Camp. I'd spent my summers taking Tyler to the library to get out of the house before swinging by our school to pick up the lunches they provided to all the free lunch kids when schools were out.

"No, my camp didn't have them."

"Even better. You'll get to experience it. A camp day with booze. Everyone will love it." His head shot up. "Does that already exist as a business? You could make a mint on alcohol-soaked nostalgia." Slipping his phone out of his back pocket, he tapped away at the screen with the ball tucked under his arm. "Shit, it exists, but that doesn't mean..." He scraped the tip of the football against his chin.

"Can you focus? We're not talking about drunk adult campers here. We're talking about Winthorpe employees who'll be evaluating us on our performance and determining whether or not we're jobless after this."

"Sam's not going to fire me." Leo scoffed. "Hell, he isn't even paying me."

"He's...not paying you?"

Leo squeezed the back of his neck. "I'm helping out. It's a long story. We've come to an arrangement and it'll all get worked out."

"Nepotism at its finest."

"If I were truly trading in nepotism, I wouldn't have let myself get stuck with you."

"Lucky me. You've decided not to cash in that chip."

He crossed his arms over his chest and stared down at me.

"You can glower at me all you want, I'm not giving in."

Our stare down continued.

Some things completely deflate the point you were trying to make. Like when you storm off and trip over your own feet, or shout a comeback, but it gets jumbled in your head and you blurt out a Pig Latin version of your awesome burn.

At that moment, my roaring stomach announced just how tough I wasn't—loudly.

His gaze dropped from my eyes down to my stomach and then back up.

"No use fighting over this on an empty stomach."

I squeezed my forehead. "What the hell does that mean? We finish now and we'll start early tomorrow?"

"It means, I'm not a robot like you pretend to be. I'm hungry and that sandwich was hours ago. I'm getting food. You can either come with me or stay here, I don't care, but I'm leaving." He shrugged on his jacket, flicked out the lights and left.

I dropped my head to the table, banging it a few times. What had I ever done to deserve this? I'd been a good sister. Sure, the first year going away to college and leaving Tyler at home had been hard. Guilt had been my constant companion as I'd tried to be a normal college freshman and failed miserably, but then I'd gotten him into a great school and he was flourishing. All I wanted to do was take care of my little brother and not be homeless. Was that too much to ask?

A sharp knock broke through my pity party.

"Gingersnap, you coming or what?"

A sheet of paper stuck to my forehead when I raised my head from the desk. I knocked it off and stared at him with his arms braced in the doorway. If this were another time, I'd think about how strong his jawline was, half-shadowed and backlit. Or how well his coat clung to his biceps, or maybe even how good I knew he smelled from being in such close proximity for the past six hours.

Instead, I was plotting where to hide his body.

There were plenty of places just over the bridge in Jersey where they could make it happen.

I grabbed my coat and my bag, slinging it across my body. "I'm coming to work. Not eat. We'll finish this up on the way there and then I'm going home. It's late." Walking to the office exit, I took a calming breath as he stepped up beside me, matching my hurried strides. Not hard to do when he was a solid half-a-foot taller than me.

He held the door open. "Have it your way. Difficult as usual."

"I'm not the one who refused to sit down and go over the menus."

"We don't need menus where we can't pronounce half of what's on there."

I jabbed the elevator button. "I didn't have any trouble reading any of it."

The elevator dinged and he stepped in front of the doors, letting me pass.

Once out on the street, he looked around at the lights with a big smile on his face. "Don't you love breathing in fresh night air and going for a walk?"

Things were cooling off in the evenings, although the afternoons were still warm enough to break out into a sweat.

I scrunched up my nose like someone had smacked me in it with a three-day old salmon. "Yeah, night skies really get my engines revving. Have you been drinking? Was your coffee mug filled with bourbon? We have a deadline."

His eyebrows dipped. "How'd you know I drank bourbon?"

I shrugged. "You seem like a bourbon guy."

Leo tugged his collar up and, considerately, never took off down the sidewalk like I'd have tried to do if my legs were as long as his.

"The lunch menu, Leo. If we decide, I can finalize it and we move onto dinner."

"The blue cheese is outstanding here. I know some people go with ranch for their wings, but that's blasphemy. They might as well douse them in motor oil. The blue cheese is where it's at, and they make it in house at The Griffin."

Was he having a stroke? Did he have a food fetish? "Are you listening to me?"

"But there's also the mini cornbread. I could use those as a pillow. Damn, are they fantastic."

"Can you focus?" I snapped my fingers in front of his face, but he was in a food coma and he hadn't even eaten anything. So much for finishing up on the walk.

He crossed to the other side of me when we turned the corner. I'd have thought it was a ploy or some weird patronizing thing, but he didn't even seem to realize he was doing it. Opening doors, stepping out in front when walking through a cross walk. Always repositioning himself to the outside of the curb. It was annoying as hell to find myself the least bit grateful to the enemy.

I repeated the mantra in my head. *He's screwing with you. He isn't trying to protect you. It's an* Art of War *thing to throw you off your game and get you to let your guard down. Do not let your guard down.*

He stopped abruptly and waved his hand overhead like the glowing red sign meant anything to me.

Huzzah. "Now can we go over things?"

"But first, food." He turned to enter. "Actually, you never laid down those rules you were talking about yesterday."

"Leo, I don't have time for this." I spun around, going back the way I came. This was my only shot at keeping my head above water right now, and he was fixating on food and screwing around.

"Where do you have to be? What do you have to do? There's no boyfriend waiting for you and you expect me to believe you've got friends to hang out with? I don't think so."

Out of left field. Why didn't he just crack me over the head with a two by four, instead of reminding me how pathetic my life was? I turned around slowly with my chin lifted high. "I have better things to do than screw around with you."

"You're the one who said you wanted to finish up our work."

Crossing my arms over my chest, I counted down from five in my head. "If you eat, then you'll cooperate?"

I needed to get the lunch order in by 8am. And confirm the paintball company could handle a game of this size on such short notice, but looking at everything they provided was like Greek. It had been Leo's idea, so I needed his input so I didn't fall flat on my face. This couldn't wait until tomorrow whenever he rolled in.

"I'll be putty in your hands." He opened the door to the bar.

My fingers squeezed the strap of my bag until they ached.

I stepped inside.

There was a small stage at the back. A long bar ran along the right side of the space. There were twenty different keg taps and bottles lined up on the glass shelves behind it.

Tables and booths took up the front of the bar, leaving a little room at the back for seats in front of the stage. It wasn't massive, but it was busy. Glasses clinked and people laughed, digging into their plates piled high with meat, cheese, and other assorted bar staples. My stomach rumbled, but over the dim of the customers, thankfully no one else heard it.

He waved to the bartender with a towel slung over his shoulder and slipped into a booth toward the back, not far from the stage.

He drummed his fingers on the table. "Their wings are outstanding. I've been here at least twice a week for the past few months."

"I'm sure your cholesterol thanks you."

He held out a menu.

I clasped my hands in front of me, glaring as he slid the slightly sticky laminated menu under my thumbs. "I said, no thank you."

This wasn't in my budget, like, not even a little bit. I had a stale catering tray of mini burgers back in my apartment. My mouth watered at the greasy, fried smells wafting through the air. It had to be better than my reheated, possibly gone bad wilted lettuce and shriveled tomato sliders.

I hadn't had bar food, real greasy, calories be damned, not reheated from a plastic container food in so long. Fries, mozzarella sticks, wings, I'd bathe in a vat of blue cheese. But my bank account was sitting at almost less than zero.

He'd heard my stomach, I couldn't pretend I wasn't hungry. "I'm not in a wings mood."

"Fine, I can see if there's sparkling wine and a cheese menu you can look over, if you prefer."

I squeezed my forehead. "Can we finish up our work for today?"

"And that's why all the boring is coming from that side of the table." He waved his finger in my direction.

With my tablet on the table, I flicked through to the To Do list. It was long and scary and unwieldy. The angry red circle on my inbox with the number of unread messages climbing by the minute would have to wait.

Apparently, working on this event didn't mean my other grunt work responsibilities had been handed over to anyone else. No, I was expected to do this on top of my regular work, which made every minute I was here one less minute of sleep I'd get tonight.

Going over the items, I chose the ones least likely to end in disaster if Leo fucked them up.

A server walked over and set a beer down in front of both of us.

"I didn't order this." My words fell on deaf ears to her already retreating figure. Leaning across the table, I whispered to Leo, "I didn't order this."

"Of course you didn't, I did." He sat back and lifted his beer bottle with a wink.

"And why would you do that?" My teeth clenched like a vise grip that had been cranked two times too tight.

"Because you needed it. Every minute of every day can't be work. There has to be some time for play."

The text messages from Bill and Valerie didn't scream "play" to me.

Scrolling through my tablet, I copied over the ten things off the list he could handle—and if he didn't, they wouldn't ruin everything—and emailed them to him. I'd triple check his list. My finger hovered over the send button.

"Do you want to do it all yourself? Weren't you the one telling me there weren't enough hours in the day?"

I jabbed at my screen and closed the cover to my tablet.

"There's a list in your inbox. Look at it. Finish it by the time we meet up at ten tomorrow. I'm serious, Leo. You can't throw things together last minute for a client like Winthorpe. It all takes time and attention."

How the hell had he ended up working for Simply Stark? They had an amazing reputation, and Felix passing away didn't mean there weren't still good people there. But Leo didn't fit the mold at all. He'd probably break the mold if anyone tried to shove him into it. He was less Play-Doh and more granite. I shoved my tablet back into my bag, my stomach knotting at all the delicious –smelling things that weren't currently in my mouth. My hatred for Leo burned a little brighter because he'd made me come here when I couldn't afford to indulge.

"It wasn't hard to share." He leaned back, watching the stage as a guy stepped up with a guitar in his hand. He looked barely out of college, smiling at the crowd like he'd never been happier.

People were out laughing, drinking and eating food with their friends. The best I had was occasional pizza and WrestleMania whenever Stella dragged me across the hall. I'd always repay her with food I'd snagged from an event during the week—when it was still relatively fresh.

I didn't want to be the person always bumming food or drinks off someone else. Indebtedness wasn't my thing, unless you counted my student loans. I'd already been bent over that barrel enough—any further and I'd be looking up at my own butt. Never owe anyone anything had always been my motto.

After packing up everything, I checked my phone again. The numbers in the little red circle kept climbing. Didn't people ever sleep?! "You have your list. I'm leaving." My escape was blocked by the server balancing three red plastic baskets with white greaseproof paper cradling the food inside.

The food had arrived. Was there a puddle of drool on the table? The way my mouth watered there should be.

Wings. Coated in buffalo sauce with a side of celery and three cups of blue cheese.

Sliders oozing two types of cheese stacked high with pickles, lettuce, tomato, and mini onion rings.

And my ultimate weakness. Chili cheese fries. No beans, because why pretend we're being healthy? The cheese sauce was topped off with shredded cheese, scallions, and—sweet mother of pearl, was that bacon?

My foot was halfway out the booth. My bag was on my shoulder. My coat was still on, but the chorus of deliciousness was whispering to me from those evil baskets.

You're going to walk away from us, Zara?

How could you abandon us?

We're so delicious. You're missing out.

My hand had a mind of its own linked directly to my mouth. Before I could stop, I'd grabbed a cheese-and-bacon-coated fry and shoved it in my mouth. A creamy, salty, crunchy, bacon fry explosion.

Closing my eyes, I tilted my head back and savored every bite. The invention of a dish like this wasn't even fair. Stopping myself became the last thing on my mind, and before I knew it I had cheese-covered fingers and was caught in Leo's amused crosshairs.

"Not hungry, huh?" He cleaned one of the wing flats in a single magical motion.

"Have one of these." He held out a mini onion ring coated in sauce.

My ass was off the seat before I could think. I bit into the fried crunchy coating, my eyes fluttering closed. My arteries were probably crying out, but at this moment, I didn't give a fuck. The sauce was perfection.

I opened my eyes and my gaze locked onto Leo's.

He stared back at me with his lips slightly parted. His hand was still outreached, less than an inch from my face.

His fingers were coated in that delicious Buffalo sauce, and a hungry, primal part of me wanted to lick each one of them clean. And I wasn't completely sure it was because of how hungry I was. My heart was pumping overtime and it wasn't from the oil.

He dragged his thumb along my bottom lip.

I gasped and fought the urge to lick his thumb. I rocketed back in my seat.

He cleared his throat. "You had some sauce on your lip."

I wrenched twenty napkins from the holder and rubbed at my lips.

What in the hell? *Get a grip, Zara.* A man orders you bar food and you're ready to ride him into battle. The way he was built, it would last all damn night.

Was I high? Had the food been laced? The bacon chili cheese fries had turned on me. All those endorphins were screwing with my head, crossing the pleasure of food with the company of Leo, which was nothing short of painfully irritating. I shoved the basket away from me.

"Leo Wilder?" A woman squealed and rushed over to the table.

Exactly what we needed. Him to be distracted by an old girlfriend, ha, who am I kidding? One-night stand was much more likely.

Leo looked at her like he'd been caught with his pants down. Oh, how I wished I hadn't stashed the ring in my purse—I could have made this a truly uncomfortable interaction for him.

He coughed into his napkin and wiped his hands.

"Can I have your autograph?" The woman bounced at the end of the table with a Sharpie held out to him.

Autograph. I looked from her to him.

"Do you have a piece of paper?"

"No, here." And the woman lifted her miniaturized football jersey to give everyone, including me, a full bra shot. Wow! My hand shot up to shield my face from an unsolicited motor boating. Her cup most definitely runneth over. She was seconds away from climbing onto the table to get close to him. I was invisible to her.

"Sure." His smile was tight, he shot me a mildly apologetic look.

"And can you take my picture?" The woman shoved her phone into my hand. Apparently I wasn't completely invisible—I made for a convenient camera woman.

Leo nodded. Taking the pen, he scrawled his name across her—there was no other word for it—heaving bosom, and snapped the cap back on the marker.

None of this made sense, but nothing in my life made any sense since Leo had steamrolled me on the sidewalk. Up was down. Left was right, and Leo was someone who signed autographs.

I held her phone out in front of my face, capturing the two in frame.

The event-planning fan turned to Leo. "I cried for two days straight when I heard you retired. The team isn't the same without you."

When I tapped the screen to take a picture, it did a rapid burst, capturing thirty shots at once. I was sure she'd use them as a flip booklet to replay this moment for the rest of her life.

Then her words burst through my near flashing-induced haze. "Team? Retired?" I returned her phone.

"Yes, this is Leo Wilder. Defensive lineman for LA Storm. He won a national championship last season."

The phone dropped short of her fingers. "You're a football player!"

Leo winced. "Was. I was a football player. Now I'm—"

"Trying to ruin my life." I snatched up my bag and stormed out of the bar.

Leo called my name, following me through the crowd that had gathered once the guitar player took the stage.

I didn't even worry about the bill. I'm sure with his professional football player money it wouldn't be too much of a burden on him. Up was down. Left was right. And football players were event planners.

Fuck my life!

14

LEO

I threw some bills onto the table. The woman who'd stopped by the table kept stepping in front of me, blocking the retreating Zara.

"Do you recognize me? Marie Hudson. From high school? I was in the drama club when you did the play." She hopped backward a couple feet every time I tried to pass her.

"Hey, Marie. I didn't, but thanks for reminding me. You've grown into a"—I cleared my throat, trying to get around her— "well-rounded woman, but I've got to go."

Zara was already halfway down the next block by the time I burst outside.

Cupping my hands around my mouth, I called her name again.

Her step faltered for a second. She heard me. She absolutely heard me.

Finally, I caught up and stepped in front of her, mimicking the backward *not letting you go* moves Marie Hudson had used.

"Where's the fire?"

Zara's eyes narrowed and her lips pursed. "The fire is my life and career now that I've been stuck with someone with absolutely no planning experience for the biggest job of my life. You've been giving me shit for every idea and you don't even know what the hell you're doing." She stepped up, jabbing her finger at me for emphasis on the last part, driving home exactly how incompetent she thought I was.

Only, I wasn't clueless here. My ideas—*most* of my ideas were solid. "I've thrown my fair share of parties and been to a hell of a lot more than most people."

"Someone rolling a keg down some deck stairs, a plastic tablecloth, and chicks in bikinis is hardly event planning."

"How'd you know my favorite way to celebrate?" The words were so dry, she had to smack her lips to regain some moisture.

"My career hangs in the balance with this job."

"So does mine." This was so much more than a job to me.

She clenched her fist on the top of her bag. "A job you don't need."

Little did she know. "I'm not going to screw it up on purpose or drop the ball."

"Why are you doing this? What's in it for you?" She locked her arms over her chest, leaning hard, judging the shit out of me.

It would be easy to tell her to go screw herself. Or that it was none of her damn business. But working together was the only way we'd beat Oren & Co.

"Sam is my uncle by marriage. This business meant everything to my late uncle. I want this place back on its feet and thriving again. I don't want to lose the legacy Felix built. Neither does Sam. This is just as important to me as it is to you."

Her head tilted to the side, sizing me up, like she was trying to determine my level of giving a shit about everything we'd worked on for the past two days.

"So this is about family." Her stance softened a little.

"Yes. It's about the family I lost and the family I have left."

Her eyes closed for a second, like she was deciding something. "Okay, then we can do this, but you need to let me take the lead."

"I wasn't lying when I talked about throwing parties and going to a shit-ton. I can't tell you how many kill-me-now corporate snoozefests I've been to. Take the lead, but you can't discount everything I say."

"Fine. Get the list done and then we can talk about appropriate levels of trust. I'll see you tomorrow at eleven. I have to go into work first thing, and then I'll meet you at Stark."

"See you there."

She gave me a tight nod and walked past me. "Leo—"

I turned to face her.

Every inch of her was tense as she took the two steps back to me. Her lips parted and closed like she still hadn't decided on what or if to say something. Then the tightness was replaced with resolve and an exhale. "Don't make me regret this." Her mouth opened again. "Goodnight." With a 180-degree turn, she was gone again, off marching to destroy anything and everything between her and her destination.

Inside my apartment building, I waved to the doorman and headed up. The hallway was quiet on my floor. There were only three other units. I'd bought it with my money before everything had been locked away in my investments and a trust that doled out livable installments each month.

My agent hadn't been a bad guy. He was actually one of

the best. Cared about his clients and wanted to make sure the sacrifice we put our bodies through wasn't for nothing. Most pro players lasted three years. Most were also broke within five years of retiring. At nearly four years in the pros, I'd already been past my prime.

Popping open a bottle of ibuprofen, I downed a couple pills dry. Lingering throbbing had been an on-again, off-again companion since my retirement. My longest-running relationship ever. Lucky me. But the doctors said it would all clear up by the first anniversary of my career-ending concussion and crushed vertebrae.

Some guys would've kept going. The blips of memory loss would've become worse and stretched on for longer periods of time. Re-injury and possibly paralysis waited in the wings for their chance to take me from a walking, talking, almost-one-hundred-percent guy, to—something else. The paycheck was nice, but not nice enough to risk life and limb.

But it left me in a situation I hadn't found myself in before. Without football. Living, breathing, playing the sport to the highest level possible had been my singular goal since I had discovered it existed. Emails to contacts trying to get myself in front of someone at Sports Central hadn't been returned now that I wasn't the guy who could get them seats on the fifty-yard line.

Helping Sam staved off some of the hollowness that had carved into my chest when I signed my name on the dotted line, officially ending my professional career, but it wasn't a long-term fix. A favor to help family. A favor that should've been in the form of a check to Felix, but now it would be in sweat and putting up with the pain in the ass that was Zara, until I got the call I'd been waiting for.

My mindless scrolling through Netflix stalled when I

remembered the list Zara had sent me. Digging out my laptop, I fired it up and found her email.

Printing out the list, I decided on my plan of attack. Jesus, this was only part of the list? How many things were on hers?

This was a hell of a lot more than linen napkins and menus.

I cracked my neck, flicked on my desk lamp, and got to work. This was going to be a long night.

I got to work finalizing the paint ball. The list was long, but most were basic tasks Teresa could've handled.

My phone buzzed on the cushion beside me.

Gingersnap: Have you started on the list yet?

Did the woman sleep?

Me: No.

Gingersnap: Why not? I can take a few things off your list. I finished up at work and I can take on a few more things.

Me: Go to bed.

Gingersnap: If you can't handle them, I can do it.

I tapped her name above the message.

She picked up after the fourth ring with a tentative. "Hello?"

"Zara. I'll say it again because it doesn't seem like my messages are getting through to you. Go to sleep. I have it handled."

"But—"

"No buts. You sent me the list. Everything on the list will be completed by the time I see you tomorrow. I'm holding up my end of our deal. Go to sleep."

"But—"

"I'm turning off my phone now. If anything on my list has been completed by anyone other than me, I'll maybe tell

Kathleen we've hit a rough patch and have called off the engagement. I'll let her know the stress of all this work was getting to you, but Simply Stark is more than happy to take on the account to give you a break."

"You wouldn't." Her voice became a high hiss.

"Try me. Go to bed. Let me handle it."

The boiling, three-seconds-from-bursting vein that throbbed in her neck was probably thumping out hatred for me in Morse code. "I've got some time."

"No, you don't. Goodnight, Zara."

Her tinny far away voice was silenced when I touched the red button on my screen.

"Everything is ready for Friday. So we have time to get a jump start on the next event."

"Are my bloodshot eyes not enough information on how that's not happening today? We have another day." I rubbed my eyes and squinted at my phone. It was already after ten. We'd been at this since ten this morning.

"You said last night you were on board." She rubbed her eyes and dropped into the chair opposite me at the table.

"I was, but every time we get through one of your lists, you come up with three hundred *new* things to do. No one is going to notice handwritten tent cards for a table. People don't care if the fake pumpkins are hand painted for extra realism." I picked at the orange paint stuck to my knuckles. "How about your bloodshot eyes?"

"They're not bloodshot."

I slid my tablet with the camera over to her side of the table.

She shoved it away without looking. "Even if they are, it

doesn't matter. There are so many things that can go wrong. We can keep things fluid until we see how the first event goes, but a basic idea will cut out half the work once we're ready."

"Celebration is part of life."

"We can celebrate when Kathleen says she loved everything we did so much we're getting bumped up to the big leagues."

"When you go for my jugular?"

"I don't need to. You'll get bored and tap out before we're done with this."

"What makes you say that?"

"The fact that you've looked at your phone fifty times in the past hour."

I glanced up from my screen. The message I'd sent out to an email I'd found for a producer at Sports Central hadn't gotten a response yet. "Maybe I'm googling ways to off myself using office equipment. But if you're so assured of your win, we don't need to keep up the engagement pretense. We can walk up to Kathleen tomorrow and tell her you lied during our pitch to get on her good side."

The blood drained out of Zara's face.

It wasn't that I took pleasure in her pain—no, that's a lie. I found her freak-outs hilarious. The way her nose scrunched up and her eyes got saucer wide. Her lip would usually fall free from her teeth and her gaze narrowed. It would be a wonderful look when I signed on the dotted line with Winthorpe when we finished.

There wasn't anything to even feel bad about. I was beating her at her own career. Every new idea had come from me. Everything tired and boring came from her.

Cocktails. High hat tables. Waiters passing hors d'oeuvres. Another boring stringed quartet playing songs from long dead composers everyone pretended to be able to tell apart.

"Let's compromise. One idea from you and one from me. We can keep that coming and give them something they've never seen before."

She dropped her head and squeezed her forehead. "If you say—"

"Axe throwing," we both said at the same time.

"What the hell is it with you and axe throwing?" She slapped her notepad down on the table.

"Have you ever done it? Taken the wooden handle in your hands and launched a piece of sharpened metal at your target and gotten the satisfaction of seeing splinters of wood fly out as the weapon you wielded flew through the air and hit its mark?"

"That's some testosterone madness right there. Did you take a few too many hits to the head out on the football field?"

My fist tightened around the mug, cracking the handle. "I'm out of here." I grabbed my coat from the back of my chair. "You run yourself into the ground if you want. Stay up all night. If you fall asleep in the middle of the campfire on Friday, that's on you."

"Sorry about what I said." She rested her head on her hands, driving her thumbs into the corners of her eyes and pressing on the sides of her nose.

Had I said I found her hilarious? Scratch that. "Save it for someone who cares."

15

LEO

Dragging myself out of bed, I felt like I'd been run over by half my team from last season. Mentally, I'd put Zara up against any opposing QB and watch him break. But she wasn't the only reason I'd popped two ibuprofen this morning.

I rolled up to the house, idling in the driveway for a while trying to decide if I wanted to go in here. The lone vehicle in the driveway was a truck with a Wilder Landscaping logo on the side. It looked smaller to me than it had growing up. Inside those walls had never felt like a place I could breathe, but there were happy memories there, too.

August and me playing touch football on the front lawn. August and Jameson's punt return in seventh grade that had landed on the roof of the house next door. We tried every tree in their yard to get up there. Once we found a ladder and scrambled onto the roof, it was nowhere to be found. It had probably melted into the shingles by now.

Get it over with. If you go in, you can be out before we're not alone anymore and that'll make it even worse.

Hesitation stalled me on the front steps. The paperwork

sat in my coat pocket. I grabbed the delivery package sitting on the steps. Shoving my key in the lock, I turned it—or tried to. A cold front washed over me. I pocketed my key and knocked, standing outside like a stranger on the porch.

The door opened and the man everyone said I looked so much like stared back at me. Only, I'd never seen the similarity.

"Hey, Dad."

"Hey, Leo." He stood in the doorway like I was a vacuum salesman trying to sell him the top priced model.

"Can I come in?"

He jolted and stepped out of the way, letting me in and closing the door behind him. "What brings you here?"

Setting the box down next to the pile of others by the front door, I bit my tongue before responding. "I can't come by and see my old man? See how you're doing?"

"Of course you can. Did you want a beer?" He was already halfway to the kitchen. Whether I wanted one or not didn't matter.

"I'm good."

The unmistakable crack of two bottles being opened came from the kitchen.

"I drove here, Dad."

He scoffed. "One beer isn't going to hurt." Shoving the bottle into my hand, he dropped into his favorite recliner, flipping the leg rest out.

"How many jobs did you have this week?"

"Not enough. We've reseeded everyone, so now it's waiting around until the snow shows up."

I'd hated my summers lugging soil from the truck to flower beds and gardens all over what felt like the tristate area, but was actually only a few towns where my dad had carved out enough clients to keep him running—barely.

Other kids went to summer training camps in football states, I helped with the family businesses. During the days, I'd sweat through two t-shirts a day sodding, mowing, and seeding lawns. At night, I'd rush off to catering jobs Felix would throw my way, and load up on mini foods while trying not to fall asleep during droning speeches or award ceremonies for salesman of the year.

"Maybe you need to pull back from doing the work yourself. You're not getting any younger. Look at Felix, he was younger than you."

Dad let out a disgruntled chuckle. "Felix was soft."

My jaw clenched. "He wasn't soft."

He leveled his gaze at me.

I scrubbed my hand down my face. We were not getting into the Felix argument again. They'd never been close, and once Felix had married Sam, their strained relationship became even more tenuous. But I hadn't missed the brush of Dad's hand against Felix's cheek at the funeral. My dad's fucked up way of showing emotions was nothing more than I'd expect from him. He'd fallen into a 1950s view of what being a man was and how you showed you cared. Wasn't this insanity? Coming back when I knew what the outcome would be?

But I'd made him a promise.

"What you said about work. That's part of the reason I am here."

He jumped forward, spilling some of his beer on his shirt. "The team will take you back?"

Disappointment cratered in my chest. Take me back. No matter how many times we went over this it came back to when would I play again. "I quit, Dad. After talking to my doctors, I decided I'd rather walk, talk, and run for the next sixty years or so."

Grumbling about quitters never winning, he leaned back in his chair.

My hand tightened around the cold condensation of the beer bottle. I slammed it down on the table, not caring about the foam spray.

I shook the paper and a pen free from my coat pocket. "If you want the last of the money, you need to sign this."

That got his attention.

"When will it be here? I have a lot of plans for that money." He snatched up the paper and scribbled his name across the line with a yellow sticky note behind it.

"They'll deposit it in a few days."

"Doesn't make any sense how you locked yourself away from your own money."

My dad had lived invoice to invoice for as far back as my memory stretched. "Savings" and "cash flow" had been foreign words to him. He also had no idea what it was like to have people crawling out of the woodwork thinking that being a pro player meant I'd won the lottery. If only it was that easy.

Protecting my money for future medical expenses and a long life ahead of me meant keeping it from myself. I thought back to the day my dad came to ask for my help. Before that, he hadn't spoken to me since the announcement that I'd be leaving the team.

But he came to me, teary-eyed about losing his business, letting his employees go, and hurting all the families who depended on him. The choice had seemed simple until Felix showed up a week later. But the money Felix had needed and the money I had access to would've been like flinging a cup of water on a house fire. If I'd had to make the decision over again, it's hard to know which way I would have gone.

Felix dying shook me to my core. If my career hadn't already been over, I don't know that I'd have lasted much longer on the other side of the country, worrying about my dad and Felix. But he was gone now, so my dad was all I had left.

"It means no one's stealing any money from me and I can make choices in my life that aren't driven purely by bills."

"Must be nice. All those practices I took you to."

We were in a time loop. His words, the same look of disappointment, and his own memories of what it was like growing up.

"All those practices, Dad? I walked or got rides to all but maybe three. And those were because you were on your way to plowing."

"Some kids were taken to none. You should be happy I found time to take you to any."

I squeezed my eyes shut and took a deep breath, the throb in my head getting worse. "Can we not do this?"

"Do what? You're the one bringing up the past."

The front door flew open.

"Oscar, can you help me with these bags?" Faith came in with her arms filled with department store bags. She stopped short when she spotted me. "What are you doing here?"

For a moment, I'd been the golden child—back when she'd gotten to post pictures on social media in the club boxes or sit beside my dad for interviews with the local paper about a hometown hero. Then she'd been glowing, talking about how dedicated and driven I'd been growing up.

Nothing but praise for the same kid who'd had to go live with Felix and Sam for half of my junior year when things got too strained at home. She'd hung a banner on the front of the house with my picture on it to celebrate the draft and my championship, even deep in Philly sports territory.

"I thought you changed the locks." Her gaze narrowed and she set down the bags.

"Leo was here for me to sign the papers for the last of the money we needed."

Her dismissive snort grated my nerves and the headache I'd thought I'd gotten rid of came flaring up.

"We wouldn't be in this position if he hadn't thrown away all our hard work."

I snapped up from my seat. "All your—" Shoving my fist against my mouth, I took a deep breath. "See you later, Dad."

"Let me know if the money is going to be delayed." He called after me on the way to my car.

If I had the chance to make that decision again...

The angry vibration of my phone ripped me from the silent simmer session I'd been swimming in, sitting in my car. Who the hell called anymore? Telemarketers and my dad.

"What?"

There was a stalled hello. "H-Hi, Leo. It's Zara. You... completed everything we had left on the list."

"Is that an accusation? Sorry for pulling my weight, Zara. I'm sorry I completed more tasks than a trained chimp could do and did something without you telling me to do it."

"I was calling to say thank you, but now I think of it, you're right. How condescending of me to call and see if you needed anything before we head up to Bartram Manor tomorrow. I'll see you at seven." She ended the call.

I slammed my hand against the steering wheel, clipping the horn and startling some older ladies walking across the parking garage of my building. They stared at me like I was deranged before rushing for the elevators.

Waiting in my car until they were gone, I got out my phone again and sent off a message.

Me: Went to visit my dad today

August: On my way

Me: I didn't say it **to get you to come over**

August: Maybe not, but I still am

Inside my apartment, I felt antsy and ready to hit something. Staring at the old frame on my bookcase, I took deep breaths, holding them for longer and longer until my heart rate slowed. My mom's glowing smile and bright eyes stared back at me. She cradled me in her arms, both of us wearing hospital arm bands. It was the only picture I had of us together.

Me: Thanks

I grabbed my jump rope and opened the French doors to the minuscule balcony that hung off my building like it was clinging on for dear life. Falling into the rhythmic slap of the rope against the floors, I let the sweat, anger, and frustration leak from my pores and roll down my back.

My apartment door swung open.

"Cheddar, Caramel, or Butter?" August set an oversized blue striped tin a few feet in front of him and nudged it toward me with his foot like I was a crazy zoo animal ready to rip his arm off.

"How'd you know it was three alarm popcorn day?"

"Mr. Pro Football, you seem to forget I was there in the third grade when you discovered this magical tub. And I took half the blame when Mrs. Fitzpatrick realized the whole thing had been devoured before anyone could get seconds."

"She shouldn't have left it unattended during recess." I sat on the floor and popped the lid. The flood of sweet, salty, and cheesy goodness lifted my mood.

"Definitely her fault for leaving it in a locked classroom while she supervised the class for thirty minutes."

The first handful of caramel corn was a sugary-sweet explosion. Nothing topped this—well, not nothing, but right now with August my options were limited.

"I'd say her supervision skills needed some work. I snuck away, didn't I?"

"Come on, I don't need a replay of every kernel that makes it into your mouth. Let me get some."

I knocked his hand away and clutched the tin to my chest. "And this is why they called me Rollie Pollie until eighth grade."

He wrestled the tin away from me mid-bite.

"Growing a foot in a couple months in seventh grade certainly has a way of shutting people up."

"It did. Back then, that nickname was the biggest worry I had."

"Times change, huh?"

I looked around my brand new three thousand square foot apartment, with shiny top-of-the-line appliances, and exposed brick walls. "They sure as hell do."

"You have permission to feel sorry for yourself."

"I'm not."

"You think I didn't see that re-centering you did? You looked around your place and said, 'I've got no right to feel sorry for myself.' There's no suffering Olympics, and no one's getting gold medals for it. We all deal with our own shit in our own way. You can bitch to me. No judgement."

I stole the tin back.

"Okay, maybe a little judgement. But, seriously. You've been so quiet since 'retirement'." He added air quotes.

"What's there to say? I got my bell rung one too many times. I left the team. Gave up on my dream. I—"

"I lied. Judgement totally incoming. You didn't give up on your dream. You lived it. No dream like that is forever unless you planned on dying out on the field. It's like happiness." He held up one fully popped kernel. "One second it's here." He stuck it into his mouth. "And the next it's been devoured by a heartless creature, never to be seen again."

"Are we talking about you or..."

Tilting his head, he grabbed another handful of the cheese flavor. "We're talking about life. When it takes a steaming dump on your chest, you wipe it off and keep on chugging."

I shuddered at the brown lump in my hand. "Nice visual." I dropped the caramel corn clump back into the tin and pushed it away.

"It's why you called me."

Snapping at Zara right before our first big day out wasn't a great plan. Of course she'd called trying to be nice at exactly the wrong moment. I didn't need another jewel added to my crown of failure, but here it was.

Halfway through our lunch of a double XL pizza and a couple beers, August handed over another slice.

"Is this only about your dad?" He folded his pepperoni and double cheese slice in half, determined to fit even more into his mouth.

I tapped out after three oversized slices. August ate like a linebacker, but looked like a surfer. I'd need to get back into the gym before Rollie Pollie returned.

"Do I have a giant scroll screen across my forehead?"

"No, but you've looked at your phone five times in the last ten minutes. Since I'm here, I know you're not anticipating a witty message from me, and your dad barely uses the phone. Is this about Zara? The one with the ring?"

I balled up my napkin and set it down, wanting to throw it. "She called right after I left my dad's house and I flipped on her. We've got this thing to do tomorrow where we have to be a pretend fake happy couple and I wouldn't be surprised if she didn't knee me in the balls the next time she saw me."

August chuckled. "Couples do that."

"Not happily engaged couples."

He downed more of his beer. "Can't help you there."

"You two were happy."

"Were we? You don't stand up in front of all your friends and family with your best man at your side, not even able to stand still because you're so happy to see your soon-to-be bride, and watch your doom walk down the aisle toward you, if you're actually happy." He drained the rest of his beer and arched the can through the air, watching it clatter into the empty recycling.

"Whatever was going on with her, you were happy."

"I was delusional." August dragged his hands down his face. "Mid-day drinking is already beyond me. We're getting old. And I'm ordering a taxi."

"If you pull any 'we're getting too old for this' shit—I swear."

"Fine, I only feel like an old man, but know we are in fact way too young for this shit. You're at the end of a career and I feel like a bitter divorced man, only I never got married."

"At least we know our roles."

"I have back-up popcorn tins at my place if you need

them. I'm only a call away. We took for granted being able to hop on our bikes and walk into each other's houses growing up."

"What do you call what you just did?"

August laughed and picked up his keys. "True. I need to get back to work."

"You serious?"

"I can do it with my eyes closed." He closed them and touched one finger to his nose, missing, and poking himself in his eye. "My tolerance is gone." Hanging his head in shame, he let the door close behind him.

At least there's someone out there who has my back and a ball pit full of flavored popcorn.

Bracing myself, I sent Zara a text.

Me: Do you need me to do anything else for tomorrow?

Ginersnap: No.

Me: I'll be at your place at 6am tomorrow

Gingersnap: Fine.

Her single word answers seethed even over text. Who'd said this was supposed to be easy? Oh, that was me. What a moron.

Better head to bed early tonight to prepare for the clusterfuck headed my way tomorrow.

16

ZARA

"**D**o you have everything?" Leo called out the second I opened the passenger side door.

I slid into my seat and turned to drop my things into the back seat. Turning to him, I held up one finger—not the one I wanted, but the one that wouldn't send our tenuous truce spiraling and ruin our first chance to prove ourselves. "One time. I forgot something once."

"Which happened to be the most important set of documents. Can't fault me for double checking. What was it you said?" He tapped his chin. "It's not personal. It's business."

I jammed my seatbelt on, simmering that he'd thrown my own words back at me.

"This will be the first time we'll see Kathleen since we won the job. Let's set some ground rules."

"This'll be good." Leo pulled into traffic and we started our hour-long drive out to the estate. He had on his favorite work uniform. A light blue button-down rolled up so his sinewy forearms flexed every time he moved. There were muscle groups there I hadn't known existed. "I'm all ears."

He cupped his hand around his ear, once again reminding me how infuriating he was.

"You took a few liberties at the presentation when—"

"When you made the unilateral split-second decision to fake an engagement to dupe a client and win us the advantage." His gaze cut to mine. "I think I wasn't the only one taking liberties." He added a hands-totally-off-the-steering-wheel set of air quotes to the last word.

"Hands on the wheel." I reached for it.

He pushed my hands back over to my side of the car.

I huffed. "I've apologized, but we're in it now, so I'd like to set some ground rules so we're both on the same page."

"Go for it, Gingersnap."

"Number 1: No more use of Gingersnap."

"No."

"What do you mean 'no'?"

"I mean the opposite of yes. No. I don't know why you're so offended—it describes you to a T. Plus, Kathleen has already heard me call you that a few times. If I never use it, then she might think something is up. We wouldn't want her to think we're fighting, would we, Gingersnap?"

My jaw clenched. "Fine. You can use it up to twice a day and only in front of Kathleen."

He let out a huff of amusement, but no further response.

"Number 2: Hand placement is exclusive to the hand, shoulder and back from the waist up."

"Kathleen's going to think you're giving me the cold shoulder."

"Couples who work together must appear professional, or it gives the wrong impression. I trust your acting abilities with these constraints."

"Don't worry. I wouldn't want to hold onto you too long —my hand might freeze off."

My anger kicked up from simmer to roar. "We're working together for now, but don't forget what this is: every man for himself when it comes to being the lead on this account."

"Thanks for clearing up exactly where we stand. Here I thought we could collaborate. Find a way to work together as professional adults to decimate Oren & Co. And then use the final presentation as a cage match to decide who will be the reigning champ."

After everything, was he freaking kidding me?

He tilted his head, catching my gaze. "Can we get through the next few weeks without drawing blood, and then you can go for the jugular after we beat Oren and Co.?"

A slow smile spread across my face. His smile dropped a bit. It was my chew-you-up-and-spit-you-out smile. The one that meant the shit list just got another name. The one Bobby Fallon saw in the seventh grade when he snipped my hair in shop class and I used a nail gun to pin him to the classroom door by his underwear.

For the past two years this grin had been locked up and I'd been on my best behavior, but now Leo had cracked open the cage and it was fucking *on*. He, Oren & Co., Bill and anyone else who doubted me would see what I was made of.

"Fine. Let's shake on it."

His gaze darted from me back to the road. "What's with the look?"

"What look?" My voice was sugary sweet, dripping with un-ironic dedication to our task.

He swirled his finger in front of my face before putting both hands back on the wheel. "The Stepford Wives look you've got going on."

"Whatever do you mean, dear?" I put the backs of my hands against my chin and batted my eyelashes at him.

"Don't look at me like that." His hands tightened on the wheel.

I leaned in closer. "Like what?"

"Come on, Zara. It's creepy, all doe-eyed..."

Laughing, I flopped back into my seat. "Fine, I'll save it for Winthorpe. But I agree to your terms as long as you agree to mine."

His unnerved glances ended. His lips tightened and he held out his hand. "Your terms are accepted."

Our hands clasped, his enveloping mine whole like an animal out on the savannah wolfing down its prize. The rough pads of his fingers brushed against my wrist.

My pulse jumped, kickstarted by the heat and strength of his hold. I tugged my hand away and sat straight in my seat. All that tension and barb-laced energy was playing tricks with my head. The enemy of my enemy in this case wasn't exactly a friend, but I'd play along.

A bump of my head against the window woke me up. I squeezed my eyes closed and covered my yawn. I'd fallen asleep? It wasn't often I was a passenger in a car. Public transportation and walking got me everywhere I needed to go, unless I was flying to see Tyler. Growing up, I'd always fall asleep within a few minutes of pulling away from the curb, even if it was a short ride. Something about the steady rock of a car meant nighty-night for me.

I rubbed my eyes and sat straighter, stealing a glance over at Leo.

He didn't make any comments about me taking an unscheduled nap, so maybe he hadn't noticed. Or maybe he was holding it back since we were on the official teamwork train.

We drove down a tree-lined entrance. The branches of the trees created a twenty-foot-tall tunnel effect, driving up to the main building of the estate hotel. Glamping on steroids. There were fancy yurts sprinkled around the property. Each filled with plush carpets, electrical outlets, the best camping bathrooms I'd ever seen. Not that I'd ever really been camping, but I could certainly use my imagination.

Instead of heading to the large double doors at the top of the white and slate gray lobby, we pulled into the parking lot.

My phone and tablet were filled with unread messages even though I'd cleared them all before I'd gotten in the car.

Leo tensed when his gaze hit my screen. "Are all the vendors here? Has the paint tag company messaged you?"

I quickly scrolled through messages. "They're here and getting set up. Everyone is here. No emergencies. We're good to go."

Leo's body relaxed and he nodded, looking out the windshield although the car was in park, staring like he was getting ready to head into battle.

I set my hand on his arm. "Calm down. We've prepared. We're going to kick ass today."

He glanced down at my hand on his bicep. "You're out of bounds, Gingersnap."

Sliding my hand off his arm, I bit back my retort. I'd have to be the grown up for both of us, if he couldn't. All my electronics went back in my bag into their padded pockets. Turning around, I grabbed my things from the back seat.

My passenger side door opened, flooding the interior with fresh forest smells and a cool breeze. Had it been this hot in here the whole time?

Leo stood in the open door, leaning against the metal

before taking the bags from my hand. We were stalled in a silent tug-of-war with my hands still wrapped around the handles being tugged up to his height. His scrutinizing gaze raked over me.

Don't let him see you squirm. He's just fucking with you.

"Don't forget the ring, Gingersnap."

A breath escaped my lips. A mental head shake followed. I looked down at my bare finger. Ducking back in the car, I rummaged in my bag for the gigantic ring and slipped it on. "Ready, dear."

He shuddered. "Don't call me that. It freaks me out."

"You keep calling me Gingersnap, I get 'dear.'"

"Fine."

"Wow, you love pushing my buttons that much, you'll let me call you the shudder-inducing 'dear', so you don't have to give up Gingersnap? Are you so commitment-phobic you can't even pretend to be in a relationship?"

He slammed the door closed behind me. "You know about my relationship history?"

I didn't need to. "You don't scream 'long-term committed guy.'"

"You don't know the first thing about me. Maybe I'm Monogamy R Us. Wouldn't that blow your mind?" He touched his fingers to the sides of his head and moved them outward like an explosion.

"So are you?"

He squeezed the back of his neck, avoiding my gaze.

"Exactly." I forged ahead, my shoes sinking into the soft grass. One thing I'd say for this whole camping thing we had going, it meant I wasn't trapped in sky-high heels. Jeans, a blouse, and black shoes. It wasn't the ideal combo, but everyone else was going to be in jeans, so it would be okay.

Even Leo in his jeans and button-down looked more laid back than I did.

Maybe my top was a bit too formal. Looking from him to me, I had the realization we weren't playing pretend for ten minutes in front of Kathleen. We'd be interacting with how many people today? At least no one was supposed to know we were together—we wouldn't have to flaunt anything. That helped me relax. No one was supposed to know we were together. No one would notice. Everyone would be too busy being blinded by paint balloons, relaxing in a massage chair or eating the amazing food to spare me or Leo a single glance.

We were the help. Background noise put here to ensure things ran smoothly.

I scrolled through my phone, checking on all the messages rolling in. Lucky me, handling this job and still being required to keep up with all my normal work, which seemed to grow every day. Andi at least shared memes of her interpretation of Valerie's facial expressions and attitude when I was away from the office.

Simply Stark had become a safe haven in many ways. Would kissing the ground when I showed up there next be an overreaction? No. No, it would not.

Kathleen's voice broke through the serene landscape. "You're fired. Pack your things and go." A woman in a business suit with a gold nametag stared at her, slack jawed.

"But..."

"No buts. You've mixed up two guests' key cards since I've been here. That's unacceptable."

"Kathleen, it's her second day."

"And you're the manager. I'd have hoped you'd have chosen better staff... Do I have to do everything around here?"

Leo and I exchanged looks. Dread settled deep in my chest.

Kathleen turned from the two shocked employees and broke into a wide smile.

"I'm so happy you're here." She bounded up to us the second we made it to the bottom steps of the lobby building like she was lighter than air, not like she'd just fired one employee and threatened to fire another. "I love this place. You know how things are in the hotel world. You're growing or you're dying." She laughed.

I smiled and pretended I knew exactly how things were. We'd been here a few days ago and no one had said anything about them being purchased. Things did move quickly, and if they were acquiring more properties it meant their budgets were expanding, which meant even more for event management. Even more opportunities if I nailed this account.

"It's lovely. Didn't I say so, Leo?" I placed my hand on his arm.

"You sure did, Gingersnap." Leo stood beside me and slid his arm around my waist, never passing up an opportunity to make me squirm. Only it wasn't with discomfort which irritated me even more. The weight of his arm and pressure of his fingers through the fabric of my shirt sparked a flicker of something I didn't have time for. He was the guy trying to push me off this project just like I was trying to do to him. A fragile trust was as far as this went until we crushed Oren & Co. and turned on each other. Until then, we'd play as nice as we needed to.

Deliveries arrived and people scurried through the lobby of the newly-acquired hotel, a small two-story main building surrounded by luxury cabins.

"We visited earlier this week to make sure everything could be set up as we needed it, so we can get to work."

"Where are your overnight bags?"

"We figured we'd—"

Kathleen leaned in with a conspiratorial look. "Have you decided yet on your wedding venue? You two have been working so hard to put everything together for us."

A small sound escaped my mouth.

Leo jumped in. "We haven't yet. We've been so busy these past few months, working to provide our clients with the best experiences possible, that other than the night I slipped the ring on her finger, we haven't been able to do anything else."

"Then you have to take this 'night together' tonight." Kathleen pressed the small key with a dangling wooden plaque into my palm.

We looked at each other, trying to justify–and gently explain—a plausible reason we would not, as an engaged couple, be sleeping in the same room in the same bed tonight.

"I plan on staying as well. We can have breakfast tomorrow." Her smirk widened and she did a mischievous shoulder shimmy. "Let's make it brunch. Your yurt is cozy and perfect for a pre-honeymoon night." She winked and walked off.

I waited until she was out of earshot before I spun to face him, panic rising. "We're not sharing a room."

"Do you want to give up a chance to chat with Kathleen over brunch? Pump her for more information? Butter her up? Or do you want to come clean now and piss her off?"

"We'll figure it out later. We've got a lot to get done. I'll check on the food and indoor events. The outdoor stuff is all yours."

"On my way." He saluted me and walked off, disappearing out the doors onto the flagstone patio.

A group of the catering staff craned their necks to watch him go. Their flirty laughter and obvious staring shouldn't have gotten to me, but I was wearing his fake engagement ring, dammit.

How dare they ogle my fake fiancé?

The first half of the guests trickled in. Some showed up in their own cars while others arrived in a bus chartered by the hotel.

We'd gone over everything twice, if not five times, walking through the set-up until we had the transition down between the first and second set of guests.

The compromise we'd set was for the first half of the day to be more laid back, fun, low stakes activities more focused on health and beauty, while the second set would be where we'd do the paintball fun, giving everyone a bit of what they wanted.

Zara would take the lead in the morning and I'd step up in the afternoon. But the open bar was a fav with both crowds. Who didn't love top shelf booze? My eyes had bulged when I'd seen the budget line for alcohol.

Winthorpe wasn't skimping on the fun their employees were having—as long as no one screwed up the key cards. The servers were dressed casually in button-downs and jeans, which helped everyone blend in more, and kept it from feeling stuffy.

There were a few furtive glances here and there, but I prayed they were for my height and not because they recognized me.

One of the servers walked in a slow circle, checking the trays as they passed.

"If you're looking for the restocking station, it's past the massage tents." I pointed in the direction. The older gentleman turned with his eyebrows furrowed and I cringed. Odds were we didn't have any servers over fifty.

I smiled. "And you're not working today, are you?"

The older man laughed and shook his head. "Not exactly, but I'm flattered you thought I could be."

"Don't stand too still or someone like me might shove a tray into your hands. It happened to me earlier."

"You weren't offended?" He leaned against the white fence ringing the event space.

"I got to eat a whole tray of the bacon-wrapped shrimp!" We laughed. "It was an honest mistake. Were you offended?" Insulting a guest wasn't the best way to kick off a good client relationship.

The corners of his eyes crinkled and he laughed. "No, not at all. And those bacon shrimp were something to write home about."

I leaned in. "After paint ball, come to the server station and if there are any left over, I'll score you some."

"That would be nice of you. I'm Clint Waverly." He extended his hand.

"Leo." Our shake was quick and hearty.

He seemed to be waiting for me to say something else.

My phone buzzed with messages from Zara. "I've got to get back to work keeping everything on track, but definitely let me know about the shrimp. Enjoy the day, Clint."

Ten steps later I didn't have to find her.

She rushed toward me with a frantic look in her eyes. "None of the masseuses are in the tents."

"They're all here. The reservation system went down."

Her hand shot out and her fingers tightened on my arm.

I peeled her fingers off before she snapped a bone. "I handled it. They've reset everything. We didn't lose any reservations and they're scheduled to start in thirty minutes after the first team-building game."

"You handled it." The shock in her voice dug under my skin.

"Like I said I would. I want this to go as well as you do. So far everyone's having fun. The weather is on our side. Take a breath."

She turned with her hand shielding her eyes. There were groups of people doing various camp-inspired activities. Their laughter traveled across the open field. Heaters were set up near the massage area for the late afternoon into evening.

"The campfire will start a little after four. I'll save you a s'more, but I need to make sure everything's ready for capture the flag after that."

She whirled around and looked at me, silently nodding like I'd been replaced by a pod person.

"Thank you, Leo."

"We've still got a long day ahead of us. You can thank me later."

By two I was beat. Lunch had gone as planned. We said goodbye to one group and the next arrived with energy to spare. At four my eyes were like an iron curtain being propped up by two toothpicks.

Two-a-day practices had nothing on being one hundred percent on and putting out fires all day while keeping a smile plastered on my face.

Evading phone numbers was also a hazard. It took me a full five minutes into a conversation with one guest to realize she was flirting. If Kathleen had seen, I'd have had my ass handed to me by Zara.

I needed a fake engagement ring of my own.

Zara and I had crisscrossed paths all day, never getting more than a few minutes before we were off to the next thing. At five, I sat for the first time since we'd arrived.

"What are they doing here?"

Zara stared at them, nearly missing the low, polished, half-tree trunk bench I'd reserved for us. "I got you this." She placed the full plate of food on my lap, never taking her gaze off Oren & Co. They were next down in the pecking order. The gala they were throwing would be next week, but it looked like they were checking up on us. Kathleen had mentioned we could attend any of the other events to get a feel for what had already been done. We'd thought it was to give us an edge, but she must've offered the option to everyone else as well.

"You got this for me?" I held up the reinforced paper plate.

"Did you eat already?" She reached between my legs to the bag of marshmallows I'd ripped open and shoved one onto a stick, holding it out over the ground beside the fire.

"No, I haven't eaten." One or two appetizers at a time was all I'd been able to scarf down. During meals we were racing onto the next thing, making sure everything went smoothly once people finished.

"It's always impossible eating. You're like a bride at a

wedding, everyone wants a piece of you, so you never get a chance to sit down long enough to eat."

"Did you have some already?" I held out a pig in a blanket to her.

"Yeah, but I'll never turn down one of these. So, what's up with them? How long have they been here?" She tilted her chin toward the two hanging back from everyone else, in their designer suits with their arms locked across their chests. Every few minutes they'd pull out their phones at the same time, like they were doing a Shining twins impersonation, and jot something down. There wasn't a hello, a friendly wave, nothing but sunglasses and blank expressions.

"They've been here all day. This is the first you're seeing them?"

I pushed her arm a few inches to the left to get the end of the stick in the way of the cracking flames. My fingers brushed against the smooth skin of her arm just above her wrist.

"I've been occupied," Zara responded. My throat tightened.

"They got here at noon and have been lurking the whole time." She leaned in close, her breath caressing my ear and sending shivers down my spine. I swallowed, my mouth suddenly dry.

"They tested out all the food, even stole a spot for a massage. Sizing up the competition."

She didn't say anything.

I glanced down at her and she jolted, tearing her gaze away from my lips before clearing her throat and facing forward.

My mind shot back to the night in the bar with the onion ring. Her lips had brushed against my fingers when she'd devoured the onion ring. Being this close to her again brought back the same crazy, blood-rushing high I'd had that night.

"Is there something on my mouth?" I wiped at my face with the back of my hand.

With wide eyes, she shook her head. "There was, but you got it. Don't worry about it."

"Don't worry about them."

"Who?" She tilted her head.

"Oren & Co. We'll be sizing them the hell up at their event too."

Recognition lit up her face and her eyes narrowed with determination. "Hell yeah, we well." She knocked her fist against mine before checking out the flaming piece of charcoal that had at one point been her marshmallow. Waving it around and blowing on it, she finally put it out.

I dug into the bag filled on the ground. "Need a new one?"

She sighed, ripping the charred one off and nodding.

"Don't worry about them. They can scribble down all the notes they want, but they don't have our secret weapon."

"What's our secret weapon?" she asked out of the corner of her mouth, keeping a watchful eye on her marshmallow.

"Me."

She snorted, covering her face with the inside of her elbow and shaking her head. "You don't lack confidence one bit."

Little did she know. "Of course not, Gingersnap."

Our team was winning. When I threw on my blue pinnie, my competitive surge couldn't be stopped. It wasn't my fault the teams were uneven and they needed me to step in. Armed with as many balloons as I could hold, we gathered around and set out our game plan then broke into position.

We were in the end game now. Both teams down to their final numbers. One of the sales guys darted across the field toward the flag. I needed to cover him. I dug into the bag at my side. I only had two balloons left. Letting one fly, I took out someone steps away from our best chance at a win.

"Leo!"

It was instinct. Pure and simple. I whirled around and launched my last balloon, staring in horror at the floppy morphing shape on a collision course with Zara's head.

Everything slowed down. The latex balloon hit her face, wrapping almost completely around it. For a second I thought maybe it would bounce off and hit the ground unbroken, but the rip happened. Once the first drop of paint was free, everything sped back up.

She stood with her hands out by her sides, not even having had enough time to react to bring them up to protect her face. The coveralls everyone had been handed before the game were nowhere to be seen. Her white shirt and jeans were splattered with paint. Red strands of hair stuck up through the blue mask of paint plastered to her head.

With her eyes and mouth squeezed shut, she stood there for a solid ten seconds not moving a muscle.

Gingerly, I pulled a remnant of the balloon from her collar.

She let out a half-growl, half-scream and batted my hands away from her face. "Don't. Touch." Slamming her lips closed, she spun around and walk-shuffled away with her arms out by her sides.

I pressed my fist to my mouth, not wanting her to get too far. "Zara! Our yurt's the other way."

She stopped and turned, her eyes spelling murder, and walked past me. "See you when you get there, sweetheart."

Pain. There was a lot of pain in my future. And possibly a castration.

~

A blue handprint marked our yurt before I even confirmed the number dangling from the metal marker staked in the grass in front.

The shower had been going since I arrived. Not a full downpour like a standard shower, but intermittent downpours like someone tipping a bucket over their head repeatedly. I changed and lay back on the thick, layered matting and rugs, awaiting my fate.

Guilt nibbled in my stomach. I hadn't meant to hit her with the balloon. An honest mistake. I'd taken her clothes out of the laundry bag in the closet and sent it out for cleaning. It would be here in the morning in time for our brunch.

She stepped out of the bathroom cubby, squeezing the ends of her hair with the towel. A hint of blue paint lingered on her forehead. Maybe it hadn't been as non-staining as I'd thought. No one else got hit nearly as badly as she had. Maybe it was something about redheads. But if we turned up tomorrow and there was a squadron of Smurfs, I had no doubt she'd be baying for my blood.

I averted my gaze to the ceiling with my hands behind my head. The plush floor wasn't as uncomfortable as I'd thought it would be, but the chill after the sunset made it feel like we were a few degrees from seeing our own breath.

She swam in the Bartram Manor pajamas they'd provided us, whereas I'd only been able to fit into the pants, and wearing my sweaty button-down wasn't at the top of my list of comfortable ways to sleep. I was past goosebumps at this point, but no one had told that to my nipples. Thank god it was dark in there. The dim light from the bathroom area was the only light we had.

She dragged the plush blanket down the bed. "You don't have to sleep on the floor."

"We had a deal." My teeth chattered through my words. Once the sun disappeared below the horizon the temperature plummeted.

"That was before we knew we'd be sleeping in a meat locker." She shivered and jumped into the bed, pulling the thick, probably insanely warm blanket up to her chin.

"I'm good down here." I pulled the robe half covering my body up higher, which left my feet completely uncovered.

"Your chattering teeth are going to keep me up all night, plus the guilt would give me nightmares."

A night on the soft and fucking freezing floor, or getting into a big warm bed, even if it's beside Zara, who wouldn't think twice about a punch to the sternum over an accidental brush. I'd take my chances on the one that didn't involve a frostbitten penis.

I slipped into the bed, holding back my moan at the warmth radiating from under the blankets. "Does this mean I'm forgiven or do I need to watch my back?"

"You mean for when you splatted an entire paint-filled balloon over my head?"

"It was part of the game. If you didn't want to get covered, then you shouldn't have come in there."

Her head dropped to the side and even though I couldn't see her eyes, I knew the daggers were being sharpened.

"Sorry."

"At least everyone loved the event. Kathleen came up to me on my way to the tent and told me she loved how playful we are." Her snort-huff mixed with the cricket sounds from the other side of our yurt.

"I'll have to keep a paint balloon in my back pocket from now on." A pillow whack came from her side of the bed with no warning. "Good thing those are soft." I pulled a feather out of my mouth.

She dragged the pillow back to her side of the bed and shoved it under her head. "Off the bed."

"Too late now, you invited me. I'm a mattress vampire."

"If I'd known the pillows were so soft, I wouldn't have."

"You only invited me up here to beat me up."

"Beat you up? What are you, thirteen?"

"I imagine you sprung from the ground as a fully formed twenty-something, complete with tablet and heels. What would you know about thirteen-year-olds?"

"If only growing up were that easy. And my little brother is thirteen—well—fourteen now." The smile in her voice shone through the dim light inside our tent.

"Does he live nearby?"

"No, he's at boarding school in Illinois."

Boarding school. Wow, she came from one of *those* families.

"Is it the same school you went to?"

"No. Not even close. He's there on a scholarship—well, he *was*. They changed his financial aid package." Frustration leaked from her words.

So, *not* one of those families at all.

"It's hitting your parents hard?"

She let out a humorless laugh. "If they crawled out of their bottles they might realize he's gone before he graduates."

Silence reigned between us. Sadness and anger brewed in each second.

"That sucks. Do they live around here?"

Even more silence. Maybe I'd pushed her into territory she didn't feel like going over with the guy who'd clobbered her with a paint bath earlier today.

My eyes adjusted to the darkness. With her lips parted, a finger-traceable outline of her face was backlit against the low light on the other side of the tent. Beside her in bed, there was a tug deep down, tapping into something I'd never felt before. She was already out cold. Dark spots speckled her hairline against her skin.

Flipping on my side, I shoved my arms under my pillow to keep from dragging her close against my chest.

"Night, Zara."

18

ZARA

Had it warmed up outside? I could feel my toes again. The warm cocoon of the bed was the most comfortable I'd been in a long time. The pillow top mattress conformed to my body. Opening my eyes meant another day of work, and I wanted to stay here all nice and snuggly. Only, my pillow wasn't exactly a pillow. It was too hard to be a pillow. Firm, but warm.

And also breathing.

My eyes shot wide open as my senses returned and the steady heartbeat under my ear clued me into exactly where I'd been resting my head.

Leo's eyes opened at the same time. We both yelped and shot to opposite sides of the bed. I caught myself with the blanket, nearly dragging it off the bed, completely uncovering Leo.

He shouted and sat straight up, hunching over, but that didn't mean I hadn't seen his little morning surprise. Only, there was nothing little about it. The flames fanned my cheeks, down my neck, and my back probably looked like I'd been out sunbathing all day in the middle of July.

I averted my eyes and wiped the lovely morning drool from the side of my face.

With a half turn, he grabbed the blanket and rubbed at his chest, sending the heat even higher. Was it coming out of my eyes yet?

"Sorry," I mumbled.

The beats of silence ratcheted up the awkwardness by a factor of ten.

Clearing his throat, Leo swung his legs over the side of the bed and mumbled a *good morning* and something about an *unexpected shower*.

"Morning." Mine came out way too chipper and fake.

"What time is it?" He rubbed his eyes and tried to push down his bedhead.

The glow of my phone broke through any sleeplessness I might've been fighting.

We whipped around at the same time, screaming, "We're late!"

Leo jumped up and rushed to the flap masquerading as a door.

"Get dressed," I hissed. Not that his body wouldn't be a distraction for Kathleen—hell for any woman, with those smooth planes and hard lines.

Focus, Zara. I searched for the clothes that I'd shoved in a laundry bag last night. They'd be crusty and paint-covered, but I didn't have a choice.

"Here." Leo shoved a hanger with a plastic laundry bag over it at me.

Holding it up, I looked back to him. "What the hell's in here?"

"Your clothes from yesterday. I had them laundered. They were hanging outside our tent."

"You sent them out." He'd gone out of his way to do me a favor. Was that a flutter in my stomach?

"It was either that or have you show up in the yurt pajamas. We have to make a good impression on Kathleen, and reminding her that I sucker slapped you in the face with a giant balloon isn't a good look."

A good look. Right, he didn't want to look like the bad guy.

We both threw on our clothes. None of those hard to place fuzzy feelings were there anymore. They'd been replaced with a determination to win the brunch and move onto our final camp-inspired event.

On the dew-soaked walk over, what we were pretending to do kept gnawing at me. What if we slipped up? What if Leo's handsy exploration went a little too far and I had to amputate a limb? What if waking up against his chest was one of the most serene moments I'd had in too long and I became obsessed, breaking into his apartment just to cuddle with him? "What if we fessed up to Kathleen?"

"About..."

I twirled the ring around my finger, slipping it over my knuckle.

Leo jogged ahead a step and turned, stopping me in my tracks.

"Are you trying to blow our shot?"

"No. Of course not, but yesterday was a success. Everyone loved it. Almost everyone who was here yesterday signed up for our next one. If that doesn't prove our worth, I don't know what does."

"And you think she'll be fine with us lying to get a leg up on the competition?"

"She'll understand." Getting this close to him wasn't okay. The touches, the looks, the late nights working together and last night's talk. It was too close. He was too close. I pulled the ring off and slapped it into his palm. "It'll be better this way. Trust me."

He shot me a disbelieving look, shaking his head, but he didn't fight me on it. Instead, he slipped the ring into his pocket and we walked to the restaurant in silence.

A man pushed open the wood and glass doors at the top of the wraparound porch. Their eyes lit up when they spotted us. "You two did an amazing job. Our team won." He high-fived Leo and jogged down the stairs like he was about to run a marathon.

A woman with blonde—well, it *used* to be blonde—hair, patted Leo's arm as we walked into the main dining room. "Yesterday was the most fun I've had in years. You two make a great team. Thank you." She grinned before running off to the buffet line.

He seemed a bit stunned. "They actually liked it."

"Wasn't that the whole point? You were going on about how much fun everyone would have and how we needed to shake things up and you weren't even sure yourself?"

"Fake it till you make it." He shrugged, laughing.

I'd put this whole thing on the line with him fighting me for every inch, and he wasn't even sure. If we hadn't been surrounded by people I'd have throttled him.

Kathleen waved us over, standing before we got to the table. "It looks like you two had a wonderful night under the stars." Her innuendo wasn't lost on either of us. The crimson flush of Leo's ears proved I wasn't the only one a little uncomfortable at someone broadcasting my sex life, whether real or imagined.

I patted down my hair and kept my head down.

Leo pulled out the seat for me and I sat, shielding my face with my hand.

"Kathleen..." I looked to Leo for back up, he nodded at me to continue. "We—"

"Sorry, I don't mean to embarrass you two. I remember those days. When my husband and I could barely keep our hands off one another. But then he couldn't keep his hands off anyone with a set of breasts and a working vagina, so I guess it wasn't all that special." She shook out her napkin furiously and sat it in her lap.

"It's probably why I have such an allergic reaction to liars. Once I've found out someone has lied to me, it's over and done with. They're dead and buried to me."

As panic seized my chest, I squeezed my fingers into my thigh and tried not to let my eyes bug out. Had she seen I wasn't wearing the ring? Had I blown our cover? Why had a clear conscience suddenly become more important than keeping Tyler in boarding school and a roof over my head? Leo tapped my leg with his foot to get my attention as he slid the ring out of his pocket and slipped it back onto my finger.

Some of the panic subsided, but the fear lingered in the back of my head. If we didn't pull this off, we were screwed. If she knew we'd lied, we were screwed.

"It was a little chilly." Leo ordered his coffee and a cappuccino for me.

"Thanks, sweetheart." I covered his hand with mine. "We had the thick blankets, so it was fine."

"Look at you two love birds, not using the heater to snuggle up to one another." She made a swoony face and sliced up her pancakes.

Leo and I stared at each other wide eyed, mouthing *heater?* at the same time.

"I can never get enough of her." Leo smeared butter onto his croissant and smiled at me.

For a second, for a split second, this was real. He was looking at me adoringly. The ring on my finger wasn't one his friend had gotten through questionable means, and we were chatting with a woman who loved that we were in love—and held the key to our financial security in her hand.

It was a boot to the chest once I zipped back to my reality. Leo was as good an actor as he was a football player. Maybe he'd be up on the Oscars stage one day.

Kathleen's mouth was moving, but I hadn't heard a word. "Sorry, I missed that."

"She was asking how we met."

I took his insistent gaze to mean I'd be in charge of supplying the story. Maybe we should've spared a little time in the hours of prep for the event into creating a little background on us.

A spark of inspiration.

"Fate. You could say the universe threw us together. After our scalding hot introduction to one another, he offered me a bite of a chocolate croissant over my coffee and the rest is history. We've been together ever since."

"How long ago?" She sliced into her fruit.

"A year."

Her head shot up. "Oh, I thought before you said it was a whirlwind romance?" Her gaze narrowed.

I sputtered.

"We spend so much time together, sometimes it feels like it's been a few weeks, and other times it feels like we've known each other forever."

I brightened my smile and gazed at him adoringly, hoping Kathleen bought it.

Leo leaned in and wrapped his arm around my shoulder, pulling me in close. "When you know, you know."

Her smile was back in place and she swooned, actually swooned and winked at us.

The panic-induced hysteria remained locked away in my chest.

Brunch ended quickly when Kathleen was called away to put out a few fires of her own, but we got plenty of information and more than a few knowing winks from her about our chances to pick up more projects after this. Maybe even together. There could be more than enough to go around.

"It's ours to lose." Leo threw his fist into the air on the way back to his car.

"Which we won't do."

"No, we won't." He opened the trunk, dumping everything in there before I made it to my door. "Don't you do it."

I balanced my bags in my arms. "Do what?"

He jogged from the back and opened my door, holding it open.

I ducked inside, hiding my smile from him. This one felt different than all those at brunch or yesterday when we were surrounded by people.

"You never know who might be watching." He smiled one of his own, like he had all through brunch and closed the door. My heart sank a little more than it should have.

And the award goes to...

He got in his side and turned on the radio. I was happy to let the music fill the silence between us, but being stuck with my thoughts was never a good thing. They always veered into worst case scenarios and imagined catastrophes. It was a habit after all these years. What would be on the other side of the door when I walked into my house? What would be in the fridge when I opened it? What song would I sing to Tyler to drown out the shouting matches?

Catastrophizing my life kept me prepared for whatever

shit sandwich had been shoved into my packed lunch, but here I was, once again, clinging to the hope that things would work out. How stupid was I?

Things didn't work out for me. They'd worked out for Leo and like any other person living in the beautiful-people bubble, he'd blow past any hurdles that jumped into his way. I'd sure as hell make sure Tyler made it into that group. At boarding school, he was being invited on ski trips with classmates and overseas trips where those parents footed the bill. Almost eighty percent of his class went to Ivy League colleges, straight into a job with a company with a stellar reputation arranged with one of those wealthy parents. He'd make it. I'd had to claw my way to where I was now, but he'd have it easier than I ever did.

I'd do everything I could to make it happen. And I wasn't letting anything or anyone get in my way.

19

LEO

"Cookie?" I held up a plastic-wrapped cookie.

The mix of spiciness, sweetness, and mouth-watering fried chicken, egg rolls, and shrimp wafted up from the table like a blanket of comfort. I kept myself from ripping into the boxes like a foraging bear. Shouldn't I be less hungry, no longer burning thousands of calories on the field and in the gym? Somehow Zara seemed to run me as ragged as any coach I'd ever had before.

I'd thought after our night in the yurt things would have changed, but less than a week had passed and she'd snapped right back to her rigid self, not a bend in sight.

Hunter grabbed the bag and passed out the individually wrapped fortune cookies. "Do you even need to ask?"

"I got these before they mysteriously disappeared from the bag."

August dried his hands on his jeans and searched the table for his beef and broccoli. "Oh, they included the fortune cookies this time. I kept telling them to stop forget-ting them." He rubbed his nose with the back of his hand. Classic tell.

I grabbed my cartons of brown rice and chicken. "How interesting that they always seem to forget them when you're the one unpacking the food."

He dragged his chair out. "Weird, right?" Keeping his head down, he snagged his noodles and fork.

Hunter cracked his open first. "*Nothing seems impossible to you.*" He grinned and shoved half the cookie into his mouth. "In bed. Damn right."

Everest opened his next. "*You love Chinese food.*" He frowned. "How insightful." He crumpled up the paper and tossed it to the center of the table.

August broke his in half and slipped the paper out. "*Change can hurt, but the path leads to something better.*" He ripped his up into small pieces and sprinkled them onto the table.

I opened mine and handed over both pieces to August.

His head snapped up and he smiled. "Never say I wasn't a good friend."

"*Note from future self: Follow your love and you'll never be led astray.*" I stared at the small white piece of paper.

"Anyone want a drink?" Jameson pushed back from the table.

"Open your cookie first," Hunter said around a mouthful of beef and broccoli.

"Yeah, open it and give it to me, if you don't want it." August tried to put up a nonchalant front.

Jameson held it up to the light. "*Bold adventures are in the future.* Ha, tell that to my CPA exams. A bold adventure indeed." Jameson shook his head and slid the paper into his jean pocket.

We clinked bottles together and dug into our food, exchanging minimal talking until the edge of hunger was gone.

"You want to do commentary." Hunter held the chopsticks up high over his head, dropping the noodles into his mouth.

I shrugged. "I've thought about it. I've even sent out a few resumes."

Hunter scoffed. "That's not how you get on TV. It's all about who you know."

"Too bad I don't know anyone."

Pressing his hand against his chest, he covered his mouth and shook his head like he couldn't hold back the emotions. "Am I chopped liver?"

"You can get me in front of someone at ESPN?"

"Maybe not right this minute, but give me time and I'll see what I can do." He shoveled another mouthful of noodles into his mouth.

"When are you going to learn? Hunter is the man who can get anything." August clamped his hands down on my shoulder before taking the seat beside me. His face paled and he cleared his throat. "You saw what he did with that ring."

Hunter set down his carton of lo mein long enough to steeple his fingers in front of him. "I have a particular set of skills."

"If you can pull that off, I'll never doubt you again."

"Challenge accepted."

"Are those connections how you got this swanky as hell apartment?"

I'd sworn I was in the wrong place when I'd shown up at the address sent to the text group. This place didn't scream late-twenty-something party guy, which was what Hunter's appearance screamed.

Jameson set down the five beer bottles on the table, sliding them into our open hands. "No, it's his grandma's place." He seemed to take an extra level of enjoyment out of letting that nugget drop.

"That makes a lot more sense." It was the floor below the penthouse. A couple bedrooms, but the decor screamed monied older lady. I'd have expected it to be Everest's, not Hunter's.

"When she moved to Florida, she wanted someone to look after the place, and I offered up my services." Hunter took a swig from his beer. "My own fortress of solitude, where I never need to worry about anyone else invading my space."

Everest laughed and gulped from one of the Dutch beer bottles he'd brought over and stuck in Hunter's fridge. "I'm sure rent-free doesn't hurt either."

"Like you'd know what it's like to actually pay for something." I shoveled my General Tso's chicken into my mouth. Something about his face just irked me. Like it was too symmetrical or too perfect. Never a hair out of place. Everything always came so easily for him. Not a care in the world.

"I paid for dinner, didn't I?" Everest lifted a smug eyebrow. Such a punchable face. He'd also paid for every spring break the guys went on during college. The one week I'd had off from conditioning and training for the next season, and he'd whisked them off somewhere kickass.

So, I'd had to retaliate. A group trip to Hawaii right after I'd been drafted.

Hunter somehow got our rooms upgraded to suites. And Everest, who hadn't been invited, showed up at our hotel and arranged a helicopter tour of the island, finished up with lunch on a yacht. Was I an ungrateful asshole? Possibly. Was I still pissed at Everest for trying to show me up? Hell yeah.

Jameson stood and put his hands out. "Can we have one meal without fighting?"

Everest picked at the fried egg roll dough and mumbled, "He started it."

The rest of the dinner was uneventful. Hunter left to take a call or two as usual, when not responding to texts on his phone.

Jameson headed out to watch Teresa before his mom headed to work. Everest 'Everested' around the apartment, which meant looking at artwork on the walls and scanning the bookshelves.

Staring out the almost floor-to-ceiling windows with sculpted Versailles-worthy window frames, I ran my hands down my face. Everyone down there was going about their life, some of them totally sure of where they were headed, and others wandering in circles consulting their phones every few seconds to make sure their destination still existed. Guess which one I was?

August's reflection popped up behind me. "Why do you always screw with him? Lay off Everest. He's having a tough time lately."

"Doesn't know which shoes he needs to buy to match his belt?"

August punched my arm. I rubbed the sore spot. "You're not the only one who's dealt with things not turning out how they'd planned."

I winced. Standing beside August in front of hundreds of his friends and family and watching the father of the bride walk down that aisle alone, asking to speak to August in private, was up there as one of the worst moments of my life. One thing we'd all agreed on, even me and Everest, was that Helena hadn't been right for him. But no one wants to say that to a friend who's in love and can't be happier. Until the moment when it seemed like he'd shatter into a thousand pieces, I'd never doubted they'd make it work, even if things had always seemed off.

"I'm being an asshole. I know." I rubbed my hands on my legs.

"A little, but I'm used to the low-level asshole that you are. After twenty years, it's sort of a given."

"I wasn't an asshole in first grade."

"How about when you replaced all the paste with white paint on paper mache day?"

I laughed. "Mrs. Banks was so pissed."

"Yeah, she was." He laughed, taking another gulp of his beer and rocking back in his chair. "So I've always known those tendencies were there."

"Everything is a blur right now. Going pro was supposed to solve all these problems. It's been the one thing I've fought for all my life."

"The one thing you thought you wanted, and then it was snatched away from you at the last second."

Somehow I didn't think we were still talking about my pro career. "Exactly. I've lived and breathed football my entire life. And now I've got to switch gears? Starting all over with something new? Even this TV thing is a pipe dream."

"What about Simply Stark? Things seem to be going well."

"Half the time I don't even know what they're talking about. Zara's driving me nuts, always picking apart everything I do, even though we had a great first event. We're turning people away for our next one."

"Then what the hell's your problem. It sounds like this is something you could be good at."

My eyebrows shot sky high. "Event planning?"

"What's wrong with that? You talked about throwing all

these parties in college. Who doesn't love to drink and eat great food? If you can make it even better than the boring corporate shit I'm dealing with right now, more power to you, I'll be the first to sign up. If I have to listen to another droning speech standing at cocktail tables, surrounded by people in suits all trying not to spill minuscule food on their ties, I'll grab a bottle of Moët and bludgeon myself."

"Things are going well at work..."

He shot me a wry look. "How could you tell?"

"What exactly do you do?"

"Hell if I know. I move numbers from one spreadsheet to another, generate reports, email those reports to my boss, who repackages them and sends them to his boss, until it sits in someone's inbox to languish forever."

"Sounds thrilling."

"At least you can see you're affecting people. You can watch their expressions as they slam paint-filled balloons into each other's faces, or smear marshmallows all over one another."

"It's a gift, what can I say." I gave him a knowing shrug. Going into this business wasn't even supposed to be more than a temporary stop on my way to something more, something better suited for me. Something I'd enjoy, but hadn't I liked the late nights with Zara? Well, maybe not with her specifically, but doing the work. It wasn't the instant gratification of the gridiron, but watching people smile and laugh when they ate food I'd picked out, and having fun at games I'd picked hadn't been a bad thing. In fact, it had felt damn good.

Hunter emerged from the hallway. "Where'd Jameson go?"

Everest pulled a book off the shelf and flipped it open. "Babysitting duty."

"Damn, I'll have to text him the good news. I got us all tickets to the Without Grey concert. Jameson loves them."

The book fell from Everest's hand. He recovered it quickly and slipped it back into the slowly closing gap on the shelf. "Without Grey. As in Madison's Without Grey."

Hunter's face fell. "Oh shit. Fuck dude, I totally forgot. I'll cancel."

Everest's jaw clenched before he took one of those calming breaths the anger management consultant who had been brought in for the team after a bench-clearing brawl my first season told us to do. His eyes opened and the tension fell off his face. "No, don't cancel. It's fine. You guys should go." Another deep breath. "Actually, let's all go. It's a concert like any other. We'll be in a sea of many."

"We'll be in the front row." Hunter winced.

Another deep cleansing breath from Everest. "Fine, the front row, but it's not like—"

"And we'll have backstage passes." Hunter peeked out at Everest through one eye, his shoulders up high.

Everest stared blankly out the window behind us. "Backstage passes."

Hunter picked up his phone. "You don't have to go. None of us want to go."

I raised my hand. "I want—"

August elbowed me in the stomach. "We don't have to go, man. Jameson wasn't in Milwaukee, but he'll understand. He didn't get the full details about what happened with Maddy—Madison. The rest of us haven't listened to their music in years."

"Except for that song last summer. It was catchy as hell." Hunter's smile morphed into a look of contrition at Everest's glare. "It was all over the radio and in a couple commercials."

"No. We'll go. And you can listen to Without Grey as much as you need to. Madison and I are older now. It's been four years. Water under the bridge. She's with Without Grey and I'm living my life too. Let's go. I'm in. Let's do this." Everest cracked his neck and rolled his shoulders like he was about to step into an MMA ring, completely outmatched by his opponent.

August pressed his fingers against his lips, gingerly walking toward Everest. "When's the concert, Hunter?"

"One week."

"We don't have to make any decisions tonight, Everest. Sleep on it and let us know in the morning. No pressure, no promises. Whatever you decide, we're there to back you up."

"It would be an awesome concert, he's—" I swallowed the words when I caught August's glare.

"Totally up to you either way, Everest."

"I need a walk." He grabbed his jacket off the back of his chair and was gone, the door slamming before anyone could say anything.

20

LEO

The Philadelphia Museum of Art housed some of the world's most well-known pieces of art and served as the location for the Winthorpe staff gala. The façade of the column-fronted architectural wonder was illuminated.

An oversized greenhouse-type structure took up the infamous landing near the top, where tourists from all over the world stood, pumping their arms in the air and throwing fake punches while humming "Eye of the Tiger" to themselves.

Cars pulled up along the front letting out people dressed up in business suits and cocktail gowns. I tugged at the collar of my shirt, tempted to ditch the tie before we even got inside.

Zara climbed out of one of the taxis, tucking a strand of hair behind her ear. Her pale pink dress skimmed her knees and fit her perfectly. Not like she'd been poured into it or had it painted on, but it hugged her waist and curves, providing the slightest tease of her breasts under the conservative square neck. She was stunning.

I should've picked her up from her house. Greeting her curbside felt wrong. I could imagine her sitting beside me with her legs crossed and my hand resting on her knee, brushing against her smooth skin in slow circles.

Her greeting was a curt nod and a dip of the edges of her mouth.

Daydream dead. Warming up to me wasn't the same as wanting to get anywhere near me. And why should she? She was all business and that's what I needed to be.

Slipping her bag under her arm, she tugged and fussed with my tie, only this time it didn't bother me at all. Was there glitter in her makeup? She had a shimmery glow to her skin. Her full lips had a hint of gloss to them, but nothing overdone.

"This is the first time I've seen you all dressed up."

"It said black tie optional." She fussed with a hemline and looked as happy as I felt to be in my suit. "We're trying to blend in. It fits you well. Tailored?"

"There aren't many fitted for someone built like me."

She huffed out a laugh. "True. And you're not going to do us any favors tonight."

"Sorry, I forgot my shrink ray in my other pants."

"It'll be fine. We'll get in. Check out their setup and include ways we'd do things better, if they choose us for their events next year. And get out."

"Aye, aye, Captain." I saluted her and offered her my arm, but she charged ahead, not taking it until the top of the first staircase landing.

Kathleen stood at the entrance. Her barked orders made their way directly to us.

I leaned down, whispering into Zara's ear. "Try to at least pretend to like me tonight."

"Don't I always." She tilted her chin to her shoulder, in a

gesture most people would take as a loving snuggle, but I'd heard the bite in her tone.

"Of course." I unlocked our arms and wrapped mine around her waist, tugging her in close. Leaning in, I ran the back of my finger against her cheek. Her smooth skin was every bit as soft as I remembered from our night in bed together. "Always playing the perfect, loving fiancée."

"You forgot doting." She made a snap bite for my finger, which I wasn't entirely sure was playful.

Chuckling, I led us through the entrance with a wave to Kathleen and toward the bar. We were going to need it.

A woman with bright red curls stepped in front of me. "Leo Wilder? Wow, it's really you."

"Every freaking time," Zara muttered under her breath and rolled her eyes, smiling at the woman. "Hi, I'm Zara. Sorry, Leo's here with his fiancée and doesn't have time to flirt tonight. He's working." Zara grabbed my hand from her back and pulled me away.

The woman's smile faltered. "Fiancée? I didn't know you were engaged." She fumbled inside of her minuscule bag and pulled out her phone.

"It's complicated," I called out over my shoulder.

Zara's eyebrow lifted when we made it to the modern and contemporary art wing. "It's complicated? What happened to playing the loving couple?"

"I can't help it if I'm recognizable. That woman grabbed her phone and probably took a picture of the ring. For all we know it's posted on social media. I'm retired now, but that doesn't mean people don't still talk and start digging and asking questions."

Her face paled. "I didn't think about that. Sorry for over-reacting."

Another apology. Who was this woman? "Welcome to

my life. And don't worry about it. Most people don't see the circus attached to playing pro sports."

"What kind of circus?" She took a sip of her drink.

"After we won a game in Cincinnati, I walked into my bedroom and there was a naked woman sitting in the middle of my bed, spread eagle."

A fine spray of champagne shot out of her mouth. At least we were far enough away from the art we only got a glare from the security guard at the far end of the room.

"Naked?"

I lifted my glass to my lips. "Naked."

"What did you do?"

"I backed the hell out of there and called security."

She raised a brow, skeptically. "You weren't tempted?"

Because all every man cared about was getting laid… "If someone is batshit crazy enough to show up in a stranger's hotel room, they're crazy enough to do any number of things that could've gotten me in deep trouble with the team. I wasn't putting my career in jeopardy for a piece of ass."

"Crazy ass."

"Exactly." I clinked my glass to hers.

"Why did you retire?"

"You haven't googled me yet?"

"No, then I'd feel like a weird stalker."

"You aren't already, with the way you message me almost constantly?"

"That's for work." She waved it away as if work communication existed in a parallel universe where your phone didn't buzz at two in the morning, ripping you from sleep. "I don't want to forget something and have things implode because I messed up."

"Sometimes you have to roll with the punches when things spring up."

"That's why I have my roll-with-the-punches back-up-back-up plan included in every standard plan. Did you not get your copy?"

I scanned my memory. Had I missed a whole alternate plan she'd put together?

"That was a joke. I know I don't make them often, so maybe I'm rusty."

We walked along the perimeter of the room, not paying attention to the art, lost in conversation. Our recon work fell by the wayside as the night stretched on. Oren & Co. were old school boring; we didn't have a thing to worry about.

Zara told me more about her little brother, Tyler, and his love of superheroes and music. And asked about my time in the pros. Getting an inside peek into the world of professional sports wasn't something I thought she'd be interested in, but her questions kept piling up and I was happy to supply her with all the stories I had.

"They made you do what?"

I took her empty glass and mine, setting them down on the tray of a passing waiter.

"Left me and another rookie with a six-figure bill."

"Those assholes. How could they do that to you? You're brand new, finally living your dream and they steal all that money from you."

"It wasn't stealing."

"It's dining and dashing and leaving you with the check. That's so...fucked up." She shook her head, her fingers tightening around the stem of her glass. Her outburst warmed me deep inside my chest. Her outrage on my behalf was genuine, and she barely liked me.

"It's tradition. It was done to them, so they do it to the

next group." It had sucked at the time—hard. The check split between me and two other rookies had been a fifth of my entire salary for the year. Not everyone signed multimillion dollar football contracts, but I wasn't going to be a statistic cited in Sports Illustrated about washed up athletes becoming destitute.

"No wonder you're working a regular job now, and no wonder so many of those players are broke after they retire. With irresponsible spending like that, they're lucky they don't retire with no money at all."

We hadn't gone into the details of my current financial situation and now didn't strike me as the time.

"People think everyone is set for life, but between medical and financial issues, a lot of guys never fully recover."

"Then I'm glad you got out early." She patted her palm against my chest, straightening my lapel.

I wrapped my arm around her back, tracing a figure eight with my thumb against the small of her back.

A hand looped around my other arm.

"Excuse—" Zara whipped around, freezing when she spotted Kathleen.

"Look at the two lovebirds cozied up in this corner."

Kathleen's eyes twinkled. "I'm so happy you're here. What do you think about this for a venue?"

We exchanged lightning fast glances. Zara's fingers tightened on my arm before she relaxed and slipped back into a relaxed posture, but no longer leaning against me like she had been before Kathleen arrived.

"It's beautiful."

"I've only run up the steps before and come on school trips. Seeing it like this is a different experience." And I wasn't only talking about seeing the artwork when the place was nearly deserted. Being here with Zara made everything new.

"It would make a lovely location for a special event in your future." Kathleen had never been subtle about her dreams for our not-going-to-happen wedding. At the end of this, I wouldn't be surprised if she didn't ask for an invite and a prime spot, either in the front row or the wedding party itself.

"It certainly would, and we'll be sure to add it to the list."

That won us another huge smile. "I wanted to see how you two were doing. I have to go give a speech now. Seems like someone didn't pay attention." She rolled her eyes and walked off.

I waited until she'd left the wing. "She didn't seem happy about that."

Zara grabbed both my lapels, dragging me to face her. There was a look of crazed excitement in her eyes. "It was in the event debrief. She said she didn't want speeches."

"So why's she agreeing to do it? She's the boss."

"It gives her the ammo she needs to choose us. She's letting them hang themselves."

Zara held her hand up and I gladly took the high five, wrapping my hand around hers. "Let's scope this thing out and see if there's anything we can make better for our next event." Her switch had flipped into seek and destroy mode now she'd smelled blood in the water. Would the same thing happen once this was finished and we went head to head?

"Are these bales of hay supposed to be their way of ripping off our event?" Zara ducked her head low with her gaze darting around the enclosed space we'd walked past when we came into the museum. Her face scrunched up and her lips were pinched tight.

"There was an attempt." I laid my hand on her arm.

"A shitty, second rate attempt. Did you see these deconstructed s'mores?" She held up a spoon with crumbled graham cracker flakes, a bit of chocolate barely bigger than a chocolate chip and an unknown white substance balanced on top.

"What the hell is that?"

"It's a marshmallow foam. Who the hell would want to eat a s'more like this?" She shoved the mini mountain of deconstructed s'more sadness into my mouth.

Plucking the spoon out, I didn't have any other choice but to chew and swallow the 'food'. "You could've warned me first before going *here comes the airplane* on me. And that's terrible."

"I know. I already had one."

Containing my laughter in the face of her furtive glances and seething voice was the most fun I'd had all night. I covered it with a cough, happy her ire wasn't directed at me for a change.

"Does this mean you're ready to go, now you've seen they're no match for us?"

"Just a little bit longer," she said over her shoulder before setting out on an even longer recon mission.

I grabbed another drink—at least there was an open bar —and observed the room. It was stiff backs and stilted conversation even the free-flowing booze couldn't help.

A couple walked up to the bar beside me. The man placed their drink order.

"How much longer do we have to stay? Let's leave now."

"It wouldn't look good if we did."

"Can you set a timer? My feet are killing me in these heels. If we wanted to come out at night I'd have rather done a date night, not some work thing. At least the other event got us out of a day of work."

"Their food was better."

"Can we get a cheesesteak on the way home?"

He handed over her drink. "Absolutely."

These whiners were our competition? If we hadn't already had confirmation, this was all I needed.

We had this in the bag.

21

ZARA

The night air was chilly in the garden area outside of the greenhouse. I ran my hands up and down my arms, trying to ward off the goosebumps.

The weight of a warm, silky fabric dropping around my shoulders nearly made me stumble. Leo stared with determination and focus at the people milling around in the glass structure.

Instead of shrugging the coat off and handing it back, I gripped the sides and pulled them tighter around me. The temperature was dropping, plus, it smelled like him. The clean, fresh smell he always wore—or was that just him?

"We need to have mini cheesesteaks next week." Leo bit into a cracker before making a face and bumping it into a bush nearby. "How are even their crackers terrible?"

"You want mini cheesesteaks for lunch?"

"No, for the block party." That's what we'd taken to calling our event.

"Does anyone do them? I'm sure we could get one of the restaurants to—"

"No, it needs to be somewhere hometown. Not a culinarily-exquisite representation, I'm talking greasy bun, grilled onions, whiz, the whole deal. I'll see what I can find out, and maybe we can get a favor from Jim's."

"We can make that happen." I slipped my phone out of my bag and typed out a few notes, adding them to our shared document.

"This..." He looked around at the clean elegance of the evening. "Has got nothing on what we put together." His confidence was maddening, but it was also a comfort. While he didn't have much experience, his instincts about how much everyone would enjoy our camp recreation had been right. The competitive drive that had served him well on the field was being channeled into our work.

As harried as I'd been, running around at our minicamp, I didn't miss how there wasn't a bored, 'get me the hell out of here' face, except maybe from me when I'd been covered in blue paint. I'd never heard so much laughter from a corporate event. Everyone was paint-splattered and roasting marshmallows on sticks. Pairing childhood favorite snacks with booze had been a winning combination.

Walking around the museum, I couldn't help the itch of boredom attaching weight to my eyelids. Were the events I'd proposed so unbearably boring? Had Leo been right?

Everything was in its place. Trays of champagne. Waiters in tuxes. Silver trays with mini-unidentifiable food stacked high. It was posh, polished, and *perfectly plain*. There wasn't a hint of excitement or anticipation. People milled around having the same conversations they always did, talking about work meetings. More than a few people discreetly and not-so-discreetly checked their phones or watches for the time.

A string quartet at least played pop music from their slightly elevated platform in the glass enclosure with an obscured view of the stars. This would have been so much better standing under them with nothing in the way around a fire, roasting hot dogs. Leo stood on the other side of the room at the bar. Women flocked to him, hung off his every word and he soaked up the attention, used to it after being at the center of one of the biggest sports in the city.

But that confidence didn't only mean he plowed ahead without thinking of the consequences. It also attracted women like bees to an ice cream sundae in the middle of summer. Every time I went out with him, he was recognized and flirted with right in front of me.

Jealousy was a bitter fucking pill, especially over my not-even-real fiancé, but as far as everyone here knew we were blissfully happy, secret lovers ready to recite our vows at our earliest opportunity. I needed to keep it in check if it put our chances in jeopardy. Also, this wasn't real. I needed to repeat that mantra over and over.

Tonight I was wearing the ring and on his arm, and that woman had still come up to us with her lip biting and sexy eyes trying to steal away my man. Well, not my man exactly, but she didn't know that. Hadn't I heard it before? The attractiveness factor of a man went up to some women once they knew he was taken.

Talk about fucked up. Back off, ladies.

But he wasn't up for anything with anyone. He'd left a naked woman in his hotel room—allegedly. And he did look uncomfortable.

I crossed the room to rescue the man who looked nothing like a damsel in distress. "Is that for me, dear?"

His lips twitched as he tried to contain his laugh. "Yes, Gingersnap. I was talking to a new friend about her work as a wedding designer."

He handed me the champagne flute. "She's the architect

of a woman's dream wedding and partners with event companies to bring the vision to life."

The tension eased from my shoulders, still wrapped in his coat.

"Nice to meet you. Leo was telling me he put on the camp event everyone here has been talking about."

"*We.*" Leo gestured between us. "We put it together."

"My mistake. Everyone's been talking about how lovely it was, and fun. While some of my brides love the stuffy type of events like these, there are just as many who love the rustic and adventurous type of wedding. They want people to feel comfortable and excited for what comes next, not waiting for another fancy tray of stuffed hors d'oeuvres. If you two are looking for more clients, let me know." She held out the card between her two fingers, directly at Leo.

I reached for it and shoved it in my bag.

The woman sauntered off, glancing back at him over her shoulder before disappearing back into the crowd.

"She was nice."

"She was flirting."

He bent down, his lips a hairsbreadth from my ear, caressing it with each exhale. "I know."

The heat of his body and the smell of him... I was in Leo overload, short-circuiting. I was part malfunctioning computer, part jello. Why did his voice have to do things to me? Make me feel all melty and delicate. I bit my lip.

"Are you two here to see what a professional can do?"

We both jumped, springing apart like we'd been doing something we shouldn't have and turned like a single unit, facing the snide voice crashing through our moment. No, there was no moment. There was just an overworked and undersexed me picking up on the general lady-attraction vibes of Leo. It was this damn ring.

My inner wrestling match back to sanity was ended when three sets of eyes turned my way.

"What'd I miss?" I whispered out of the side of my mouth to Leo.

"I was informing our Oren & Co. colleagues of how we've enjoyed ourselves immensely, and have been feverishly taking notes to figure out how to fix the clusterfuck of an event we're throwing together last minute with no attention paid to our clients and their enjoyment of said event."

"And we wanted to be sure you didn't rip us off completely next week. Had you gone first, we'd have had to watch you flounder and bastardize what we've created." She opened her arms gesturing to the glass and metal surroundings like they were the Seventh Wonder of the Modern World.

"So, s'mores and hay bales were two things you came up with all on your own?" Leo tilted his head, squinting like he couldn't quite hear through all their bullshit.

"We thought we'd show people how homey things could be elevated."

Leo bristled. "Elevated right up your—"

I knocked my hand against his chest. "Down, boy." Biting back my smile, I nodded and kept a solemn look on my face. "We can tell when we're clearly outmatched, but thank you two for showing us how it's truly done. Let's go, Leo."

I took his hand and dragged him away, barely keeping my laughter at bay.

Bursting out of the greenhouse doors, I bent over, gasping for breath, hiding behind one of the shrubs and holding onto the edges of Leo's coat.

"What did they say? I was hypnotized by the deadness in their eyes."

"Blah, blah, blah, I'm a complete asshole who's never had an original thought and this is my male clone. Something like that." Although Leo covered his mouth with his hand, his yawn came out as a muted roar.

"I'd have thought you could party all night."

"This isn't the type of place to kick anyone's stamina into high gear."

Oh boy. "We should go. It's late. Sorry for making you stay so long."

We walked down the stairs to the street below. "I can't wait to get out of this thing and out of these heels," I added.

"You didn't enjoy yourself? I'd have thought you'd be happy among your people. The pastel, bubbly, prim-and-proper crew." He nudged me with his elbow.

My taxi app showed no one in the vicinity. "Is that who you think I am?" I walked backward to see if changing locations helped.

His gaze traveled up and down my body with his arms crossed over his chest in a know-it-all, I've-had-you-sized-up-since-day-one kind of way. And he knew nothing about me. Absolutely nothing.

"You're wrong."

He smirked. "I'm not wrong."

"I'm not one of them." I jerked my thumb over my shoulder to all the corporate types who'd swarmed this party versus our event where there had been a mixture of people from all walks of life, who did less posturing and had more actual fun. "You think I can't be spontaneous and fun." I flung my arms out, whacking a man in a suit passing by. "Sorry."

He glared at me before going back to his phone.

Leo shrugged a shoulder. "You can be, as long as it's happening according to schedule."

"I can be spontaneous. Check this out." My bank account wasn't overflowing, so I wouldn't be hopping a plane to Italy, but I could find spontaneity anywhere. Anywhere... My gaze ping-ponged around our surroundings. A food cart sat on the corner. Perfect.

"Look at me. Eating street food. You think I'm so stuffy and I'll only eat *foie gras*, well look at me now."

"I know you eat normal food. I sat across from you while you inhaled those chili cheese fries, and the s'mores, and the pigs in a blanket."

"Too late. I'm being spontaneous, remember? You can't stop me. A chili cheese dog, please." I held up my arm like I was hailing a taxi, shouting to the guy who seemed startled I'd approached him, like a major part of his business wasn't people coming up to him and placing an order.

"Zara, what if we try spontaneous somewhere else." Leo tugged at the back of his jacket, trying to guide me away. "Like a place without a free side dish of E. coli and salmonella."

Shaking free from his hold, I stood my ground and looked over my shoulder. "So refined and elite, you can't eat what everyone else eats?" I teased. "Do you want one?"

"Zara." His chest bumped up against my back, once again hitting me with the melty words against my neck. "Look at his hands."

I swallowed hard, watching his grimy fingers handle the tongs and open the vat of—was that supposed to be chili? Oh god. *You've eaten worse.* Once I did this, Leo would never be able to call me a prima donna again.

Juggling my bags, I handed over my cash and took the hot dog smothered in 'chili'.

Leo tried to take the hot dog from my hand. "I get it, you've proven your point."

I skipped away. "Oh, Leo's so scared. It's okay, it won't hurt you."

"Zara, I wouldn't."

Turning around, I took my first bite and grimaced at the texture. Oh god what had I done? I faced Leo and kept my face neutral, taking another bite.

He crossed his arms over his chest and shook his head. "You've proven your point. Stop eating it."

"Why? It's delicious?" I choked down another bite and cautiously swallowed another. Once you got past the initial smell, taste, and texture it wasn't horrendous. Would I be doing it again? Hell, no.

But the look on his face was worth it.

Leo kept shaking his head and muttering, while staring at me like he expected an alien to burst out of my chest.

I shoved the last piece into my mouth, and bit into something hard. Way harder than those mystery bits that sometimes pop up in a hot dog that you pretend aren't there. My formerly iron stomach decided to stage a revolt.

I raced to the nearest trashcan, dropping all my bags on the way and burying it as far down as it could go. This had been a mistake.

A big fucking mistake.

22

LEO

Zara rested her head against my shoulder with her eyes closed, moaning and holding her stomach. There had been a time when I'd never have gotten this close to her without the threat of bodily harm. The bag the taxi driver had given us was clutched in her hand, sloshing its unholy, and warm, horror against my leg. She whimpered and I lifted my bag-ladened arm to rub her forehead, hitting her in the nose with her own purse.

"Hey." The word came out drained and only slightly angry.

If I hadn't known she was sick already and been witness to her *Exorcist* impersonation, I'd have known for sure right then.

I hated this.

I hated that I couldn't stop her pain and hated that I hadn't been able to protect her from herself. Yes, old hot dog water from a street vendor sometimes made them taste like heaven in a roll, but not from *that* cart. If there had been a used band aid floating in there, I wouldn't have been surprised. And she'd eaten the whole thing. To prove a point. To prove to me, she wasn't like Oren & Co. Like I could ever confuse them.

"Which number?" I shook her shoulders.

Moaning, her face drove the buttons into my chest. I was seconds from picking her up and taking her back downstairs.

"Thirteen. Lucky number thirteen." She pushed her head into me even harder, clutching her stomach.

"We're almost there." I tightened my arm around her waist and shifted our weight to get the keys into the door.

"Zara, what happened?" A short woman in a robe and rubber duck slippers darted out of her apartment across the hall, her wide eyes turning suspicious immediately.

"Ate something bad. Leo's helping." Zara patted her hand against my chest. "I'm okay." Lifting her head for a second, she offered a smile to her wary neighbor, who was wearing the sparkler I recognized from our Winthorpe pitch session.

This was the friend. The one with the ring. An irrational part of me had been worried there was a guy waiting in the wings somewhere and she hadn't wanted to tell me. "Congratulations on the engagement."

Her lip fell free from her teeth and her face softened as she cradled her hand. "Isn't it pretty?" She held the engagement ring up to the light.

"Gorgeous. I need to get her inside."

The friend backed up and nodded, holding her door open and waiting for me to take Zara inside.

Unlocking the door, I pushed it open and reversed my hold on pressing her up against the wall inside the entrance.

I flicked on the light and my stomach dropped like *I'd* eaten the bacteria infested hot dog.

Covering my body with hers, I put my arm under hers

ready to get her out of here in case whoever did this was still here.

I scanned the ransacked room searching for the intruder. Room clear, I whispered, "Zara, someone broke into your apartment."

"What?" She nudged at my chest, pushing herself away from the wall and from under my arm. "Why would anyone?" And for a second, she looked up at me with pursed lips. "That's how it always looks." Her face was once again seafoam green and she shoved past me, bolting through the entry way and down the darker hallway.

A door slammed shut and the unmistakable sounds of every molecule of food she'd ever eaten evacuating her body filled the small apartment. Closing the front door, I took in Zara's allegedly non-broken-into home. For someone so meticulous about their work she lived like the love child of a football team and a frat had who had never been taught to pick up after herself.

I pulled a piece of bright green fabric from behind the ripped couch cushion before shoving it back into place. This wasn't how I'd thought I'd get my hands on Zara's underwear. Not that I'd thought about it before. I mean, lying next to her in bed when she'd rolled over in her sleep with her hands tucked under her face had unintentionally shown me more of her non-hard ass. But the symphony of puke going on in the next room didn't scream '*Come look at my silky-to-the-touch panties with a delicate frill along the edges.*' No, I definitely hadn't burned the feel of them into my frontal lobe.

Righting the couch cushions, I made a pile of clothes on the single chair in her living room. The plastic lawn chair. Blazers, button-down shirts, the previously touched underwear. There were five shoes in the living room, none with their mate. I grabbed them and lined them up alongside the wall by the doorway.

The sounds from the bathroom had quieted down. There were half-filled cups of water on the counter. I could see her now, getting a drink when an email or text came in about work—she'd drop everything, rushing to get it done before her next breath.

Rummaging through the cabinet under the sink, I grabbed a sponge and then cleaned out the last of the cups stacked on the counter before drying them and putting everything away in the empty cabinets.

Every so often I'd turn off the water and listen for the symphony of sickness. She couldn't possibly have any food left in her system.

I rapped my knuckles against the bathroom door. "Zara, how you doing?"

If her moans were any indication, not the best.

I performed the sniff test on a pile of laundry in a basket in the hallway, grabbed a wash cloth from the top, let myself into the bathroom, and ran it under the faucet. At least the bathroom was clean. The lights were off, but it smelled of disinfectant. Well, disinfectant, and the new smell layered on top.

Her head rested on the seat, her body crumpled up and sagging against the porcelain.

"What are you still doing here?" She limply lifted her arm, trying to wave me off. "Go. I'm home. I'm good." She rested her head against the toilet seat and shooed me away without opening her eyes.

I placed the cool, damp cloth along the back of her neck.

The noise that escaped her mouth was halfway between a moan and a whimper. Helplessness drove me to action. I walked back to the kitchen and grabbed one of the clean cups, filling it with water.

"You're not good. I brought you some water." Taking her hand, I wrapped it around the cup.

She gulped it down like she hadn't had a drink in weeks. The top buttons of her dress had come undone. One of her shoes was on and the other was against the wall. Her dress had ridden up, nearly over her ass.

I focused on her eyes. "This should make you feel better."

She made a murmur of appreciation and opened one eye, squinting at me. "You're being so nice."

"You're hurting. I'd be an asshole if I didn't help you out. I'm not all bad, Zara."

"You're not bad at all. Actually—" Her eyes bulged and she shoved her head deep down in the toilet bowl.

It seems her body had a visceral reaction to paying me the slightest compliment. I stepped out of the bathroom, turning to the only other door in the hallway.

She needed to get out of her dress and into something that made puking from the bathroom floor a little less terrible.

If her living room was a disaster, her bedroom was the rubble of a bombed-out city. How the hell did she live this way? There were clothes everywhere. On the bed. Scratch that, it wasn't a bed, it was a mattress on the floor. On the floor.

On top of a dresser that gave the Leaning Tower a run for its money, cups covered every surface not covered with clothes. Some were half filled with water, some completely empty, but it was like once they came into this room they were never allowed to leave.

I approached a pile of laundry cautiously. With another

tentative sniff test, I found a clean t-shirt and pair of flannel pajama pants.

Her latest bout finished, I stepped back into the bathroom, which was the only clean spot in her whole apartment. Sticking my arms under hers, I helped her off the floor.

"Rinse out your mouth and we'll get you changed."

She didn't even fight me. Her forehead rested against my shoulder. That scared me. How bad did I let her get before taking her to the hospital? Her skin was clammy but cool. Usually after eating something bad, you bounced back, but the hotdog from hell had done a number on her. Fear rode me hard that the evil dog had done something beyond food poisoning.

Doing most of the work, I unbuttoned and peeled her dress off, keeping my eyes averted as much as possible. It doesn't mean I didn't get an eyeful. The plain black of her bra did nothing to take away from the perfection that was her breasts. The perfect overflowing handful.

Snap out of it, Leo. She's puking. Don't be an asshole.

There wasn't a barbed comment or threat from her. Only a moan every so often and the smallest bit of assistance in getting her clothes off and the pajama pants on. I tugged the top over her head and her hair fell over her face like a curtain. I brushed it away, letting my touch linger on her cheek.

"Is that better?"

Her eyes fluttered open and I got a half nod before she flung herself back at the toilet.

Holding her hair back, I rubbed up and down her spine. There was a stack of black hairbands on the counter. I took one. Gathering her hair up, I looped the band and put it up into the world's worst ponytail. It would have to do.

While she rested, I crossed the hallway back into her bedroom and shoved everything off the bed. Shuffling clothes out of the way of the closet door, I found a set of neatly folded sheets on the top shelf. It was like she was allergic to anything neat and organized. I shook the sheets out and quickly made her bed and swapped out the pillow cases.

A trashcan by the side of the bed and corralling the clothes into a pile beside the door, and the room was ready for her.

She rested with her head against the toilet seat with a soft snore from her lips. Her cheeks were rosy and flushed as I helped her up and to the sink to brush. With one swish of her mouth while she was practically still asleep, I lifted her up into my arms.

The short trip stretched on for way longer than the eight steps it took me to get to her bed. She was nestled close, her long limbs dangling from my hold, but it wasn't awkward. Her cheek rested against my shoulder, with her Dr. Seuss hairdo courtesy of me.

I set her down and she curled into a ball, clutching her stomach. Tugging the blankets up over her, I pushed the trashcan right against the side of the bed.

"Zara."

She moaned in acknowledgment, keeping her eyes closed.

I sat on the edge of the bed. It dipped under my weight and she rolled closer. Flexing my fingers, I pulled her hair out of her sloppy ponytail. A brush teetered on the edge of her sock-covered night stand. I grabbed it and ran it through her hair.

"There's a trashcan right next to you."

Another whimper.

"I'll put your hair up, so it doesn't get in your way." Dragging it through her sun-kissed waves, I slipped the hairband around my wrist.

Her lips parted and she shifted her head to the side, so I could get to the rest of her hair, all without opening her eyes like even the dim light from the hallway was too bright.

Each pass of the brush seemed to relax her more. She wasn't the tight ball anymore, more curled up on her side pressed against my thigh like she might be if we shared a bed.

If I hadn't run into her that day on the street, how would things be different between us? What would working together be like if we weren't constantly butting heads and planning on working against one another as soon as possible?

I brushed her bangs back from her forehead to feel her temperature in case it wasn't food poisoning, but a sudden and vicious bug. Still fine, and she was less clammy. Her room was still a disaster zone, but at least her bed didn't look like a tornado had ripped across it. The rest of the room, however...

I stood and she grabbed onto my arm.

"Don't leave." She opened her eyes and held onto me, her fingers weak, but determined.

"It'll be okay. I won't. I'll go out into the living room and work on our plans for next week."

She nodded and tucked both hands under her face.

On the way out, I gathered up all the clothes I saw in a bundle with the old sheets. I closed the door behind me and took stock of the rest of the apartment.

I'd start working on our plans, but first I'd pick up a few things.

23

ZARA

A knocking invaded the blackness of my sleep. Slowly, I woke up, rolling over on my side. My stomach ached. Not like before, when I'd blasted into my apartment like a rocket set to explode, but my muscles were sore. The driving, twisting pain that had made me want to slam my eyes shut and never open them was gone.

The insistent knocking continued, only it wasn't the door. Climbing out of bed, I stared down at the comfy pajamas I thought I'd lost months ago. The warm flannel pants and t-shirt weren't what I remembered wearing to sleep.

Something was off.

My leg banged against the trashcan beside my bed. Thankfully it was empty, not filled with whatever had shot out of me from the pits of spoiled food hell.

I took two steps and it dawned on me.

My floor was spotless.

There wasn't an article of clothing anywhere. It wasn't just the floor that had somehow received a makeover. My dresser no longer tilted at an odd slant that made it impossible to fit the drawers in it—and every drawer was closed. It looked like the day I'd found it on the curb and not how it had ended up by the time I pushed and shoved it into the elevator and into my bedroom.

Memories from my arrival to my apartment flashed back to me. Leo asking if I'd been robbed. Had I been robbed? Why the hell would they have wanted my hand-me-down clothes?

I wished I'd kept a baseball bat or something in my room for protection—not like I'd have been able to find it. I flung open my closet door and grabbed one of my heels, all of which were sitting nicely in a row with my other shoes along the back wall.

After two more steps, it dawned on me.

A robber wouldn't straighten my shoes. Had Leo dropped me off and let Stella into my apartment to take care of me? Embarrassment burned my cheeks. I'd managed to divert every opportunity for her to come inside, but I guess if there was one time for her to do it, it would be when I was puking my brains out for hours.

I set the shoe back in its place. All my suits were hung up in the closet. How long had I been out?

Walking to my dresser like I'd expected a maniacal jack in the box to pop out, I tugged open the drawer. My shirts were neatly folded and organized by color. In the next drawer, my jeans and pajama pants were folded the same way. Bracing myself, I pulled on the top drawer. The bundles of fabric were dropped inside, not meticulously transformed into origami swans.

Of course she'd do this. Everything about her apartment screamed PTA mom who'd make everything from scratch, including decorations for the school dance. I'd owe her after this.

The knocking continued and I walked out into the hallway. Metal on metal clanged behind the slatted accordion door next to me. I yanked open the lid half expecting to find a serial killer, not the overstuffed load of laundry I'd been jamming in there for weeks. Everything was bunched up on one side. I shifted things around, including a handful of my underwear, and closed the lid. It rumbled back to life without any more knocking. I jumped back when the dryer buzzer went off. This was *The Twilight Zone* crossed with a slightly disconcerting fantasy I'd often had of waking up and finding everything magically done for me.

Stella had outdone herself, and the pit in my stomach opened even wider. What had she thought when she'd walked in here and seen the way I lived? I could never face her again. I'd have to leave and come back to my apartment only when I knew she wouldn't be awake, or was watching wrestling. Why'd she have to be so nice? A whole case of Tastykakes were in her future to make up for this, and I'd set them down on her doorstep under the cover of night.

The front door swung open.

"Stella, you didn't have to—"

Only it wasn't Stella.

"You're awake." Leo smiled, walking in with his arms full of brown paper grocery bags just like in the movies. He kicked the door closed and dropped the key ring on the kitchen counter before unpacking the bags.

"And you're here." I stepped out into the living room, acutely aware of how disheveled I looked, how run down I felt, and the fact that my breath could peel the paint off a car.

He pulled open a cabinet and stuck some boxes inside before closing it again. "I stepped out for a bit for supplies."

"You didn't have to."

"I know, but you needed it." He nodded toward the ramshackle shitstorm that was my home.

Tears threatened at his attempts to get this place in order. It's why I'd left it like this too long. Can't look at it if you never turn the lights on, or aren't here for longer than it takes to get a little sleep and do it all again tomorrow. Anything was better than facing it. But no one was supposed to see this. Hell, I hadn't even let Stella in here.

A scream of 'just leave, don't look at the shambles' caught in my throat. "I don't need or want your help."

"Good thing I don't listen, right?" His smile and his eyes didn't hold a hint of pity. "Because you're getting it."

"Leo..." Misery leached from that one word. It didn't even come close to when I'd said it with my head plunger-deep in the toilet.

He pushed ahead with his kitchen organization. "Let me help." Turning his head, he braced his hands on the counter. "Please, Gingersnap."

Only, this time when he called me that it didn't make me want to rent a car exclusively to run him over with it.

"Why are you being so nice to me?"

His hand froze halfway to the drawer beside the stove. He hung his head for a second. "Maybe things got off to a rocky start. We're both coming at this from opposing sides, forced to work together, but we don't have to fight. We can do this together, beat Oren & Co. at their own game, and figure out what we do about Winthorpe once they're out of the picture. Maybe we can find another way and actually be friends."

I crossed my living room and fell in step beside him,

helping him put away the dishes he'd obviously cleaned last night, and unpack the groceries he'd bought this morning.

Squatting, I stuck the package of paper towels under the sink and leaned on the open cabinet door. "You even cleaned under the sink?"

He shrugged. "It needed it. I've got the rest of this. There are bagels and bacon in the bag on the counter. And some chocolate croissants. They're fresh." He ducked his head. "I figured I owed you."

This swell of emotions was too much after everything that happened between us. Chocolate croissants. He'd remembered.

"You need to hydrate and have something to eat. How's your stomach?"

I stood and dropped my hand to my no-longer-churning stomach. "Completely chili dog free and no longer pissed as hell at me for eating poison."

"I warned you." He opened another cabinet.

"Trust me. I won't forget anytime soon." I dug through the bags, setting everything out on the counter. Half a dozen bagels. Three types of cream cheese. A couple bagel sandwiches. And a big bottle of orange juice.

"What bagel and cream cheese did you want?"

"I can make it."

I sawed mine open. "I know. But I want to."

He chuckled. "Everything, with the Philly cream cheese."

"On it." I set out his bagel and poured us both a cup of OJ.

He finished putting everything away.

Picking at the seeds on my plate, I took a bite of my bagel now that he was no longer distracted by putting away the multitude of groceries he'd bought.

"So..." Leo rocked back on his heels with his gaze roaming my apartment and his hands in his pockets.

I picked at the sesame seeds on the top of my bagel, unable to hide the heat of embarrassment burning in my cheeks. "How'd I end up living in such a shithole?" I chanced a glance up at him.

He leaned against the counter, trying to keep his face neutral.

I scrubbed my hands down my face. "It's a long story."

Picking up his plate, he took a bite of his bagel and stood across from me in the cramped kitchen. It had never seemed too small before, but with Leo standing there, it suddenly felt undersized.

Trying to think of the best place to start, I sipped on my juice, trying to buy myself a little more time. "When I left college, I didn't have many friends. Other people moved away or moved in with their college roommates, keeping the party going, but I didn't have that luxury.

"I had a roommate. Technically, a roommate, but...my name is on the lease because I didn't want to be at someone else's mercy once I finally had my own place. She was a friend of a friend in college. And we lived together perfectly fine for the first year. We never fought. She was quiet and kept to herself and I was working all the time. Everything was kept clean and we'd set up a schedule to split the household duties.

"Things were going so well, I signed another 2-year lease at the reduced rate and things were perfect. Until she got a new boyfriend. You know how some people live a sheltered life in high school and go buck wild in college? This was her delayed version.

"He was her first real boyfriend. Things were off immediately. Stuff would go missing. Things were broken. I'd come home after a late night and there would be a hole in the wall or they'd be having sex on the couch. And I didn't miss how she'd fallen behind on rent. The joint account we deposited our rent and utilities had been overdrawn and I'd had to pay the fees. Finally, I told her it was enough. He wasn't allowed to come over anymore. The next night, I came back here and the place was trashed."

Talking about it even now brought the tears back. I blinked them away. This had happened over a year ago. I should be over it. How not over it I was could be seen all over my still-trashed apartment.

"Most of my stuff was taken or destroyed. I called the cops, but—" I shrugged. Walking into my apartment after a long night of work had been one of the worst moments of my life. I'd finally started to feel like this was my real home. I'd been so proud, scouring flea markets and secondhand shops for fun or unique accents to make the apartment mine. And someone I'd trusted had dismantled it in a matter of hours.

Cleaning up everything I could, I'd fallen asleep on my comforter on the floor, since my mattress had been wrecked. Shredded, with springs bursting through the foam and fabric. Bits of glass from the busted light bulbs and dishes were all over it, like they'd taken special joy in making it unsalvageable.

My tears had blinded me as I swept up the broken glass and shattered plates, sneaking everything out after the cops had taken my statement and made their report.

Leo ran his hand down my arm. The comforting gesture was almost a step too far in pushing me into blubbering territory.

"They caught them." A chunk of bagel met an unfortunate end from my poking and prodding finger. "But junkies aren't notorious for taking care of their stuff, and they sure as hell don't take care of other people's stuff."

She'd at least left my picture of me and Ty his first day at The Mercerville School. It had been a portrait taken by a photographer on move-in day. The frame was shattered and the corner ripped, but I still had one reminder of why I couldn't give up.

"I bought a new mattress and found the rest of furniture you see here." I couldn't even look at it. My neck was on fire like I'd been out in the blazing sun for hours. Lawn furniture held together better than what I had. Another reason heading home after a long day of work didn't hold the same charm to me as it might for others.

But owning nice stuff was another opportunity for it to be taken away. Even if I had the money, buying new things would've put me on edge, afraid it would disappear in a snap. "After that, I couldn't really look at the place. It brought back too many bad memories. All the little touches I'd put into making this my home had been taken away from me."

"Are you sure you don't want me to hunt them both down?" From the look on his face, he was completely serious.

It made my heart happy he cared so much. I shook my head, my throat clogged with a waterfall of emotions.

"It doesn't matter. What's done is done." I stole a glance over my shoulder at the ruins of the home I'd tried to build. "I gave up on it. It wasn't a safe place, and every time I turned on the lights it reminded me of what they'd done to me, so I stopped turning them on. I'd dump everything when I came in and try not to look too hard at anything."

Wiping angrily at my face, I hoped the floor would open up and swallow me. Weepy wasn't a good look on me and I'd already cried more than enough tears over the things in my past I couldn't change. "It's stupid, I know. I'm safe and healthy and that's what matters." *There are worse things out there, Zara. Much worse.*

A pair of strong arms wrapped around me. He smelled like bread, fresh from the oven, and I couldn't help myself.

"There are worse things, but they took something from you and made you feel unsafe. They stole your peaceful place, and it does matter."

My head rested in the crook of his neck. I wrapped my arms tight around him and let myself believe for a few seconds that I didn't have to have all my shit together all the time and maybe, just maybe, someone would give me a little help, even if I tried to pretend I didn't need it.

I patted his back and then dropped my arms. "Sorry about that. And thank you for the bagels and the croissant." My voice dropped and I started cleaning up.

"Maybe I can help with the furniture situation."

"Really, it's okay. I'm barely here anyway, right. It's not like I've been inviting friends over. And I'll be moving to someplace smaller once my lease is up. It would only be more to pack." I closed the lids on the cream cheese and put them and the bagels back in the bag.

Closing it, I held it out for him to take. "Thank you for everything. I appreciate it. I really do."

"No problem. Keep them." He nudged my hand back toward my chest.

I walked him to the door with the bagels clutched against me like my own protective barrier. The back of my hand tingled where he'd pressed against it. Gratitude swelled in my chest, not only for the bagels, but everything he'd done for me from the hot dog horror warning to staying with me all night to the groceries.

Opening the door, he turned to me. "I'll see you tomorrow?"

"Of course. We've got to plan another event to destroy Oren & Co. with. I'll meet you tomorrow at ten at Stark."

"Make it nine. We've got a lot to get through."

I couldn't hold back my chuckle. "Look at you, workaholic. Nine, then."

Leaning against the closed door, I banged my head against it. *Don't even think about having feelings for your fake fiancé, Zara.* Who had time for that anyway? Not me.

But a small part of me piped up. Maybe...

24

LEO

"You want me to come up with another front row ticket to one of the biggest concerts of the year with less than twenty-four hours' notice?" Hunter splayed his hands out on the counter, leaning forward with a take-no-prisoners look on his face.

When I'd found myself in the elevator on the way up, I'd tried to talk myself out of it twenty times, but here I was in Hunter's pre-war apartment feeling like an asshole. Zara had popped into the office today looking back to normal after four days of harboring a slight green tinge and a non-existent appetite. Every night I'd stayed up, itching to call her and see how she was doing, but I'd kept calm and confined our calls and texts to business only.

"I should've asked when we played basketball on Monday."

Hunter scoffed. "No shit."

"I've been thinking about it more and more, so I thought I'd ask. If it's impossible, don't worry about it."

"No, don't back down now. Have a seat." He dropped back into the chair behind his desk. I felt like I'd come in to make a deal with a mob boss, asking for a favor in exchange for hiding a body at some point down the line. "You'd like a ticket for..."

"Zara."

"The shrew I got the ring for, who was making your life a living hell."

"She's not a shrew."

"Your words not mine."

"We had a rocky start."

"And that's smoothed out now." He steepled his fingers, resting his elbows on the arms of the wingback chair.

"We've come to an understanding."

"And you think a concert would be an olive branch."

"Exactly. We're friendly, and this could make the rest of our time together easier." She'd dealt with a lot and rode herself harder than anyone else. A fun night out with music, drinks and dancing would be just what she needed.

"And you want to bang her."

I jerked back in my seat. "What? No."

He tilted his head, giving me a 'do I look stupid?' look.

I scrubbed my chin. "Once you cut through all that intensity, she's a woman who knows what she wants and isn't going to let anyone stand in her way."

"Does she want you?"

"We're friends."

"So, no. But you want her to."

"What the hell is with the million questions? If you can't get the ticket, just tell me."

"I'm only trying to figure out how much the ticket is worth to you." He leaned back in his chair like a super villain.

"Do you want a kidney?"

"Do you have one to spare?" He glanced down at my

right side, before holding my gaze for another beat. What the hell kind of shit was he into? Milwaukee had been one thing. How deep did his acquisition skills truly go?

His grim lips parted into a wide grin. "I'm fucking with you. Give me a second." Picking up his phone, he held up one finger while tapping away using with thumb. "Sent."

Eight tense seconds later his phone buzzed. "Done. She's on the list."

I huffed out a laugh. "That's it? She's got a ticket?" I dragged my fingers through my hair, relief washing over me. "No kidney needed?"

"Not today." Even harder laughing. "The look on your face. I do not trade in black market organs. Would you prefer I sucked at getting things done?" He chuckled, wiping away his tears.

"No, I much prefer things this way, but that doesn't mean I'm not still a little afraid of you."

His chest puffed up like it was a point of pride.

"I need to let Zara know. She'll be floored."

"Yeah, not the tiniest bit of attraction there at all." His words and nod dripped with skepticism.

"We've hit a stride in our relationship."

"Ahhh, a relationship, is it?"

Asshole. "Our working relationship."

"A relationship where you'll be striding into someone's panties after the encore from Without Grey."

"No panties will be gotten into."

"Not by you, anyway." We left the office. The hallway stretched on past five doorways on one side and three on the other before opening to the living room we all took over for our weekly Chinese food feasts.

"It's not weird living in this place alone?"

"I prefer it this way. I get in late at night and don't have to worry about waking anyone up. No dirty dishes other than my own. It would drive me crazy to have to tiptoe around someone else."

The floorboards creaked under our steps. "Plus, the ghosts would hate to have to share you with anyone else."

"There's more than enough of me to go around." His hand shot out like he'd just had the most brilliant idea. "Do you want to get a drink?"

~

Giant floodlights painted a pattern in the sky as we got closer to the brightly-lit multistory structure up ahead. There were huge nets stretching up higher than I could see beyond the building.

"Where are we?" I leaned forward between the driver and passenger seat of the cab. A line of people snaked their way down the path in front of the building.

We got out of the taxi and Hunter jogged up the steps, slapping hands with the security guard at the front of the line before walking in like there weren't fifty people staring daggers at us. Who needed a former celebrity when you had Hunter?

Instead of stopping at the check-in counter like everyone else, we took the elevator up to the third floor. There were bays filled with groups of people at low-backed couches and high tables, drinking, eating, and golfing. Golfing?

"This wasn't what I thought you meant when you said out for a drink."

"I like to mix things up."

We ordered food and drinks and got set up. While Hunter was pulled away to schmooze, I grabbed my phone.

Me: Hey Zara, are you at home?

Gingersnap: No, I'm out.

On a date? Was she out with someone else right now?

Me: Having fun?

Gingersnap: Not in the slightest.

I let out the breath that had caught in my chest. At least it was a shitty date. Not that I wanted her to put up with an asshole, but the thought of her out with some guy with his hands all over her made me want to punch something. Namely the fuckwit who thought he could go out with my fake fiancée in the first place.

A moment of indecision rushed through me before I tapped her name.

"Bad date?" I said, before she could even say hello. But it was the question I needed answered, even if I didn't want to know at the same time.

"If only. I'd rather be on a date with Hannibal Lecter than where I am." A spark of laughter ran through her words.

"Where the hell are you?"

"I was at a symphony cocktail reception for corporate sponsors."

"Lucky you. That sounds drier than a box of Saltines in the Sahara."

"I've already fallen asleep standing up twice. Are you at a club?"

"It's a driving range nightclub combo, Vertex Golf."

"It opened recently, right? Ads were all over the radio."

"Opening night was tonight."

Her words were whisper quiet. "Are *you* on a date?"

Why did it make me so damn happy she'd even asked? I suppressed my smile. "In a way."

"How's your date feel about you calling me in the middle of it?" Her words were a little clipped.

"I'm sure they'd be fine with it. They'd probably want you to join us."

She gasped. "Don't even—"

"I let Hunter talk me into coming out with him. We're shooting a few buckets of balls."

"Oh! Thank him again for getting the ring."

"Why are you working tonight?"

"After the reception, I remembered there were some things I forgot to do in the office, so I'm currently being blinded by a copy machine and getting paper cuts that'll last until next year." She sighed, her weariness coming through the call. "My boss's daughter doesn't want to do anything that's not one hundred percent fun all the time, so I'm stuck here."

She worked harder than anyone I knew, including quarterbacks who have multiple championship rings.

"I've got some news to make it easier to get through your night."

"Lay it on me."

A particular part of my anatomy jumped at the sleepy, sultry tone of her voice and phrase.

"Hunter had an extra ticket to the Without Grey concert tomorrow and I wanted to know if you were up for it?"

"What? Hell, yes!"

I jerked the phone away from my ear.

"Shit, I'm in trouble." Her voice dropped to a whisper. "Yes, that's amazing. Text me the details and I'll be there. Thank you and thank Hunter again." She ended the call.

He showed up with two beers, sliding me one.

I chose the dartboard version of golf. My thoughts kept drifting back to Zara. Was she still in the office? How was her stomach after her night of adventurous eating? Could I help her fix her place up without her threatening me with bodily harm?

"You'd be winning right now, if you were paying attention to what you were doing." Hunter's voice pulled me out of my Zara-filled thoughts.

The scores were almost tied up.

"You've always got tricks up your sleeve?" I took a swig from my beer, lifting the driver out of the golf bag.

"Nah, you're going to want this one." He handed over a 3-wood. "Of course, I need to keep things exciting. Making an appearance at their grand opening is a favor I'm doing."

I lined up my shot. Outside of a few 'celebrity' tournaments, my golf experience was lackluster to say the least. "You showing up here is a favor? How are you connected with this place?" Keeping my head down, I followed through with my shot, connecting with the ball. It sailed through the air and landed in the outermost ring of the net target. A point appeared on the computer screen tracking our progress.

Hunter shrugged, tugging on the bottom of the rolled sleeve of his button-down shirt. He gave Everest a run for his money in the well put together department. But Hunter was scrappier than Everest could be. He didn't ooze money, but he could wear the look like a coat depending on what circles he was around, and I had no doubt they were varied. "You meet people and things happen."

"Only for you. I've never met someone who could wheel and deal like you. You were the campus dealer, weren't you?"

He laughed into his beer. "Sort of." Grabbing his club, he took his spot at the ball dispenser and set up his shot. It made mine look like I should've broken out the Little Tykes plastic play set. The ball blasted off the platform. I couldn't even track it, but the computer told me all I needed to know.

A damn bullseye.

He holstered the club like the lethal weapon it was in his hands, and grabbed one of the sliders off the table in our low seating area. Club music vibrated the floor beneath our feet.

"How's it feel no longer being a pro athlete?" He lounged on the seat with his arms along the back edge.

I stood for my turn. "Weird as fuck. I can't even lie. I've spent the last twenty-one years of my life devoted to football. From pee-wee leagues up until five months ago, I lived and breathed football. Every off season I was in the gym keeping up my conditioning. My singular goal was to make it pro. The odds were against me, but I was determined. Gave it my all in every practice…"

"And now it's all gone."

"This is why I've never dedicated my life to a singular purpose. I like to spread the love."

"That's one way to put it."

"That's why you're thinking of the sports TV thing."

"It was an idea, but I figured it was a long shot."

"Not entirely." Hunter wolfed down half his quesadilla.

Sitting on the edge of my seat, I was seconds away from giving him the Heimlich, just to get him to spit it out. "You haven't said anything about it."

"I don't like to confirm anything until I'm sure. Pieces are working in the background, and I'm close."

"If you pull this off, I swear I'll owe you fifty favors."

He tilted his head in my direction. "Fifty, you say?"

"Why do I feel like I just made a deal with the devil?"

Laughing, he lined up his shot. "Better the devil you

know." Following through, he tracked the ball sailing through the air.

"How do you think tomorrow will go?"

"As in, do I think Everest will either not show or absolutely flip his shit?"

"That."

"Toss up. It'll depend on whether Madison and the band are there or not. For every one the band shows up to, there are five they don't. Half the parties are for the road crew who've been killing themselves for the past two years they've been on tour."

"What happened? Right after he lost his mind."

"When your girlfriend starts fucking one of the biggest bands in the world it's hard to keep it together."

Beer spurted past the lip of the bottle. "She's screwing the whole band?"

He laughed. "No." A thoughtful look crossed his face as he looked up at the ceiling like he was flipping through his mental rolodex. "At least, I don't think so."

"I'll be prepared to tackle him if need be."

"You'd do that on a Tuesday."

"True."

"Don't worry. You two are past the angry phase. You've slid into the hostile phase. Next up is acceptance, and then finally love."

"Everest can find another group of friends to hang out with instead of mine."

"What about me? I'm the newest to the crew. Are you going to kick me out next?"

"You're way too useful, man. Plus, you don't piss me off like he does."

"And you piss him off just as much."

"Good. I don't know why he hangs around."

Hunter shook his head. "It beats the alternative."

"What's that?"

"Being alone."

We finished our beers and headed out. The entire meal and three rounds of golf were on the house. He hadn't needed to spend eighteen years putting his body on the line, and he still got all the celebrity perks.

Back in my apartment, I was tempted to call Zara again and make sure she'd made it home. Instead, I settled for a text in case she was in bed already. Not that the mattress counted. She needed a bed. A soft bed, up off the floor. A comfortable place after a long day.

I ran my hand over the cold side of my bed. We've barely made it to friends. Fake fiancée or not, we had one more event, one more week to our truce, and then the gloves came off. But did they have to? Maybe we could figure out a new arrangement entirely.

25

ZARA

Flashes of light shot out the sides of the copy machine. Two reams of paper later, the last of the collated copies shot out. Heat from the overworked machine turned the cramped room into a sauna. Being stuck in here wasn't as terrible as it had been ten minutes ago.

A concert. Leo had invited me to a concert. The wheels were spinning in overdrive. I hadn't been to a concert in... ever? There had been some free ones when I was at college, but spending money on tickets to music I could listen to for free never won out over Tyler's tuition and my food, rent, and student loan payments.

But tomorrow, I'd be going to one with Leo. Hunter the Fixer had a spare ticket, and maybe Leo had figured since I didn't have many friends my evening would be wide open. Instead of being offended, I was flattered that he'd asked. Maybe we were turning a corner. What did that mean for things between us once we won? What did it mean if we lost?

The door banged open behind me.

"Are you printing out the entire Encyclopedia Britannica?" Andi strode into the room balancing four long boxes in her arms.

"If only it were that exciting."

"Toner's low and I replaced these three days ago."

"Sorry."

"No problem. It gets me out of my desk for more than coffee and snack runs. Plus, I promised the guys I'd buy them Tastykakes all next week if they did the server migration by five pm and guess who came through? Which means I need to stock up on the way home."

"That's a work incentive I can get behind."

The copies finished and I set the last few on the massive stacks I'd run off already.

"You haven't been around much." Andi crunched behind the printer, opening the massive side door and tugging out the toner.

"The Winthorpe account has been a lot."

"Is that what this is?" She gestured to the huge stacks of paper I'd be lugging out of here.

I stared at the stack of over three hundred proposal packages I'd had to format and copy, which had landed on my desk at 4:58pm. "No."

The door flew open again. This time there was a much less welcome visitor to the cramped copy room.

Valerie swanned in with her arms crossed over her chest looking like she'd rather be anywhere except here. Take a number. "Are you finished yet?"

"Yet?" I bit my tongue. She was the boss's daughter. It had been less than an hour. Boss's daughter won out. "I'm almost finished."

"Better late than never."

Was that blood I tasted?

"Winthorpe should be my account."

I heard it was until they asked that you be removed.

"I'm sure your dad had his reasons for making the decision he made." *Like the fact that you're an incompetent coattail-rider who wants nothing more than to boss people around and lord her perceived power over them.* Only it wasn't perceived, since I wasn't shouting all this in her face right now.

"Once I'm finished, I can set them on your desk like always."

I grabbed a copy off the top.

Valerie gasped behind me.

"Where did you get that?" I lifted the top packet off and held it out to her. "These are the documents you said you needed for tomorrow."

She snatched the packet and flung it onto the counter. "Not that. That." Twisting my wrist—ow! —she shoved my hand back in my face.

Oh. That. After my night of puking, I hadn't taken the ring off like I normally did.

"It's nothing." I tried to tug my hand free from her iron grip.

"It's a three carat Emerald cut VVS1 diamond engagement ring." Did she have a bionic jeweler's eye installed in her head? And there was no way this was real. Was there?

I shook her grip off my hand and snatched it back. "It's nothing."

"You're engaged?" Shock and outrage reverberated through her voice. Like the very idea of me being engaged with a ring like this was a sick cosmic prank. Joke's on her.

"I'm not engaged. Do you want me to drop these copies off in your office?" I gestured to the stack sitting behind me.

"I'd like to leave. I don't want to be stuck here checking up on you."

No one said you had to stay. "Everything will be on your desk by 8am."

"I heard the Winthorpe event was interesting?" Every bit of her entitled, belittling arsenal was on fire tonight.

"It went well. Everyone enjoyed themselves."

"They're not a bunch of pre-teens, Zara." She laughed throwing her head back.

"Maybe not, but they had fun and there haven't been any complaints."

"Not to you."

Andi slammed a toner cartridge in place.

My stomach dropped. "Someone complained?"

"My father mentioned a message from Winthorpe. I can't imagine why else they'd call."

Andi responded, but only loud enough for me to hear. "Maybe that's because no one calls with anything other than complaints for you. But there's these crazy things called compliments. People get them when they do their jobs properly." She slammed the large plastic panel on the side of the machine closed and stood beside me.

"Hi, Val. So nice of you to stay late to help Zara bring all your copies to your office." She hefted one of the stacks in her arms and dropped them into Valerie's unsuspecting grasp.

Valerie yelped and teetered, nearly toppling over.

"They're insanely heavy, you should drop those off asap." Andi turned her by the shoulders and showed her out of the copy room as collated packets slid off the top of her stack.

"Don't let her get to you. I'm always here for back up."

Without Andi, I'd have lost my shit at least a year ago. She channeled my inner rage, saying and doing the things I couldn't because I needed this job.

"Thanks for saving me from saying something I shouldn't."

"Oh, you most definitely should."

"Not when I've got so much hanging on this job. This is my first primary planning position." I lifted the second stack.

"You mean the one Bill promised you within six months of starting." She followed behind me with a smaller bundle of papers under her arm.

"Don't let them walk all over you."

"Like I have a choice." I stopped in front of Valerie's door. Locked and the lights were off.

"That—" I seethed, turning in the opposite direction to set everything down in my office.

"One day you'll say the word to her face and I'll dance around the office with a feather boa and tiara." Andi set down her stack on my desk.

"You'll be the first to know if I win the lotto."

My phone started ringing a block from my apartment.

"Hey, Tyler."

"I made first chair." I didn't even get a hello. The words spewed through the phone.

"All that practice paid off."

"I know, I know. Of course, I listened to you because you're my wise, all-knowing big sister, and I did it. One week from today, we're performing at Carnegie Hall. Can you make it?"

"One sec." Checking my calendar, it was the night before our final presentations to Kathleen. "I have a big work thing the next day."

"Cool, so you can come, right?" Why did he sound like he was jumping on his bed? How many fourteen year olds wanted their big sister hanging around them? But I got it. We were all we had.

When had I ever been able to tell him no? And breaking promises wasn't something I did.

"If I can get through everything I need to get done before that, then I can come, but that's not a yes." I waved the couple waiting behind me on as the elevator doors opened.

"Yes! I'm first chair playing at Carnegie Hall."

I laughed, his happiness was infections, and so precious from the boy who would barely look at anyone other than me through the long hair covering his eyes three short years ago. "That wasn't a yes."

"Of course it was. When have you not finished something early? You're always twelve steps ahead with everything. I can't wait for you to see me play."

"Stop jumping on your bed and get some sleep."

"How can I sleep when I'm so excited?"

"Soundly. Good night, Tyler."

"'Night, Zara. I love you. You're the best."

He ended the call and was probably seeing if he could touch the ceiling in his dorm room. He'd been through a lot. Hell, we'd both been through a lot.

I jabbed my finger into the button, and the doors popped back open. Leaving him behind had been like ripping out a piece of my heart. But that piece kept beating, growing, and making a life neither of us could imagine. Carnegie Hall. How many high schoolers got to do that?

Steps off the elevator, Stella's door swung open, but the dread I used to feel when I stalled at my apartment door was gone. She continued to be my wacky neighbor, I continued to be the one who had her shit together—at least in person

—and nothing between us needed to change. I loved her for that.

"An early night for you." She blew on her steaming mug.

"My slacking gets the best of me sometimes." I pulled the flat pink box from my bag. "But it doesn't mean I fall down on the job."

Her eyes widened and she snatched the box from me. "The B&B caramel chocolate chip." Dropping the mug and box inside her apartment, she came back out clutching the oversized cookie in both hands. "It's so beautiful."

"Please don't cry."

"No promises." She took a bite, closing her eyes and bracing herself against the doorway.

"I'm happy you like it."

"I love it. I'd marry it, if I weren't already taken."

"Is Adam traveling again?"

"More interviews. But they'll be over in a couple weeks." Each word was punctuated with a nibble.

"You're hanging out alone tonight?"

She shrugged. "I'm already in the robe and fluffy slippers, plus I've got my cookies now, so I don't need to leave for at least three days."

I chuckled. "Sounds like a wonderful night."

What Andi said stuck with me. I'd been trying so hard to keep everyone at arm's length.

"Hey, Stella?"

She popped back out her partially closed door and stared at me expectantly.

I bit my lip willing myself not to chicken out. "Can you help me with what to wear for tomorrow?"

"You wanted to borrow something?"

I glanced back at my closed door, sticking the key in the

lock and turning it. "Maybe you can help me go through my stuff and find something?"

Her face was a slow-moving transformation from surprise to unbridled joy. "Holy, shit! Yes!" She jumped up and down clapping her hands together. "Yes! A thousand times, yes!"

She stepped inside like she'd wandered into a vault over-flowing with shiny gold coins, instead of my no-longer-ransacked, but insanely sparse and sad apartment. But she hadn't said a word, if she was thinking of how crappy things were inside.

An hour later, I was regretting my invitation.

"You've got to show some skin for your date."

I snatched the tube top from her hands and tossed it in the 'hell no' pile. "It's not a date."

"A hot guy who nursed you back to health invites you to a concert. How is this not a date?"

"He never said it was a date."

"Probably because he knows there'd be a Zara shaped hole in a door exiting the room if he did."

"You don't know Leo. We're not playing the same sports."

"Because he's an ex-pro football player." She held up another shirt in front of her face at a half attempt to hide her laughter.

I tugged it out of her grasp. "How'd you know?"

"Did you think wrestling was all I watched?"

I flopped onto my mattress. "Apparently, I'm the only one who didn't know."

"You're busy." She lay down beside me. "You've got Tyler and work and everything else you're trying to do."

Those old feelings gnawed at my stomach. Embarrassment. Guilt. Shame.

"You don't have to tell me anything, of course, but I'm

your friend. What kind of shitty friend would I be, if I weren't there for you when you needed me?" She wrapped her fingers around mine.

Staring up at the ceiling, I blinked back the swelling tide of emotions threatening to make me cry. "I know." I dropped my head to the side. "Thanks, Stella."

"Any time." She popped back up and picked up a skirt, so short it must have been Jeannie's. "Plus, you're my catered mini foods hook up. I can't have you moving out and cutting me off from my supply."

"The truth comes out. Before you even ask, hard pass on this one."

"You've got to give me something to work with here. We're on a mission."

"A mission to what? Freeze my eggs without needing to go to a doctor?"

She waggled her eyebrows up and down. "Mission: Get Zara Laid."

"No. It's not that kind of night out. Absolutely, no." I swiped my arms in front of me.

"That's what you think. Wait and see, Z. Wait and see."

26

LEO

Squadrons of people flowed through the street heading to the main entrances of the stadium. Cars honked, not realizing the mistake they had made coming this way an hour before the concert started. The green walk light became more of a suggestion than a strict rule. Groups of girls and guys, parents being dragged by their kids, and couples out for a date night all mingled together for an evening of alternative pop rock that everyone found themselves humming along to without even realizing it.

But we were in the throngs of people headed to the front of the venue. We were at the side entrance where a few people trickled in through an imposing metal door that always seemed to open as someone approached, despite there being no way for anyone to see in or out. That was our door. The one that would take us into the belly of the beast. At least it was Everest's beast.

He glanced around, folding and unfolding his arms like a junkie looking to score. "Are we going in? Can we go in? What are we waiting for?" His pace-and-observe routine had been ruined by us having nothing more than a brick wall to stare at since we'd gotten here.

"You can go in. I'm waiting for Zara."

August grabbed Everest and pulled him aside, their heads close and August's emphatic hand gestures punctuating his words. His hands only came into the conversation when he really wanted you to pay attention.

I should've picked her up. But then it would have been closer to a date, and we weren't dating. She'd made that insanely clear. So now I waited. Her text had said she was ten minutes away, but that had been fifteen minutes ago. How long should I wait before checking in on her?

Jameson stared down at his ticket afraid it would disappear. "What kind of merch do you think they have? Teresa wanted a keyring for her train keys and I promised my mom a water bottle."

"You know those are going to be a thousand dollars each." I checked up and down the street, tempted to walk to the cross street to see if she was on her way.

Hunter leaned against the brick wall near us, tapping away on his phone, setting up who knew what kinds of others deals. He was either getting nuclear launch codes for a cartel or arranging a cupcake delivery for a children's hospital. His fixing and finding skills didn't know good or evil, only the challenge of making things happen.

"What's the point of having all this CPA money if I don't splash it around?" He brushed his hand against his palm, like he was doling out hundreds at a strip club.

I laughed, looking over his shoulder. "Baller."

He smiled and grabbed my shoulders, turning me around.

Breaking free from the flow of the crowd, Zara rushed toward me with her heels in her hands. She was in jeans, and a t-shirt, but, damn, it looked nothing like that simple outfit would have on anyone else. The front of the t-shirt was slit to just between her breasts and stitched back together with black thread or a cable or something, which made it impossible not to look at the swell of her breasts from my height.

Our group had kept it low key. Jeans and button-downs with rolled up sleeves, or a t-shirt in August and Jameson's cases, but her jeans hugged her body in a way that made the thought of cupping her ass while peeling them off—with my teeth—unshakable.

"Sorry, I'm late. The bus broke down and I had to run a few blocks." She waved to the rest of the guys and walked straight up to me. Putting her hand on my shoulder, she leaned in.

My heart skipped a beat and started racing like I was running a 100 for pro scouts.

Her hand slid down my arm and she ducked her head.

I sucked in a breath, not sure what the hell was going on.

It wasn't until the first teeter that I snapped out of my ice-block impersonation.

She brushed off the bottom of her feet and used me as her steadying post to slip one and then the other shoe on. Flipping her hair back, she grinned up at me, slightly out of breath and with a glowing sheen of perspiration.

"There. I'm ready."

"Awesome. And your outfit looks amazing." Why did *I* sound like I'd run from a broken-down bus to get here?

"Thanks, you guys clean up nice too."

She brushed her hair back from her face, still taking those heavy panting breaths you need after maximum exertion. The kind of breaths that kept my thoughts drifting to where else her hands might be when she was slightly sweaty and out of breath.

"Hunter, we're ready."

He nodded and approached the door, which swung open just like it had for everyone else who'd approached it. And we were in without a hitch.

"How'd you get these tickets again?"

Hunter laughed and waved his phone as though it explained anything. "I know people."

We walked down the aisle of the floor seating area to find our seats. They were numbered oddly down here and were only folding chairs on a rough mat laid over the cables and other tech needed for the concert.

There was a team of people behind mixing and lighting boards on a platform raised a little over our heads.

"This is the most amazing thing ever." Zara held onto my arm, not wanting to get lost in the milling crowds of people, looking around at the lighting rigs and scaffolding along the sides of the stage. This close, we'd be able to see every droplet of sweat from Without Grey.

Everest walked toward his seat, but he flicked the antique lighter that was always with him open and closed against his pant leg. He'd paid extra attention to his always-perfected appearance tonight. Had he used tweezers and an oversized mirror to get each piece of hair perfectly placed on his head?

If the sportscasting thing happened, I'd ask him for hair tips. Hopefully it wasn't susceptible to melting under TV studio lights.

Jameson practically bounded down the aisles. He'd stopped by the first merch table we'd seen, even though Hunter told him there'd be one with a lot fewer people exclusively for those with floor seating.

We found our seats. Five minutes before the start of the show, someone showed up with a tray of multicolored cups, and Hunter passed them down to our group.

The wristbands we'd gotten in our VIP packs flashed in time to the drummers count-off. The flashes flared in quicker rhythm as the floor rumbled under our feet.

Overhead, the lights roamed the crowd before zeroing back in on the front of the stage. The band took the stage one by one, amping up the crowd with each entrance. They launched into their biggest hit of the year so far. Although I didn't listen to Without Grey much, the words had been imprinted on me by almost constant airplay and even a movie and commercial placement.

Zara stared up at the stage. The lights reflected off her eyes and she glanced over at me with a wide grin. "This is amazing!" she shouted over the driving, blaring music, wrapping her fingers around my arm.

Whatever favor Hunter called in for scoring me another ticket was one hundred percent worth it for the look on her face.

We were on our feet for an hour and a half and I only felt even more energized when the band finished their second encore.

Hunter huddled up our group as rows of seats emptied behind us. "There's an after party, but we don't have to go."

"Where is it? A hotel suite?" Everest clenched and unclenched his fists.

"Backstage. They put together a makeshift nightclub to celebrate the end of the tour."

Jameson leapt forward. "Yes." Covering his mouth, he cleared his throat and looked back at the rest of us. "I mean, I'm good with whatever the rest of the group wants to do. We don't have to go. It's just that I haven't had a whole night to myself in five months, and I might never get another chance to party with my favorite band. But I'm cool with doing whatever everyone else wants."

August shook his head. "Real subtle."

"What are the odds Madison and the rest of the band will even be there? They've probably got a private party going on somewhere else."

Everest made a noise. It was a cross between distress and full-on berserker rage. The only place I'd heard it before was in Milwaukee, and we all knew how that had turned out.

I looped my arm around the back of Jameson's neck. "Maybe we go and you stay."

Everest piped up, ruining my attempt to deflect us from a train wreck. "No, we should all go."

"Dude—"

"What? Let's all go to the fucking party," he snapped.

Zara came down the aisle, rejoining the group and adjusting her bag across her chest. "Hey, where to next?"

"After party." Everest took off, following the few people headed toward a line of burly security guards scrutinizing laminates.

Zara leaned in closer, and the silky-smooth fabric of her t-shirt brushed against my arm, raising goosebumps even though it was still piping hot as we got closer to the back-stage area. "Is everything okay?

We walked down a black-fabric-lined temporary hall-way. Darkness blanketed us except for the light at either end of the long walkway to the after party. "Ghosts. That's all."

She grabbed onto my arm and looked up into the rafters. "What?" Her head whipped from side to side and her steps collided with mine.

"Figurative ones from Everest's past. Not actual ones."

Her grip loosened slightly, but she kept her hands around my arm. And I didn't mind one bit. Becoming someone she could depend on or use as a human shield against poltergeists was a role I could settle into quite easily. The floating stage floor under our feet rumbled the closer we got to the end of the long stretch. Music and lights strobed, and people milled behind the velvet ropes.

It was familiar and foreign all at once. I hadn't been much into partying once I'd gone pro. It went stale pretty damn fast when you knew most people were only looking for a free drink or an even longer 18-year free ride. Those parties had been non-existent once I'd been injured.

"I need a drink." Everest broke off from our group rushing the bar the second the security guard finished checking our credentials. They took this shit as seriously as anyone on the sidelines at the games had. Maybe more. I didn't expect any streakers to come blazing across the room, though, and if they did, I didn't think they'd get tackled to the ground. More like handed a drink and helped up onto a table to perform.

The bartender poured Everest a drink. He power-chugged it and made a motion to keep them coming.

Zara slid up next to me. "He's really thirsty."

August *thwipped* his backstage-pass laminate against his palm, keeping his gaze on Everest. "He's something."

Hunter took the lead, pointing to the far end of the pop-up room. "Our booth should be over there, I'll go get us all some drinks before Everest drains the bar."

We found our booth. Zara slid in and I sat beside her.

"How the hell does Hunter do this?" Zara leaned in close, her lips less than an inch from my ear. A flush of desire thumped through my veins. Fuck, that outfit on her was insane. It was an everyday outfit, but on her an award show dress couldn't have looked better. It hugged her body. Teasing me with a neckline that made me want to run my tongue along the curve of her breast down to the nipple—

My head shot up, and so did my dick. I dropped my hands into my lap to adjust the growing new arrival beckoned by my daydreams about Zara.

"He's always had a way of getting whatever anyone needed. Asking too many questions would only get us an answer we wouldn't like, so we don't. But it was handy for the guys in college. He had a way of opening doors no matter where they went."

"A modern magician." She looked around the table at the rest of the guys. "It was a great show, wasn't it?"

"Amazing." August said, distractedly scanning the room full of beautiful people, bottles of champagne, and one impressive food display.

Jameson looked around with a huge smile on his face, like a kid out on his first field trip. "They said they're heading into the studio in a couple months, after a break. Twenty-three months. That's how long they've been on tour. It's all on the back of our laminate." He held it up and the mini spotlights from the dance floor caught the heated plastic, nearly blinding us all. We needed to get him out more.

"I'm sure their break will be quite relaxing." Everest had a death grip on his tumbler. Ballsy of a place like this to have actual glasses. I'd expected plastic beer bottles and red Solo cups, but they'd taken a step up in the world. Were those King crab legs?

I leaned over to Zara. "We should find out who the caterer is."

She jumped and looked to me. "Are you reading my mind? I thought the same thing when I saw the seafood display."

I was rewarded with a huge smile. "They've kept the club vibe." I looked up at the exposed rafters, lighting and tech dangling high above our heads. "But a bit of color would've brought it all together. Maybe something from their album work."

Zara's lips parted and her mouth fell open. "If someone didn't know any better, they'd think you were a pro at this event planning stuff." Her grin was infectious.

"Nah, I've just learned from one of the best." I nudged her with my shoulder.

Hunter came back to our table with three servers balancing platters full of bottles and glasses.

The music shifted from a club mix of Without Grey's latest radio hit to a '90s staple.

"I love this song." Zara clapped and raised her arms above her head, nearly whacking me in the head. She was more relaxed and happy than I'd ever seen her. I let my thoughts slip before I could think of a good reason to hold them back.

"Do you want to dance?"

27

ZARA

"Do you want to dance?" Leo's deep gaze held mine.

The words were so simple I found myself nodding before I could sputter out a denial. Why should I say no? I deserved a dance. With Leo? That was a whole other ball of craziness, but it didn't stop me from sliding out of the booth and following him out onto the dance floor.

My stomach flipped, the butterflies suddenly swallowed up by hummingbirds amped up on Red Bull. Outside of a couple of college parties, I'd never danced with a guy. And calling that dancing was a stretch. It was usually the unexpected slam against my back of a guy's sweaty body and overeager dick until I flipped him off and found my way back to whoever I'd come to the party with. So my track record wasn't stellar.

The pop-up dance floor wasn't crowded like those college parties. Who knew the after parties of one of the biggest bands in the world were ultra-exclusive? Sitting in the front row, rocking out as Without Grey ripped through their hit-packed set list had already had me pinching myself at least three times throughout the night.

Whose lap did these things fall into? Certainly not mine. But whatever switch had been flipped temporarily in the luck factory, I'd take it. Was this how being with Leo felt?

He took my hand for a second to pull me to a vacant spot in the center of the dance floor. His gentle, strong grip brought back memories from my night of culinary misadventure. He'd held me close and carried me into my bedroom. Instead of embarrassment or shame that he was seeing my place, I'd felt warm and safe in his arms. I'd also been on the verge of passing out, but it didn't feel as scary as I would have imagined when he was there.

But now we weren't in my shitty apartment. We were dancing backstage after one of the best concerts I'd ever been to. The vibe of the crowd was kinetic energy rolled together with a gleeful communal experience. Those feelings spilled over, and keeping a smile off my face was impossible.

We danced throughout the rest of the song and straight into the next. I'd never been a party-all-night person. Tonight could be the exception.

Leo's body moved like a man who'd spent his whole life honing it into a well-oiled machine. Dammit, now I was imagining him shirtless and well-oiled under these lights. That image would require mental filing for the next time I needed some inspiration.

He never crowded me or did the bump and grind —only a brush here or there that drew me up to the tips of my toes trying to prolong the contact. Shaking my head, I took a step back. What was wrong with me? This was Leo. As in the guy who was trying to take away the biggest account I'd ever have the chance of landing. Except it didn't feel that way right now. Maybe...

Cheers broke out from the far end of our private club. People rushed forward.

"The band has arrived." He didn't even have to crane his neck to get a view. Staring intently like he was looking for something, his grim look turned apocalyptic. "Fuck," he mumbled, barely over the driving dance beat that had replaced the 90s hit. "We should go back to the table." He took my hand without another word and pulled me through the throngs of people who'd poured in now that the band was here.

I hopped up trying to get a look at them. I didn't need to look very far, because they were standing right at our table.

Slipping into the booth, I tried to figure out why Without Grey was at our table and no one looked happy about it.

"Some nerve showing up here and ruining—"

A woman pressed the back of her hand against the chest of the lead singer. His face was blustery and his glare melting.

"I'll handle it. Go enjoy the party."

One of the other guys cut in. "You sure, Mads?"

Beside me, Everest flinched.

Her black hair was blown out, making her look like a red carpet was missing a starlet. Big cascading curls made me want to reach out and touch them. She wore a champagne bandage-dress and heels laced up her calves.

"I'm sure. You know me." Her hands were up on her hips. Even though she was petite, she exuded big-balls energy. Holding her own didn't seem like it was something new to her.

The band seemed to know it too. Her words pacified

them and they backed away from the table like we were sporting bats wrapped in barbed wire and broken bottles. "If you need us."

She held up her hand over her shoulder. "I won't." But her gaze never strayed from our table.

"Hunter, I should've known it was you who would ask for an extra ticket the night of a show."

Extra ticket? Was that extra ticket for me? I looked to Leo, but his gaze was trained on Mads, the woman with amazing hair.

"You know me, Maddy."

She chuckled. "Good to see you." She bent, kissing him on the cheek. A locket she had on a thin chain around her neck, slipped out from between her cleavage dangling in front of her.

Everest's gaze snapped to it.

Hunter picked up his drink and held it up for a toast to himself. "I know."

"The correct response is 'good to see you too'." She laughed again.

He shrugged. "Is it?" His wink was playful, but the rest of his face was set to fight or flight.

She looked at the merch bag sitting beside Jameson. "I'll have a swag pack made up for you to take. Everything is insanely overpriced, but the merch vendors get to set their own prices."

"August." A nod, that was all. He'd shifted in his seat so his shoulder pinned Everest's to the back of the booth.

"I don't think we've met. I'm Madison." She held out her hand to me.

This was awkward as fuck. Half the table seemed cordial with her and the other half ready to jump across it and throttle her. I went the diplomatic route.

"Zara. Leo's friend."

"Friend?" She tilted her head at my hand, looking at my ring.

"It's nothing." I pulled my hand away and dropped it under the table, my cheeks burning. I kept forgetting to take it off. For some reason leaving it on didn't freak me out like it had before.

"And you must be Leo. What did you call him, Everest?" She tapped her finger against her chin looking off like she needed to recall the exact words when there was no doubt she had them locked and loaded. "The overgrown high schooler clinging to his old friends because he wasn't interesting enough to make new ones."

Leo tensed beside me. Great, now everyone was tense except me. I was confused as hell.

"Are you fucking all of them now? Or only Camden?" Everest's fury was so thick I could taste it.

"No more fucking than you did in Milwaukee. And who *I* fuck has never been any of your business."

"For a couple years it was, until you decided it wasn't."

"*I* decided." She lurched forward and the table rocked, slipping a few of the drinks. Taking a deep calming breath, she opened her eyes and painted an easy smile on her face. "Have a wonderful night, guys. I hope you enjoy the party."

"Will you be enjoying it later tonight? Who gets the first round? And who's stuck with sloppy fourths?"

Her smile widened. "They trade off. We've got a rotation going so no one feels left out. And *everyone's* satisfied. But you wouldn't know anything about making sure someone else is satisfied, would you?" She smirked and her arms crossed over her chest.

"I satisfied you enough. You're still wearing that." He nodded to the locket that had fallen free earlier.

Her hand shot to the rose gold metal. Her fingers tightened around it for a second before jerking it down, snapping the chain. Holding it out, she released her grip and let it clatter to the table. "It matched the dress, but you're right. It belongs to you." She left and the volume of the room came roaring back.

The bubble around the table evaporated and the too-loud voices, clinking bottles and driving bass snapped me out of the display that had made me want to turn and bury my face in the nearest hole.

Everest touched the locket like he expected it to burn him before sliding it off the table and into his waiting hand. All the barely-contained anger evaporated, replaced with a palpable grief.

"I'm out of here."

Both sides of the booth had been vacated, which gave him his choice of escape routes.

People screamed and laughed, unaware of the implosion taking place steps away from them.

He stormed out of the backstage area, August heading out after him.

Leo touched the small of my back, jerking me from the bystander role I'd taken on in someone else's life. "You ready to go?"

I nodded. At the bar, the woman, Madison, who'd been the storm cloud to our night out toasted, surrounded by the guys in the band, but I didn't miss how she watched the door closing behind Everest, or how her face didn't scream smug satisfaction.

We gathered our things, but Hunter hung back. "I've got some people to talk to. I'll see you guys later. Zara, as always, it was a pleasure." He lifted my hand and kissed the back of it. Somehow when he did it, it wasn't smarmy or creepy or dorky. It was Hunter. No wonder he always got whatever he wanted.

Leo steered me away from him.

Jameson dropped in behind us after we made it outside, his arms laden with swag. "I couldn't help it. I love their music and I promised my mom and Teresa. I'm catching a cab. Do you guys want to share?"

Before I could respond, Leo jumped in. "It's cool, I've got it."

Jameson climbed into the taxi and was gone. Then it was me and Leo. The street, which had been swarming with fans, was empty now except for a small crowd outside of another of the stadium doors.

"I can get the bus, there might be one running this late."

"Come on, Gingersnap. Don't make me fight you on this."

"I'm not trying to be difficult. I can make my own way home."

"Of that, I have no doubt. It'll help me sleep better and wake up more refreshed if I see you get home safely."

A taxi I didn't know he'd ordered pulled up to the curb. He opened the door and held it open for me. "Your trusty steed awaits."

Inside the car, the questions piled up so high they'd come toppling over at any second.

"Was that as much of a train wreck from the outside as it was from the inside?" He laughed and squeezed his forehead.

"Only slightly. It was intense."

"Everest and Madison have history even I'm not fully in on. College sweethearts. Something happened in Europe."

"And Milwaukee?"

His body went rigid like he'd seen a predator. "And

Milwaukee. Let's not let their drama ruin the night. Did you have fun?"

"It was the most fun I've had in a long time."

"That's a shame."

We pulled up outside my building.

"Why? I shouldn't have a fun night?"

"No, that it's been so long since you've had one."

"If we can get the presentation ready early for next Friday, I'd really appreciate it."

"Hot date?"

"And cheat on my fiancé? I'd never." I pressed my palm against my chest. "Tyler has a concert in Carnegie Hall on Thursday. I'd like to be there for him." I'd opened my door and had a foot on the sidewalk.

"We can make that happen." His fingers landed on top of mine on the door handle.

My pulse thumped out the insistent beat of anticipation. Of what? I wasn't sure.

A beat passed between us. One where, in a rom-com, I'd trip and fall back into the car and our lips would meet. But I wasn't the klutzy girl who was adorably awkward and cute.

"'Night, Leo." I dropped my gaze and shot out of the taxi.

"'Night, Zara." He called after me.

I shoved the door closed and rushed into my apartment, not looking back.

Putting my party girl outfit into my hamper, I climbed into bed. I stared up at the ceiling—I couldn't stop thinking about him. Every touch. Every word. I couldn't afford this kind of distraction. One more event. One more presentation, and then he'd hate me forever. What was the point of daydreaming about him now, when this was all going to end in disaster?

28

LEO

My steps faltered on the walk up to the house. It had been too long since I'd been here. California was on the other side of the country, but that was no excuse. I'd found time to travel in the off season. Why did I only stop by once or twice a year?

So much for the big celebrity I was. I switched the bottle to my other hand and started to knock.

The door swung open before I could. "What are you knocking for? You don't have your key?" Sam hugged me and swatted me on the back.

It was in my pocket, but I hadn't wanted to try. Not after what had happened at my dad's.

In the company, Sam mainly kept to his office, never leaving other than to remind me and Zara how late it was or ask if we'd eaten. From there, he juggled the few accounts Simply Stark still had, and directed the part-timers.

I'd taken over some of that as I learned the ropes. My time with Zara had shown me a lot of what went into the business, and I hoped I could take some of the load off Sam, but for how long?

"Someone's glowing." Sam ushered me through the door and into the small craftsman nestled in the quiet neighborhood outside of Center City. Garlic and onion scents from the kitchen drew me in by my nose. Felix had been the decor man. Everything from the curtains to the pillows made the house look like a homey version of the ones on the covers of interior design magazines.

After working with Zara, I could see how much work he'd put into making their house inviting and beautiful. She'd helped me see a place I'd been in hundreds of times in a new way. It also explained why Felix used to jump on my case about cleaning up after myself when I'd been here. My gear didn't exactly match the decor.

"Who's the girl?" He inspected the bottle of wine, pretending he wasn't watching my embarrassment grow.

The tips of my ears were glowing now. "There's no girl. How are you doing?"

"Fine." He waved away my question. "The woman, then? I might not have picked up Felix's fashion sense or knack for floral display, but I can tell when my nephew is smitten."

"There's no one. It's not a thing. I went out with the guys last night. It's probably my hangover or bleary eyes you're picking up on."

"Yes, because a hangover and goo-goo eyes look so similar. Thanks for the wine. Dinner's almost ready."

"Did you need help with it?" I tried to walk into the kitchen, but he turned me around, shoving me toward living room.

"I'll call you when I need you."

This was the first time I'd been back since Felix died.

Shame burned bright in my gut. I should've come by sooner. Checked up on Sam. Now, at least working at Simply Stark, I got to see him every day and see if there was anything he needed—in between the marathon sessions with Zara.

Only now those marathon sessions didn't fill me with the dread of hours on end fighting tooth and nail—they made me imagine a different kind of session. *Don't cross that line, Leo.*

Last night in the taxi, there had been a moment. Trying to describe it made it feel inadequate. Dancing together. The taxi ride home. When our hands brushed as she went to leave, I'd wanted to drag her back into the car to learn firsthand how soft those lips were, but she'd bolted.

Next time, I wouldn't let indecision stop me.

Decisive action had been how I'd run my life. In a play on the field, knowing where I needed to be and adjusting at a split second when things changed was how I'd stood out. My ticket had been written by my ability to make lightning-fast decisions before anyone else could recover.

It was also why I'd agreed to give my dad the money he'd needed instead of waiting. It was what had made me fake right and not left, ending my career. The split-second decision meter hadn't been working in a while, but with Zara last night, it had felt like it had clicked back into place.

Pictures lined every wall of the house. Sam and Felix's trips all over the world. Events Felix had pulled off. Their wedding. A bunch of me with Felix when I was little, including some of us picking up a pumpkin for Halloween and our attempts at carving it. The jack-o-lantern's half smile hadn't been nearly as menacing as I'd hoped.

Sam was in the later ones, once I made it to middle school. He and Felix stood smiling beside me at my eighth grade graduation, where I was already a few inches taller than them. I'd been able to see over the sea of kids and parents to find their smiling faces. My dad had been at home watching football.

One of last photos we'd taken all together hung outside the entryway, almost to the kitchen. It was draft night. I'd slammed that California hat down on my head when their logo appeared on the screen behind me. My smile was huge and full of the promise my future held.

"He was a blubbering mess that night. I had a box worth of tissues shoved into my pockets."

"It was a great night." And here I was four years later, trying to find my new place in the world—just like Sam was trying to find his now, too. "Have you been cooking a lot?"

"Not too much. Help me with the sauce." He nodded toward the stove. "Open the wine first."

I grabbed the corkscrew and poured a glass for each of us. Garlic bread went into the oven and the old memories came rushing back.

Sam laid the last of the freshly-made pasta across the small gap on the drying rack and gestured to another photo from my senior year of high school. "Do you remember how nervous you were on opening night?"

"It was even worse than my first college game. Those pants were so tight. Plus, the dance moves—it was a minor disaster."

"Not from the way all the ladies in the audience were screaming your name." He added more salt to the water before it reached a boil.

"You mean Conrad Birdie's name."

Somehow, my senior year, the drama teacher who'd hounded me since I was a freshman finally convinced me to take a part in the spring musical. Football season was over, I'd gotten my full ride, and there wasn't much else to do. At least the late-night rehearsals had kept me busy.

When she'd said I'd have a part, I thought I'd be a tree or something, not Conrad-freaking-Birdie in *Bye Bye Birdie*. The guys on the team had given me shit about freezing on stage, so I couldn't back out.

"I meant yours. Trust me, they weren't worried one little bit about a missed step. You did a wonderful job." Sam patted my arm, going back to stirring the pasta. "Who knew you had such a wonderful singing voice?" He covered his barely-contained laughter with a cough and a dash of garlic salt into the sauce pot.

"I couldn't have done it without all the help from you guys."

"All we did was run some lines with you."

"And helped me get my costume together. Felix went over the dance steps with me so many times."

Sam lifted two handfuls of pasta from the rack and dropped them into the pot. "You were also there in the front row, cheering me on at every performance."

"It's not every day we get to see someone we know up on stage with their name in lights." He framed his hands in front of his face, mimicking a marquee.

"The ticket booth kiosk in front of Reed High hardly counts as a theater."

"That's what you think. We had a ball and we were happy to be there to support you."

"I'm glad someone was," I mumbled, stealing a piece of garlic bread from the tray.

"Your dad probably had perfectly valid reasons to not make it."

"To any of the shows?"

Sam went back to stirring furiously. "He was always there for your football games."

"So was Felix. He was always there to support me no

matter what." And I'd let him down. I hadn't been there for him when he'd been there for me from the time I was little. When everyone had shoved me into the football box, never to escape, he'd encouraged me to do whatever I enjoyed. It happened that was football, but I'd never felt like I'd let him down by trying other activities.

Plating the heaping bowls of pasta with a side of garlic bread, Sam grated what looked like five pounds of parmesan over the steaming dish.

"Do you think that's enough cheese?"

Sam looked from me to the bowls and picked up the block of parmesan again.

"I was joking, Sam. This dish is 80% cheese as it is."

"You can't beat a good parmesan."

"You can when homemade pasta's on the menu."

"What are the rest of the gang up to?" He scooped up a spoonful of sauce.

"August? He's hating his job and trying to figure out what the hell to do."

"Being an adult's not as easy as you all thought, right?" He smiled. There was a sad glint in his eye. Some things never got easier.

"Jameson is doing his accounting thing and helping his mom with Teresa. I showed you pictures of the cake, right?"

He scooped up a bite of pasta, choking on it when I showed him the photo on my phone.

I thumped him on the back.

"Is that a spider?" He wiped the pasta sauce from his mouth with a napkin, trying to catch his breath through the laughter-filled tears.

"No, it's a train, obviously. Teresa's big into trains." I snatched the phone back and looked at it again, squinting. It didn't look like a—oh dear god. It was absolutely an unholy abomination when I tilted my head just right. My phone dropped to the table and I flipped it over.

"I'm sorry." Tears streamed down his face. "I'm sure you all worked so hard on it." His shoulders shook so hard, he could barely get the words out. The hand banging on the table was the nail in the coffin of my composure.

"Teresa was so happy when she saw it."

"Was she afraid if she wasn't, it would devour her soul?" He took a few deep breaths, his gaze darting toward my phone. "I'm sorry, that was a wonderful thing you did for Jameson's sister. She's lucky to have so many people around her who care so much."

"She wants us to make her cake again next year." I twirled my spaghetti with my fork.

"That poor child will have nightmare fuel for the rest of her life. What about the rest of the guys?"

"Who?"

"You know who. Hunter and Everest."

"I wouldn't classify them as the rest of the guys. Well, yeah, Hunter is cool. He can be part of the rest of the guys."

"You always give Everest such a hard time."

"How do you even know him?"

"You got us tickets to a club box every time you played in town and he was there. After four years, we were bound to chat."

"I didn't know he came to the games with the rest of the guys."

"He always seemed very impressed with you whenever we were there."

"Probably trying to butter you two up."

"Or maybe he was impressed that you were out there on the field living your dream. You wanted something and you took it."

"I don't think that's why."

"It's what he said."

"Everest said that? Everest van Konig?"

"That's what he said." Sam shrugged and cleared the plates from the table.

With an oversized container of pasta and garlic bread, I was sent on my way.

Back home, the silence in my apartment filled my ears. I chucked my keys onto the table and slipped my food into the fridge.

Grabbing my football, I tossed it from hand to hand and paced.

29

ZARA

Popping into the coffee shop around the corner from Simply Stark—the one where Leo and I had had our explosive first meeting—I slipped on the ring like I did whenever Leo and I were working together. The weirdness of having it off had eclipsed the weirdness of having it on, which was insane, and told me Leo an I had been working together too much, putting in too many hours. But this was our last event. Finally!

Already...

Once it was finished, we'd put together the final presentation and things would change. The truce would be over and the no-holds-barred grab for the Winthorpe account would be on.

There were whispers and more than a few discreetly lifted coffee cups pointed at the tall, broad man who stood nearly a head above most people. The same one who filled out a white button-down better than anyone I'd ever met. The same one who was mine—well, not *mine,* mine. I threw the brakes on that brain blip. Leo wasn't mine. Pretend-mine.

He stood three people from the front, talking to the woman behind him. I grabbed my free coffee cards from my bag and stepped out of line. The quicker we got our coffee, the quicker we'd get to work. That was the only reason I felt compelled to hand these over—not to find out what he was saying to the woman with the killer chestnut blow out who kept smiling at him.

"Hey, Leo." I stayed out of line, so no one thought I was cutting. "Can you get me—"

He started, but smoothed his look of surprise once he saw it was me. "A medium cookie crumble cappuccino?"

"Yeah, that. I have these cards." I held out my small stack of free coffee cards.

"Gingersnap, come on." He pushed them back to me.

"Oh my god, that ring is freaking amazing." The woman who'd been speaking with Leo looked at him and back at me and down to the ring. "Are you two engaged?" Her voice at the end of *engaged* shot up like she was trying out for a falsetto role. Heads turned our way.

Before he could jump in to let the woman who'd been twirling her hair around her finger know that under no uncertain terms would he ever think of me as his girlfriend, let alone fiancé, I flung myself on the self-dignity pyre and beat him to it.

"What? No! No, no, definitely not. We're one hundred percent not engaged. We're just friends—barely friends. Right, Leo?" I laughed and nudged him with my elbow.

He stared at me for a beat before turning back to the woman in line. "She's absolutely right. We're definitely not engaged, we've barely made it over the hurdle of being able to stand one another. Right, Zara?"

I kept my smile plastered on my face even though it suddenly felt bitter and strained. We'd gone to a concert and had a few drinks. Maybe a little flirty, but here he was flirting with a woman in line. And now he's saying he can barely stand me. Flirty was his natural state, like breathing, or a reflex, like a flinch when someone hit you in the face with a water balloon.

"He's so right. Sometimes looking at his face makes me want to run screaming from the room. Or hail a taxi to get away from him by jumping in front of it."

"This one." He jerked his thumb in my direction. "She'd rather gnaw her own arm off rather than leave her tablet alone for more than ten minutes. If it was fitted with a few extra attachments, she'd probably consider it the perfect boyfriend."

"And let me tell you about the way he goes to bed at night with his football. You know how some people have a stuffed animal from childhood. Not Leo, he cuddles up with a worn leather ball at night."

We looked to the woman Leo had been talking to, but there was no one there. Only an empty spot and a slowly closing front door that jangled as it slammed behind her retreating figure.

An older woman poked her head into the empty space. "Are you two finished? The line has moved and I saw you try to cut." Her squinty glare ended the pissing-one-another-off competition Leo and I had fallen into.

I shoved the cards into his hand and stepped back, waiting outside. With my arms wrapped around myself, I shifted from foot to foot. The day had started so well.

"Here." Leo handed me the plastic cup and my free punch-out cards. "And keep these, I don't need them to buy you a cup of coffee."

"I never said you did," I snapped, my wounded pride

being overridden by the smell of the cookie crumble cappuccino shoved under my nose.

That was the rest of our day.

Leo ducked out to take the fourth call in the past two hours. Calls he'd taken in front of me before he now took outside the room. What the hell was he up to? Our moment after the concert hadn't amounted to more than a stalled, sputtering hello this morning, and then, while I'd been thinking about what might've happened if I'd turned back around, he was flirting with other women.

I needed to focus.

After the success of the camp day, we'd gone similarly fun for the final event, planning a scavenger hunt. Clues with puzzles led to activities, which would lead to more clues, food and drinks until everyone met up for a dance party at the end.

I grabbed the destination clue and crumpled it up, dumping it in the trash. Was it petty? Hell yeah. Did I care? Not right now. I'd incorporate more of my ideas and when someone asked who'd come up with them, it wouldn't even be a lie to say it was all mine.

Going over the clues for the scavenger hunt, I didn't look up when he walked back in. I squeezed the bridge of my nose. These riddles made me want to rip my hair out. They'd take the guests through various tasks, some adventurous and others relaxing.

The map we'd laid out with the overhead view of the property showed us where the teams of ten would be going throughout the day. Each of the ten teams had a different path to follow This let us avoid any traffic jams, but it meant we had to plot out all those paths, make sure the color-coded clues made sense, and set them all out on the property.

We also had to make sure an advanced degree in English composition or thermodynamics wasn't required to solve the problems.

I pinned the next clue up on the board.

"Why's this in the trash?" Leo held up the crumpled piece of paper.

I opened my tablet and dug into my inbox to field some of the questions for the day after tomorrow.

Leo cleared his throat. "I'll say it again for the people in the back. Why is this in the trash?"

"It must've fallen in." Not even looking at the paper or him, I went back to my work.

"Crumpled up into a ball."

"Look at this table. Does it look organized?" The table was littered with scraps of paper and half-filled and empty cups. It looked kind of like my apartment had.

"The trash can is halfway across the room."

"Can you focus and get to work?"

"I want to know what your problem is."

"My problem is that we have a lot to get done and not much time, so instead of running off to field phone calls every three minutes, how about you focus so we can get this done? Then you can go off and do whatever the hell you're planning with whoever you're planning on doing it with." Pun not intended.

"You're jumping all over my case, but we're almost finished."

"We could have been finished already if you'd focus."

He tilted his head. "Did you want to be a drill sergeant when you grew up?"

"No, I wanted to be an interior designer," I shouted, flinging the stylus onto the table.

"Really?" His head reared back.

His genuine surprise threw me off. "What the hell is wrong with that?"

"But your apartment..."

I winced like I'd been shot. "You think I don't know that? You don't think every day walking through that damn door hurts my heart and makes me want to cry? Why do you think I don't turn on the lights? Sure, it's clean and not a horror show, but it's an empty reminder of everything that happened.

"Why do you think I try to get out the door every day while it's still dark and try not to go home until midnight? Being there kills me, but right now, I'd rather be there than here." I picked up my things, shoved them into my bag and was out the door before he could say another word.

I'd finish everything myself.

Back in my terrible apartment, I grabbed some chocolate from the cabinet. Sitting on the floor with my back against the wall, I reviewed our progress for the day. The chocolate—which Leo had snuck in with the rest of the groceries—didn't taste nearly as good now, as I scanned through everything we'd gotten through. The task list wasn't anything that couldn't wait until tomorrow. Leo had been right. That had been a frequent refrain over the past month. Why did he have to be right? Why'd he have to make me feel like this?

I'd never dealt with a guy I couldn't handle. Men did not intimidate me, and there'd never really been an outlier. Having feelings for someone had always been an inconvenience I thought I could control.

Guys in high school were never a temptation.

Guys in college were even less so; combine the *I'm a badass* attitude with Daddy's money and they couldn't have paid me to sleep with them.

But a guy like Leo? A man who could be cocky one second and thoughtful the next, who wasn't scared off by my snark—who even challenged me (and was often right)? I wasn't prepared for that kind of man.

I looked around my sad apartment, flicked off the lights, and headed to the one place that didn't make me want to run screaming into the street. Turning on the shower, I braced my hands on the sink, keeping my eyes averted from my reflection.

If I looked, I'd see the stupidity up close and personal. Why had I blurted out all that crap about us barely even being friends? We weren't dating, but to say we weren't even friends was rude. Why had I let what he said afterward get to me at all?

My ring tapped against the sink. I took it off and set it on the counter. It wasn't my ring. It was a ring. A ring with no meaning or importance to me or to Leo. And I wasn't going to forget that again.

Tomorrow was a new day. I'd slip it on, play my part, and do everything I needed to keep swimming, so those six-foot swells didn't drag me under. I'd made it this far; I wasn't going to let a pesky thing like feelings sidetrack me.

She'd talked about the thought of dating me like she'd been asked if she'd like to join a leper colony or have her head shaved.

But we had a whole day to get through today.

Leaves crunched under my feet and I shifted the picnic basket in my arms. The weather hadn't taken its full fall turn yet. Some days were colder than others, but none as cold yet as our night in the yurt. I'd left my jacket back at our station, needing only my thermal on my search for Zara.

The *thunk* of metal against wood clued me in to her location. I'd helped the company set up earlier in the day and she'd been nowhere to be found. We'd fallen into a pattern where no matter what I was doing, she was always needed as far away as possible to help figure something out.

She flung the ax at the wooden target like she hated it. If there had been a picture of my face on it, I wouldn't have been surprised.

Another throw and a miss. "Hell. Come on, Zara, you can do this. It's throwing something sharp into some wood. It shouldn't be this hard." She didn't give up. She stomped over to the fallen axes and snatched each one off the ground. They'd have no choice but to fly straight after the stern looks they were getting.

I stepped from beside the tree. "Let me show you."

A yelp and wild throw that thankfully wasn't in my direction were my welcome. Her body went rigid like I'd shown up in a ski mask and broken into her fortress of solitude. Watching her chuck the axes at the target and retrieve them from the ground had been fun, but she was also beating herself up about not getting the hang of it, which wasn't going to make our day any easier.

At least that's what I told myself. It wasn't because I hated seeing her kick herself when she was down.

She never wanted anyone to see her sweat. Never wanted anyone to see her lose. Every throw was followed by a grumble and angry stomp to retrieve the projectile. Come to think of it, what I'd thought before was wrong. I was surprised there wasn't a picture of *herself* taped to the target.

After seeing how hard she was on herself when she made a mistake, I didn't take her reactions to my screw-ups nearly as personally. Compared to how she treated herself, I'd barely gotten a slap on the wrist.

"Do you think I don't know how to throw an ax?" She whirled on me, brandishing the wood and metal weapon.

I was ninety percent sure she didn't plan on using it on me. I set down the basket at the base of a wide tree that had to be at least a hundred years old. After all our time together, it was easier to see the difference between pissed-as-hell Zara, and I'm-fucking-with-you Zara.

Poor word choice. Ever since the night I'd helped her get undressed after puking her guts out, I hadn't been able to stop thinking about her. Once she was in bed with her head on the pillow and her eyes closed, it had been an act of sheer will that had driven me from the room and kept me from curling up behind her on the mattress to give her comfort or be close in case she needed anything.

Instead, I'd thrown myself into overdrive cleaning her horror show of an apartment. I had a magic-maker working on some solutions, but it would take a little more time.

"Those weren't my thoughts exactly. I didn't want you to hurt yourself."

Her eyebrows shot up, a cocky smirk curling her lip. "Hurt myself? Do you think I can't get the job done?" She was always up for a challenge and never backed down. It was equal parts infuriating and hot. Right now, it was all heat.

"You've been known to drop the ball before. A certain presentation mishap."

"One mistake." She shook the ax at me.

"A pretty big one."

"You've never dropped the ball? Figuratively and literally? Mr. All-American Football Player. They probably hoisted you through the hallways in high school like a Maharajah, didn't they?" There was fire in her eyes, and the tension was growing with each angry word.

"College, too." Why was I provoking her?

Because her fire was better than her freezing me out.

She whirled around, cocking her arm and letting the ax fly. It sailed through the air, clipped the edge of the wooden target and fell to the ground. "Damnit," she cursed under her breath and picked up another ax from the pile.

"Now will you let me show you?"

Flipping the ax handle first in my direction, she let out a begrudging, "Sure."

"It's all in the wrist. It'll be easier if I show you this way." I stepped behind her, wrapping my hand around hers. A jolt shot through my palm. The dick problem was becoming more evident every second. Something about the way she was always ready with a comeback, never letting me get away with anything, painted a picture in my mind of what it would be like to have her under me. Or over me.

Her breath caught. She glared at me over her shoulder through the soft, strawberry-scented strands of hair brushing against the curve of her neck. She straightened her shoulders.

"Always so agreeable."

Her lips slammed together and she stared straight ahead, flinging her hair into my face.

I pulled it out of my mouth.

The strands were soft, and I couldn't shake the thump in my chest and the daydream of her moaning my name. Pressing my chest against her back, I lifted her arm over her shoulder, bringing the ax up by the side of my face. My fingers skimmed the curve of her wrist. "And follow through with an explosive release."

"I'm sure you know all about those," she grumbled.

"Take a breath. And when you let it out, follow through." I guided her arm.

She filled her lungs and let it out, whipping the ax toward the target.

Thunk.

Her mouth opened in a ring of surprise, she turned and hugged me tight around my waist, squeezing like she wanted to lift me off the ground. Pure, unadulterated joy practically vibrated off her. And at something so small. She really never let herself have fun, did she? Just sneaking in a moment for herself here and there. I hugged her back, letting her happiness blanket this late fall afternoon in the middle of the woods.

Her smiling face looking up at me from my chest sent my heart racing. It was a hard-won smile, and that made it even sweeter. The green of her eyes was even more stark and brighter than usual, filled with excitement and accomplishment. "Will you be giving lessons like those to all the women today? Awfully handsy."

"You're supposed to be my fiancée. That wouldn't look good."

She stepped out of my arms. "Oh, so now I'm your fiancée again." She flung another ax and, proving once she learned something she never let it go, it sunk into the wood in almost the exact same spot. Impressive as hell.

"What do you mean, *so now* I'm your fiancé? We've been playing this game for long enough. I haven't forgotten."

"It seemed like news to the woman at the coffee shop."

"Am I supposed to shout it from the rooftops to everyone I meet that I have a fake fiancée?"

"You were flirting with her."

"She was flirting with me. There's a difference." Wait a damned minute. Why was I feeling guilty? "And so what if I'm flirting? Even if we were engaged, engaged men can flirt."

"You're right. You can do whatever the hell you want." Her next ax hit the target faster than before. "You can flirt with, kiss, *bang* whoever you want. This"—she gestured to the rock procured by Hunter—"doesn't actually mean anything outside of these things." She waved her arms around the event we'd put together.

And then it hit me like a 400-pound offensive lineman. "You were jealous."

Her throw went wild and she picked up another one. "That's insane. No I wasn't."

"You were ear-steamingly, can't-stop-yourself, *jealous* of the woman I was flirting with at the coffee shop."

She shot me a blisteringly hot glare, but it only heated up the fall weather even more, setting my skin ablaze.

"I thought *she* was flirting with *you*, not the other way around." She cut her gaze to mine before gritting her teeth and flinging the ax.

I closed the space between us with a playfully predatory smile. The trap had been laid and neither one of us had been paying attention. We'd set it for ourselves and I was ready to spring it even if she wasn't secure enough to dive in. I stepped in behind her again, this time no longer feeling like I had to hold back. I let the words skim along the curve of her neck. "Wow, Gingersnap all you had to do was admit it."

She straightened her shoulders and kept her gaze straight ahead, but I didn't miss the way goosebumps that had nothing to do with the weather broke out on her skin down the valley of her breasts, highlighted by the v-neck sweater I couldn't wait to get off her.

"There's nothing to admit." Her voice came out husky. "I'm not now, nor have I ever been, jealous of anyone shoving their barely-covered boobs into your face and asking you to sign them, or servers checking out your ass when you walk away, or women in coffee shops who want to score a free coffee."

My smile widened with each replay of past events. She'd catalogued it all. "For someone who's not jealous, you definitely kept a file of every time a woman has talked to me around you." I dropped my hand to her arm, running it down the length of the soft fabric barrier between our skin.

Did she realize she was leaning into my touch? She shivered. "Damage control is a thing. I need to know what level of a potential shitstorm I'm working with when it comes to you." She hefted the ax and I dipped my head to the other side of her face to get out of the way.

Letting my body blanket her back, I whispered in her ear, "You're not my babysitter." I plucked the raised ax from her grip and let it fall to the ground.

"No, I'm not. I'm your fake fiancée." She spun, pushing me back, glaring, her breathing heavy from the exertion of throwing. But the maelstrom brewing in her eyes told me it was the same thing that made my skin prickle with awareness at her closeness and crave more of her warmth.

"Damn right you are, and don't think I haven't seen every time a guy checks out your ass when you walk by. Or at the concert when they couldn't stop looking at you. Or how my daydreams are now filled with you in the shower washing blue paint out of your hair. My erection could've held that yurt up all on its own. What do you think about that, Gingersnap? Still jealous?"

Her eyes shifted from wide and comical to hooded. Birds chirped overhead. Fiery crackling had always been there, but it had transformed into a beast that would only be sated by one thing. How long would it take to get back to somewhere private? Somewhere I could make her scream my name?

"People are only jealous of things they can't have."

I didn't have a chance to debate the meaning of those words before her lips crashed into mine.

Recovery of my senses took a whole half a second, and that was too long. Like a rubber band held taut, stretching the lengths of its ability to withstand the pressure, we snapped, colliding.

Her hands were around my neck, in my hair, and her tongue danced with mine. A forceful and hungry kiss. Her lips were soft and sweet, so much better than I'd imagined all those times I'd caught myself staring at them.

My hands were up and under her sweater, wrapped around her back and pressing her soft, supple body against my chest. Through her sweater and bra, her nipples were hard and I needed to taste them like I needed to devour every inch of her.

She made a mewling sound that sent even more blood rushing to my cock. The denim confines were a torture I'd endure for the sake of touching and tasting her.

I broke our kiss. "Do you want to—"

"Yes." She strained to press her lips to mine again.

I leaned back. "My cock is so hard for you I can barely walk. We're not going to make it back to our room."

"I don't care." She held onto the sides of my face and delved right back into the kiss.

Barely breaking our kiss, her shirt was up and over her head, her hair flopping into her face. I brushed it back and drew her back in and against me.

Her hands tugged at my shirt, making quick work of the thermal. And her fingers were like magic, unbuckling my belt, the jingle of the metal sending shivers down my spine.

"Where?" She bit her lip, tugging down my zipper.

My gaze zeroed in on the flat surfaces available. The leaf-covered ground. A tree. The ax-throwing targets.

Lifting her off the ground, I wrapped her legs around my waist. I kicked out the legs of the target and slammed my back into it. Leaves fluttered around us as the flat, heavy target toppled over like a felled tree, giving me a raised platform off the ground. Keeping one hand on her ass, I pulled my shirt up and over my head. I flung my shirt over the smooth wood.

Zara worked her hand into my boxers. The cold rasp of her fingers against my skin sent my pulse skyrocketing.

"Good god." Her eyes widened as she worked her hands up and down my length.

I had to get my hands on her. I had to taste her. I had to have her.

31

ZARA

Outdoor sex? Who knew it was my thing? I sure as hell hadn't. Or maybe Leo was my thing. The throbbing between my thighs hadn't faded for a single second since Leo had wrapped his arms around me, leaving me breathless and electrifying my skin.

"Zara, I need to fuck you."

My mouth watered as I rocked my hand down over the thick crown of his cock. Fuck, I couldn't wait to get him into my mouth, but we'd save that for round two. Right now was all about the main attraction.

"For once, we're in complete agreement."

Leo tugged me forward by the waistband of my jeans. Damnit, I should've worn a skirt. He didn't waste any time dragging them down my legs and pulling me down onto him. With a practiced move so welcome I didn't even have time for jealousy, he produced a condom and rolled it on.

He tightened his hands around my waist, dragging me forward until my bent legs were on either side of his. "Next time we do this I'm eating you out until you come on my lips screaming my name."

"Again, no argument from me."

"Then come here, Gingersnap." His fingers sunk into my hips. Thick, callused fingers crafted over years of dedication and hard work were now devoted to my pleasure.

I ran the head of his cock up and down my soaking seam.

His grip tightened, fingers teetering on the edge of painful. He was at the end of his rope. So was I.

But the heady power of having him on the brink heightened my excitement. The goosebumps all over my body intensified every stroke and rub.

A happy sigh broke free from my lips as I dropped my weight, allowing the mushroom tip of his cock to stretch me. The blunt thickness of him stole my breath away and made it hard to concentrate on anything except where our bodies were joined. Being on top, I had complete control of my descent, but the shallow thrusts of Leo's hips sent my back bowing.

Every inch, thick and weighty, set off nerve endings I didn't know existed, and I sank onto Leo, shuddering as his stomach ground against my clit. Fully seated on his cock, I tried to gather my senses and remember how all my limbs worked. Everything in my universe was now centered on the desperate, demanding race for the blissed-out feelings coursing through my body that I never wanted to end.

"You're killing me. I'm fucking dying you're so tight." He locked eyes with me saying it like an accusation. As if death by outdoor sex had been my plan all along.

"Are you going to talk or are you going to fuck me?"

His hooded gaze snapped open with fingers biting into my ass as a pleasurable punishment for teasing. In a fluid motion that disoriented me, he stood, taking my full body weight with him and settling me back onto the thermal-covered target.

"Always challenging." Bracing his hands on the ground behind my head, he traded the shallow thrusts he'd used when I'd been on top of him for powerful driving action, keeping my thighs pinned back by his hips colliding with mine.

Dirty. Demanding. Delicious.

The coursing pleasure overwhelmed my senses and licked an ever-growing intensity up and down my spine in time to the efficiently ruthless strokes that hit my every plea-sure center.

He held onto my neck, cupping the side of my face, drag-ging his thumb over my lips. "You're beautiful."

The crescendo raced higher, the notes growing in inten-sity until they broke. My back arched off the wood, my legs locked around his waist, not wanting him to move an inch or I'd be thrown into overload, but wanting him to keep going to push me there.

He ground his hips harder into me, setting off another cascading orgasm triggering his own. He swelled inside me, feeling impossibly larger, his last thrusts sloppy and fierce, wringing the last drops of pleasure from us both.

Unrestrained and wild. That's how he made me feel. If you'd told me a month ago I'd be having sex in the woods with Leo Wilder, there wouldn't have been a bank account big enough to make me believe you.

Clinging to him, trying to catch my breath, I laughed at the inevitability of this moment from the moment he'd stepped on my breakfast that first morning.

All that anger, all those emotions coiled and ready to strike, but instead of a viper or a cobra, it was a sexual explosion that made every other guy I'd been with feel like a fizzled-out sparkler.

"That's a first." He shifted his weight so he wasn't crushing me.

"Sex in the woods?"

"No, laughing."

"Sorry." I pushed the hair off my face. "I was thinking about the coffee-and-croissant version of me seeing us right now."

"She'd probably kick your ass."

"Right after she kicked yours."

He trailed his finger down my neck. "I don't want to move."

"I don't want you to move." Not just because the sex heat was wearing off and I was naked. I stared into his eyes.

There was a tenderness that shot a lump straight into my throat.

"Zara—"

"...and these trees have been on the property for nearly two hundred years. Their massive trunks and serene foliage providing shade for visitors such as yourselves."

We gaped at one another, scrambling up off the felled target. I rolled off onto all fours, grabbing my inside out pants and shoving my legs into them.

My shirt hit me in the face. I grabbed it and threw it on while searching for my shoes. I spotted one and tugged it on.

The tour guide continued his droning speech.

I peeked around one of the trees. A group of twelve people walked along with him, staring up at the fall foliage that hadn't already littered the ground.

Every leaf crunch sent my heartrate racing back to mid-sex speed.

Leo's belt jingled. We both froze, staring at one another.

"We host a number of corporate and private events like weddings, family reunions and more." The guide's voice and the crunching of leaves got louder.

Where's my other shoe? I mouthed.

Leo grabbed it, shaking the leaves free before handing it over.

Crouching low, we scurried away. Leo grabbing the basket I hadn't even seen him bring along.

Running alongside a former athlete was a surefire way to send a person to heart attack city, especially after the work out—and subsequent shock—we'd just had.

I panted, clutching at the front of my shirt, sure there was an outline of my heart there.

Our eyes met. The madness of what had just happened, and our last-minute getaway, cracked through the blind panic and sent me straight into full-on laughter. I dropped to my knees, a cramp in my side and generally unable to breathe after running for what felt like ten miles back to the hotel.

Leo braced his hand on the column on the side of the sweeping porch, wiping tears from his eyes. "They were feet away."

"Had they shown up two minutes earlier..." I leaned against the wooden railing beside Leo.

"They'd have gotten quite a show. Unless there had been a bear or mountain lion, I wasn't stopping."

I batted at his legs. "Never again."

His head jerked back.

I clarified. "No more outdoor sex for me. I can check that off my list."

He turned, sliding down the column to sit beside me, one leg on the stairs we'd run up. "There's a list, is there?

You can't hold out on me."

"There's not an actual list. It was a joke."

He picked a leaf out of my hair. "Maybe you need to work on making one."

A shiver raced down my spine at the way his eyes smoldered with the same hunger I'd been treated to back in the woods.

Ducking my head, I looked down at myself. "Maybe I should." I grinned at him, brushing my fingers through his hair, flicking the small twig out of it before remembering the picnic basket.

Shooting to my feet, I flipped open the lid.

"You had a blanket this entire time?" I pulled out the massive fluffy blanket and shook it at him.

"I forgot. I was a little distracted." He took it from me, shaking it out and draping it over my shoulders. "I'll remember next time."

"Next time? Sex outside isn't my thing, remember?"

"Like I said, from the way you ripped out half my hair, you need to reevaluate your sex list."

"We need to reevaluate how to get past everyone and to our room when we obviously look like we just had sex."

"Follow me." He threaded his fingers through mine and took off around the back of the hotel.

Heading in through the service entrance, we made it up to our floor with only minimal eye contact. Kathleen had once again reserved us a room at the lodge, only this time it wouldn't be an awkward inconvenience.

Leo slipped the key out of his pocket.

"We have three hours before anyone else gets here."

He stopped so quickly, I slammed into his back.

Whipping around, he caged me between his arms and pressed my back against the wall. "Are you suggesting we

don't spend the next three hours going over and over everything we need for today?"

My breathing picked up. "I'm sure things are under
control. We only need an hour, tops, to make sure everything is good to go."

He dipped his head, our lips less than an inch apart.
"Two hours."

The promise of those two words sent shockwaves
through my core. A needy ache was back, even though he'd
been inside me less than twenty minutes ago.

"I'll set an alarm." I fumbled for my phone.

"You do that, Gingersnap."

We rounded the corner, skirted past the housekeeping
trolley, and nearly broke into a sprint on the way to our
room.

He shoved the plastic key card into the lock which
flashed an angry red twice before I yanked the card from his
grasp, flipped it around and stuck it back in. His inability to
focus made this moment even sweeter.

The green light flashed and we flew into the room,
hands all over one another.

A toilet flush broke through our quest to explore one
another's bodies for the next 120 minutes. We jumped apart.

A small, older woman came out of the bathroom with a
toilet brush, yelping when she spotted us. "I'm sorry. The
front desk said no one would be here until later."

"We came back early."

"I just started on the room. I'm so sorry. Had I known
you'd be back early, I'd have cleaned this one first."

I tore my gaze away from Leo's, barely keeping my smile
in check. "It's okay. We have a lot of work to do. Take your
time. Is it okay if we stay while you work? We'll keep out of
your way."

"No problem at all."

Leo's gaze narrowed. His hand wrapped around my arm as I brushed past, letting my fingers graze the large problem he had stuffed into his jeans.

"The payback for this will be repaid between your legs later tonight." He dropped a kiss on my neck.

I looked at him over my shoulder. "I'm counting on it."

Trying to focus, I dug into my list of tasks we needed to complete, completely aware of Leo watching my every move. He was the predator and I was the prey, and I was more than happy to tease him and myself for the next seven hours.

I'd never felt like this before. The crazy, can't-wait-to-rip-your-clothes-off, ready-to-die-happy feeling made my skin tingle and my pussy throb in anticipation.

Tonight would be a night I wouldn't forget. I'd focus on sexy anticipation instead of everything else that turned me into a neurotic mess whenever it was time to run an event. He made me want to forget it and pretend we were a couple —my chest seized and I looked down at the ring on my finger.

Tugging it off, I set it on the desk, staring at the sparkling, shimmering stone.

Leo was the best distraction I'd ever discovered and I couldn't wait for another taste.

But what happened when we stopped playing pretend?

32

LEO

An insistent buzz pulled me out of sleep. I fumbled around on the nightstand, grabbing my phone.

Hair brushed against my chest. Last night had been the longest foreplay in the history of man. The scavenger hunt had been another killer success. No back-ups at any activity. One team did attempt to cross a stream at one point, but I found them and got them back on course.

Kathleen commended us both and told us we'd have a bigger audience at our presentation for which events we could handle for Winthorpe next quarter. Well, that Simply Stark and Zara could handle next quarter.

Leaving felt wrong, but this wasn't where I was cut out to be. No matter how high I'd felt yesterday beside her, keeping the day on track. We made a great team, but I'd learned those never lasted forever. It didn't mean I'd give up before we won the championship ring, though—not with how crazy Zara made me.

We'd barely made it through the door before I was inside her again. Against the wall. On the coffee table. The floor. The bed was the last place we'd made it, with my face buried between her legs. My scalp would need a solid week to recover, but, damn, had it been worth it.

"Who died?" My voice was groggy and laced with sleep.

"Good morning, Sleeping Beauty." Hunter's mildly amused voice pulled me out of my fog.

"Hey, Hunter, what's up? Why are you calling so early?"

"It's eleven am. And I thought I was the night owl."

I pulled the phone away and checked the time. Shit. We'd need to check out soon.

"It was a late night."

Zara groaned and snuggled in closer to my side.

I wrapped my arm tighter around her. The weight of her against my chest made getting out of bed seem like an impossibility.

"Since I can hear you're not alone, I'll make this quick. You've got an interview in two days at Sports Central in New York."

I shot halfway up before sinking back down and rubbing Zara's back. "You serious?"

"No, I called you on the phone like a psycho to screw around with you."

She rolled away, snuggling deeper into the blankets and pillows, leaving a cold spot on my chest.

"What time?"

"Eleven. Try to be awake before noon that day."

"You did it." Could Hunter hear the awe in my voice? Because it was there.

"Pulling strings is what I do best. You're in the door. Now get it over the goal line."

"I will."

He ended the call and I sank into the pillows. This was my shot. A Hail Mary pass. In two days, I'd have my chance to get back to the game I loved, even if it was in a different capacity.

Zara flipped over and brushed the hair out of her face. "Morning." Her voice was rough and sleepy and sexy as fuck. "Who was that?"

"Hunter."

"Was he trying to get you to smuggle parakeets across the border?"

"No." The words stalled in my throat. If I told her about the interview and I bombed, it would be another tally mark on the *Leo's a fuck-up* score board. "It was a party invite."

"So early in the morning." She scrunched up her face in disapproval.

"It's almost time to check out."

She shot up, clutching the blankets to her chest. Blowing her hair out of her face, she stretched over me to look at the clock, rubbing her body against me. "I haven't slept this late in forever. Someone kept me up late." Her hands brushed along my chest.

My body hummed in anticipation of another taste of her. "Someone brought this on herself with her *let the cleaner stay* foreplay."

She bit her bottom lip. "Are you saying it wasn't worth it?"

I wrapped my arms around her and flipped her over, settling my hips between her spread legs. "I wasn't the one complaining about sleeping in."

She looked up at the clock again, a hungry mischief filling her eyes. "It'll only take us ten minutes to pack."

"That gives me nearly fifty minutes with you."

She hitched her legs around my back, digging her heels into my ass. "Yes, it does."

Insatiable, and I fucking loved it.

~

I sat in the lobby full of two-story TV screens running last night's Sports Central prime time broadcast in my suit, Windsor knot, and resume. It was a sparse, sad piece of paper. Barely three lines. Catering server and professional football player were my only qualifications. My degree in communications might win me a point or two. At least I'd graduated. It was more than a lot of guys could say.

The train was easier than driving. No traffic or parking to contend with. I could plan everything out and I'd be back in Philly to meet up with Zara and complete more work on our final presentation with time to spare.

With all the information from our two events and the Oren & Co. bomb, we could pitch something that would keep everyone coming back for more. Maybe make the Simply Stark and Easton Events collaboration a permanent thing. At least until there was enough money for Sam to bring her on full time. We could...what the hell was I talking about? *We* couldn't do anything. The whole reason—

"Leo Wilder." A man in a gray suit walked into the reception area and grabbed my hand, pumping it up and down enthusiastically. "Killer name. I'm Charles."

"Thanks for inviting me up here."

"No problem, we're always excited to have new blood fresh off the field around here. Half the time I feel like it's nothing but fossils who don't remember what it was like to play."

"I practically still have grass stains burned into my knees."

He guffawed, swiping his badge to call the elevator. "Hunter didn't say you were funny. Most of the guys barely talk and seem afraid of their own shadow. But you might do all right." The elevator doors closed behind us.

For four hours, I bounced from office to office, studio to studio. After thirty uncomfortable minutes in hair and makeup, they put me in front of green screens, LED screens covering an entire wall, and sat me down with a few recent additions to the channel for a mock play-by-play.

Talking with guys who'd run the pro gauntlet, I should've felt right at home. But my mind kept drifting to who their craft services caterer was and how Zara would love to pick apart the green room design. The table blocked everyone's access to the room and the food. And more than one person had run their shin into it.

I checked my phone. Two hours until my train. Plenty of time.

I sent off a quick message.

Me: How much actual work do you plan on getting done tonight?

Zara: All the work, but there will be a reward at the end of our long grueling night

Me: Tease

Zara: That's only if I don't uphold my end of the bargain. And yes, I plan on upholding it

"Leo." Charles calling my name broke through the wild thoughts dancing through my mind of the torture Zara had in store for me. I couldn't wait.

"Sorry."

"Did you have somewhere to be?"

"No, checking the scores."

"Those scores?" He pointed to the glowing screens in front of me, showing every score for every sport and every game being played across the country.

"Force of habit. Did you have someone else for me to meet?"

"Yeah, but we like to get to know people outside of this place to make sure they're a good fit with the whole crew, so we're going out for a drink."

"Out."

His smile slipped. "You've got a problem with going out?"

I slid my phone into my pocket. "No problem at all. Lead the way."

Half the guys I'd met that day piled into four sleek black SUVs. Out wasn't to a bar around the corner, but a "secret" speakeasy set up behind a laundromat. Apparently, expensing drinks as part of the interview process wasn't something any employee wanted to miss out on.

One drink turned into three which turned into five. Leaving wasn't an option. This was my break.

The third time I checked my phone one of the guys grabbed it from me and plunked it down inside a full glass of beer. "What the fuck, man?" I shot up from my seat, blood coursing through my veins, seconds from diving at him over the fucking table.

He laughed, letting a woman lead him away by his tie, wrapped around his head like a headband. "We're here having fun. Once you leave we have to start paying, so get comfortable."

Grabbing my phone and heading for the bathroom, I took one of the neatly folded towels on the counter and wiped down my phone. The screen was a mottled mess.

Charlie popped his head into the bathroom. "Hey, sorry about Drew. He gets a bit carried away sometimes. We'll have a new phone shipped to your house tomorrow."

The door closed behind him.

"Thanks..." Running it under the hand dryer didn't do a thing, but seemed to lock in the full screen fritz. I spent the rest of the night, nursing a seltzer and plotting the deaths of everyone who ordered another round from the bar.

This was what I wanted right? My big break?

So why would I rather be anywhere but here?

My fist thundered against her door and I cringed at the volume and echo in the deserted hallway. There weren't many people out at seven in the morning. Bracing my arm on the door, I leaned my head against the smooth wood.

"Zara, I know you're in there. I'm sorry. I got here as soon as I could. I took the first train this morning."

I banged on the door again. "If I—"

The door flew open and my hands shot out to the frame to stop myself from pitching forward into her apartment.

She stood in front of me with her arms crossed over her chest, looking gloriously furious with a hint of bedhead and a heaping helping of pissed off.

"I waited for you until midnight." She bit out. "Not a phone call. Not a text. Not even a comment on social media."

"I didn't have my phone—"

"Were you shipwrecked off the coast of Madagascar?" Her gaze traveled up and down my wrinkled suit. "No, it looks—*and smells*—more like you had a 'flirty' night out." She threw up air quotes. "Take your walk of shame to your own apartment." Her lips clenched and she tried to slam the door closed in my face.

I shoved my foot into the rapidly shrinking opening. "It wasn't like that."

"What was it like, Leo? You tell me you're going to meet me and then you don't show. I get one message that you're running late and then nothing. You show up at my door at the hairy crack of dawn looking like you've had a wild night, reeking of booze. What am I supposed to think?"

This is what I got for coming straight here from the train. I should've gone home and taken a shower. Gone and gotten her half a dozen of the everything bagels she loved so much, and maybe something from B&B, before coming to plead my case. But from the second the train pulled into the station I'd had one goal. Let her know I was okay and explain.

Only I hadn't gotten to the whole explanation part. "I had an interview."

"An interview?" She looked back at me dazed and confused.

I took the opportunity to slip past her and close the door behind me. At least now if she started throwing things, innocent bystanders wouldn't be caught in the crossfire.

"What kind of interview?" she enunciated.

"With a sports station."

"Where?"

"In New York." No backing out now.

Fury and brimstone flared in her eyes. "So when you texted and told me you'd be here soon, you were lying."

"I wasn't lying. It was a ten am interview. I figured I'd have loads of time."

A flicker of realization sparked in her eyes. "The morning phone call. You said Hunter was inviting you to a party. He was telling you about the interview."

Damn her insane level of recall, even before noon with a sex hangover.

"Yes."

"Why'd you lie?"

"It wasn't a big deal."

She re-crossed her arms, tighter than before. "If it wasn't a big deal, then why didn't you tell me?"

She wasn't wrong, per se, but my aversion to explaining myself when I hadn't fucking done anything wrong flared up anyway. "Since when are we sharing every aspect of our lives with each other?"

"Since we started fucking," she screamed, throwing her hands in the air before resting them on top of her head. "I'd at least hope for a text or a call when you're going to blow me off, so I know you're not dead in a gutter."

"*I tried!*" I dragged my fingers through my hair. "The interview went later than I expected and they wanted to take me out for drinks after. Some asshole broke my phone and I couldn't leave or I'd have blown my chances by seeming uninterested."

She kept talking like I hadn't said a word. "I waited up until midnight last night, and you were at an interview for another job in a different state, living it up and drinking with your new co-workers."

"I thought I could make it. I missed the last train down and got the first one this morning."

"Wait." Her head snapped back. "Is this why you've been nice to me all the sudden? Because you're leaving? You don't care about winning Winthorpe all by yourself anymore because you're not even going to be here?"

"That has nothing to do with it. I didn't even find out I'd gotten the interview until the morning after the scavenger hunt."

"But you'd been trying for it. You had that in your back pocket."

"In my back pocket? This is TV we're talking about. I'm a

shitty, slightly-above-no-name linebacker who washed out in four years. I'm hardly anyone anybody is banging down the door to get on the air. Hunter pulled a few strings to have someone look at my resume and a tape I put together. The fact that they didn't laugh and throw it in the trash is a minor miracle." But when I looked to her for understanding, fury still blazed in her eyes.

"You're leaving."

33

ZARA

"Three weeks ago, you'd have been clicking your heels together that I was."

"Things are different now." The one guy I'd opened up to. The one I let into my damned apartment, to say nothing of my pants, and he was planning on moving out of state without telling me. I wasn't ready to put a label on this, but I'd hoped we'd figure it out when we wrapped the project and the dust had settled.

"Nothing is happening right this moment. They said it'll be weeks until they know."

"Then you'll leave." I tightened my arms around my waist. Why delay the inevitable? People loved him. Women flocked to him. Of course he'd get the job and his stint helping out Sam would be over and I'd be left a wreck in Philly as the girl he used to bang.

"And then I decide what I want to do." I spread my arms out at my sides. "Are you telling me you haven't put out resumes? That you haven't been searching for an out from Easton? You hate it there. You hate them."

Of course I did, but my options were limited. The sky

was the limit for him. The world was his oyster and mine was a flaming dumpster filled with week-old takeout.

Whatever this was between us had barely begun; why had I thought that gave me any special say or right to know what he was doing with his life? Once again, it was me painting a pretty fantasy picture that was never coming true. Just like with my old roommate.

He shook his head like I was being obstinate, which really got my back up. "Yes, but every application I put in falls into a black hole."

He frowned. "So you're pissed at *me* because you can't get another job?"

I fisted my hands at my sides. A fiery maelstrom of emotions rushed through me. Yes, exactly. All I'd ever done was scrape and scrimp to get by and Leo had waltzed into this job, and one of the biggest accounts I'd ever seen had fallen straight into his lap. And in a couple weeks the sports channel would call him back and offer him the job because of course they would. He'd lived a golden life touched by King Midas, and I was suddenly, utterly done.

"Get out." My arm shot out directing him to the door.

His face fell, but it was too late. "Zara, I'm sorry."

"Leave."

"I wouldn't be here if I didn't want to be. I'm in this until the end. Hell, Sam's not even paying me. I don't need to do this job, but I want to do it."

"You don't even need this job?" That inferno had another heaping of lighter fluid sprayed onto it. He didn't even need the money. All his bullshit fighting me every step of the way, and for what?

"Fuck."

"Is this a joke to you?"

"Have I been treating it as a joke?"

Every day, I busted my ass. I wrung every bit of energy and did mental gymnastics to figure out how I'd balance everything like a waitress at a greasy spoon during the lunch rush, and he *didn't need this job*. My best shot at keeping Tyler and myself above water could be ripped away by someone who was doing this for shits and giggles?!

Leo cupped my shoulders. "Calm down."

Bull, meet the red flag of someone who's pissed you off telling you to calm down. I yanked out of his grasp. "Screw you."

"Exactly, it's what we've been doing. Have you considered maybe I'm doing this for reasons other than money? Maybe I'm here because I want to be?"

I had the fluttery pulses of energy telling me to stand here and fight or take flight, maybe crossing state lines before I looked back. "I don't want you here, and you need to leave."

His jaw clenched and he took a step back.

"I'll go, but this isn't over, Zara."

"It's well and truly over. You and I can coordinate the presentation by email. I'll meet you two hours before, and we can go over it, present it, and go our separate ways. Kathleen will decide who gets the account."

"What about that?" He pointed to the ring on my finger.

My chest tight with anger and hurt, I twisted it and tugged it off. Of course he'd want it back.

What the hell was wrong with me? Playing pretend was all this was. I grabbed his hand and smacked the ring into his palm. "You can bring it to the final presentation. Tell Hunter I said thanks."

"What happens when Kathleen finds out we lied?"

"People break up all the time. We let her know our whirlwind romance is on hold for now."

"Zara…"

"You need to go."

His lips parted. He slammed them shut and turned, walking out without another word.

I gave myself a second to feel all the feelings. I clutched my chest and bent at the waist to shoulder the weight of what had happened. Staring up at the ceiling, I blinked back the tears. It was one night. This was always only ever supposed to be temporary.

"He's leaving?" Stella released the ice cream scoop handle, adding another ball of coffee ice cream to the cup. Popping open the microwave, she pulled out the two jars and waved them in front of my face. "Hot fudge or caramel?"

"Do I have to choose?"

She looked at them and back at me with an assessing head tilt. "You deserve both."

I'd come over asking for a corkscrew for the single bottle of wine in my cabinet left over from an event last year.

She'd taken one look at my face and dragged me inside. Since white wine didn't pair well with ice cream, she traded me a six pack of cider, cracking one open on the counter top.

Using two spoons, she drizzled—more like doused—the two bowls of ice cream in sticky-sweet syrups.

"Do you want walnuts or peanuts?

"Peanuts." I stole a spoonful of ice cream from the overflowing dish on her counter.

She opened a cabinet and set two containers on the counter.

"Chocolate or rainbow jimmies?"

"Jimmies?"

"Sorry, it's a Jersey thing." She stuck out her tongue. "Rainbow or chocolate sprinkles?" Her face scrunched up like saying the word was painful.

"Do you run an ice cream parlor that I don't know about?" I peered over the counter from my stool on the other side. "Rainbow."

"I used to work at one down the shore. How do you think I got these incredible forearms?" She flexed.

I laughed around my second spoonful of ice cream.

"And now for the pièce de résistance." She spun around, kicking the fridge closed, shaking a can of whipped cream in one hand and holding a jar of maraschino cherries in the other.

"A goddess. Have I told you that's what you are?"

"No, but I can't say I mind." She winked as she whirled the whipped cream high on top of the fudge and caramel that was ending up mainly on the counter. Fishing out a couple cherries, she set them on top and pushed mine toward me.

"Hey, Stell—" Adam walked into the room and froze, holding up two different ties. "Fudge *and* caramel? What happened? Who died?"

"No one. Zara's having boy troubles," she said around the spoon in her mouth.

"I'll leave you ladies to it. Let me know if you need me." He backed up like he'd walked into a pen of ravenous lionesses. I swear there was a smoke plume behind him.

Oh no. "Were you guys going somewhere? Sorry to barge in."

She waved me off. "I invited you in. It was either go to a stuffy resident's dinner where I'd be one of the only people without an MD and no one would speak to me no matter how much Adam tried to pull me into the conversation, or stay here with you and eat ice cream." She held up her spoon.

I clinked mine against hers and dug back into it. Warm fudge, cold, creamy coffee goodness, the crunch of peanuts, and smooth whipped cream. I was wallowing in perfection.

"He's really moving?"

"To New York. He had an interview up there. He was out all last night doing who-knows-what with who-knows-who, standing me up."

She *tsk*ed and inhaled her sundae. "Bad move. Are you going to let him squirm some before you forgive him?"

"He's leaving."

"I thought you said it was an interview. He might not get it, right?"

"Look at him. They're not turning him down." I sure as hell couldn't. Neither could half the women in the city who approach him every day. He probably came home each night emptying his pockets of slips of paper with women's numbers scribbled on them, or deleted ten old phone numbers a day from his phone to make room for even more new ones.

Stella waved her spoon at me. "I see. I get what this is. It's not you worrying about a long-distance relationship, it's you shutting this down before one can even form."

"We've slept together once. That's hardly the start of a long term relationship."

"Why the hell not? You've been heads-down together for nearly a month, spending almost every waking minute together. That's more time than most married couples spend together. When Adam's on rotation it feels like we go days without seeing each other."

"Leo's not my boyfriend. Hell, a couple days before we slept together he said we were barely friends, so me being the dumb-dumb I am, I decided to have hot, angry sex with him in the woods." I squeezed the bridge of my nose, wishing the headache was brain freeze and not my own stupidity coming back to haunt me.

"That doesn't sound like Leo."

"How are you taking his side on this? You met him once."

"It was twice. The night he carried you into your apartment, and then the next morning. He asked about your favorite foods and was so worried about leaving you at all. I offered to get breakfast for you, but he wanted to do it. I'm not taking sides, but that doesn't sound like a hit-it-and-quit-it guy to me."

"That was before we'd even slept together." Instead it was when he'd brought me a cool wet washcloth while I prayed for death, carried me to my bed, and cleaned my apartment. Why did he have to be so damn charming and caring?

"Even better. He wasn't even swayed by all your sweet, sweet loving then."

"Who are you?" Was there a wacky neighbor handbook? If not, she needed to write one. Chapter 7 was offering advice with cringe-inducing phrases.

"Just Stella!" She poked her finger into her cheek and flung the other hand with her spoon out, recreating a freeze frame from her imaginary '80s TV show.

I stabbed at my ice cream.

"You're pissed, I get it, but maybe a part of that anger"— she ducked her head to catch my eye—"is because you're upset he might be leaving?"

"It doesn't bother me." I tried to shrug it off, but even my shoulders didn't want to cooperate with the farce. "I don't care."

"Yeah, you're drowning your sorrows in cider and coffee ice cream because everything is one hundred percent fine."

"Dairy is good for the bones." I shoveled another spoonful of whipped cream and fudge into my mouth. "All we have is one more presentation and then things are finished."

"Maybe, just maybe, think about talking to him. Tell him how you feel. Tell him why you're upset."

"I'm not upset."

Talk about my feelings. I held back my shudder. That sounded like the absolute worst idea. I'd rather go up against a chainsaw-wielding horror movie villain than slide down that rabbit hole. Letting him know how much it hurt to hear he might be leaving made it more real. Then it wasn't something in my head, it was a living breathing thing I'd have to deal with. I'd have to deal with my feelings for him and those were way scarier than anything I'd faced before.

34

LEO

The elevator door opened. I took a deep breath and entered the Easton Events offices.

A short woman with blondish hair stopped and backed up, eyes wide.

"Hello there." She extended her hand.

"Hi. I'm looking for Zara Logan."

The woman's gaze narrowed and her bright smile dropped. "Zara? I don't think she's in, but I'm more than happy to help."

Another woman stood up from the cubicle behind her. "She's here. She's been here all morning. I don't think she's left her office once. I can show you." The woman came out to the hall. Her jeans, *Star Wars* sweater, and sneakers didn't fit with the Easton Events look.

I liked her immediately.

"Thanks." With a nod to the woman who'd tried to intercept me, I followed my *Star Wars* savior.

"Don't mind Valerie. She was probably going to invite you into the supply closet to suck your dick or get you to bang her."

I tripped over my feet, catching myself on the wall and staring back at my guide, wondering if everyone in this place was a little batshit crazy.

"Don't worry. The supply closet is in the opposite direction. I'm not luring you into a trap. But I can certainly see why Zara's been in a better mood lately."

"That's probably not because of me."

"It is. Except for this morning. She came back as her normal cat-got-run-over-by-a-taxi self, so whatever you did..." She rounded on me and jabbed her finger into my chest. "Fix it. She's my only friend around here, and I won't have someone fucking with her head. Feel free to fuck other parts of her to your heart's content—as long as you have her consent."

I choked on my own spit.

The madwoman patted me on the chest and walked off, leaving me alone in the hallway.

Dragging myself from the depths of my stunned brain wipe, I checked the nameplate outside the office she'd abandoned me in front of.

Zara's name was printed on a cream piece of paper. I peered through the skinny window to the side of the door.

Inside, behind a stack of papers that reached mid-chest, she squeezed the bridge of her nose and refocused on her computer screen.

I moved out of sight to grab my phone and send off my back-up text. The heavy arsenal was needed at a time like this.

Stepping into the open doorway, I knocked on the door.

Zara's head snapped up and she shot up from her chair. The look on her face transformed from startled anxiousness to bristling anger. "What are you doing here?"

The elevator dinged at the front of the office.

"I came to give you this." I slipped the ring out of my pocket and held it out to her.

Her gaze bounced from me to the sparkling diamond glittering even in the dim light of her office. "You're supposed to give it back to me on Friday."

"You're going to want it now."

"Is this Zara's office?" Kathleen's voice broke through the simmering tension in the room.

Zara's head whipped to the open doorway and the familiar voice getting closer with each step.

"What did you do?" she seethed.

"What I had to."

She rounded her desk and snatched the ring from my fingers, shoving it on seconds before Kathleen appeared in her open doorway.

"Zara. There you are—and Leo. I wanted to invite you two to lunch, but Leo said the only way we could drag you away from your desk was to show up and surprise you."

I could see the gears whirring behind Zara's eyes. *Leo's been talking to Kathleen behind my back?* This was supposed to be my Hail Mary, but it might end up being the nail in my coffin.

Zara brushed past me. "I'm glad you did. I'd love to go out to lunch with you, but why don't we make it a girls' lunch?" She linked her arm through Kathleen's, leading the older woman toward the door.

Kathleen stopped in the doorway, keeping Zara from abandoning me in her office. "And leave poor Leo all on his own? I wouldn't do that to you, especially when you've been working so hard that he barely gets to see you. You don't have to protest too much with me—I know you're dying for more time together. It will be my treat."

The abandonment plan had crashed and burned hard.

I sent my silent thank you to Kathleen. "My treat. I don't get to take two lovely ladies out for lunch every day."

She blushed and swatted at my arm. "Such a charmer."

Zara would need a full mouth of veneers from how hard she was gritting her teeth. What a charmer, indeed. I'd be lucky if she didn't push me in front of traffic and use the sympathy to clean up with Kathleen.

The whole office was scrutinizing us as we walked out. The woman who'd accosted me when I arrived wore a scowl and a questioning look. No wonder Zara had always come to Simply Stark to work. This place was fish bowl central.

There were a few restaurants within a couple blocks of Zara's office.

Four blocks wasn't long enough. Once we sat down, the true challenge would begin—getting Zara to speak to me while not letting on to Kathleen that anything was up. It wasn't my brightest idea, but if I had shown up on my own, a slammed and locked door would've been my only reception.

Maybe Kathleen would take a long time in the bathroom, giving Zara and me a chance to talk.

I rested my palm on the small of her back, loving how the curve of it fit my hand perfectly. My fingers brushed her elbow before we crossed the street, watching for insane bike messengers and taxis who seemed to be staging chariot races around the city. Before, I'd done it to irk Zara. Now I did it because I missed the chance to touch her.

Kathleen chattered on about all her plans for the next year, but I couldn't stop watching Zara. Every time Kathleen looked back, I'd smile and nod like I'd been paying attention, but I couldn't drag my focus away from Zara.

The swoop of her hair across her forehead before it was tucked behind her ear. The hug and fit of her skirt, teasing me with the legs she'd draped over mine while we'd slept.

The unpleasant way she hadn't been distracted by having me so close, but was listening carefully to every word Kathleen was saying—or maybe she was just better at pretending than I was.

We beat the lunch rush and found a spot at a restaurant. I pulled out the seats for both of them and sat myself beside Zara even though she tried to force me into one across from her.

After the server took our orders, we settled into an uneasy silence. Zara maintained her plastic smile that didn't reach her eyes and continued to exclude me from the conversation by redirecting everything back to Kathleen.

"The end of the year will be here soon. Have you two given any more thought to the big day?"

Zara sliced into her chicken. "We're still taking it one day at a time. Life moves so quickly and we're never sure what's around the corner, so we're holding off so we don't get our hopes up."

I toyed with my food. "But we also know sometimes surprises come up we can't avoid and we have to be ready to change at a moment's notice."

"Change is fine as long as everyone is on the same page. If you're not rowing the boat together, then no one goes anywhere. Or one person rows full steam ahead and the other person is stuck in a place they don't want to be." She set down her fork.

"I didn't know the boat had more than one person on it. Everything up until this point has been about how this is absolutely a solo mission." Any time I'd hinted at getting close, she put so much distance between us I couldn't even think of what we could be, but now it wasn't just about New York. It was about why she's been the closed-off hard ass in the first place.

Kathleen cleared her throat, breaking up the not-so-stealthy argument. "I'm confused. Are you two planning a boat trip somewhere?"

Our heads snapped to Kathleen and we smiled wide.

Zara grabbed her drink. "It's a mutual friend. They're having some trouble and we're not sure how to help."

"Excuse me, ladies." I got up, texting Hunter on the way to the bathroom. I hovered in the hallway as he helped me put my plans in motion. He was a magician. Sam could use someone like him to make things happen and win over clients. Had he ever not come through? Why hadn't I thought of this before?

Because I hadn't found a good enough reason to get over myself.

The expense would make things tight for the rest of the year, but I didn't mind keeping close to home to give Zara something she needed. One thing I'd learned from my past mistakes was to do what I could for the people I cared about when I could. People I loved. That stopped me in my tracks three tables away from where the two of them were sitting and waiting for me.

I loved her. The prickly, surly, caring, infuriating, driven, talented, and beautiful woman who hated me.

Sitting back down in stunned silence, I tried to keep up with their conversation. We ordered dessert. Kathleen gushed about all her ideas for next year. The job was ours to lose. She also hinted at some big news that would change things for the better for us, but I couldn't concentrate on anything other than Zara.

Outside, I draped my arm over her shoulder and we waved to Kathleen when she stepped into her taxi. The second the car disappeared from view, Zara shrugged my arm off her shoulder.

"I'll email you the draft of the presentation I have so far. Let me know your notes and I'll incorporate them."

"We can work on it together, Gingersnap."

She flinched like that word hurt her now. "No, we can't. Bye, Leo." She kept her gaze down, taking a half-step before committing to her escape.

My stomach pitched and knotted.

I stood outside the restaurant long after she was gone, trapped in my own head, trying to figure out what the hell I'd do if she couldn't love me back.

35

ZARA

I stared out my office window. At least I had a view, even if another building obstructed eighty percent of it. The lunch with Leo had been a mistake for sure, but he'd tried to use Kathleen against me. How was I supposed to push forward with everything when I couldn't stop thinking about him? And while I was mooning over him, he was having conversations with Kathleen behind my back.

A voice broke into the back and forth in my head. "Zara, can I see you in my office?"

I jumped up from my chair.

Bill stood in the doorway. He never came to my office, he always sent Valerie to do his fetching. "Now."

I scrambled, grabbing a notepad and pen off my desk. "Of course."

He was gone before I stood back up.

Rushing down the hallway, I stepped into his office as he sat in his chair.

"Things went well with Winthorpe."

"Yes, Bill. They're going well. Kathleen came by today for lunch to discuss how much everyone enjoyed themselves."

His head dipped slightly. "And Stark? Have you maneuvered your way into a more favorable position?"

"About that." I stepped forward with my notepad crushed against my chest. "We're working on a pitch to win more business than what Winthorpe is currently offering. With the relationship we're building with Kathleen and an increased roster of events, it would be possible for both companies to work together to maximize profits."

"Are you sure I don't need to assign someone else to help?" He wrapped his fingers around his chin.

And steal my commission? "I have it handled. One hundred percent."

"Don't let me down, Zara."

"I won't. I promise." Backing out of his office, I barely kept myself from whacking my notebook against my head. Why the hell had I done that? Under-promise and over-deliver had always been my motto, and here I was running my mouth to Bill about how I had this all locked down. *Screwed*, that's exactly what I was.

My day went too quickly after lunch, the hurtling roller-coaster setting me down in my apartment alone. Stella's words had rung in my ears the whole time Leo and I were sitting beside one another—pretending to be together, but never feeling further apart. When I'd shut down my computer and left, all the lights were off in the office. The last one to leave once again, only this time it felt way too early.

In the lobby, the slurred shout of my name made me wish I'd stayed upstairs longer, at least until she could've been poured into her taxi after the booze had been put on the company tab. The bar and grill connected to the lobby was quick and easy for business lunches and dinners for most people in the building. For Valerie, it was a convenient spot to get blitzed Monday through Friday without spending a dime.

"Leo Wilder's your fiancé?"

I tucked my hand inside my coat. Why hadn't I taken off the ring? "It's late, Valerie, and I'd like to go home."

"You badger my dad into giving you a raise and making you a full-time planner and you're getting married to a pro football player." She sipped from her martini glass, stumbling with each step.

"He's retired. Can I go now?" I bit the inside of my cheek. Couldn't one of her sloppy friends come out here and get her to buy them another round?

My escape was blocked when she got in front of me, more gin splattering on the floor between us, each of my steps matched by a wobbly one of her own.

"You think you're so much better than me."

I knew I was. Not because she worked for her dad's company—plenty of people did—but because she lorded it over everyone and coasted on the hard work other people put in. Screwing others wasn't a game I played even though I'd been on the receiving end multiple times—and not the pleasurable kind. I bit down so hard I tasted blood in my mouth.

"Go back to the bar." I stared straight ahead, which only seemed to infuriate her more. People like her always wanted to provoke a reaction so they could play the victim. Fight or flight isn't the only coping mechanism when facing down a threat. Scientists have also discovered freeze as a natural reaction like a deer in your headlights in the middle of a quiet country road at night. But I couldn't blame this on instinct. This was me curling up into a ball letting a drunk bear with claws out bat me around until they got bored. Survival took on a different form when the predator had a direct line to the guy writing my paychecks.

"You don't get to tell me what to do. I'm running things here."

A man with an earpiece walked out of the bar toward us. "Ma'am, we need you to step back into the restaurant."

I took the momentary distraction to make my escape. But it didn't stop is-this-Vegas Valerie from spewing even more vileness before being escorted back inside with her completely empty martini glass.

Work tomorrow would be a barrel of laughs. I gave it fifty-fifty odds that she remembered any of it. Wouldn't be the first time she'd forgotten a conversation with me.

I opened the door to my apartment. My keys fell from my hand. The jingling clink was the only sound other than my gasp. It wasn't dark and dim inside. There was light. Lamps, a coffee table, and a sofa. I stepped inside, covering my mouth with both hands.

In the center of a coffee table, there was a piece of paper with a gift card taped in the inside.

"Leo ordered it."

I jumped, yelping, and spun around.

Stella stood in my doorway behind me. "His name was all over the paperwork."

"He did this?" The room had been transformed. Earth tones with pops of color. It radiated warmth, comfort, relaxation and an unworried lifestyle I'd yet to taste—but here I felt as though I lived it. Some things I wouldn't have chosen for myself, but for him to do this for me? It was perfect.

"The delivery guys got here a little bit after lunch. They were rushing, but I told them they had all day with the hours you've been working."

Everything in the room exuded 'Chill the hell out, Zara.

Relax and get comfortable. You've had a long day, don't worry about what's out there, just hang out in here.'

Inside the cabinets were neatly stacked cups and plates. Everything matched. Simple classic designs I could layer my own style on top of.

Stella wandered around my apartment.

I walked to my bedroom. A queen-sized bed with the softest mattress topper filled more than half the room. I pressed my hands into it, ready to fling off the sheets and jump up and down, pulling a Tyler. My barely-held together dresser had been replaced by gorgeous light wood pieces that didn't crowd the area and made it feel bright and open even with the limited space.

There was a sleeper sofa, which would be perfect for Tyler. He could stay with me this summer—for a couple weeks, even. I'd never been able to do that before. Leo had given me more time with my brother, and that alone was worth everything.

Stella poked her head into the room. "Wow, can I stay here? Adam can have our place." She hopped on the bed, bouncing up and down and running her hands over the insanely high-thread-count sheets.

We walked back to the living room. Everywhere I looked there was something new to see. The lamps. Empty picture frames ready for new memories captured and preserved. "I was such an asshole to him today." Staring at my phone, a lump formed in my throat.

"All the more reason to call him now." She nudged my phone toward me. "Do it!"

I laughed at her creepy whisper voice.

Trying to come up with what the hell to say, I held my phone in both hands, staring at the screen as if the words to

a script on how to thank a guy for refurnishing and redeco-
rating your entire apartment would appear there.

Squeezing the bridge of my nose, I tapped on his name
and waited for him to pick up.

"Hey, Zara."

"Thank you." Blurting it out like that seemed appropriate, given how I'd left things this afternoon.

"For what?"

"You didn't have to."

"Of course I didn't. But you needed it." *Why was he so
sweet? Why was he so sweet to me?* Trusting people had never
been my strong suit. Someone like him who could pull off
something like this in a day could have anyone he wanted.
I'd been snarky, bossy, pushy, and all around pain in the ass.
Why me?

Cue those miserable, guilty feelings. "Not after what I
said today."

"You were upset and I screwed up."

"Stop being so understanding. You're not making this
any easier." There were people who deserved something
like this and I wasn't one of them.

He laughed. A deep, rumbling one that made me smile.
"Fine, I'll send you a bill. And I never want to see you
again." A *bing* sounded on his end of the line.

"Where are you?"

"Outside."

"My building?"

"Your door." My head whipped to my front door which
seemed to be beating like a telltale heart—but I think that
was my own. With the phone up to my ear I opened it.

Leo stood in the hallway looking every bit as good as he
had this afternoon, but now he held a single rose. The pink
petals looked even more delicate in his giant hands.

"You're here." The words came out shaky and breathless. Swallowing past the lump in my throat, I stepped back and let him into the apartment.

He handed me the rose, his fingers brushing against mine.

"I'll let myself out." Stella did a giddy high step, sliding past us and winking before closing the door behind her.

"Stella helped you set this all up?" I gestured to the gorgeous furniture behind me, still vaguely afraid it would disappear in a cloud of smoke like a magic trick gone wrong.

"She was excited to help."

"You didn't have to."

"It was my apology for standing you up."

"What happens if you do it again? Do you buy me a car?" I laughed.

He tilted his head to the side like he was running a mental calculation.

I held up my hand. "Don't answer that."

He set the flower down on the table beside the door, which was perfect for my portfolios, keys or anything I needed to drop off when I stepped through the door.

His teasing smile slid off his face, transforming into a different look. One that made my stomach flip and my heart skip a beat.

"Maybe there's something else I could give you." His hand looped around the side of my neck and his lips stole away the last of my protests about deserving the apartment makeover.

I met his hungry kisses with a craving of my own for his lips on mine and his arms around me. But Stella's words from our ice cream extravaganza came back to me. 'Tell him how you feel. Tell him why you're upset,' echoed in my head.

Separating us and taking a step back, I tried to catch my breath. It should be illegal to kiss like he did. "This wasn't only about standing me up. Or about the interview." I kept my head down.

"It was about you leaving." I stared down at my hands, twisting the ring around my finger. Once I'd returned to my apartment, I hadn't taken it off. Taking it off was getting harder each time, and that scared the shit out of me. Playing the part had been so easy; it had helped me cling to the anger.

Anger was easy, it was safe. A blanket I could pull over me to crowd out those overwhelming emotions I didn't let in until ignoring them any longer wasn't an option. But this. Sadness. I wasn't prepared for this. "It hit me harder than I thought it would. We're...new."

He reached for me, running his hand along the side of my face. "We are new, but that doesn't mean we can't be old eventually."

"It does if you're leaving." I peered up at him before settling my gaze on the center of his chest.

"My mind isn't made up. I don't have an offer, and I'm here now. Worrying about a future that might not come only steals away the happiness we can have today."

Sadness rippled through my chest. This would leave a mark once he was gone, but did I want to miss out on whatever time we might have together? No tomorrow was ever certain. I lifted my head and stared into his eyes, wanting to dive headlong into whatever this was, but still unable to let go of the fear that had been ingrained in me. "Wise words from a jock."

"I have my moments." His smile threatened to melt me with only the curve of his lips. The lips I'd missed, even after they'd been on mine a minute ago. "Plus, I'm sure someone else said it better than me."

But this wasn't only about us. There was so much else on the line other than whatever this thing was between us. I had responsibilities to more than myself.

"What about Winthorpe?" I dropped my gaze. Bringing it up felt wrong right now, but I needed to know. Lay all the cards out, pull back the curtain, and reveal every little thing holding me back from being with him.

"We have to win more jobs first. We have three days until the presentation."

A zip of panic raced through my chest. "I'll never make it to Tyler's concert." Misery rippled through me at the thought of letting him down.

"We can do this presentation." He dipped his knees to look me in the eyes, capturing my chin and lifting my head. "And once we do, we'll convince Kathleen that this partnership will be best for Winthorpe, and there'll be enough business for both companies." He slid his hand down my arm, lacing his fingers through mine.

That the bonus would keep me treading water for the next year flooded me with hope. The idea of working with Leo for the foreseeable future made my stomach flip. And being here with him now. I pressed my hand against his chest.

His heart thudded against my palm. The soft fabric of his t-shirt was the only barrier between us.

"You make it sound easy."

"You're always making things so much harder."

I laughed, looping my arms around his neck. "Was that a dick joke?"

"No, but it can be, if you want it to." His hand slipped around my waist, tugging me closer.

"I'd be okay with that change of plans. Take me to my brand new bed, Mr. Wilder."

He scooped me up in his arms.

I yelped, clinging to him.

"With pleasure."

36

LEO

I got off the elevator with the box tucked under my arm. Sticking the key Zara had given me into the lock, I paused and waited for the arrival ritual. After what I'd been through on the football field, you'd think I'd have learned that life can change quickly. In a blink, where you thought you were going was gone, and the tide was surging in a different direction.

We'd worked non-stop on our final showcase. We'd spent every night at my place or hers, never apart for longer than absolutely necessary. A week ago, I'd believed I was in love with her—now I knew.

I smiled as the door across from Zara's opened. "Hey, Leo." I hadn't believed Zara about Stella's uncanny ability to know the second she was in the hallway, but it seemed her superpower extended to me as well.

"Hey, Stella."

"Are you coming to see Zara?"

I turned, resting my hand on the knob. "No, I was in the neighborhood and thought I'd go for a walk."

"Oh." She slumped back, her smile falling off her face.

"Yes, I'm here to see her. I have some good news, so I thought I'd do something special for her tonight."

Her smile was twice as bright now. "That's so sweet. You two are adorable together. I've never seen her like this with anyone else before. Come to think of it, I've never seen her with anyone before. Every so often there were a few guys." Her eyes widened and she waved her arms in front of her face. "Not all at once. I didn't mean she had a quarterly gang bang or something. I meant a date or two—with one guy. One guy at a time." She continued sputtering and I kept quiet, letting her flail for a bit before finally putting her out of her misery.

"I get you, Stella. Thanks for looking out for her."

"She needs it, you know. She's always so good at pretending she never needs any help, but everyone needs some help sometimes."

"You're right. I'm glad she has you as a friend."

"Once you get past the prickly exterior, biting sarcasm, face melting staredowns, and general grumpiness, she's so sweet."

"You can say that again." Mouthwateringly sweet and I couldn't wait for my next chance to indulge. "I'll see you later. Have a great night." I ducked inside Zara's apartment and closed the door.

I gathered up the half-filled cups of water, and stuck them in the dishwasher. Some things didn't change. But everything else had. Lamps were on. Her work was spread out on the table. It felt like a home where someone lived and enjoyed relaxing. Not just anyone. Zara. Giving that to her was something I couldn't put a price on.

The drumbeat of the shower meant it was the perfect time to enact my plan. I shrugged off my jacket, put the box down on one of the kitchen chairs and laid my jacket on top of it.

Even with the interior designer making most of the decisions, Zara had put her own spin on the apartment, as well as putting the gift card to good use on things Tyler needed for his dorm room until he'd finally told her he literally didn't have room for anything else.

Sitting, I grabbed the pink cardboard bakery box from the center of the table and slid it closer to me.

The shower shut off and the sounds of Zara moving around in the bathroom sent my pulse pounding. She was in there completely naked. Wet, glistening, gorgeous. I bit back a groan. Patience.

"Leo, are you here?"

"I'm here." I opened the box in front of me and pulled my find out.

"These are phenomenal." I peeled the paper off the cupcake. The rich, buttery, vanilla scent made my mouth water, but not as much as Zara stepping out of the bathroom dripping wet.

"Is that the last cupcake?" She came down the hall, drying her hair with a towel while another one wrapped around her body. A gap had formed at the bottom, so her thigh peeked out from behind the green terry cloth that matched her eyes.

I looked between her and the sugary sweet, icing-topped, fluffy cake in my hand and took a bite. "Maybe."

Her jaw dropped and she threw the towel in her hand on the floor, rushing toward me. "It is! You're eating my last cupcake?"

Turning my back to her, I lifted the cupcake overhead. "I've had a long day. I deserve it." My long-suffering sigh was cut short by another bite of the cupcake.

"I've been saving that since yesterday." She jumped, grabbing at my arm, trying to snatch away the vanilla-bean goodness.

"Saving it for me? How sweet." I craned my neck, bringing it closer to my mouth.

"Don't you dare take another bite." She held onto my arm like she was trying to do pull-ups.

"I'm sorry, did you want a bite? Why didn't you say so?"

She fell off my arm the same time I dropped it, accelerating the speed of its descent and sending my cupcake filled hand straight into her face. The cake and icing smeared across—and up—her nose, cheek, and halfway in her mouth.

Her stunned, wide-open mouth was partially filled with cupcake and icing. The rest was plastered all over her face. Pretty sure that didn't count as me sharing the last cupcake with her.

The towel hit the floor with a small thud, and her shocked gaze shot from my icing-covered hand and back up to my face.

"Oh shit." I searched the counters for a paper towel, completely aware that Zara was glistening and naked. My dick hadn't gotten the memo that a naked Zara wasn't above a knee to the groin now that I'd bathed her in buttercream and sugar. The paper towel holder was empty.

Wiping the cupcake off the side of her face, she stared at it and back at me in disbelief. "Did you just shove a cupcake into my face?" She closed her mouth, swallowing the mush that had made its way inside before sticking her tongue out and licking at the icing from the corner of her mouth.

I cringed. "Not on purpose. Where the hell are the paper towels?" I opened and closed the cabinets and found a new roll. "It's good though, right?" Ripping a sheet off, I held it out to her as a peace offering to save me from impending doom.

"It really is, maybe you should have some more." Her cupcake-covered hand shot out at a speed that would have made any wide receiver proud, and she smeared the icing across my face from cheek to cheek.

She smiled and laughed, picking up the half of the cupcake that had fallen to the counter and adding to the face mural she'd started. Her laughs were punctuated with snorts that made it hard to stop my own grin.

I dragged my thumb across my face and into my mouth. "Say what you will, it was worth it."

"You're the worst." Her eyes sparkled with laughter.

"I have my moments." I stooped down and picked her towel off the floor. Now that there was no longer an imminent threat of death, the picture in front of me was too tempting to turn away from. A naked, sugar-coated Zara.

"You dropped this." I dangled the cloth from my fingers.

She reached for it, lifting the corner of her mouth still smeared with icing.

I jerked my arm back, keeping it out of her grasp. I raked my gaze across every bare inch of her. My pulse pounded, fueled by a sugar high and headed straight to my cock.

Her lips pursed and she made another play for the towel.

But I was faster.

Her gaze narrowed and she tried to fake me out, but I saw it coming from a mile away—until I didn't. She planted her lips on mine and the towel was forgotten, falling from my fingers as I wrapped my arm around her waist, and tugged her against me.

The natural sweetness of her lips was multiplied by the B&B treat.

She wrapped her arms around my neck, her fingers threading through my hair.

My back hit the fridge, rattling the contents inside, but I didn't stop kissing Zara. I palmed her ass, lifting her, until she got my intention and wrapped her legs around my waist —not before unbuckling my pants like a quick-change artist.

But I'd never been happier for her speedy fingers than when the seam of her pussy teased the head of my cock through my boxers. The hot, wet heat of her sent my pulse pounding like an offensive line returning a punt.

Her happy sigh sent shivers down my spine. It was a sound I'd never tire of hearing. Music to my fucking ears. Snagging my wallet from my pants pocket halfway down my thighs, I slipped a condom out.

Zara kissed her way along my jaw, probably getting the rest of the icing from my skin.

I put just enough space between us to shove down the waistband of my boxers and roll the condom on. The driving need to be inside her was only second to staring into her eyes and feeling how much she needed this too.

Shifting our weight, I cradled her ass and ran my other hand along her neck. "You're beautiful, Gingersnap."

She lifted her head and stared into my eyes. A fiery desire, her sweet lips, everything about her made me never want to let her go.

"I need you, Leo. Now. Don't make me wait." Always so demanding.

We were at each other's throats in a completely different way now. Burying my face in her neck as her pussy clenched around me and her fingers yanked at the hair at the nape of my neck. I wasn't going to last long.

"Being inside you and making you come are my two favorite new hobbies."

She covered my mouth with hers. Her soft lips and the nips from her teeth drew a shudder out of me.

I tightened my grip on her. My fingers clenched, shudders racing up and down my spine. The neighbors would probably knock to find out if we needed help moving any furniture, but that wasn't going to stop me.

Spinning around, I pinned her against the wall. Canting my hips and hitching her legs up higher, holding under her knees and thrusting, I powered into her and drank down every moan from her lips. Sweat rolled down my back. I'd never been happier for those grueling gym sessions and weekly basketball games. The threads of me were fraying. Zara's body and touch were ripping me apart at the seams.

"Leo!" She threw her head back, staring into my eyes with a look teetering on the edge of shock and awe. Her pussy clenched around me as every muscle went rigid, her back arching off the wall.

I couldn't hold back a second longer. I exploded into her, filling the latex between us. Spots danced in front of my eyes and I pinned us both to the wall, slowly letting her legs down and wondering if this was what it felt like seconds before your heart exploded.

Panting, covered in a fine sheen of sweat, I kissed her with a Super Bowl-wide grin on my face. I was crazy about this woman. I was batshit, losing my mind crazy about her. A lump lodged in my throat at the sobering thought.

Her eyes opened and she smiled back at me, pushing away those scary, crazy fears that rushed in right behind the tide of endorphins.

"And that'll teach you to steal my cupcake." She let out a wrung-out chuckle and loosened her arms around my neck.

"In the spirit of full honesty..." I rubbed my nose against hers, maintaining eye contact. "I brought another half dozen cupcakes. They're on the chair under my coat. Freshly made today." I leaned out of smacking range and used my finger to close her slack jaw.

Her face morphed from shock to outrage to a bright wide smile. "You jerk, you did that on purpose." She shoved at my chest, laughing and searching for her towel.

As much as I wanted to, I couldn't keep us pinned against the wall for the foreseeable future, exploring her body, and sating this growing need for her touch. We'd have to eat at some point. Neighbors probably wouldn't appreciate the round-the-clock sex Olympics. And there was always the job we needed to get done.

Snagging the towel off the floor, I held it out to her. "I can't say it didn't work out well for both of us. We even got to share the cupcake."

"I'm not sharing the new ones. They're all mine." She rushed out of the kitchen to the chair, knocking my coat onto the floor and grabbing the box.

"Oh no, you don't." I raced after her, ready for a rematch on the counter, floor, or wherever else she'd have me.

With lightning speed, she stole a cupcake from the box in a mad dash for the bedroom. "It's mine. I deserve it." She snuck a glance over her shoulder, taking a bite of the blue icing top.

"You're going to pay for that, thief!"

She crossed the threshold to the bedroom. "The things you promise me."

I stalked into the room.

On the bed without her towel, she peeled off the paper and took a huge bite of one side.

I crawled onto the bed and tugged her down off the pillows by her ankle.

She held the cupcake up high like that would be enough to keep me away.

Our game of cat and mouse was one we'd both win. Over, and over, and over again.

37

ZARA

I traced my finger down his chest, hiding my smile as I circled the flat disk of his nipple, letting it pebble under

"You're teasing again." My touch. We'd had no trouble getting dirty again after a shower.

I pushed up from his body, pressing my palm against his chest. "I thought you liked it."

"It drives me fucking crazy." He palmed my ass, kneading and squeezing the supple flesh I'd never thought of as particularly sexy until he couldn't keep his hands off it.

"That's the point." I nipped at his pec.

His fingers flexed against my sides, bringing his own retribution against me.

I laughed and wriggled out of his hold. Flopping back on the bed, I stared up at the ceiling with my hands over my chest. My laughter died down, and, like they always did whenever he wasn't touching me, the thoughts kicked into overdrive. Lists upon lists. Backup plan after backup plan. "We need to get to work." My heartbeat slowed from 100-yard dash to its normal, steady rhythm.

"Not right now." He walked his fingers across my stomach. His mastery of distraction would be my downfall.

"Yes, right now. We've lost two days already. Oren & Co. might suck at creating events people love, but their presentation skills are next level. We can't leave anything to chance." I rolled off the bed, thumping straight down to the floor. Hopping up, I rubbed my butt. I kept forgetting it wasn't just a mattress on the floor anymore.

"Kathleen loves us. We've got it in the bag." He placed his hands behind his head with a yummy sleepy smile, swaying me to abandon my mission in the race to the finish line.

"And I don't want to drop that bag." Slapping my hands over my eyes, I ripped the blankets off the bed, dropping them to the floor. *Do not look directly at the man candy.* He deserved a large flashing sign over the bed. *Hazardous to productivity and thinking straight.*

"Always so demanding." He swung his legs over the side of the bed and stretched his arms over his head. Every muscle and bulge tempted me to drag him right back into the sheets, and screw the bag.

Rent. Tuition. Student loans. "Put some pants on. You'll poke someone's eye out with that thing."

He laughed. A drawer opened and closed. "Your modesty is safe. I'm covered."

I dropped my hand, heat cranking up a notch. "Gray sweatpants? And no shirt? Why not whip your dick out and rest it on my forehead?"

He tripped in the doorway, swinging around staring at me, stunned, before bursting into laughter.

Opening the drawer again, I pulled out a t-shirt and flung it to him. He'd already taken over a drawer at my place and I had one at his. Things were moving so quickly, I could barely catch my breath. Did I want to catch my breath? "At least put this on."

"Had I known this look got you so hot, I'd have changed into it sooner." He wrapped his arms around my waist when I passed by, burying his face in my neck, nipping at me.

I yelped and wriggled out of his hold. Keeping myself on the opposite side of the table, I fired up my computer and tablet and read through where we'd left off the night before.

We spent the rest of the afternoon and evening poring over all our documents, laptops, and design ideas. I brought the more classic, tried-and-true to the table. Leo supplied the off-the-wall ideas we could refine into something unique that no one had experienced before.

The focus was on what we could provide Winthorpe's employees and clients who came to the hotel looking for something outside of their norm. We emphasized the local flair and flavor, and how we could customize everything to suit their needs.

Feedback from the event attendees was also prominent. It wasn't about us. It was about them and everything we could do to make their lives easier and more enjoyable.

Tyler's name flashed up on my phone as it rumbled across the neat stack of paper beside my laptop. The call I'd been dreading. And I'd been slacking off, sleeping with Leo, and now there wasn't enough time. We still had so much to finish. The bulk of the presentation was ready, but I hadn't practiced. Leo hadn't practiced.

I'd let my baby brother down.

"Hey, Ty." I stood, stretching, my back cracking all the way up to my aching shoulders.

"Hey, Z. We're flying into New York today. I wanted to know if I should tell them to leave a ticket for you. Everyone gets one free one."

I stood from my seat and walked to the hallway. "I'm sorry, Ty. Going to New York on Thursday night would be hard. I have a big presentation on Friday morning, and there's a lot more to do." My stomach churned. I'd been having so much fun with Leo. If I'd focused a bit more, we could be done by now, and I could've gone to New York.

"I'll still tell them to leave a ticket anyway. It's free. Sometimes I get through things way faster than I expected!" Hopefulness burned brightly in his voice, and I hated disappointing him. But I'd be crushing him more if he couldn't go back to school next term. I had to win this contract.

"Have a safe trip and I'll do whatever I can to make it." I ended the call and rested my head against the wall. So many things had changed, but so much more had stayed the same.

I opened our lunch pizza box. Three lonely crusts stared back at me.

"Should we eat? It'll be a late night. There's some leftovers in the fridge."

"Chinese food?" Leo looked up from his laptop. "I know just the place." He took out his phone, rolling right over my leftovers question. Fine, it meant even more leftovers for my fridge.

Not wanting to leave the slightest smudge or stain on any of the new furniture, I took the pizza boxes out to the trashcan.

Returning, I took in my apartment—the same one I'd dreaded setting foot in for so long. Every time I opened the door now, I held my breath, expecting it all to evaporate in a blink. Instead, Leo sat at the new cherry wood table with matching green-and-blue upholstered chairs, rubbing the back of his neck while he pored over the last quarter of our presentation.

Standing behind him, I wrapped my arms around his

shoulders, burying my face in his neck. I'd skirted this talk, blanketing it in gratefulness, not able to talk much more about it because of all the feelings it brought up.

He'd done this for *me*. The money. The time. The care. How did my heart stand a chance against someone like him? And he hadn't gotten any old furniture, even though I would have been equally happy with curb alert leftover furniture no one wanted—what he'd gotten was pinch-myself beautiful. "How *did* you know?"

He ran his hands across my arms, the rough pads of his fingers sending tingles down my spine. "About what?"

"About all this." I held on tighter, afraid even now that I didn't deserve it. "The colors. The fabrics. The wood."

Hooking his hands behind him, he shifted in his chair and swung me down onto his lap.

"You told me?"

My eyebrows dipped even as I kept my arms around his neck.

He twisted his head. His brownie-batter gaze made me hungry for so much more than the ice cream in my fridge. "You mentioned wanting to study interior design."

My head jerked back. Mentioned? More like shouted it in a flash of hurt anger. "You remembered?"

"This might surprise you, but I don't get into screaming matches too often. Ours have burned lasting memories into my brain. I figured being in this place the way it was when that was something you cared about had to make it even harder."

"But the design. The furniture. How'd you pull that off?"

He looked away. "I take absolutely no credit, other than pulling together some of your designs for Winthorpe and using them for inspiration. You definitely have refined taste.

Hunter found someone to put it all together on short notice."

"What the hell can't that guy do?"

"I have no idea and I'm a little scared to find out. His connections can be frighteningly responsive."

"Looks like I owe him even more thanks."

"What about me?"

"I thought I'd been thanking you for the past week." I peppered his jaw with kisses.

"It's been convincing. But like I said before, I don't need any thanks. I could do it and you needed it."

He was so sweet my molars ached. "I did. I'd spent so much time making it mine before…"

His embrace tightened at the unspoken pain of having it ripped away and trashed. Everything was perfect now. The flowers on the table hadn't even wilted yet.

"What happened to wanting to do interior design?" He tucked a strand of hair behind my ear.

I held Leo's gaze and slid off his lap. How would things have gone for us if we hadn't had our run-in? If that hadn't started off one of the most stressful days I'd ever experienced? Would I have melted into a puddle the first time I saw him, instead of wanting to give him papercuts between each one of his fingers?

His arms tightened around me for a second before he let me go.

"Unpaid internships are required to get your big break. With Tyler in school and student loans, I didn't have the luxury of spending months or years being underpaid in a job, even if I loved it. There was no one pulling strings for me, so I gave up on that dream and kept my designs to paper and in my head." I straightened a stack of papers.

He leaned forward, trying to catch my eye. "Let me see them."

"See what?" I asked, stalling for time. No one had seen the designs. I hadn't even seen them in over a year. With the destruction Jeannie had rained down on me, thinking about creating beautifully designed spaces while living in a violated hovel hurt too much.

"Your designs. Do you still have them?"

I shrugged. "Unless your movers threw them out."

"They didn't take anything that wasn't broken. Everything should be here."

The folio I'd shoved everything in had been crammed into a makeshift bookcase made from broken milk crates. Flicking open one of the doors at the bottom of the beautiful cherry wood cabinet, I looked inside.

Beauty had been superimposed over the top of my crappy taped together versions.

"Don't laugh." I slid the battered edged folio onto the table. "I took inspiration from all over the world. Paris. Spain. London. Tokyo. It's why they're so eclectic."

"You've visited all those places?" He didn't look up, but kept flipping through the pages, spending a couple minutes on each, soaking up the work I'd put into them.

I sat on my hands to keep myself from snatching it back and shoving it under the kitchen sink. "No, I've never even been on a plane. But the internet is handy for daydreaming."

"You've *never* been on a plane? How's that possible?"

"Everyone can't hop on a flight and jet set across the country or the globe. Flights. All-inclusive resorts. International travel. Unpaid internships. They all need one thing."

"Money." The word was whisper quiet like it threatened

our very existence. And it did. They said money didn't buy happiness, but not having money sure bought a lot of pain.

"Ding, ding, ding." I rolled my pencil between my hands, the familiar money insecurity rearing its ugly head. My college roommates, spending hours searching for the perfect resort and the perfect bathing suit that cost more than I made in a month, had never invited me along. Could they smell the sale-brand shampoo and spot my discount-store backpack and notebooks from across the quad? Not everyone at my school had money, but almost everyone seemed to have more than me. Even if they were only taking a week off to go to the beach or hanging out at home—I didn't have the luxury of either.

"Everyone else went on spring break. I stayed and worked. I figured I'd have the chance when I got older."

His lips tightened for a flash before he dropped his gaze back to the folio.

"I know nothing about interior design, but every room in here is a place I'd love to hang out."

"Even the one with the four-poster bed?"

"Can't I want to be swept off my feet too?"

I shifted in my seat, checking him out from the side of the table. "I'd need a lot more time in the gym to pull that off."

He laughed. "I have no doubt you could, if you set your mind to it. Determination is your middle name. Do you want ice cream?" He got up and opened the freezer. "Stella gave me some tips on making your favorite."

"You're making me ice cream sundaes too? Next time you're naked, I'm checking your head for a microchip."

"I can't help it if I'm just so damn smooth. One scoop or two?" He waved the ice cream scooper at me.

Smooth he was. "Two."

He grabbed all the sundae supplies I'd somehow missed in my cabinets and got to work.

"How did you end up working at Easton?" He looked up from the intense study in chocolate fudge pouring.

"The same way I've managed to never get on a plane. In college, I'd worked catering jobs. I'd helped organize some events on campus. A little embellishment on my resume, and event planning fit the bill. They had an opening and the pay was enough, so I jumped at the chance. Being choosy or hoping I'd luck into something wasn't an option. Once I was there, there was barely enough time to breathe, let alone apply for other jobs."

"Sorry, I didn't think about you not having a chance to travel."

I waved off his apology. "I'm used to it. I live such a glamorous life, I can see how you'd be confused." My attempt at joking didn't stop the crease in his brow. "I'm overpaid for my experience, as I've been told many times before." Using my thumbs, I smoothed out the ridges of his frown.

"By who?"

I wasn't saying her name in my place of peace.

He wrapped his hands around my wrists and kissed my knuckles. His lips pressed against the ring he'd slipped on my finger. "Someone at work."

I nodded.

He set down the mountain of sugar in front of me. "You're not overpaid. Even someone as inexperienced as I am can see your talent's wasted there, and your designs are gorgeous. If you want, I could see if some of my old teammates—"

I held up my hand to stop him. "One thing at a time. Let's get through Friday night. Then you can tell me the whole plan for how I can fix my life—in bed."

"I'm not trying to railroad you. You deserve more."

"You thinking that is enough to get me through all the bullshit." He didn't understand, but I couldn't expect him to. Being on my own was my normal. If you didn't count on anyone else, then no one could let you down. Working with Leo had shown me that maybe there was another way. Maybe I could trust someone else. Maybe I could trust him.

38

LEO

My apartment door swung open. Zara tugged the key out of the lock and closed the door behind her.

"What are you doing here?"

She took off her coat and hung it in the closet like she'd done it a million times before.

"You aren't supposed to be here."

She made a face. "Why not? We still have work to do."

"No, we don't. Remember last night when you sat on my lap and kicked off the celebratory 'we're finished' make out session?"

"There's finished and then there's ironclad." She approached the table.

I sighed. "What about New York?"

"What about it?"

"Tyler. I overheard you. He's performing tonight."

She tried to pull out a chair at the table.

I looped my foot around the leg and held it tight so it wouldn't budge.

"Would you let me sit? Tyler will understand. He knows

how important this is." Her gaze narrowed. She'd play tough tonight, but tomorrow, when she thought about not being there for him, she'd punish herself. Force herself to work harder, push further, and burn out faster to justify it. Her patterns were obvious the closer I looked.

"But does he know how important he is? I've got everything handled."

Her lips pinched. "There will be last minute changes. You need me."

And there it was. The creeping insecurity she covered with engines on full, powering through so fast there was no time to see anything except the goal.

I stood, wedging myself between her and the chair she kept a death grip on. "My beautiful, determined, unstoppable, stubborn pain in the ass." I ran my hands down her arms before pulling her close, hugging her and pressing my lips against the side of her head. "Of course I do, but not right now. Your brother needs you now. He's performing at a place most people work their whole lives to perform in, and still never get to. And he's going to look out at the crowd and see his big sister smiling up at him."

"He won't know I'm there. That place is huge." She held onto me tighter.

"He'll know. Don't worry about tomorrow." I pulled my phone out of my pocket and pulled up a site while still holding her against me. "You've taught me well. I've proven myself. It's final touches. I can handle this. Save everything to my computer and two back-up drives. All the documents are printed. There's nothing left for either of us to do, really." I clicked *pay* on the screen.

"I—"

Holding up my phone, I released her. "Your train leaves

in forty minutes. It'll take you twenty to get there. Have a soft pretzel and enjoy the ride."

"Leo..." Her phone pinged.

"I'm serious. That's your ticket hitting your email. Be there for him."

She paused, dropping her gaze before flinging her arms around my neck. "Thank you." When she let go, there were tears in her eyes. She smiled and blinked them away before rushing for the closet.

A quick trip back to me, and a kiss that would have to tide me over until tomorrow, and she was gone.

The quiet of my apartment didn't feel so empty anymore, not with Zara in my life.

Kathleen sent a text letting me know to bring at least fifty copies of our handouts for tomorrow. That struck me as odd after the initial meeting with only a handful of people in the room, but I responded and ran off the copies she needed.

After another hour of combing through the presentation, I closed my laptop. Every slide had been spellchecked. Spellchecked backward. Printed out and checked again. Squeezing the back of my neck, I pushed back from the table. Organizing all the papers, I uncovered my phone which had been buried at some point. I tapped the home button and a message from Hunter filled the screen.

Hunter: You saw the news about the acquisition?

I unlocked my phone.

Me: No? Was this message for me?

Hunter: Winthorpe was acquired by the Waverly Hotel Group today

Me: Winthorpe? Like the hotels we're presenting to tomorrow?

Hunter: No, Winthorpe from Trading Places. Who the

hell do you think I'm talking about. Yes, the company you have your big presentation for tomorrow.

Me: Oh shit.

Hunter: Google text alerts, damnit. Use Them.

I pulled up the website and fell back into my chair. A press release from noon today. Winthorpe had been acquired by The Waverly Hotels Group. What did this mean for tomorrow?

No new messages from Kathleen or anyone at Winthorpe. So we were still on? This could be massive for Zara.

Waverly had over two thousand locations on every continent, including a luxury seasonal hotel in the works on Antarctica. There were over eight hotel chains that made up the entire company headquartered in Toronto.

Hunter's name flashed on my phone screen. "How do you not know this stuff is going on with your clients?"

"How do you know about any of this?" I scrolled through the corporate website trying to get a feel for their tastes. This wasn't only a pitch to Kathleen anymore. This was about bagging a client that could transform Simply Stark and cement the future. They already had ten other hotels in the city.

"It's my job to know."

"What exactly is your job?"

"Irrelevant." His dismissive, hand-waving tone even worked over the phone. "All that matters is you have the chance to show your shit off in front of one of the biggest hotel groups in the world tomorrow. Are you ready?"

This was the Super Bowl all over again. Only, I wasn't on the field as part of a team of 11. It would just be me and Zara under the lights.

She'd freak. I checked the time. She'd be twenty minutes

outside New York. If I told her now, she'd turn straight around and be on the next train back. She'd missed Tyler so much and he needed her there for his big night. I could handle this.

Researching a multinational corporation and a complete revamp of the entire presentation in the next twelve hours? "I'm ready. Well, I'll be ready."

"When was the last time you pulled an all-nighter?"

"It's been a while."

"I'll call the guys and we can help."

"You don't have to."

"Of course we don't, but we can't leave you hanging. Jameson will run the numbers. August can help with design. Everest's got the high end knowhow and I'll do what I do best."

"What's that?"

"Come through with whatever anyone needs. We'll be there in twenty."

"Thanks, man."

39

ZARA

Running on absolute faith in our performance tomorrow, I took a taxi from the train station to the hall. New York cabs were not cheap.

An usher handed me a program for the evening. I wished Leo could've been there with me, but knowing he was handling everything back in the city for tomorrow meant I could shut off my phone and watch the performance without the anxiety and fear that had always plagued me before any public speaking. I'd be up on stage with Leo. He'd be the calm yin to my neurotic yang. Before, I'd cursed his cool exterior, but now I needed him there to keep me from losing it.

Parents and other orchestra buffs found their seats. Pre-show chatter filled the storied room. I'd never been here, and Tyler was performing as a ninth grader. Once again the divergence of our lives hit me hard. There hadn't been anyone to look out for me, but I'd never stop looking out for him.

The house lights dimmed and the crowd quieted as students filed out onto the stage. Phones were pulled up, their screens filling the audience like a high-tech version of lighters calling for an encore.

Tyler's curly mop was pulled back, but I could tell it was him. He took his seat without looking out at the crowd. All the other kids searched the audience from the stage, although they had to be blinded by the lights, but he didn't.

He didn't think I'd come, and I'd never been happier for Leo stating in no uncertain terms that I was getting on the train. Tyler would've covered his disappointment on our next call, but it would've been there.

Shoving down the embarrassment that would normally keep me in my seat, I cupped my hands around my mouth and shouted his name whooping. "You've got this, Ty!"

His head shot up. Even if he couldn't find me in the sea of people, from his grin, he knew I was there.

I sat back to enjoy the performance, ready to shower him with hugs and praise the moment they finished.

The conductor stood and they launched into the first song. Orchestral versions of popular movie themes took us from the jaws of summer hysteria and horror to interstellar travel with a few watchful guardians.

Tyler's heart was in every note, and his happiness radiated throughout the concert hall. He wasn't planning to become a concert cellist, but he could be. Opportunities surrounded him, and tomorrow I'd be able to secure them for myself as well.

Less than twenty-four hours until our lives changed forever.

I led the charge to the standing ovation at the end. Every musician putting their all into the performance had paid off. Not that I knew the first thing about classical music, but every song was beautiful.

Parents swarmed the aisles and kids abandoned their instruments and fanned out to find their cheerleaders in the audience. I lost sight of Tyler behind the family hugs, program flinging, and bouquets of roses handed to other students.

"Zara, you came." His bushy curls had escaped his contained stage hairstyle and bobbed as he darted down an aisle toward me. His arms were longer than I remembered, and he wrapped them around me and hugged me tight. He wasn't so little anymore.

"I told you I'd try." I hugged him back even harder.

"But you're always so busy with work. I didn't think you'd make it."

Burying my head in his floral-scented hair, I sent up a silent thanks to Leo for getting me on that train. Tyler would've told me it wasn't a big deal if I'd missed it, not wanting to lay on the guilt, but based on his excitement now, he'd have been crushed if he'd wandered the aisles with no one to celebrate him.

I brushed back some of his curls. "Who did your hair?"

His cheeks reddened and he ducked his head, trying to smooth it back down. "One of the first chair girls did it on the bus ride over. She said everyone would be mesmerized by the sway of my hair if she didn't do something with it."

"It looks good. But I think the lights melted some of the product." I patted my hand against his head. "You're half-porcupine, half-curly fry."

He swatted at my arm. "You're making it worse." Annoying older sister was a job I never minded being on duty for.

"My friend's parents invited me out to dinner with them. Can you come?" He held onto my hand, dragging me down the aisle.

"They didn't invite me. We can go get a bite somewhere else together."

"No, Z. I want you to meet them. They're going to this awesome restaurant. He said normally you have to get reservations six months in advance, but his mom called and they had a table right away."

"And that's exactly the reason they wouldn't want another person tacked onto their reservation." I tried to dig my heels in, but the carpet was too smooth and soft and Tyler was now too strong. He pulled me forward.

Turned out the parents were happy to have me along. I'd hoped they'd be snooty assholes, so Tyler and I could grab a bite at a sandwich shop before my train ride, but they were gracious and lovely.

What wasn't so lovely were the prices at the trendy tasting-menu-only restaurant in Tribeca. If they'd been printed on the embossed and personally-signed-by-the-Michelin-starred-chef dish listings, I'd have probably fallen out of my seat.

The next time I picked up Tyler from school, we'd take them out to dinner. Not somewhere this amazing, but not a place with laminated menus. After tomorrow, that would be possible.

After a full seven courses, a glass of wine, and all the hugs I could get from my little brother, I was back at the train station, texting Leo to see how his night had gone.

No reply. Sitting in the station waiting for my train, I nodded off more than once. I set the timer on my phone for every ten minutes, so I wouldn't miss the last train.

Safely on board, I set another alarm, so I wouldn't miss my stop.

"Ma'am." Someone rocked my shoulder.

Groggy, I opened my eyes and looked up at the conductor.

Snapping up straight, I squeezed the bridge of my nose and rubbed my eyes. "Are we in Philly yet?"

"Philly? Sweetheart, Philadelphia was five stops ago."

I shot up out of my seat. The train car was empty. Out the window, the blue and white station sign hung above the platform. Washington, DC.

I gathered everything up and bolted off the train. Scrambling for another ticket, I was back on my way to Philly too late to show up at Leo's. As much as I wanted to sleep beside him and check over his work, I stopped myself. *Trust him —he can do this.* Instead, I went home and crashed, sleeping well, knowing he had everything handled, and that tomorrow would kick off something bigger than I'd ever worked on before.

40

LEO

I jolted awake. Pens and pencils were sprayed across the table. Fuck, my neck was killing me. That's what I got for sleeping at my kitchen table. I scrambled for the laptop, opening it and releasing a grateful sigh that all the work I'd done last night was saved and backed up.

My phone buzzed the angry song across the paper-covered table top. I rubbed my eyes and cracked my back.

Shit! It was already 8am.

Zara: Are you on your way?

Me: In a taxi now. I'll be there in a bit.

Zara: I'm on my way too. Wait until I tell you what happened last night. But don't worry, disaster averted. I know you got everything handled.

She must've heard the news already. Leave it to Zara to have a Google Alert on everything under the sun, but she hadn't turned right around and come back. She'd left it to me to handle and enjoyed her time with her little brother. This upped my confidence even more going into this presentation.

I needed to get the hell out of here. I triple saved everything and closed the laptop. After gathering up the papers, I rushed into the shower, threw on some clothes, and was out the door in less than fifteen minutes.

Working my fingers into the kink from hell in my neck, I gave Zara my ETA.

And then a bike messenger zipped out in front of the taxi, rolling up onto the hood of the car. He wasn't hurt. He expressed his level of not-hurt by jamming his fist into the hood of the taxi repeatedly, screaming, and swearing at the driver, finally topping it off with a head butt to the windshield, cracking it.

The driver threw open his door.

Fuck. I dropped a few bills in the driver's seat and got out. It was eight blocks to the hotel. Running like I was charging up the field for an eighty-yard touchdown, I skidded into the lobby with sweat making my shirt cling to my chest.

Zara paced outside the doors of the room, squeezing the bridge of her nose. She spotted me and her eyes widened. "What happened?" Rushing over, she took the laptop and papers out of my hands, so I could fix my jacket. "Are you okay? You're so sweaty." She darted into the women's bathroom and came back out with a cold, wet towel. "You're alright?"

"My taxi driver only hit a bike messenger. That's all. Everyone is okay, except for his windshield."

"Sounds like you've had quite a morning." She straightened my tie, smoothing her hand down my chest.

"And quite a night."

She rushed to throw away the paper towels and came back to me.

"Zara, there were some changes I needed to make to the presentation."

The blood drained from her face. "What? Why?"

Kathleen opened the door to the small auditorium. "Great, you two are here. We're ready."

There was no more time and I couldn't explain in front of Kathleen. I guided Zara toward the door. "Follow my lead. Trust me."

She looked up at me, her lips tight. "I trust you." With a nod, she fell in stride beside me and we took our place up on stage.

41

ZARA

L eo's panicked, sweaty appearance had sent my adrenaline spiking. He always had things under control, although a bike-messenger-slash-taxi-driver accident was enough to throw anyone off.

A look of determination and resolve came over his face when he asked me if I trusted him. I did, even with worry creeping in that there was something I didn't know.

The lights were bright in the conference room. As the smallest company, we presented first, which gave us the chance to impress everyone before presentation fatigue set in. Our big shot had arrived.

There were many more suits with Bluetooth ear pieces and a video conferencing set-up with faces on the screen in front of us in sixteen different locations. London. Madrid. Paris. Dublin. Zurich. Way more than I was expecting.

I tugged on Leo's suit jacket and leaned in. "What is going on?"

"You'll see. Don't worry. I've got it handled." Leo smiled and squeezed my hand reassuringly.

He'd said there were some changes, but this was already

more than I'd been expecting. Worry edged into my mind, but I pushed it aside. This was Leo. He'd come through for me more than once. I could trust him.

The Oren & Co. robots sat at the front of the room on the side farthest from the door.

From the back of the room, Sam waved and gave us a thumbs-up.

Kathleen stood at the center of the conference room table and smiled wide at both of us. Her tartan scarf had been replaced by a navy and gray one.

"Thank you everyone for being here today. I know we're already well into our day, but we'll be changing gears for a bit. It's exciting work we'll be doing and we can't wait to join the Waverly group and show them what it means to be part of the Winthorpe family."

Leo's jaw clenched and he mouthed words silently like he was running through the presentation in his head.

Wait, '...join the Waverly group?' What?

"To give you an idea of how we work, I've invited you here today into a review of all the teams we've worked with over Q3 this year to manage our staff and guests' exceptional experiences. We have a number of companies presenting and some of you have been to their events, so that'll give you an idea of the level of care we take in ensuring our employees and guests feel like family. First up, we have Easton Events and Simply Stark. Leo and Zara, take it away."

Keeping my smile, I whispered through my teeth, trying not to draw attention to us. "Leo, what happened? Did you know about the acquisition?"

He leaned in, smelling like soap and cedar. "Yes, I found out. I've handled everything. The presentation has been updated."

How had he found out? When? How long had he known? The questions flew through my head and I tried to focus on Kathleen's speech. My foot shook, rattling my chair before Leo slipped his hand under the table and squeezed my knee. Sleep-deprived and on edge about Leo's mad dash here today, I blinked hard and struggled to keep the neutral smile on my face.

"Relax." His whispered word soothed me the tiniest bit. He scribbled down a note on a notepad. *I have it handled. Don't worry.* With a smiley face drawn under it.

I nodded and clasped my hands in my lap to keep the nervous bounce out of my legs.

Leo pushed back his chair and I went to join him, he dropped his hand to my shoulder. "I've got this. Let me handle it."

His presence alone drew back the attention of some of the more distracted suits in the room and on the screens.

"I'm Leo Wilder. Yes, I'm the same guy who got carted off the field at the last national championship, in case you had an inkling you'd seen my face before. But today I'm here as part of a collaboration between Simply Stark and Easton Events to show you why there hasn't been an event planning outfit like this before.

"There are many ways we can develop the perfect experience for guests, colleagues and high-profile visitors to the city and the hotels."

He flicked through the screens and pointed to the boards behind him.

I recognized none of it. My chest felt like it had been hollowed out. Cavernous and empty, and it only got worse as he continued.

He'd changed *the entire* presentation. None of the things we'd discussed to win over Kathleen were there. Leo focused on international flexibility, bringing groups in from abroad, and touring them through the city and a different set of objectives than we'd laid out.

"Thank you, Leo. This is a unique take on what you could bring to Winthorpe and Waverly. The coffee has arrived, if anyone wants to take a break. We'll reconvene in a few minutes." She got up and patted Leo on the shoulder before leaving the room.

"How was that?" He sat beside me with his eyes on everyone else in the room.

I stared back at him. "Where was the presentation we worked on?"

"Those were the changes I was talking about." He scanned the room, looking everywhere but at me.

"Those weren't changes, you threw out everything we worked on."

People milled around the room chatting, grabbing cups of coffee and breakfast pastries.

Leo tried to cover my hand with his, but I dropped it into my lap.

The door opened again and Kathleen strode in. Not an acknowledgement or wave to us like she usually did. Maybe she was taking the veneer of impartiality in her decision more seriously with so many people in the room.

Then the door opened again and Bill and Valerie waltzed in, both on their phones. They'd finally showed up. The management of all the companies presenting today had been invited to attend.

Valerie's smile at me tightened the knot in my stomach. Her happiness always came at someone else's expense.

Kathleen stood in front of her chair, but didn't take her seat. "While there was some consensus about bringing on a new provider to handle bigger events for us this year, the roster is full."

She directed her gaze at us. "Leo and Zara, we won't be bringing you on for more events. Let's move on to the rest of the presentations."

Everyone else went back to what they were doing, unaware we'd been tossed into chummed water.

Kathleen leaned over toward us, bracing her hands on the table. "You two should be ashamed of yourselves," she hissed. "Pretending to be together. That's low, and I don't abide liars. You can leave."

I sat in my seat, doubly stunned. Frozen like I'd been welded in place.

We'd lost. Our lie had blown up in our faces at the worst possible moment. How had she found out? Had Valerie remembered our last confrontation and told Kathleen? But that didn't make sense. If so, she'd lost her dad tens, if not hundreds of thousands of dollars.

I looked down at the glinting ring on my finger and wanted to launch it across the room. All our work. All my work was gone. Leo had erased it, shredding it and flinging me in front of the wolves from Easton.

I sat beside him, every fiber of my being wanting to fling my chair back and rush from the room as Oren & Co. walked through their presentation.

Why would he do this? How had he done this? He hadn't completed this presentation in one night on his own. He'd sabotaged me. We'd worked together for a week nearly non-stop when we hadn't been falling into bed together—this presentation wasn't a slapped-together job. I squeezed my forehead. What had I been thinking, trusting him?

Kathleen cleared her throat. "Thank you everyone for your attention this morning." She tidied her stack of papers.

"Everyone else, we'll start the tour of the grounds in ten minutes. We'll meet you outside of the Barnes Room."

Kathleen left the room.

Leo shot up out of his seat and rushed after her before the door could close.

How long had he been working on this behind my back? Had it been his plan the entire time? How long had he known about the acquisition? I glared at his retreating figure through the closing door.

42

ZARA

I sat in my seat with my copy of the presentation gripped in my hand.

Leo's hands flexed on the arms of the chair beside me. His gaze was trained on Kathleen and he jerked forward in his seat.

I could almost laugh. His big plan had failed. The words floated on the page as the crushing ache in my chest stifled each breath. If only his failure hadn't tanked my chances of holding the pieces of my life together.

My spot on the end of the table with the full morning glare of the sun shining on me should've felt hopeful. A new day with a new beginning. Instead, I felt like I'd been transported to the surface of the sun. Blood *whooshed* through my veins, thumping out the erratic heartbeat that had started the second the words had left his mouth.

I'd drive to tell Tyler tonight. I squeezed my eyes shut. He'd be crushed. That devastating disappointment that only came from the people closest to you letting you down. I clutched at my chest, the ache growing, burning, searing me.

I'd trusted Leo with not only my future, but Tyler's.

"Zara." Leo's voice assaulted my ears like drumming on a metal trashcan. The crowd leaving the room was thick and heavy with excited conversation. Their acquisition would mean even more expansion. Even more money. Maybe there was something else I could do. I could sell the furniture. As quickly as that flashed into my head I dismissed it. I'd rather sleep in an empty apartment than know that I owed anything. I'd have to find another way to pay for it. I'd hung everything on the hope of winning this job.

Every beautiful piece of furniture was going back to Leo. I'd slept on the floor before. Besides, it would be less to deal with when I was evicted. Maybe I could crash with Stella for a bit. That would give me more time to set up a payment plan and figure something out for Tyler. I could donate plasma. And maybe my eggs to make extra cash.

Pushing my chair away from the table, spots danced in front of my face. Was this what it felt like just before you passed out? The door to the conference room opened again. Everything was drowned out by the desperation filling my veins.

Leo broke through the haze of doom I was trapped in. "Zara." But I couldn't be the least bit relieved. My rescuer had turned into my villain.

"What did you do?"

"I had to call the guys in after you left. Hunter gave me a tip, so I redid the whole thing. I was up until 5am working on it with them."

"You let him handle this?" Bill's glower drilled into me. Valerie stood behind him with her arms crossed, wearing a smug look of satisfaction that turned my stomach and fanned the flames of embarrassment glowing like a beacon in my chest. "You said you had this handled, Zara."

"I told you, Daddy. She wasn't up to it." Her snide voice was nails driven into my eardrums.

"It seems you were right." Bill's disapproving tone barely scratched the surface of the groundswell of emotions eating away at me. "This is unacceptable, especially since this could've led to a partnership with the Waverly Group." Bill seethed, keeping the simmering rant low enough for my ears only. "You're fired."

No crying. Breathe. A shortness of breath threatened to collapse my lungs. Valerie had said far worse to me, but that didn't hurt nearly as much as Leo's hammering the final nail into my coffin with his words.

The certainty in my future. My job. Leo. All of it had all been set alight, and I was standing outside the raging inferno, trying to decide whether to throw myself on the blaze next.

I wanted to slam my hands over my ears and run screaming from the room. All the times he'd whispered his sweet words, ones I'd always felt were only for other women, in my ear at night. His hands trailing along my side, tickling my skin. Had it been worth it? Had it been worth letting him into my bed and my heart?

Tunnel vision took over. All the sounds in the room dulled and morphed into Charlie Brown adult speak.

One final sneer from Valerie and Bill and they were gone. My heart thumped against my ribs and my stomach threatened to revolt. I'd need to keep whatever I'd eaten down since it would be some time before I'd have a full plate again.

"Zara." Leo stood beside me.

I stared at him, almost unable to place his face in the fog in my brain. My body wasn't my own. My arms and legs wouldn't move. The plan I'd just made with a fragment of a glimmer of hope had died. Now I had zero months and no chance of keeping Tyler in school and my head above water.

Leo cupped his arm around my elbow and walked me toward the exit. I stumbled and he wrapped his arm around my waist, guiding me out of the room.

He led me to the stairwell, pressing the exit bar and letting it close behind us. There was a temperature drop the second we stepped over the threshold and it snapped me out of my stupor. The weight that had built up in the last three-and-a-half minutes crashed into me like a time-lapse video slammed into my face.

"Bill fired me."

We were enveloped by the dim seclusion of the concrete and metal steps. My voice echoed off the walls, dialing it up to surround sound.

"That sucks." He rubbed his hands up and down my arms. "But you hated that job."

Was he kidding me right now? My chest tightened and my blood hammered in my ears like it could start spilling out of them any second. I'd been *fired*. There was no upside, no silver lining. I shook his hold off my arms and took a step back.

He broadcast it to Bill and Valerie about staying up all night alone to work on today's presentation. How had Kathleen figured out we weren't engaged? Had she seen a picture of him cozied up with some woman's cleavage, or had our over-the-top denials exposed our lie?

My cheeks heated and my hands trembled. I hadn't even had a chance to help with his new presentation. Maybe I could've seen something that would have improved our chances. He'd taken the whole thing on, leaving me hanging there as the shitty lab partner no one wanted to get stuck with, not even telling me there was an issue.

"You got me fired." My clipped words barely made it past my clenched teeth.

"It'll be okay, Z. You can come work for Simply Stark." He smiled and took a step closer like it was no big deal.

Newsflash, it was a huge freaking deal. "With what accounts, Leo?" I shrugged and shook my head.

"We'll make it happen. We're a great team. It'll take us a few months to get things up and running, but we pulled it off. If the Shining Twins hadn't gone to Kathleen, we'd have won the job."

Accounts like Winthorpe and the Waverly Hotel Group did not fall out of the sky. Simply Stark wouldn't have been on its last legs if it were so damn easy to come up with events jobs in this city with no effort, capital, or experience.

"Do you think I was with Easton Events because of the warm and welcoming atmosphere and friendly coworkers? I was there because it paid. I needed a job and it paid what I needed. Sam hasn't even been paying you. You don't even know if *you'll* still be there and you're family."

"I'm not saying it'll be easy, but we'll figure this out."

"Figure this out?" I dragged my fingers through my hair until they caught on my bun. I ripped them out, probably making myself look like a psycho in the process. But the look on his face, like everything would be just fine and dandy, sent my blood pressure skyrocketing. "I can't afford a temporary stopgap. I can't even afford a fucking cup of coffee. And you want me to take a chance on a company that can't even pay its single full-time employee?"

"Calm down, Gingersnap." He stepped closer.

I shoved both hands against his chest before balling them into fists. I snatched them back and clutched them against my chest. My heart rabbit punched against my ribs. "I don't have the fucking luxury of calming down." I pressed the heel of my hand against my forehead. "Tyler's tuition is due in a week. My rent is due in three weeks, and I have one paycheck left. If I'm lucky, unemployment will keep me going for another month, but even so, my brother will have to go home, crushing his spirit and destroying everything he's worked for. I can't believe you did that to me. I can't believe you got up there and fucked me over like that."

"Zara—"

"No! You could've told me what was happening. You could've given me the chance to help."

"You were already on the train. You needed to spend time with your brother."

"I needed to protect him. I needed to pay his tuition. I needed my chance to save my life, not you trying to save it for me," I barked at him, blinking back the tears. "This is why I don't trust people," I spat the words fast and furious before spinning on my heels and rushing down the stairwell. My ring scraped against the painted metal on the way down, adding to the echoing call of my name from above.

I rushed for the exit and out into the street, where the bright sunlight blinded me. A taxi screeched to a halt in front of me, and I rested both hands on the hood before jumping in the back. I rattled off my address.

"There are easier ways to get a cab." The driver looked at me through the Plexiglas divider.

I brushed the tears from my face.

"Are you okay?"

Staring out the window, I watched everyone else walking around, looking at their phones, laughing, grabbing a hotdog from the street vendors like my world hadn't just imploded. The loneliness crowded in on me, threatening to swallow me whole.

"No, I'm not."

43

LEO

The tin of popcorn beside me needed to be a hell of a lot bigger. August left it on my doorstep. I don't even know how he knew, but he did. Leaving the Winthorpe presentation, I'd come straight back here. I couldn't face Sam. I'd had one shot and I blew it. Not only had I blown the job, but I'd lost the girl.

Sam had found me after she left, hugged me and told me that it was okay, I'd tried my best. Only it wasn't okay, and he was too damn understanding.

I'd been holding onto so many threads, trying to keep everything together, and it had collapsed all around me, taking my heart with it. The anger and disappointment shining in Zara's eyes killed me. I was just another person added to her list of unreliable people she couldn't count on.

My phone rumbled across the coffee table in front of me. I brushed off the caramel and cheese dust and stared at the unknown number. Hope flared in my chest. Maybe it was Zara.

"Leo, my man," a familiar voice crowed on the other end of the line.

"Charlie?"

"Of course, who else would be calling you from New York?"

There was a list a mile long.

"All the guys got together with the producers and higher-ups. You got the job," he screamed it through the line, and I jerked the phone away from my face.

A week ago, I'd probably have been yelling my thanks back to him, but now...bro-ing down with those guys turned my stomach. Leaving Philly felt wrong—not like my feet were cemented here and I couldn't escape, but like I was finally putting down roots to things I cared about, even if they no longer cared back.

"Thanks for letting me know. When do you need my decision?"

"The fuck?"

"There's a lot going on right now, so I need to make sure I'm making the right move."

"You've got until Monday morning, if you need it." His voice hollowed out like a deflated balloon. "Show up at nine and we'll get you started"

"I appreciate this offer and your help." Ending the call, I sat back and tried to picture the future I saw for myself.

What did this call mean for me? I'd be back in the spot-light, in a place where I knew what the hell I was doing. I'd be around people who knew what I'd been through and had gone through the same struggles I had transitioning to life after football.

Or, I could build something from the ground up. Be scrappy and fight my way into a business I had no idea about and could barely compete in—but I'd be doing some-thing where I saw the happiness it brought people. Not thousands of fans going crazy in the stands, or producers in a studio, but people celebrating milestones, anniversaries, and happiness.

I was going to need another tin of popcorn.

Torrential rain pounded on the roof of my car. The cold rain matched my own dreariness. I pulled up to the curb, staring at the house that seemed to shrink every time I stopped by.

But a call from my dad was a rarity these days. Bitterness swept through me at the thought of how the phone calls had stopped once the box seats and all-expenses-paid vacations had dried up.

Getting out, I tugged my collar up and rushed to the front door. I knocked, waiting in the pelting freezing rain.

He opened the door with a wide smile and a beer in hand. "Leo, you're here."

At least he was happy to see me.

"The check came through just like you said, son. You're a lifesaver."

"I'm glad I helped when I could." I dragged my hat off my head as I stepped through the front door.

"Of course. I won't keep you too long." Dad set down his beer and clapped me on both shoulders before muting the TV he hadn't had last time I was here. The one covering a third of the wall, with a huge sound bar installed below it.

A sinking feeling punched at my gut. *Don't jump to conclusions. Don't read into things you don't know are true. Trust him.* Isn't that what I'd harped on Zara for? *Don't always think the worst of someone.*

"Is that a new TV?" I jerked my thumb over my shoulder.

He walked around me and stood beside it. "Isn't it a beauty? Got a great deal."

His words tamped down some of the ire bubbling up. A deal. Okay, maybe it wasn't that bad. He'd found a bargain and couldn't pass it up. He loved watching every game that came on TV. It was a long-term investment.

"Dad, I could use some advice." Why was I doing it? And why couldn't I stop myself? Why did I keep going to this well although every indicator pointed to it being dry?

"I have an offer."

"With another team?" He threw his arms over head, bowing his back and shouting at the ceiling in celebration. "That's my boy!"

His pride almost made me wish it were true. Almost. "No. I'm not playing again. It's not happening. But there's a commentator spot at Sports Central."

He gave me an assessing look.

Maybe he'd—

"How much does it pay? Will they give you an advance? If you're making TV money that could be even better than football money."

"This isn't about the money."

"Of course, it is. Come here." He smiled over his shoulder, walking down the hall to his office. "Money is the key to happiness."

I followed behind him, not sure I wanted to hear the rest of this story.

"And money can buy you things like this." He shoved a brochure in front of my face.

My fingers tightened around the edges of the glossy boat brochure.

"Are you going to rent this for a few days over the

summer?" The muscles in my neck tightened, throbbing and pulsing as I struggled to keep my shit together.

"Hell, no. We don't want something someone else has beat to hell."

"You bought a boat." I stared, blinking extra hard to make sure this wasn't the result of one too many hits to the head.

"She's a beauty, isn't she?" He took the brochure from my hand and stared at the shiny paper showcasing the *fucking* boat he'd bought—*I'd* bought.

My fists clenched at my sides and anger rolled through me like the waves of a rising tide.

"After the year I've had, Faith and I deserved it." A shit-eating grin spread wide across his face.

He didn't see one thing wrong with this. All my life, I was an annoyance until I was a meal ticket. A slot machine that always paid out.

"I gave you money to bail out your business. You said the ten guys who work for you would've lost their jobs." I kept the words on a low simmer. If I didn't keep my voice down, I was going to rip his damn head off. The flash of sadness in Felix's eyes when I'd told him I couldn't cover the loan stabbed at my heart like a pair of rusty cleats. He'd told me he understood and gave me a hug before making me promise I'd come to his house for Christmas dinner.

One Sam would be having without him.

And I'd let him down. I'd let them both down.

My dad plowed ahead like he hadn't ripped my fucking heart out.

"Your bail-out was just what I needed. We'd have had to cut back around here, if you hadn't come through. Selling the shore house and my two trucks to keep the business afloat wasn't something I was prepared to do."

I staggered back like I'd been hit with an illegal tackle. "You still have the shore house?" Anger raced through my veins, searching for an outlet. It was seconds from being my own father's face.

"Of course I do. We leased a slip down there for the boat. Where else would Faith and I go for our summer vacations?"

"How about nowhere, if you can't even keep your business afloat? I had plans for that money, Dad."

"Plans that should've included giving your old man a cut of it anyway." He scoffed. "You wouldn't be where you are without me. I deserved a piece of the pie too. You were getting stingy with it, but now you'll be on TV. You won't even feel a tiny pinch." His eyes flashed dollar signs, already spending the money I hadn't made.

Yeah, I'd had my money kept away from me because I was afraid I'd burn through it. But a part of me knew if I had access to it, I'd keep trying to buy my own father's love and respect. The blinders had been lifted, not only on him, but on me.

"Bull-fucking-shit. You've been pulling that guilt trip on me for years, but it's over now. I'm through with you. I should've given that money to Felix. I should never have even given you that last check—hell, I shouldn't have given you the first one. I won't make the mistake again. The next time your business is in trouble, I'll help your employees set up their own business that's not run by a selfish asshole like you."

"You'd rather have given that money to my brother over me?"

Out of everything I'd said, he'd homed in on that one detail.

"Yes!" My voice ricocheted throughout the hallway.

"Because he wasn't an inconsiderate asshole. He overleveraged himself helping people who worked for him, not buying a fucking boat and a brand new TV and sound system. And he actually cared about me."

"I'm your father, goddammit."

"You could've fooled me. But I'm not falling for your bait and switch anymore. That's the last cent you'll ever see from me again. Enjoy your boat. It only cost you your son."

I stormed out of the house, determined to make it the last time the old oak door slammed closed behind me.

Pulling into the garage of my building, my phone buzzed in the cup holder. If this was my dad trying to coax me back, forget it. There wasn't anything in the world to drag me back there.

"What?"

A sharp gasp was followed by a throat clearing. "Is this Mr. Leo Wilder?"

"Yes, sorry. I thought you were someone else."

"Is this a bad time? Sam Stark gave me this number to reach you on."

"No, sorry, it's fine. I've been dealing with some telemarketers lately."

She chuckled, some of the unease leaving her voice. "I'm calling on behalf of Mr. Waverly from the Waverly Hotels Group. He'd like to have a meeting with you on Monday morning at nine. He's using the offices at the Winthorpe."

Waverly Hotels Group. Maybe I could salvage this. If not for me, maybe for Sam and Zara. Maybe everything hadn't turned into fiery rubble.

I ended the call and rushed back to my apartment, firing up the laptop and researching their hotel development programs. Maybe...

Every step to my office was another flood of emotions. Each step threatened to send me back to my apartment, but even there wasn't safe.

Stella's muffled voice on the other side of my door, and Leo's low rumble, had kept me rooted in place in my living room. He hadn't tried to use my key. Good. I had the chain on. I couldn't even afford to change the locks. I buried my face in the couch cushions. The soft, beautiful couch cushions he'd bought me, that only made everything worse. My tears didn't stop until the timid knock from Stella.

There weren't enough ice cream sundaes in the world to fix this. Chocolate fudge and sprinkles couldn't fix a shattered heart.

Messages and calls from Leo filled my screen. My finger hovered above the block button before I broke down and tapped it. But that didn't stop the messages. Hunter's phone, Jameson's phone, August's phone—each one blocked. Leo even borrowed Everest's, although they weren't on the best of terms. Each message ended with the line. "Let me explain."

Only I couldn't. Not right now. Every text brought tears to my eyes. A reminder of my own stupidity. Once I figured out what would happen to me and Tyler, then I could— there was nothing. Only a yawning abyss of impossibility when I tried to think of how this could be fixed.

My hands shook with each message to Tyler. I'd wait to tell him. No sense killing his happiness with the news that he wouldn't be returning next term.

It was Monday morning, when I'd normally already be at the office. Instead, I was in sweats, with stringy, unwashed hair, and sneakers, trudging to the office with my empty box.

The lights flicked on when I arrived. Even at seven, I was still the earliest arrival. After two years of bleeding-from-my-eyes level of work and dedication, losing a client Valerie had already lost got me booted out.

I wrapped up the spare cables for my phone into the cardboard box. Tugging open my drawer, I brushed my hair back from my face and dumped the whole thing into the box. Chapsticks, hair ties, safety pins, bobby pins, tide sticks, and more fell like a shower of preparedness into the box. Except I hadn't been prepared. How could I have been?

After twenty calls and thirty texts, I'd blocked Leo's number. My eyes were still red-ringed and puffy. The over-sized sweatshirt, sneakers, jeans, and messy bun screamed breakup wardrobe, but I didn't care. Couldn't care.

In between crying jags, I'd put in over seventy applications over the past week. And just as I'd known when I got stuck there, it wasn't what you knew, but who you knew. There hadn't been a single response. I might as well have been drafting personalized cover letters and lighting them on fire, —which was what I'd probably be doing in another month when I got kicked out of my apartment for not being able to make rent.

All my emails to old college 'friends' had also gone unanswered. Dammit, I should've networked more. Instead, I'd worked my ass off to graduate on time, and look where that had gotten me.

A grating voice broke through my snuffle-filled solitude. "Did you honestly think you could've pulled it off?"

"Not now, Valerie." I emptied out the last drawer under my desk and picked up the picture frame of me and Ty last summer at a carnival.

"It's not like you'll be around to say this to later." She sauntered into the office with a smug smirk. "I told my dad it was a mistake to put you on the job, but he was trying to teach me a lesson about responsibility. Can I give you a little advice for your next job?"

"Can we not do this?"

"I'm only trying to be helpful." She put on a sugary sweet voice, but glee danced in her eyes.

My stomach knotted.

She was enjoying the hell out of this. "Your little lie about being engaged to Leo. You should've seen Kathleen's face when I told—"

I slammed the box down on my former desk. My back snapped straight, shock ricocheting down my spine.

"You told Kathleen." Blind fury clouded the edges of my vision. Blood hammering in my veins, making it hard to hear any of the sputtering and stammering before her cool mask slipped back into place.

"You screwed your own father out of a possibly million-dollar client all to get back at me." I jammed my finger into the center of my chest. "You ruined a man's business because of your petty, jealous bullshit. You can walk in here with your designer bags, overpriced coffee, and plastic smile, and pretend you're trying to be helpful, but you're not a nice person. I should've known when you introduced yourself the first day by telling me you hated people and everyone thought you were a nightmare." I tapped my finger against my chin. "Now, why would anyone say that about you? Probably because you are. You've been riding Daddy's coattails, fucking things up left and right. I am so happy I don't have to clean up after your messes anymore." I slammed the lid down on the box and hefted it into my arms.

There was a flicker of self-reflection on her face—or maybe it was gas. She crossed her arms over her chest without moving an inch when I stood in front of her with the box in my arms. But I wasn't her lackey anymore and I didn't have to bow down to her or kiss her ass.

"That's some other person's job now, which means I also don't have to listen to you gloat. So go right ahead with what you're doing, but some day Daddy won't be there to cover for you, and who's going to want to give a job to a..." I wracked my brain for the perfect description.

Andi popped up from her cubicle with her hand in the air, jumping up and down like a first grader who needed to use the bathroom. "Towering thundercunt?"

"I was going to go with bitch, but I like yours much better."

A drawer opened and closed behind Andi's cubicle wall, and she stepped out of her cube wearing a feather boa and tiara and fell in line with me as I walked to the elevator.

"I told you I had these at the ready for the day you finally cracked. And you get a gold star." She pulled out a shiny gold sheet of star stickers out of her back pocket and stuck it to my chest. "What? It motivates my team."

A screech sounded behind us. It seemed Valerie was

finally unfrozen. "Andi, you think you can talk to me that way?"

Andi shrugged. "I don't *think* I can. I just did," she called out over her shoulder.

"I'm telling my father." Valerie flipped her hair and stormed off.

"Run to Daddy." Leaning against the wall beside the elevator, she jabbed the button and propped up the bottom of her foot against the wall.

"I can't imagine that's going to go well for you."

The vapor trail Valerie had streaking to her dad's office created a vacuum of swirling papers in the hallway.

"After all this time, I'm ready to go. Plus, my entire team will follow me if Bill gives me any shit. I've been headhunted at least twenty times over the past few years, so I have options."

"Why would anyone with options stay in this place?"

She crossed her arms over her chest and squinted. "The food's good, the guys I work with are cool, the coffee's shit, but the pay is fine. It's also got the bonus of fucking with Valerie, and you're my best work friend. I don't have many girlfriends. So it was all good while it lasted."

I dropped the box, opened my arms and pulled her into a hug. I'd never had anyone who'd stay somewhere for me. Things made so much more sense and it broke my heart that it had taken me this long to see how good a friend she'd been to me. My go-to vent buddy. The person who could say the things I never could when I'd clung to this job.

After a second she hugged me back. "Some days, you were the only thing that made me not want to fling myself in front of a taxi. We're hanging out." I let her go. "Drinks, although you'll have to pay since I'm unemployed now." There wasn't a hint of sadness or worry in her voice. Her catlike reflexes would ensure she had a safe comfortable landing somewhere way better than here.

Guilt gnawed at my gut a little that she'd put up with this place as long as she had, at least partly because of me.

"Drinks are on me. Although, I'm unemployed as well, so happy hour special for the win."

The elevator arrived and I stepped inside.

"Wait." Andi stood in the way of the door. "Why would you be unemployed? I'd have thought Stark would've picked you up in a heartbeat. You and Leo worked well together."

"It's a long story."

"One you can tell me over drinks." The elevator doors closed, banging into her shoulders. "Tonight."

"Tonight really isn't—"

An annoyed chirp sounded from the elevator as the doors tried to close again. Andi shoved her elbows out to keep the door from closing.

Heads popped up from their cubicles to see why the elevator was now screaming like it was being murdered. "I will literally stand here until the end of time. I'm not the best at making friends, especially not girl friends, and I don't want to lose you as one, Zara." Her gaze was intent. "Tonight."

"Yes. Tonight." Maybe I could invite Stella too. There had to be a happy hour somewhere with half-priced drinks.

"Awesome. My first ever girls' night." Unwedging herself, she stepped back, waving with a wide smile as the doors closed. Over her shoulder, a fuming Bill and Valerie stormed toward her.

If she hadn't already told me she was ready to go, I'd have tried to warn her. She'd looked forward to coming to work to hang out with me? I should've invited her out sooner. Now I wouldn't get to hang out with her every day.

Maybe she had a couch I could crash on once I was evicted.

Unemployed, drinking half-priced booze, hanging with my girls. The perfect way to forget about the ache in my chest that made it hard to breathe. Somehow getting fired hurt far less than Leo betraying my trust.

45

LEO

Life is about choices. Some are big, like which college to attend. Some are small, like faking left instead of right. And some can shift the entire course of your life. Standing in front of the reception desk, there was no question mark or worry, only sheer determination to make this work.

My leg bounced up and down the entire time I was waiting in the reception area. This time it wasn't nervous energy that flooded my system, like standing in the tunnel in a stadium with the roar of the crowd rumbling the ground under my feet. It was fear like a gladiator felt, facing down a lion with nothing but a spear and a broken shield. I had to do this.

The second the call came in, my plan kicked into high gear. I put in a call to my lawyer and accountant, who at least still took my calls. One piece was in place, but there was still more to do. People flowed up and down the long hallways like this was any other day, not one of the biggest of my life.

"Leo. What are you doing here?" Kathleen's voice broke

through the nerves building inside me as I sat outside the large double doors.

I stood, buttoning my coat. "Mr. Waverly invited me."

Her lips pressed together and she looked toward the closed door. "That might be so, but this is still my hotel and I won't be working with people I don't trust."

"We bent over backward for you. Should we have pretended to be engaged? Maybe not, but we busted our asses to give you everything you wanted and more, so I won't apologize for one damn thing."

A woman with a sunny smile and a folder held against her chest stopped short when she saw the two of us. The smile slid off her face.

"Is everything okay?"

I tugged on the cuffs of my jacket. "Kathleen and I were resolving an issue between us."

She harrumphed and stormed off.

The woman turned to me. "Sorry for everything being out of sorts. Mr. Waverly doesn't generally work this quickly, but he wanted to meet with you before he left town. You'll only have twenty minutes, I'm afraid."

I nodded, gripping the folio in my hands. My heartbeat pounded in my hands. I held onto it, not wanting it out of my sight.

"Mr. Waverly will see you now." The receptionist gestured to the large wooden doors beside her.

Sticking the folio under my arm, I took a deep breath, my hand tightening on the handle.

"It'll be fine. He's incredibly nice, and hardly ever has security escort anyone out." She stood and opened the door. "It was a joke."

I stepped through the open door. A fresh paint smell lingered in the room. Leather couches—not the slick kind with chrome accents like Sports Central, but the homey, lived-in kind that were broken in and soft—made up the seating area of the office.

"Leo." A tall man stood from behind his desk, walking around it with his hand extended. "Good to see you again."

"Clint with the shrimp?"

He laughed. "I can see you're surprised. None of your research turned up a picture of me, I see."

Clint Waverly. *Holy shit.*

I swallowed those words since I was at least pretending to be a professional right now.

"No, it didn't. I can't say I was looking for it, either. I was more focused on the quirks of the company."

He sat in a wide leather chair beside the couch. "I could tell from the presentation. You put a lot of work and effort into showing us what you could bring to the table. What do you have for me?" He nodded toward the dark leather folder I had with me.

I sat up straighter, my fingers curling around the portfolio I held against my leg. "Your chance to land one of the best up and coming design professionals in the industry and bring them on board at Waverly."

The speech I'd practiced at least a hundred times with variations based on objections was delivered with a calm, cool, collected demeanor that didn't match the chaos racing through my head.

I'd gotten Sam's blessing to do this. He'd come to terms with what might happen to Simply Stark even with all the work I'd put in, but I could still save Zara. As much as she'd hate that, and maybe hate me, I could give her the choices and chances she'd never had before and to finally put herself first.

"You have..." Clint glanced down at his watch, fixing his

shirt cuff. "Eighteen minutes. I arranged this talk after seeing your vision and passion for the work, and to discuss your future with Waverly Hotels, and you're pitching someone for our interior design internship? Is this how you want to start things off? Asking for a favor?"

Fixing this was my only chance, not just putting a broken thing back together, but making it better than before.

"It would be me doing you a favor to help you get someone like Zara here at Waverly."

"This is the woman who worked with you and Kathleen." His mouth twitched "She mentioned something about an engagement."

I cleared my throat. The weight of this settled on my chest like a three-ton stone. "Our engagement...I'm coming clean to you, Clint. It was never real. We pretended to be engaged to get on Kathleen's good side and stay there."

He leveled his gaze at me.

My hands clamped onto my knees, refusing to squirm.

"And how'd that turn out for you?"

My head dipped.

"She didn't seem too happy with how things turned out."

"It was a bad day for both of us, but she got fired because of it."

Clint let out a low whistle. "Why isn't she here with you today?"

"I'm not her favorite person right now."

He leaned back in his chair, lifting his leg and resting his ankle against his knee. "So this isn't concern for a fellow colleague. This is something more."

"It's both." I looked into his eyes. Launching into the story of how we came to be fake fiancées, I laid it all out on the table for him. Everything—well, not everything, but everything PG-rated that brought me to his office.

"You didn't answer my question from before. How was it, pretending to be engaged?"

"Frustrating and hilarious and confusing and infuriating and breathtaking."

He apprised me with a look. "It may be you know a bit more about being in a relationship than you thought." And a chuckle.

I let out a huff of stifled laughter. "Maybe in a small way."

"As for getting on Kathleen's good side, I can't blame anyone for doing everything they can to stay there. We've been working on this merger for over two years. I've never seen a more hands-on owner in my life."

He rocked back in his chair, eyes boring into mine.

I held his gaze without a flinching. If this was a battle of the wills to win even a chance at getting her back, I could go all day.

"The interior design group doesn't have a home base. Did you know that? We're a global company. That team works setting up new properties whenever we acquire them, and they're on-location during the acquisition. We like them embedded to bring as much of the regional flavor to each hotel as possible."

"I understand."

"This means continuous travel. Months at a time spent in different locations crisscrossing the globe to keep us at the top of the hotel game."

"She's always wanted to travel."

"What about you? You're willing to watch her go."

I stared down at my hands, clasped in front of me, my forearms resting on my knees. If they offered her this job, she'd be gone. Globetrotting, discovering new and exciting places leaving her past behind. Leaving me behind.

"She's talented and deserves to have her chance at her dream."

"So this is your grand gesture? You plan on standing outside of her window with a boom box until she'll talk to you."

I laughed. "It's part of it. I do have a few other tricks up my sleeve."

The office door opened and the assistant from earlier poked her head in. "Clint, I'm sorry, but we need to get you in the car if you're going to make your flight."

Sighing, he pushed himself up from the chair. "It's always go-go-go. Rachel keeps me on track though." He took my hand. A firm, but friendly shake.

It was done. At least part of it. There were still a few more things to put in place—and then the whole 'getting Zara to speak to me' thing, —but I'd keep trying to make her dream come true, even as my future turned murkier by the minute.

My phone buzzed in my pocket. I stole a glance. Charlie at Sports Central. Pushing it back inside, I silenced the vibration. It wasn't what I wanted after all.

Clint's assistant rushed into the room and gathered up a few things from his desk, while he slipped on his suit jacket.

"Do I have any calls in the car?" He buttoned his blazer without a hint of worry about the time. That must be the benefit of having other people worry about that for you.

She shot a quick glance at her phone and shook her head. "You're clear until take off, then you have a couple calls once we're in flight before we land in Rome."

"Rome? I thought we were going to Berlin."

"The updated itinerary was sent to you this morning."

She opened her folder and slipped out a piece of paper holding it out to him.

He waved it off with a smile. "That's what I pay you for. If I kept my own schedule, I'd end up in Paris, Texas, instead of France."

"If I recall, that's when my new contract showed up on my doorstep." She laughed and slipped the paper back inside her folder.

They carried on with their conversation as if I weren't there. Should I see myself out? They were blocking the door. Then again, they were leaving anyway. I hadn't gotten an answer from Clint, but he seemed like he'd been on board.

"Worth every penny." Clint stopped at the door, holding onto it. Rachel narrowly averted slamming into his back. With a quick dip of his head, he swung his gaze to mine. "Leo, let's keep this meeting going. The car can bring you back once it's dropped me off. That work for you?"

"I've got nowhere to be."

"Then hurry up. If we put Rach behind schedule, there'll be hell to pay. So what else do you have planned for your no-longer-fake fiancée? I need more details on *that* presentation."

We set out to the airport in a black-tinted SUV. I laid out my entire playbook for Clint and he nodded and laughed along.

By the end of the ride, I felt hopeful that I could pull this off.

We didn't pull up to the normal departures terminal, but straight onto the tarmac.

Rachel climbed out of the driver's opened door and answered her phone, waiting for Clint to follow.

He shook my hand again. "Good luck, Leo. The next

time we're in the city, you'll have to fill me in on how it all goes."

"I will. Thanks for everything, Clint."

"Don't thank me just yet. Wait until the ink is dry and you haven't slept in a month."

"I can handle it."

His smile brightened. "I have no doubt you can."

The driver closed the door behind him and we were back on the road. Back in my apartment, I went through all the emails and documents I'd need to finalize my plans. Big plans. All I had to do was hope they didn't blow up in my face.

46

LEO

A man in a suit even more formal than my tux opened the doors to the hotel. His suit had tails. At least I hadn't gone full penguin.

"There's still time to turn around and find a less insane way of talking to her." August leaned over, slipping his finger under his collar, sweat beading on his forehead.

"You didn't have to come."

"Someone needs to be here for when you need bail money."

It had taken all my detective skills and a compelling argument made to Stella to get the information I needed to put my plan in motion. This wasn't the ideal place, but there weren't many options.

Zara had become part hermit, barricading herself in her apartment. Tonight, she wouldn't have the chance to run away. Not until she heard everything I had to say. I'd already run through each of the guy's phones—even using Everest's hadn't gotten me more than a single text or a ten-second call. Tonight was my night.

I stepped through the second doorway leading to the ballroom. One of these days I'd find a way to repay Hunter. A word was all it took for him to make the impossible possible. Not that scoring an invitation to a reception neither of us had been invited to had been any more difficult than procuring an engagement ring with a few hours' notice, but he never let me down.

Fingers tightened on my arm. For a second, I thought we'd been spotted and we were on our way to being chucked out in the gutter. August's fingers bit into my bicep. "You didn't say this was a wedding reception." He looked over at me like we'd stepped into the seventh circle of hell.

The twenty-piece classical orchestra on the stage was set up in front of the large backdrop with two interlocking initials signifying the bride and groom's new nuptials. A wedding cake large enough to feed three city blocks sat prominently in the corner under spotlights more powerful than any SWAT team.

"It'll be okay. You're not the groom, remember?"

He stared straight ahead at the cake.

Prying his fingers off my arm, I scanned the room for the only reason I was there.

Couples in evening gowns and tuxes like mine glided across the dance floor to waltzes that put my plays out on the field to shame. Was everyone here a professional ballroom dancer?

The colorful dresses created a tapestry of wealth in the room, but I wasn't looking for one of them. Servers blended in with the décor, wearing matching outfits in black and white. There were more people crammed into the room than there had been at our Super Bowl after party.

"August, can you see her? I can't see anyone." Turning

behind me, I saw that I was on my own in a sea of people shooting me strange looks.

He was standing right where I'd left him.

I stepped in front of him and shook his jacket, breaking the stare-down he had going with the fondant-covered tower in the corner. "Snap the hell out of it. It's a wedding. I didn't know either, or I wouldn't have had you come. But you're here now. Will you help me?"

He blinked a few times and shook his head. Some of the color returned to his face and he no longer looked like he'd watched an exorcism go wrong. "I'm good. I can do this."

We walked through the crowds of people that grew thicker by the minute.

"There have to be at least three hundred people here. How much do you think this wedding cost?"

"With that spread." He nodded to the carving stations, seafood waterfall made up of lobster tails and crab legs and champagne glass tower. "We're talking five times what mine would've been."

Holy shit. Even from afar I'd been roped into some of the wedding planning details as August's best man. The sting from his almost-wedding was still there, but one thing we all agreed on was he'd dodged a bullet, not that any of us could say that to his face. Not yet anyway. Five times! No wonder the wedding planning business was so fierce. Shaking off the distraction and mental calculations, I got back to my mission.

"I'll never find her in here. We need a better vantage point." Even with both of us a head above most people, there were too many bodies. And more people were looking our way. They were going to find out we had no business being here.

"What about up there?" He pointed to the stage where

the orchestra had taken a break. An unattended micro-
phone sat perched at the front of the raised platform. "From
the looks we're getting, the countdown clock is ticking. I'll
distract the sound guy, you go up there."

We rushed through the press of people, swimming
through a sea of faces until we reached the stairs leading up
to the stage.

August did his wing man duty and tripped over some of
the wires, sending earsplitting feedback through the room.
Heads turned our way.

I climbed the first two steps, getting a better vantage
point, and searched the faces. Waiters wove their way
through the throngs of people, trays balanced above their
heads in some places where the packed bodies left them
little room. I took the next two steps until I was up on the
stage. Shielding my eyes from the bright lights, I scanned
the room. Could she be in the back? Maybe she'd be on the
rotation of servers coming in later? Had I missed her?

Then I spotted her. The one moving through the crowd
with determined efficiency, never deviating from her
forward progress while still letting people take their pick
from her tray. Even from behind with her hair in a low braid
in an efficient and out-of-the-way hairstyle, I couldn't look
away. Her outfit matched all the other servers, but she
looked more beautiful than any of the women in their glittering designer gowns.

She smiled politely as people took champagne flutes off
her tray.

"Zara," I called out.

She wasn't far from the stage, but with so many people it
was hard to be heard over the background music and
rumble from the crowd.

I cupped my hands around my mouth. "Zara."

She paused for a second looking up and around, but not behind her.

Once again, I cupped my hands. "Zara!" My voice boomed through the room and every head whipped around in my direction. The mic beside me now live and cranked up to eleven.

"Sorry," I said into the mic. "Congratulations to..." I looked behind me at the custom backdrop "Marcela and Evan. May you have a marriage as wonderful as this wedding. Your dress looks amazing." The woman in white's expression changed from confused to beaming. "But I need to talk to that woman."

"Is that Leo Wilder?" someone in the crowd called out as I jumped from the stage with my gaze locked onto the woman who'd haunted every dream I'd had since she'd walked away from me.

Zara's face cycled through at least five emotions. Surprise, embarrassment, sadness, and maybe wishful thinking on my part, but a hint of longing, before settling on unbridled anger. She jolted when I hit the floor, setting the glasses on her tray wobbling.

My forward movement was impeded by the partygoers, but I dug deep into my defender skills to dodge, duck, and weave my way through them without ever losing sight of her.

Three steps from the swinging doors all the other servers kept disappearing into, I reached her. My fingers slipped around her elbow, stopping her escape.

"Zara—"

"I'm working," she called out over her shoulder, snatching her arm from my grasp.

"Three minutes. That's all I need."

"I have a fifteen-minute break in three hours." Her eyes

blazed with fiery fury but beneath it, the hurt radiated like a throbbing tooth.

"You can take a few minutes to talk to a guest. It's a wedding, isn't it?" I plucked a glass from her tray and motioned to the his-and-hers monogram on nearly every surface.

"No, we're specifically told not to speak to any of the guests and to be as invisible as possible throughout the evening.

"Did you know, none of the other companies in the city will touch me. I've sent out over fifty applications in the past two weeks. I've showed up at companies trying to get three minutes with someone who might take a look at my portfolio." Her gaze dropped and her hand fisted at her side. "I don't have many employment options right now. Please don't get me fired from another job."

"If I were trying to do that, I could think of a much more creative way."

"You could have come to my apartment."

"Been there, done that, got a warning from your building security. If you hadn't dodged my calls, I wouldn't have had to resort to this. This is for you." I pulled the envelope out of my inside jacket pocket.

"Keep it. I don't need your peace offering, and I don't need to assuage your guilt." She shoved through the double doors leading to the kitchen.

"And that's what it's always about. Leo getting his way. Not this time." She spun quickly, storming off into the kitchen, the doors silently swinging behind her.

"I take it that didn't go too well?" August popped up at my side.

I downed the champagne, needing the final bit of fortification before laying everything on the line with her. "No, but it's not over yet."

And I charged ahead after her. Where Zara's concerned, nothing is ever easy, but that didn't mean I'd give up without a fight.

47

ZARA

Halfway through the kitchen filled with trays upon trays of hors d'oeuvres, kitchen staff and servers, I could feel his presence behind me. The startled looks from everyone I passed confirmed it.

"Why won't you leave me alone?" My voice came out like a hiss above the chopping, searing, and frying going on at the stations in full force to feed the stadium full of people out there.

"I couldn't leave you alone any more than I could stop breathing, Zara. At least, not without giving you this. Will you take it?" He took the tray from my hand and set it on the counter.

I backed up trying to find my escape route. Hard to do in a room crowded with other people all staring at you. I was so getting fired.

He slipped a thick envelope out of his jacket pocket and took my hand, curling my fingers around it.

"I'm not taking your money. Once I figure out what I'm doing with the apartment I'll get you your furniture back."

"This isn't my money. Would you just stop being so frustrating for five damn seconds and look at the envelope?" He jabbed his finger toward the ticking time bomb he'd handed over.

Seeing him in the flesh was nothing like seeing him through my peephole. Leo Wilder in a tux was a crime. Women's heads continued to turn, as they always did whenever he entered a room.

I swallowed hard before venturing a peek. Waverly Hotel Group was embossed on the front of the envelope. I ran my fingers along the heavy, raised lettering, tracing the classic font.

My clammy hands fumbled the envelope, nearly dropping it. With trembling fingers, I unfolded it and read the lines. Each word blurring as tears welled in my eyes. A Waverly Hotels Group internship. A six-month paid international internship. "You want me gone."

"Not one bit. It kills me to know you'd be gone for six months. And if they take you on full-time you'd be away from here for months, if not years at a time." Anguish leached from his words.

My head snapped up. "Then why?"

"You deserve this."

"Before...why did you call me out on stage? Why show up here?"

He stepped in closer, invading my space. "I can't exactly have a grand gesture without an audience. Plus, it's our way, isn't it? I ruffle your feathers and piss you off. You don't let me get away with it and fire back at me."

"Thank you, Leo. But I can't take it." I stuffed the letter back into the envelope before I changed my mind, and handed it back to him.

"Of course, because that would be too easy." He finished his glass of champagne in one gulp, but otherwise didn't move to take the envelope I shoved against his chest.

"It's not me trying to be difficult. I can't go to Europe and leave Tyler here. He's going to have trouble readjusting to home, so I need to—"

Leo held up a finger in my face and took out his phone. "Yes, I have her here."

I batted it away. "What the hell?"

"It's your brother." He slipped the phone into my hand.

I looked from the glowing screen with my brother's name on it back to Leo.

A tinny voice came from the phone. "Zara? Hello?"

If I lived a different life and had more than cobwebs in my bank account, this would be when my tearful brother provided his proof of life before the kidnapper snatched the phone away and demanded a million dollars. Instead, I had lint and a few tic tacs, and Tyler was tearful for another reason.

"Tyler what's wrong?"

"Did you win the lottery?"

"No. What?"

"It's a scholarship. The Logan Scholarship."

"I've never heard of it."

"It's new. Everyone here thinks I've been pretending not to have money all this time. So when they said I needed to call the scholarship benefactor tonight, I...I was wondering if it would be you."

"It wasn't me, Ty. But I think I know who it was." I peered up at Leo. Tears brimmed in my eyes and I didn't blink or brush them away. They crested down my cheeks, dripping off my chin.

"It's a full ride through the school and college. It's awarded to a new kid each year, and I'm the first recipient."

"I'm so proud of you, Ty." My voice cracked and the waterworks wouldn't stop. The pressure had been like a blanket that had threatened to suffocate me. It had been lifted. Leo had lifted it. But why? Boarding school and college? That was an insane amount of money.

"This is great news, right Z? You won't have to work so hard anymore. I know you've been doing so much for me, and I was going to look for a job this summer to help out too. It's a lot of stress to pay the bills."

"Don't be silly."

"It's not silly. I know you love me no matter what. I don't need you to pay for everything to prove that. I was thinking of leaving after this year, but now I don't have to. I didn't want you to have to work so hard instead of having fun for yourself. You're the best big sister anyone could ever have."

I slapped my hand over my mouth to keep my choking sobs from blowing out his eardrums.

A linen towel was thrust into my hand.

I looked up at Leo. How had he done all this? "I'm so happy for you, Ty."

The look in Leo's eyes was part worry, and part questioning.

"It's almost curfew. I'll talk to you later. And thank Mr. Wilder for me. Love you."

"I will. Love you too."

He ended the call.

I stared down at the black screen of the phone, my reflection staring straight back.

"You did that for him."

"He's a great kid from everything you've told me, but I did it for you."

My hands shook. This scenario had never presented itself in all my fight, flight, or freeze encounters. "Why, Leo?

And how? I thought you had everything tied up and kept away from yourself. How are you going to fund him through that school and college and award this to one kid each year for the next five years?"

"There was a loophole for charitable donations and foundations as long as they were for a minimum of five years. They'll shunt off a portion to finance the fund and invest it. It'll grow."

"And if it doesn't?"

"They'll divert the money to fund it. Giving up half of what I have to give you a chance at what you need is worth it, Zara. You're worth it."

I flopped down onto the milk crates stacked up by the back door. The organized chaos of the kitchen flooded in, snapping me back to reality.

Everything I'd ever wanted. And Leo had made it all come true.

"Why?" I stared up at him, trying to make sense of what he'd gone through to make this happen.

He dragged a milk crate in front of me, looking hilarious and sexy in his tux perched on an orange, beat-to-hell plastic monstrosity a foot off the ground. "You can't tell?"

"I wouldn't have asked, if I knew. If I knew, I wouldn't be sitting here thinking about pinching myself hard enough to leave a bruise to make sure this is real. But if it's not real, I'm not sure I want to recover from this head injury."

Leo took my hand in his, threading his fingers through mine. "Since I need to be more direct, I'll lay it all out for you. I love you, Zara. I am madly, mind-blowingly, my-life-will-never-be-the-same-again, in love with you."

I sputtered, snapping my head up. "Why?"

He laughed. "That." His finger swirled around in front of my face. "That face, and your determination to protect the people around you, even if it means serving a room full of people after having a corporate job, not taking shit from an asshole who makes you spill coffee all over yourself, and never letting me get away with a hint of bullshit. It's why I love you."

Joy burned bright in my chest, overwhelming me and bringing the tears I'd finally stifled back to my eyes.

"Why else would I have done all this? Why would I have used my fifteen minutes with the President of Waverly telling him he'd be insane not to take you for this program?"

"You what?" I shot up from my seat. "Of all the insane things...you had a chance to get into the good graces of Clinton Waverly and you spent it talking about an interior design internship? Are you insane? That's time you could've spent pitching for Simply Stark. Did you think about Sam? How did he feel about you throwing away an opportunity for his company?"

He stared up at me, grinning wide.

My heart did a backflip, filling with a feeling I couldn't have placed before this moment.

He loved me. Everything everyone else hated—or at best tolerated—he loved. He loved me. All of me. The infuriating bits I used to keep people at arm's length. My inability to keep my mouth shut when I should. The way I stood up to him.

"I love you."

"How could you help yourself?" He stood and pulled me against him, running his fingers under my chin.

"This was your plan all along, wasn't it?"

"Cornering you at work where you couldn't run away? Yes. Absolutely. Showering you in coffee and crushing your croissant? Blurting out that we're engaged when you got Stella's ring stuck on your finger and pretending to be your fiancé for the next month? There's not a playbook in the world that good, but I'm certainly glad it ended up being ours."

"Me too."

He ducked his head, capturing my lips with his and dipping me.

A soundtrack of applause broke out around us. It was quickly broken up by the catering manager.

With his hands on his hips, he stood, tapping his toe, as everyone broke up and went back to their duties behind him. "Your break isn't for another two hours and forty-five minutes, Ms. Logan. And what have I said about fraternizing with the guests?"

I stared up at Leo, panting, ready to peel him out of this tux and spend the rest of the night showing him how grateful I was for everything he'd done to right the wrongs in my life and take care of me. For once, someone had stood up for me. For once, I didn't have to be the rock. He'd be my rock. I rested my head against Leo's chest, patting my hand against the solid wall of muscle. "I quit."

48

LEO

With a wide, probably goofy grin, I walked off the elevator with three cups of coffee. I slid one onto Phyllis's desk and headed back to see Sam.

Zara was sleeping in. Her sleepy moans and clutching the pillow to her chest had almost diverted me from the only thing that could've dragged me from the bed. My plan had been to stay in the apartment with her until she got on the plane, but there was one thing I needed to decide on before then.

Her day was packed with everything that needed to be done before an international move, like getting a passport and meeting with her internship coordinator. Tomorrow I'd start our cocooning in full force.

The lights from Sam's office were the only lights in the still office space.

I walked in and set down his coffee.

He smiled wide and popped the top off, inhaling the hazelnut scent. "What are you doing here? I thought you had plans to keep to your apartment for the next few weeks?"

"That was the plan, but I wanted to swing by."

Sam made a noise of acknowledgment while rummaging through his drawers for extra sugar.

"What would you think about me staying on at Simply Stark?"

He looked up at me from over his glasses, tugging them off and letting them fall around his neck. "I'd think you're crazy. I've had to let everyone go except Phyllis—she won't leave, but she also hasn't cashed a check in the past twelve years, so there's not much I can do at this point. Why would you want to do that? I thought you had the job up in New York."

"I know, but I want to try something new. Stick closer to my friends and see if football is all there is to me." I rolled the glass ball from hand to hand across the top of the desk.

"Leo, you don't have to prove anything to anyone. Of course there's more to you than football."

"It's me I need to prove it to. Make something from nothing—not nothing." My eyes widened and the ball slipped out of my hand and fell to the floor.

"I know what you mean." Sam snatched the ball up and placed it in my palm. He looked out of his office door at the empty space that had once been the hub of the business. "Truth be told, I was going to close up shop. The little jobs here and there are only enough to keep me afloat. The house isn't the same without Felix there and this business..." He waved his hand in front of the doorway. "Without him it doesn't have the same magic it once had. If you want to take it over you can, but I have one condition."

"Anything."

"You can't do things the way he did them. Change the

name. Break the mold, and never feel like you have to do this for him or me or anyone else. Do this because you want to do it. Do you accept?" He held out his hand.

"That's doable. I'll keep you on as partner if you like."

He scoffed. "A silent, silent partner. It's time I went out and did a little living of my own. I've got a new life to figure out now, too."

"A silent partner."

"Are you going to do this all on your own? Where's Zara?"

"She's leaving for Australia in three weeks." I tossed the ball in the air.

"And you want to start a business instead of following her? What the hell are you thinking? After everything you two—"

"I want to build something she'll want to come back to. Start something she'd be proud of."

"You're planning on doing this all on your own?"

I looked at him over my shoulder. "I might ask for a little help."

"Are you guys sure you want to do this?" I looked at them across the drafting desk that had taken over the main office area. "All I needed was some help getting set up."

"Some help." Hunter moved his fingers in air quotes. "How the hell was this thing limping along at all?"

Jameson looked up from the laptop. "Hunter's being a little harsh, but, fucking hell, these books are a mess."

The balloon was being pricked from all sides, the air leaking out. Maybe this had been a mistake. Maybe Zara would be cool with an unemployed and unemployable boyfriend.

August squeezed my shoulder. "But that doesn't mean it can't be fixed."

I squeezed the mini football stress ball. "It's not your mess to figure out. It's mine."

"What if we wanted it to be our mess too?" August dragged his chair beside me. "We're all here for whatever you need. Tell us and we'll get it done."

My eyebrows dipped and I looked at all of them. Everest stood in the corner, scanning the older invitations pinned to the wall as a showcase. "What about him? Are you in Everest?"

He didn't look over at everyone else. He stood there with his hands in the coat he still hadn't taken off, like he wanted to run away at a moment's notice. "I have nothing better to do. Why not get a front row seat to watch this shit show burn?"

Jameson snatched the ball out of my hand and lobbed it at Everest, hitting him in the side of the head. "Do you have to be an asshole twenty-four seven, or do you take vacations from time to time? Are you going to help or not?"

"No need to be so dramatic, Jameson. Not everyone has team player stitched into their DNA, but I'll help. It looks like you're all going to need it. What's the cash flow on this place?"

Everyone looked to Jameson from behind the laptop.

He winced and drummed his fingers across the desk. "Well...there are a few different ways we could handle this."

"Direct would be best." I swung the laptop around and looked down at the bottom line highlighted in red. "Is that months?" White-knuckling it while riding in the business owner seat wouldn't be easy, but it was doable.

He sucked in a short breath between his teeth. "Weeks."

"Shit."

"You need cash flow yesterday." Everest peered over my shoulder. "There are three types of clients you're looking for. Corporate. They're a huge pain in the ass, but they don't require too much handholding and their budgets can handle upsells. Then you have your entertainment focused clients. This is clubs, sporting events, musicians." He grimaced. "Finally, you have one of the most lucrative clients, where the sky isn't even the limit, if you've got the right person at the helm."

August and I exchanged a look. He'd gone chalk pale.

I turned to Everest. "Weddings."

He raised a finger high over his head. "Ding, ding, ding, we have a winner."

Hunter jumped in, keeping himself out of the scramble. "I can handle clubs and musicians. Those are already in my wheelhouse. I can see what's coming up and work my magic." He rubbed his hands together.

My experience wasn't huge, but I had a relationship with one of the biggest clients in the world. "Corporate, I've got locked down."

Jameson raised his hand. "I can do sports."

I nudged the laptop back toward him. "We need you on the back end handling this financial shit show. You cool with that?"

He shrugged and pulled the computer back in front of him. "Sure, whatever you need me to do."

Hunter rocked back in his chair, lifting the front two legs off the floor. "That leaves sports and weddings."

Jameson's nearly silent typing was the only sound other than the rumble of the heater kicking on.

"Between those two, I'll take sports." Everest flicked his lighter open and closed against his leg.

August shot out of his chair. It teetered on two legs before landing back down. "I'm sure as hell not doing weddings."

Jameson looked up from the screen. "You *are* the only one with any experience."

Everest sliced his hands in front of him. "I'm not doing weddings."

"As soon as things are up and running, we'll swap. Everyone will take turns learning each thing, but we need someone to be the expert out of the gate."

"I'm not doing weddings." August crossed his arms over his chest.

Hunter set his chair down on all four legs. "You did say whatever he needed. And what he needs now is a wedding planner."

August looked around the room with a mild panic in his eyes that transformed into dead set retribution. "Who knew all my friends were such fucking assholes?"

Jameson slowly raised his hand over his head, scanning the room.

I clapped him on the shoulder. "We'll order extra fortune cookies for you."

Our meeting raced into the night and I sprung for the Chinese food. We figured out the partnership agreement on the back of a napkin, even came up with a new name and logo.

"Business cards will be delivered in two days." Hunter shoveled beef and broccoli into his mouth.

Rummaging around in a grease-soaked bag, Jameson pulled out an egg roll like he'd discovered long lost treasure. "It's a bit early for spending on things like that. We need to focus on revenue-generating expenses only."

Hunter winked and grabbed his beer. "Don't worry. I got a great deal."

We set out the game plan for hitting the ground running starting tomorrow.

"Did we really do this?" I stared at the large whiteboard August and Jameson had hung on the wall.

The elevator dinged. A hooded figure strode through the open doors and into the office with something tucked under their arm.

We all exchanged stares and searched the room for weapons.

Jameson jumped up, sprinted around the corner, and grabbed a metal sign, hefting it over his head.

As the figure got closer it was easier to see their build wasn't that of a maniacal murderer. It was a woman in Converse and a superhero hoodie. Steps from the table we'd all been working at, Jameson yelled bringing down the sign for a face flattening blow.

The woman yelped, her arms flailing and the thick brown envelope she'd been carrying slid across the floor.

He recovered at the last minute, halting his swing and stopping the decapitation of our guest. Flinging down the sign, his face turned beet red.

She scrambled up off the floor, her hood falling back. "Zara said I might find you here." Her hand clutched to her chest, she panted, pushing herself up onto all fours.

We scrambled and recovered from the shift from office brawl to cleaning up our screw up. Her face was familiar. Someone I'd seen at Easton.

Five sets of hands shot out to help her up. "Thanks. I didn't get my cardio in today, so that did the trick." She locked hands with August and popped up, her hair falling out of her ponytail.

He dropped her hand and took a step back. "Sorry about that. Who are you?"

She smiled, a mischievous sneak of a grin, before crossing both her arms over her chest. "How she's going to stay away for six months, I'll never know. She's a much stronger woman than me. Anyway, ogling the man candy isn't why I'm here." That didn't stop the long lingering survey of each one of us. Was this what it felt like to be on the meat market?

"Zara said you were thinking about starting up something new of your own. I figured you could use a leg up." Holding up the envelope, she radiated exhilaration at handing over whatever was inside. "I'm Andi."

I ripped it open and slid the black rectangular object onto the desk.

The guys all looked at her and back at me.

"It's a hard drive. An external hard drive with every client, calendar, and vendor for Easton Events."

"You stole this?" Jameson's voice was steeped in disapproval.

She shot him a lopsided grin. "Do you take the fun out of everything? Technically it's all my information housed on my hard drive and paid-for accounts. Do what you want with it, but I figured you'd like to kick things off right with your company and screw over Easton at the same time."

"Is that the name of your company?" She stood in front of the whiteboard where we'd written out our plan of action and Everest had sketched out the logo.

"We already ordered the business cards."

"If you move one little letter..." She picked up one of the white board markers and rubbed out the S from SWANK—

the name we'd put together using each of our initials. She moved it to the end, spelling out WANKS.

She turned around grinning and shoved the cap onto the marker. "None of you saw that?"

Things were already off to a promising start.

49

ZARA

Taxis rushed past the entrance of the hotel. The distinctive European siren wailed in the distance. Even after so many months outside the US, it always caught my ear. I backed through the door held open by a doorman in a top hat and tails and stared out at the historical buildings across from me.

Everyone else hurried along the sidewalks, not taking any of this in. Then again, I was barely above a tourist. My phone buzzed in my pocket.

I waved to the front desk and rushed across the lobby to the elevators.

Reaching my floor, I hopped, taking my heels off. The plush carpet cushioned my feet, soothing the day-long ache in my toes. Leo would've chastised me for wearing them for so long, but I'd barely felt the pain until I made it to the lobby.

Previously, my work had been so mind-numbing that I'd felt every minute tick by like a lemon-soaked paper cut. Now, I forgot to eat. Every minute was jam-packed with projects, events and tasks I had to drag myself away from, but something was missing. I could pretend I couldn't quite place it, but it was him. Leo and I had gotten a month before I left. It had been one of the best of my life—I could relax, plan things on my own terms and spend as much time with him as possible. I'd never had someone take care of me before. I'd never *let* someone take care of me before, but with him it wasn't hard at all.

And then I made it through the metal detectors, glancing back at him over my shoulder on the other side of the security line. It wasn't until I was buckled into my seat that I let myself cry. This was my dream. This was what I'd fantasized about before I met him, and it was every bit as exciting and fulfilling as I'd hoped it would be, but I couldn't stop feeling like I wasn't in the right place. I wasn't with him.

My key card was clutched between my teeth and I held my shoes in one hand and my bag of croissants for the morning in the other.

It was sacrilege to eat day-old croissants instead of buying them in the morning, but I'd much rather eat them sitting in the doorway to my barely-there balcony in my robe than get dressed early in the morning to get freshly baked ones.

My phone buzzed again in my purse. Dropping my shoes, I grabbed the key card out of my mouth and shoved it into the lock. I kicked my shoes through the doorway and let it close behind me, juggling the phone with my free hand.

"Olivier. It's me. I'm here." I let my bags fall to the floor right beside the door. The continent may have changed right along with the room, but other things stayed the same.

The accented voice came through the speaker. "Tomorrow, I'll get the fabric samples. The company is small, but they've promised they can supply us with everything we need as long as they have enough notice." I stared out my window, soaking in the view I'd had for the past three weeks. It would be hard to leave, but not as hard as it would be to stay.

A knock clued me into how late it was. Dinner time. Usually, I went out instead of using my room service perks, but I'd spent the day in heels, which meant my feet needed a rest. It never felt like I was burning the midnight oil like it had back at Easton. The long hours were as rewarding as they were tiring. My stomach rumbled.

"Let me get a pen." Notes on top of notes, but all to execute my vision for the pitch for renovations to one of the three Paris hotels. This was my first time taking lead after nearly five months.

I opened the door, holding it open with my foot, and grabbed a pen off the desk while holding my phone against my ear with my shoulder.

"Olivier, I have to go. My dinner is here."

"It's later than I thought too. Get some dinner and we can go over everything in the morning once I have the samples."

I ended the call and dug through my purse on the desk for a tip.

Turning with the euro note in my hand, I dropped the phone to the floor. The soft thud was the only sound other than my sharp gasp.

The room service delivery guy stood beside the man I'd thought I'd have to wait another two weeks to see.

I flung myself at him. My arms wrapped around his neck and he caught me, wrapping my legs around his waist.

Waving the bill at the delivery guy, I kissed Leo, reveling in his musky scent, firm grip on my ass, and equally ravenous hunger for me.

The probably insanely embarrassed delivery guy slipped the bill from between my fingers.

"Thank you." We both let out gasping, laughter-filled appreciation to the man who let the door slam closed behind him.

Our nearly six weeks apart between his visits over the past six months had tested the limits of my love for what I'd always dreamed of doing. Each morning, I'd pat his empty side of the bed, and roll over each night staring at undisturbed blankets and pillow with a longing in my heart before I closed my eyes.

"I missed you." He set me down on the desk. The soft fabric of his pants tickled the insides of my thighs.

"You said you were on a business trip for the next two days." I slipped his buttons out of their holes, exposing his smooth chest to my gaze and fingers.

"I did. I'm here right now." His fingers found the zipper to my dress, tugging it down my back.

My fingers flew to his belt, unzipping him and slipping my hand inside his pants.

He clenched his jaw and sucked in a sharp breath as I stroked his cock.

"Too good." He knocked my hands aside and hiked my skirt up, tugging my panties to the side, and pressed the blunt tip of his head against my pussy.

A sigh escaped my lips. It melted into a moan. Every inch stretched and opened me up until he'd sunk completely into me. He rested his forehead against mine.

"I couldn't wait."

"No complaints from me." My chuckle was lost when he rocked his hips against me, grinding and thrusting. His hands slipped inside the open back of my dress, but other than that we were fully clothed, clinging to one another as we hurtled to our own personal brinks.

"Too long. It's been too long since I'd touched you." He held onto the back of my neck, burying his face against my skin and inhaling.

The desk rocked and banged against the wall. I tightened my legs around him, locking them around his hips as I held on through the rippling waves of pleasure. Every cant and buck of his hips tapped and rubbed my clit, sending a cascade of tingling feelings all through my body until I was blindsided by my orgasm. It ripped through me, stealing my breath as my walls clamped down around him.

He swelled even bigger, his orgasm triggered by my own.

I sat on the edge of the desk, holding onto him. His heartbeat raced under my hands. Panting, sweaty and blissfully happy, I leaned back and kissed him.

His hands found the sides of my face and he held me tight, letting our mouths do a talking that required no words.

"Let's get a shower." He helped me off the desk and we spent the next twenty minutes getting reacquainted again.

We collapsed onto the bed. I brushed my sweaty hair out of my face, panting, smiling, and happier than I'd ever thought possible.

"Three more weeks," he mumbled, running his fingers though my hair. "Have you decided yet?"

The phrase had ricocheted around my head for the past nine weeks, since the requirement to choose our placements within the Waverly Hotels Group had come up. Leo had only uttered it a few times since I'd mentioned it.

Sydney. Tokyo. Paris. Johannesburg. Buenos Aires. And finally Paris. Six cities in six months. Some of the places I'd dreamed of traveling to, and I'd lived in each one, working, exploring, discovering new things about myself while I went to work each day, unable to contain my excitement for my work.

But there had been a piece missing.

"I asked for a placement in Philly." I looked up at him from the circles I'd been drawing on his chest.

His hand tightened around my shoulder. "Zara, don't—"

I pressed my fingers against his lips. "You can't talk me out of it. I already turned in my placement forms."

"But look at this." He gestured to the window with a picture-perfect view of the Eiffel Tower. Globetrotting while staying at the Waverly Hotels hadn't dampened my travel itch, but scratching it occasionally was different than packing up my whole life and moving halfway around the globe.

"It's beautiful. Every night when I go to sleep and every morning when I wake up, I can't believe I'm here." The lights twinkled, lighting up the iconic structure for a celebration. "And I can't wait to come back again, but I'd like to go home—with you."

He kissed me with a fierceness and resolve that made spots dance in front of my eyes. "How do you know you'll get the spot?" Worry creased his brow.

"As awesome as Philly is, I don't think it's at the top of many people's lists. The program director was surprised when he looked at my ranking. It's pretty much a done deal. All that's left is a signature and I'll be coming back to the city in three weeks. Back to you." I dropped my gaze back to his chest. "I've missed you."

The belt on his pants jingled as he shifted to the edge of the bed.

Had he hoped I wouldn't come back to Philly? Was he trying to make a quick escape? Phone calls, texting, video chats, and some pretty steamy phone sex had tided us over in between his monthly trips to visit me. At least, I thought it had.

"Does this mean you'll finally say yes?"

I sat up, pulling the blankets with me "Moving in with you is a—"

He sat up, pushing himself higher in the bed, and held an open ring box in his palm.

I looked from him to the ring that looked suspiciously like the one I'd sported for months. It hadn't lost a hint of its shine, and it sparkled even brighter through the unshed tears pooling in my eyes.

"Is that—" the words caught in my throat.

"Yes, only this time it'll be for real, if your answer is yes."

"Leo—"

"I know I'm a semi-employed washed-up pro football player, running an event planning company that's limping into the next year, and you're poised to set the hotel redesign market on fire, but you'd make me the most frustrated, most insanely awed, and happiest man on earth if you'd agree to be my wife." His throat worked up and down. The vulnerability of his confession and the beauty of his question brought tears to my eyes.

I crawled up the bed, straddling his legs, the sheets a tangled mess between us. "Yes." My cheeks hurt I smiled so wide.

He shouted and flipped me over, grinning, and slipped the ring onto my finger. "You know what we should have at the reception?"

We gazed into one another's eyes, filled with so much love and contentment, and said the words at the same time, "Ax throwing."

EPILOGUE

LEO

"Stop talking over each other." August stood with his arms spread out at his sides. "We're all tired as hell, but we need to get on the same page for April. Who has clients booked for the next month?"

All hands went up except for Hunter. He'd been off all night.

I kicked his foot under the table.

His head shot up and he raised his hands. Ever since we'd shown up, he'd been distracted, and not by his phone like he normally was. Something else had taken over whatever madness normally churned inside his head.

August swirled the marker between his fingers, spinning it around. "Who needs help?"

All hands remained raised.

August uncapped his whiteboard marker with his teeth and walked over to the giant board beside Hunter's ornate dining room table. "Leo, your weekend workload is light."

I nodded. "Corporate keeps things to weekdays."

"Fine. You can help Everest with the Final Four events and Draft Day."

Everest's eyes narrowed.

"Can't wait to help." I slapped a smile on my face. Irritating the hell out of Everest would be a bonus.

Zara walked out of the kitchen with plates and set them in the middle of the table before sitting on my lap. There weren't any free chairs—two of them were being used as whiteboard stands.

The table was crowded with laptops, print outs, and invoices. Sprinkled in between the thick books of samples were the containers of food Zara and I had picked up on the way over.

Our weekly Chinese food dinners had become another space where work spilled over into our lives. Basketball and buffalo wings had become our official board meetings.

Zara leaned over the table to load up the plate with my favorites alongside hers. Each rock of her hips to reach another dish tested my focus and ability to think coherently.

She served as a deciding vote on something the guys were fighting about, since my brain was no longer functioning.

I squeezed my hands around her hips to keep her still.

"What? You're not up for a tease anymore?" She looked over her shoulder and bit her lip, wriggling her ass on my lap.

"Retribution when you get back will be swift and well-deserved."

"I can only hope." She took a bite of her egg roll and a few forkfuls of chicken before popping up.

I shoved my seat forward with my lap under the full cover of the table.

Everest lifted an eyebrow and took a bite of his perfectly swirled noodles. "Lap dance finished already?"

My hands clenched under the table. Our truce had its ups and downs.

"Gentlemen, I leave you to your work. I'm picking up my little brother from the airport." She pecked me on the lips. A fleeting press of her soft, full lips wasn't enough, but it would tide me over until she got back.

She grabbed her keys and left the dining room, yelping once she disappeared from view.

I shot out of my seat, rushing.

She stood in the hall leading to the front door, clutching the front of her shirt with her keys in her hand. Standing beside her was a woman I hadn't seen before. And she was in Hunter's apartment.

The crowd around the doorway all turned to look between her and Hunter, who stood on the other side of the table with his hands clenched at his sides.

"Hi, I'm Sabrina." She extended her hand. "Hunter's new roommate."

"Uninvited! Uninvited intruder," Hunter chimed from the other side of the dining room.

She rolled her eyes. "I didn't mean to interrupt. I was headed out to pick up a friend and ran into Zara. Sorry for scaring the crap out of you."

Zara smiled back. "No problem. I'm happy to have another woman around here to help handle this crew." She jerked her thumb in our direction.

"I can only imagine."

August stepped forward, rubbing his whiteboard-marker-covered hands on his pants before extending his hand. "I'm August. This is Jameson, Everest, and Leo."

She waved. "Nice meeting you all. Testosterone overload

in here, am I right?" Her hand went to the collar of her shirt and she tugged it away from her neck.

Zara laughed. "It's next level. You should've seen me the first time I met them all."

"Don't you have somewhere to be, Sabrina?"

Sabrina leaned farther into the room. "You're absolutely right. Thank you for being so helpful, Hunter." Sweetness dripped from her words like she hadn't picked up on a hint of his snappiness.

"I was headed out too. You can tell me all about what it's like to live here with Hunter."

Sabrina linked her arm through Zara's and they walked down the hall. "How long do you have?"

Jameson turned with his jaw dropped. "You have a roommate?"

Hunter gritted his teeth. "It wasn't my choice." He flopped back into his chair. "I don't want to talk about it." He folded his arms over his chest.

We exchanged looks and took our seats.

Everest flipped through the pages of a sample book. "She's cute. A little mousy, but she didn't mind needling Hunter, so I already like her."

Jameson loaded up his plate with more noodles. "She seemed nice. How long has she been living here?"

"Three weeks," Hunter grumbled.

August drew an hourglass on the whiteboard. "Great curves."

Hunter glared at him and shredded a piece of paper at his seat, but didn't say anything more.

"Back to business." Jameson squeezed his forehead. "We're going to have to bring on more staff."

August cracked open a fortune cookie. "With what

money? I'm never sure my paycheck will show up on the first."

"I've streamlined and automated everything possible. You've hustled hard the past few months and our calendar is booked solid. Check this out." Jameson flipped the laptop around. The ugly red cells of the spreadsheet transitioned to pink, then white. For the rest of the year everything was bright neon green.

I stared at the number at the bottom right hand corner. "Is that where we'll be at the end of this year?" We'd pulled it off. By the end of this year, I'd no longer feel like I'd shoved my friends—and Everest—out onto a leaky dinghy to set out on an insane adventure.

Jameson shook his head.

And the hope took a nosedive into the sand.

"That's our cash flow right now." He grinned dollar-sign wide.

I jerked back so hard, my chair nearly toppled over. My hands shot out to grab onto the table and steady myself. "You're shitting me."

"Not even a little bit. August scored those five weddings back-to-back, and that tipped us over the edge."

Our heads swung to him.

He shrugged. "When you know how obsessed people are with the perfect day and not an actual marriage, it's easy to play them like a damn fiddle."

Hunter grabbed a plastic-wrapped fortune cookie and cracked it open. He pulled out the two slips of paper. "You've got to be fucking kidding me." Our meetings were usually overrun by Hunter and his tales from the trenches of bottle service and backstage passes, but tonight he'd barely said a word.

I leaned closer. "What's it say?"

"Open your mind and be prepared to receive something special."

Jameson tapped away at his keyboard. "That doesn't sound too bad to me."

The corners of Hunter's mouth shot down. "The second says, 'Your tongue is your best ambassador.'"

Beer showered the table as August choked on his drink. "How'd they know?" he wheezed. "So that's how you score so many deals around town?"

Everest set down his beer. "Fine, someone's living with you, but you need to chill out. She seemed nice."

Hunter rolled his shoulders and shot up from his chair. "I don't know how else to say this." He stood from the table and paced, shaking out his arms like he was preparing for a few rounds in the ring. "You need to see it for yourself." He left. We exchanged looks.

I grabbed my beer and got up, following him out of the room. "You're freaking us all out. What the hell is wrong?"

The rest of the guys joined our apprehensive game of follow the leader.

"My grandma's friend said she needed a place for her granddaughter to stay since she was new to the city. I told her I could get a great deal on a hotel, but she put her foot down and said she was staying here, no ifs, ands, or buts."

We passed the living room and formal living room toward his bedroom.

"She shows up, moves in all her crap, takes over my bathroom since it has a tub, leaves her laundry everywhere, and I'm left to clean it up."

Jameson clapped him on the shoulder. "Who knew you were so uptight?"

"She's driving me crazy already." Hunter stood in front of a closed bedroom door.

"I figured, it won't be long. She'll leave in a few weeks. But she's making herself at home." He pushed open the bedroom door.

Everest pushed in first and his eyes bugged out. "Holy shit."

I nudged past Hunter and pushed Everest out of the way. Lights hung from a mini scaffolding set-up. There had to be at least ten lights set up all over the room, all spotlighting the bed.

"Holy shit."

"Exactly!" Hunter shouted as though vindicated.

The bed was stripped down and a fresh bundle of sheets sat on the floor beside it.

"She gets like twenty sheet deliveries a week."

Jameson stepped inside and looked around the room like he'd walked into an abstract painting his brain couldn't process. "What is all this?"

"Hey, guys." A sunny voice from the end of the hall broke through our gawking session.

We all bolted out of the room, but there was no playing it cool. "Sabrina!"

"We were just—" We were just shit at covering our tracks, is what we were.

"Guys, this is my friend, Rex." Her friend was a guy who looked like he could've played in the pros with me. He was ripped and towered over Sabrina, who stood there in her jeans and oversized t-shirt covered in pineapples. Rex gave us the 'what's up' head nod.

"Did you need something from my room, Hunter?"

His jaw clenched. "No, I was just showing the guys how

little light there is on this side of the apartment, and why you needed to set up your own lights."

"No, it's perfect. When natural light screws with your artificial lighting, it makes editing a pain in the ass. The darker the better." She edged past us with Rex following behind her.

He checked his phone and dropped back through the doorway. "Brina, can we get started? I only have an hour before I need to head to my next job."

"We'll get to work." She set her bag down inside the room and turned back to us. "This should only take an hour, but if you're still around, I'd love to show you our work. It'll be a rough cut, but I try to keep things simple. I don't do much fancy camera work. Who needs that when you're getting your hands dirty, right?" She tapped Hunter on the chest.

I swear they must have heard our jaws hitting the floor from the lobby.

Her gaze bounced between all of us. "It was nice meeting you all again. See you in an hour?" She closed the door in our stunned faces as Rex tugged his shirt up and over his head behind her.

August broke through the silence reigning on our long walk back to the dining room. "Hunter..."

Everest flicked his lighter. "Do you think you can get a cut since you're supplying the location? Don't people usually get paid for that?"

Jameson pulled out his chair. "I'm sure it's..." His mouth opened and closed a few times. "Tasteful."

I stared at the documents at my spot, unable to focus on the words on the page. "I guess we'll find out what she's been up to in an hour."

Hunter's jaw popped. "We sure as hell will."

Thank you so much for taking time out of your day to spend some time with Leo and Zara and the rest of the SWANK guys or are they WANKS now? :-D

There's a treat for you with an extra special day for these two. You can get your hands on that scene by clicking here (https://BookHip.com/BJNQHW).

It was a lot of fun for me to jump back into a contemporary story, but of course, I couldn't leave the sports completely behind. There's so much fun in store for the rest of the guys and I hope you'll be here for it!

Hunter's book is the next up! What exactly is Sabrina up to? Hunter's on a mission to find out.

I can't wait for you to discover it right along with him!

Don't miss your chance to pre-order The Sweetest Thing now!

Persephone has a list of firsts to tackle in her senior year of college and her biggest is lose her V-Card. Reece is a cocky football player who stumbles into her interview session for candidates can't help, but want to protect her and keep her from making a big mistake. He volunteers to help her with everything on her list--except her No. 1, but then everything changes.

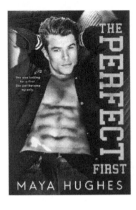

The Perfect First is available now and in Kindle Unlimited!

I hope you'll love your next read and happy reading!

Maya xx

ACKNOWLEDGMENTS

Thank you as always to my incredible husband. He's the most supportive man in the world and I couldn't do this without him.

To my editing team: Lea Schaffer, Tamara Mataya, Sarah Kremen-Hicks and Sarah Plocher, you're the best and I this story wouldn't be half as amazing without your help and guidance.

To every person out there who showed Leo and Zara so much love from the first teaser to release day, it means the world to me and I thank you from the bottom of my heart. Knowing how much you're cheering me on makes the marathon writing sprints so much more enjoyable.

I can't wait to bring you even more sweet and steamy stories in the future.

Thank you for taking the time to get to know Leo, Zara and the rest of the SWANK guys, or is it WANKS? :-D

Until your next read!

Maya xx

ALSO BY MAYA HUGHES

Fulton U

The Perfect First - First Time Romance

The Second We Met - Enemies to Lovers

The Third Best Thing - Secret Admirer

Kings of Rittenhouse

Kings of Rittenhouse - FREE

Shameless King - Enemies to Lovers

Reckless King - Off Limits Lover

Ruthless King - Second Chance

Fearless King - Brother's Best Friend

Heartless King - Friends to Enemies to Lovers

Manhattan Misters

All His Secrets - Single Dad Romance

All His Lies - Revenge Romance

All His Regrets - Second Chance Romance

Under His Series

Under His Ink - Second Chance Romance

CONNECT WITH MAYA

Sign up for my newsletter to get exclusive bonus content, ARC opportunities, sneak peeks, new release alerts and to find out just what I'm books are coming up next.

Join my reader group for teasers, giveaways and more!

Follow my Amazon author page for new release alerts!

Follow me on Instagram, where I try and fail to take pretty pictures!

Follow me on Twitter, just because :)

I'd love to hear from you! Drop me a line anytime :)
https://www.mayahughes.com/
maya@mayahughes.com

facebook.com/mayahugheswrites
twitter.com/mhugheswrites
instagram.com/mayahugheswrites

Made in the USA
Columbia, SC
28 July 2020